The Charted Systems are in pieces. *Mercy's Pledge* is destroyed, and her captain dead. With no homes to return to, the remaining crew sets off on a journey to find the mythical planet of Ardulum—a planet where Emn might find her people, and Neek the answers she's long sought. Finding the planet, however, brings a host of uncomfortable truths about Ardulum's vision for the galaxy and Neek's role in a religion that refuses to release her. Neek must balance her planet's past and the unchecked power of the Ardulans with a budding relationship and a surprising revelation about her own genealogy.

Ardulum: Second Don blends space opera elements and hard science into a story about two women persistently bound to their past and a sentient planet determined to shape their future.

D0743685

Published by
NineStar Press
PO Box 91792
Albuquerque, New Mexico, 87199
www.ninestarpress.com

Warning: This book contains scenes of graphic violence and gore, as well as brief depictions of genocide.

Print ISBN # 978-1-947139-96-1
Cover by Natasha Snow
Edited by Sasha Vorun

SECOND DON

Ardulum

J.S. Fields

For my Aunt Barbara, who always made sure I had books to read with strong female protagonists, and for my mother, who forced me to read them even when they were dry.

Acknowledgements

Whew! Books are always a huge collaboration of sorts, and so many people helped to make this one possible. Thanks, first, as always, to Lauren for all the late-night brainstorming, red ink, and concept of bipeds needing "walkies." Thank you to my editor, Sasha Vorun, for taking a chance on me as a brand-new sci-fi writer and suffering through my perpetual inability to properly use commas. To Letty, for finding time to beta read despite the demands of two toddlers, and once again, to the amazing forum readers over at 17th Shard's Reading Excuses (Bill, Robinski, and so many others) for going over each chapter until their eyes bled.

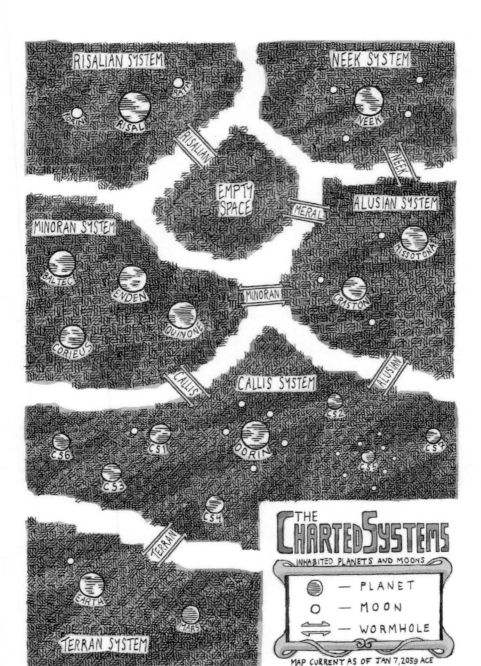

Chapter 1: Eld Palace, Ardulum

This is a Galactic News Network special report. Aid agency reports coming in outline a new species found on Risalian ships in the aftermath of the Crippling War. Our Risalian sources confirm the species as 'Ardulan,' a non-sentient beast of burden. The bipeds resemble Terrans and Neek in appearance but have unique subdermal bruising. All specimens thus far recovered have been dead; however, the newly appointed Markin request that should a live one be found, it should be turned over to the Council immediately.

—Excerpt from wideband news broadcast in the Charted Systems, December 2nd, 2060 CE

IT WAS HIS Talent Day. *His* day to be here, in the old palace. His day to meet the Eld and complete his metamorphosis.

Arik pushed a sheet of black hair from his face—streaked with red from a summer tending andal trees—and began a slow, deliberate procession towards the Talent Chamber. He passed under a high andal archway built in the traditional encased knot style, reliefs carved into each aborted branch. Reaching out as he passed, Arik ran a finger over one of the knots, noting the texture created by chisels and pyrography. He picked his way over andal floorboards, worn to unevenness from generations of youth making this same journey. The lustrous, black heartwood reflected the sunlight falling from the glass ceiling, but Arik didn't turn his eyes from the glare.

Four more steps and a turn brought Arik around the final corner. He faced the door to the Talent Chamber and paused. His heart rate increased, so Arik rested his back against the andal wall paneling, digging his nails into the soft, white sapwood. It was comforting to be so close to Ardulum's native tree, reassuring to embed himself in it, if only slightly. His pulse calmed. His breathing slowed. Arik took another two calming breaths and pushed off the wall. He nudged the door ahead with his foot, and it slid silently open, revealing the room inside.

As with the receiving hall and throne room, natural light filtered in from the glass ceiling. Here, however, it was muted. Outside, the canopy of several large andal trees swayed in the breeze, casting patchwork shadows on the floor. Arik stepped forward, trying to keep to only the darker, shadowed areas, and approached the rulers of Ardulum.

In the center of the room, the three elds sat on ornate, wooden thrones, each watching him with reserved amusement. Arik supposed humor was a good sign. Perhaps the Eld had a soft spot for young second *don*s on their Talent Day. Perhaps being the only one present meant the Eld were not tired from numerous ceremonies, and Arik would get their full attention.

Arik stopped when he was within an arm's length of the Eld and then let his gaze flicker around the hall. Towering sculptures of past elds, carved in great detail in the black andal heartwood, loomed over the thrones and stared ominously at Arik—their freshly polished faces glistened in the baronial light.

A deep male voice broke the silence. "You come before us, Arik of the second *don*, fresh from metamorphosis. What do you bring?" The male eld, who looked to be the oldest of the group, stared unblinkingly at Arik as he stroked the worn wood grain of his throne seat. His two Talents were carved into the throne base, easy for Arik to see: Hearth and Mind. It wasn't a bad pairing to have. The Eld were the only ones on Ardulum to have more than one Talent, of course, but Arik liked the balance created when the Talents encompassing protection and construction intertwined with the Talents surrounding critical thinking and mathematics. The male eld was likely an excellent architect, which, if the palace suffered any ill effects after the next move, would be a key skill to have.

Arik's stomach growled loudly, and the youth sheepishly placed a hand over it, hoping that somehow the Eld hadn't heard.

"Arik?" the male eld prompted again, his tone gentler than before. "What do you bring to offer to us, your Eld?"

Arik closed his eyes tightly for just a moment and brought his mind back to the present. Andal help him, he could smell wood cooking, the sweet odor wafting from the kitchens. Arik's stomach growled again, and his mouth started to water.

Focus! he scolded himself as he fumbled momentarily through his tunic pockets. *This is the biggest day of your life. Stop thinking about lunch!* Finally, his fingers came across his offering—the form of a small child whittled from andal from his parents' plantation. The carving was crude and made only from sapwood—Arik had never had great fine motor skills, but the figure had visible appendages and a reasonably detailed face. Arik hoped it was enough.

"I bring you this gift," Arik said slowly, his voice wavering and squeaking to a higher pitch on the last word. "May it show my devotion to my spiritual journey, so I can leave my childhood and discover my Talent. Please accept this offering and guide me onto my new path." With shaking hands, Arik knelt on the mat and held the carving up over his head. The coarse weave of the andal fibers dug into his knees, and Arik had to stop himself from reaching down to scratch.

A cool hand touched Arik's wrist briefly before removing the carving. "We accept your offering, Arik of the second *don*." The female eld reached down and put a small finger under Arik's chin, lifting his face up. "Rise and receive your Talent."

Arik got to his feet, suddenly hyperaware of these mystical individuals. He'd never been this close to the Eld before and likely never would again, so Arik took a moment to study their faces. They were old, older than the oldest third *don* Arik had ever seen—and yet, their fingers were elegant, their bodies strong and well-muscled. The male eld looked to be from one of the southern provinces. His hair still had dark streaks shooting through a mass of silver, and his skin was closer to olive in its translucency. The female, blessed with Talents of Mind and Aggression, was tall, her sharp chin well above the other elds' heads. Her hair was uniformly cinnamon save for at her temples. She, too, looked to be from the south. However, the gatoi, of Science and Hearth, was much paler, zir skin containing next to no melanin. Zie was from the farthest northern province, then, where sunlight rarely penetrated the thick andal forests. The birth rate was skewed in favor of the third-gender gatois in that region, although Arik wasn't certain whether that was a natural phenomenon or whether it came from parental selection.

The male eld cleared his throat, and Arik again snapped back to the present. The Eld were still staring at him, unmoving. Was his offering not enough? Was there another component he had forgotten? His mother and talther, his gatoi parent, had helped him carve it, staying up late each night since Arik's emergence and guiding the young man's wavering chisel with steady hands. A week wasn't much time to construct an offering. Did others bring more elaborate gifts? Should he have done something in line with what he hoped his Talent might be? Dizziness threatened to topple him, the smells from the kitchen confused him, and he had to work to control his breathing. His mind wandered. The increasingly saturated smell of cooked andal spun through his head. Was he *in* the kitchens? It certainly seemed that way now. How had he ignored the intensity of the smell before? It was almost like standing in the rotisserie himself, the scent of sweet spice invading his nostrils.

The female eld smiled slightly at the male, who gave a knowing wink. Arik teetered in a near panic, vision straying between reality and his wandering delusions.

"Peace, young one," the gatoi eld said as zie stepped forward. In zir hands, zie carried a small wooden bowl filled with a pale mucus. Zie dipped two fingers into the bowl, coating them, and then held zir hand out towards Arik. "Step forward to begin your journey."

Arik's empty stomach rolled. He knew the mucus was synthetic, but what it represented brought the taste of bile to the back of his throat. Determined to not embarrass himself further, Arik took a confident step towards the gatoi eld and closed his eyes. For the past year, he'd been instructed in the ritual that was about to take place. He would not mess things up now—not on his Talent Day, no matter how strange and ostentatious the performers or how heavily the air hung with the smell of food.

"I am Eld," the gatoi eld said steadily as zie outlined Arik's face with the mucus. "I am the vessels that transport power."

"I am Eld," said the female, taking the bowl from the gatoi. She swirled her smallest finger in the mixture and then coated Arik's nose. "I am the fibers of strength." She handed the bowl to the male, who had stepped forward as well.

"I am Eld," the male said, pinching Arik's chin between two mucus-coated fingers. "I am the rays that store our knowledge."

Arik counted silently to fifteen in his head as he'd been instructed. The tingling at the mucosal contact points radiated from his face down to his neck, absorbed into his skin, and congealed into a tight, painful lump just above his heart.

"I am Arik of the second *don*," he said when he finished the count. Gently, slowly, Arik moved his consciousness into himself to where the lump lay just under his skin, pulsing in rhythm with his heartbeat. He watched it for a moment, external stimuli forgotten. He was both slightly revolted and slightly in awe of this *thing*, this synthetic chemical compound that would, in just a few seconds, stimulate his adrenal gland and cause the production of a massive number of hormones—hormones that would determine how he would spend the rest of his life.

Arik let his mind touch the lump. The mass dissolved, its components seeping into his bloodstream and heading directly for their target. Arik's body became warm—and then hot. He broke out in a sweat, the salty liquid beading on his yellow skin and reflecting in the bright overhead lighting. He shut his eyes and was forced to his hands and knees when the chemicals hit his adrenal gland and the hormones began to affect his other cells.

Cells changed. Cells morphed. His blood circulated in the normal direction, paused for a fraction of a second, and then reversed. His metabolism increased, and his internal body temperature shot up even more. Veins bulged in his wrists and began to burst, blood seeping under the skin and forming bright violet bruises. Arik felt like he couldn't breathe anymore. The heat was too intense. He began to pant and fell onto his right side, curling into a fetal position.

As abruptly as it began, the heat began to back off. Arik could feel his cells calming, the veins in his wrists closing. Sweat stung his eyes, seeping past his eyelids, and Arik brought his left hand up to wipe them clean. When his vision cleared and he brought his hand away, Arik saw his new markings for the first time—three linked, black circles on the inside of both of his wrists surrounded by a bruised haze of extra subdermal blood. His smile grew slowly as he moved into a sitting position and looked up at the Eld.

"I am Arik of the second *don*," he said clearly, his voice resonating, crisp and strong, throughout the chamber. No wavering. He could be proud of that. "I am of Science."

"And there your Talent shall lie," the female responded. "Stand, Arik, and leave this palace. Return to your home and begin your apprenticeship."

Arik's face broke into a broad grin. He clasped his hands behind his back and stood, his previous discomforts forgotten. Arik took a moment to straighten his tunic before bowing to each eld. "I thank you, Eld, for showing me my way."

The Eld smiled back but remained silent. Remembering that he was to leave promptly, Arik turned and took several confident steps towards the door. Pride filled his chest—pride at his Talent, pride at the way he'd conducted himself, and pride that he could go home and apprentice to a Talent that would not take him away from his family or his andal saplings. With the Talent of Science, he could stay and work his ancestors' andal plantations—could tend the young trees he'd grown up with. His entire family was of Science. They would be proud of him.

Several steps into his departure, the smell of the cooked andal began to waft towards him again. What should have been a pleasant, understated smell was pungent and slightly curdled. He tried to ignore it, quickening his pace. The soft *slack slack slack* of Arik's bare feet hitting the polished andal floor was suddenly joined by the deep sounds of a heartbeat.

Slack du-dumn, slack du-dumn, slack...

Arik spun around, confused, and looked for the source of the noise. It took another three seconds of *du-dumn du-dumn* before Arik realized that it was *his* heart he was hearing, the beats becoming more rapid in his agitation.

Arik swallowed, his throat dry. His muscles twitched under his tunic, the fibers itching his skin. He glanced at the Eld, a peculiar expression on their wrinkled faces.

"I...I don't feel well," Arik said, mostly to himself. He cringed when his own voice sounded too loud in his ears. His heart was trying to escape out of his chest, and no amount of controlled breathing seemed to help. The smell of the andal wound through his head and down his throat, causing Arik to gag. Thoughts of simultaneous choking and hyperventilating filled his mind. Unsure of what else to do, he moved his consciousness back inside himself, trying to find the cause of his distress.

What he saw shocked him. This wasn't the body he knew—did not resemble anything of his. Here, capillaries burst just under his skin and leaked perpetual blood out of his circulatory system. Hormones raced everywhere, transmitting across his chest and up into his brain. Something was happening near his throat, too. Loose blood pushed ligaments around, unwrapping and changing their positions, and pooled just under his larynx. Cartilage scavenged from around his thyrohyoid ligament sidled closer, surrounding the blood.

Arik opened his mouth in an effort to call over the Eld, but was shocked when all that came out was a gurgle. He tried again, forcing more air out through what had once been his larynx. Again, only gibberish.

He grew hot, a red flush surfacing not just on his cheeks, but across his entire body. Arik watched in stunned horror as the purple veins that had always been just slightly visible under his skin—the veins that had already started to fade after his time with the Eld—darkened to black.

Once more, Arik looked to the Eld, desperate for guidance. They'd moved closer. The gatoi reached a bony hand out to Arik, zir expression unreadable.

Help? Arik sent frantically on a telepathic thread. It was unacceptable to speak to the Eld in such a manner, but he was in trouble. They had to know!

None of the Eld responded to Arik's mental query. The hand remained out and open, all elds staring at Arik expectantly. Not knowing what else to do, Arik reached out. His whole right arm was covered now in arcing black veins that grouped into geometric patterns just under his skin.

I'm dying, Arik thought to himself. *The smell of the andal is actually going to kill me.* He let his fingers touch the tips of the gatoi eld's hand, and his mind cleared. The contact sparked through Arik, and he snapped his head up, eyes wide. The gatoi eld stared back, unblinking, as pieces of emotion began to filter into Arik's mind. Discomfort, unease, disappointment... That didn't seem right. He hadn't done anything wrong—something had just misfired, that was all. He was still Arik, still of Science. A healer could fix his larynx, he was sure of it. He wasn't quite sure *why* all of this was happening, but surely the Eld knew. Surely others had had this same problem.

The intensity of the connection became uncomfortable, but when Arik tried to pull his hand away, he could not. The gatoi eld had a tight grip on Arik's wrist. The male eld moved behind Arik in two fluid steps and placed his hands on his shoulders, pushing down to keep Arik in place. The female grabbed his other hand around the wrist, her longer fingernails digging into his skin.

Time seemed to be slowing. Arik felt his heart rate depress, the blood in his veins decrease in flow rate. His mind became muddled again. Something was wrong, and he needed to speak to the Eld about it. Why couldn't he speak? Why wouldn't the words come out?

Dark spots began to swim before Arik's vision. His heart didn't seem to be beating anymore, and Arik thought that was wrong somehow. The blackness increased. Arik slumped. The male eld backed away quickly, and Arik's body hit the wood floor with a thump, his head bouncing once after the initial impact. Words leaked across the darkness: *defective, unsuitable, terminate.*

Terminate?

Arik opened his mouth to make a sound to indicate his distress, when his brain, starved of oxygen, finally shut down.

Chapter 2: Mmnnuggl Pod, Risalian Wormhole

In order to keep the Terran and the altered Risalian Ardulan alive, we need to stop at Xinar Hub on our way back to Mmnn. We will be buying bipedal foodstuffs, drinks, and clothes. We might be a while. Don't worry though—we will be back soon. Everything is going just fine. Nothing to worry about. Maybe we could bring up ceiling height at the next council meeting.

—Tightband communication from the small Mmnnuggl pod *Bysspp*, to the Mmnnuggl president's office, Third Month of Arath, 26_15

"THIS TEXT IS impossible!"

Neek slammed the plastic data pad into the wall. The glass screen shattered in a satisfying crash, and the unit went dark. A moment later, a thin gel secreted from the pad's scaffold, condensed, and hardened. The unit turned back on.

It was less satisfying to break things when they could regenerate. Exhaling, Neek bent and picked the pad back up. The text resumed where she had left off, the screen's backlighting flashing irritably.

She couldn't read any more. It had been bad enough having to go through the old Neek holy texts with her uncle during her exile from her homeworld, but at least then it had only been once a month. She might have been branded a heretic for claiming Ardulum was a stupid, religious fairy tale, but she was still niece to the high priest. Now, however, the text seemed more cumbersome than ever. In the past two days alone, she had finished two versions of *The Book of the Arrival* and was about to start the first version of *The Book of the Uplifting*. She couldn't bring herself to open another file. She only had to kill another half an hour until their diminutive Mmnnuggl pod made it to Risal, but

Neek couldn't take one more verse about Ardulan deities or an impossibly traveling planet. She had an *actual* Ardulan—sort of— onboard the ship. She hadn't been able to bring herself to believe in the old texts while still living on her homeworld under her parents' care. There was no way she could find them even remotely plausible now, despite one of those supposedly mystical beings sitting meters away from her, separated only by thin sheets of biometal and putrid green lighting.

Ardulum was a planet. A traveling planet. A traveling planet that housed a race of gods or god-like beings that had fundamentally shaped Neek civilization. It was ridiculous and unbelievable, and yet, *yet...*

Neek stood as much as she could in the low-ceilinged room and tried to stretch away the cramps from her thighs. She splayed her hands out on the ceiling, letting her mind wander to trivial things, like if her *stuk* would interact with the paint, or how her life would have been different if she'd been born into one of the older family lines on Neek, the ones with three fingers per hand instead of eight. Had that happened, she would have never been able to pilot the *Pledge* and its geriatric, piecemeal navigation systems. She wouldn't be here, on a Mmnnuggl pod, with an Ardulan and—*damn it*! If the Risalians didn't have the answers she was looking for or at least some trail of information she could follow, Neek wasn't certain what they would do. Regardless of the promise she had made to Emn, Neek couldn't find Ardulum without any leads. If they were lucky, the Risalians wouldn't shoot them the moment they emerged from the wormhole and would provide some coordinates where they might begin. The Risalians were looking for their Ardulans, after all, and had to have acquired the base genetic stock from *somewhere*. Armed with coordinates, Neek could stop sifting through mountains of religious text, looking for location clues, and driving herself slowly insane.

The ache in her thighs wasn't getting better. With a labored sigh, Neek leaned her head against the wall and cursed the coldness of the metal. She closed her eyes. The white noise was blissful. She counted her heartbeats against the thrum of the ship's engines and tried to ignore the steady, feathery presence in her mind. The presence wasn't intrusive, but thinking about it overloaded her brain, blurred her vision, and made her throat feel tight. No matter how many times Neek tried to put the jigsaw pieces of her life into some semblance of order, the pieces kept changing shape. It was hard to focus on anything except the woman in the cockpit—the Ardulan in the cockpit. The god in the cockpit. Maybe. Shit.

Memories flooded her mind.

A blood-soaked little girl tumbled from a stasis chamber, one dark triangle under her eye.

Flotsam from a Risalian cutter.

Emn's chrysalis nestled underneath a pyre of Risalian bodies. The smoky smells. The crisp flesh.

The scattered remains of the *Mercy's Pledge* drifting through space, carrying Yorden's body with them.

The Ardulan woman who ended the Crippling War, or whatever the news feeds were calling it now. Ended the lives of many Mmnnuggls, Risalians, and her own people.

The Ardulan woman who was piloting their stolen Mmnnuggl ship. The woman so covered in Talent markings that little of her translucent skin remained.

The woman she couldn't be around without her body entering into some sort of primeval panic mode, which did *not* create an enjoyable atmosphere within the ship. Her Journey youth, Nicholas, had been sure to point that out several times over. Loudly. Usually when they were all together in the cockpit and Neek couldn't avoid Emn's stares.

A soft knock on the door drew Neek away from her memories. The round panel slid into the wall to reveal a gangly, young man with thick, dark curls framing his face and even darker skin. Nicholas brushed the curls from his eyes as he stepped into Neek's room and smiled lopsidedly, surveying the wreckage.

"Don't give me that look," Neek spat as she launched a small, plastic tablet at his head. Nicholas ducked just in time to avoid impact, and the pad rebounded off the wall, landing at his feet. He shoved his hands into the gaping pockets of his flight suit and stared at her reproachfully. Neek glared in response.

"No, I still haven't found any clues for how to find Ardulum. Yes, I'm sure I don't want to come hang out in the galley or the cockpit or wherever you and Emn have set up camp, and no, we are not going to avoid Risalian space. We have a reasonable chance of not being shot on sight. The ship is valuable, if nothing else."

"Neek," Nicholas interjected, but Neek cut him off.

"They're the only species in the Charted Systems to have potentially interacted with the Ardulans, so they're a logical starting point." Neek kicked at the nearest pile of pads, this time trying to avoid cracking the screens. "If you really want to steer clear of the Risalians, start reading. There are three main holy books, four revised editions of each, and a small mountain of supplementary text written in the first ten years after the Departure. Oh, and these plastic tablets Chen gave us don't have the memory or speed of the newer cellulose ones, so each only holds half a holy book. There is a mess of oversized artwork files embedded in the text. Enjoy."

"I'm not the one that doesn't want to go to Risal, Neek, and I don't have any goals in this Ardulum thing, outside of wanting to help Emn find her people." Nicholas dropped to his knees and picked up the pad Neek had thrown at him. "How far into this are you?"

Neek sighed and tugged at the end of her braid, debating whether it was long enough to strangle Nicholas with. "I'm systematically reading one holy book at a time, starting with the original and working my way through the revisions. I'm about to start the second set of texts."

Nicholas eyed her warily. "Emn is afraid..."

An image of Emn's mother—her skull shattered, the pieces spinning on the floor—danced across Neek's vision. She pushed the image away, buried it under a million other memories she didn't need to see right now. "I understand Emn's fears. What the Risalians did is unforgivable. We'd be completely remiss, however, if we didn't at least try to get information from the Risalians. Emn deserves a home. It's a crazy undertaking, but I made a promise. And this, here, with the Risalians, is the best place to start. Surely she understands that."

"She might, if you actually explained it to her in person." Nicholas nudged Neek's boot with his bare foot. "It's been two weeks, Neek, and you've spoken to Emn maybe three times." He put his hand over his nose. "It *smells* in here. You have to leave. Walk around. Eat something. *Talk* to her." Nicholas pressed his hand into the film on the floor and lifted it slowly. A squelching noise followed as the film stretched and then popped loose. "One room can only handle so much *stuk*. Natural secretion or not, your body can't possibly have evolved to stay stationary in a tiny room all day."

"Get out."

Nicholas stared at her, his brown eyes so full of concern that she wanted to vomit. Last week, they'd spent four days on Craston, getting supplies and catching up with Chen, one of the late Captain Yorden Kuebrich's old contacts. Yorden. Andal help her, she missed that old foul-mouthed Terran and the dilapidated tramp transport she'd piloted with him for a decade. If it hadn't been sheared in two by a Risalian cutter, Yorden and the adult Arduluan woman they'd rescued from the Risalians would still be alive—and Neek wouldn't be the one shepherding the remaining crew of the former *Mercy's Pledge* through space. Damn Yorden, and damn his death!

Neek dragged her mind back to the present, before memories threatened to suffocate her. She'd seen Emn every day while in the spaceport, even on the day she'd gotten horrifically lost trying to find someone who could sharpen the strange knife-vegetable peeler thing with the hooked blade she'd gotten from Chen the last time they'd come this way, and for some reason couldn't manage to just throw away. She'd probably spoken to the young woman too, although she couldn't recall what she might have said. Nicholas was clearly exaggerating.

"I'm fine," Neek managed through gritted teeth. "Are you going to help, or are you going to leave?"

Nicholas tapped the glass screen of the pad. A chime sounded from the old technology as a start-up screen flashed on. Nicholas grimaced and brought the pad up closer to his face. "I'll help. Where do you want me to start?"

Picking up the pad she'd been working on, Neek checked her progress. The first two sentences from *The Book of the Uplifting* stared back, taunting her with hyperbole. "Tackle the extra material, and we can compare notes when you finish. That way there is no chance we overlap and you have to suffer through the same crap I just read. Also, watch out for mentions of the word 'Keft.' It keeps coming up, and I can't tell if it's a planet or food or what."

Nicholas slumped into a sitting position in the far corner, eyeing her warily. The pad wavered in his hand, moving up to his eyes, down to his lap, and then back up again. On the third iteration, he opened his mouth to speak.

"Don't," Neek warned, hoping to forestall another lecture.

"Fine." Nicholas looked down at his pad, running his hands over the plastic scaffold that held the glass screen in place. The pad flashed twice, indicating that the text was ready. Nicholas squinted against the bright backlighting of the device and then groaned. "One hundred and seventy-three books of 'encounter' stories and over forty volumes of poetry." He looked up. "Aw, not the poetry. I tried to go through some of this stuff when we were marooned on your homeworld. It's excruciating."

"Hey, there are technical reports and data from the technology the Ardulans supposedly gifted the Neek with as well. You're always babbling about how great cellulosic integration is. You should love those sections. The texts describe the whole process in detail, from andal genetic engineering to cellulosic separation and weaving cellulose into biometals."

Nicholas huffed and bent back over his pad, grumbling.

"Hey!" Neek kicked him with a booted foot. "That part *is* interesting. The Risalian company Cell-Tal is credited with developing all the cellulosic integration techniques, but if you read between the lines of the text, the Ardulans were doing it first." She tapped the pad against the floor. "Looks like the Neek people weren't the only ones who were given gifts."

Nicholas stared back at her, unconvinced. She watched the youth for another moment, making sure he wasn't going to pepper her with more questions, before she returned to her own text. The first fifteen pages went quickly, containing only a primer on wood anatomy. After the introduction, the text veered more to Ardulan encounters on the planet Neek. Likely fiction, in Neek's opinion, although her thoughts on that were certainly evolving. This passage covered sightings of the Eld, the triarchy which ruled Ardulum. Neek slowed her reading. She read the same paragraph once, twice, and then a third time, checking that she wasn't making up words as a result of eye strain.

On that day, we were treated to a most holy sight. The Eld had chosen the harvest festival to greet us in person, we who managed the andal forests. Magnificent were they, the Eld of the Ardulans—resplendent in their golden robes, the markings of their many Talents shimmered in the dawn light.

Many Talents.

Eld.

Emn and all her markings.

Neek had had enough revelations in the past two months. She didn't need another. Neek tossed the pad to the side, cracking yet another screen, and buried her head in her hands. She could just file this tidbit away, let it simmer and marinate until it was digestible. The texts did change from version to version. That was natural in any revisionist religion. The changes weren't major, but it was possible this paragraph wasn't even in any of the revised material. There was no need to overreact. No need to jump to conclusions. Nicholas was likely buried in some bad poetry and hadn't even looked up when she'd thrown her pad, and Emn was up in the cockpit right now, probably synced with the Mmnnuggl ship's mental interface and trying to figure out how to work the wormhole generator. Everything was fine.

In the back of her mind, Emn's presence stirred, nudged by Neek's errant thoughts. Their connection tightened, the wispy presence continuing to flicker but making no move to engage. Emn was keeping her distance, which Neek appreciated, but she felt the pressure of a silent question every time she reached for their link.

Neek didn't know what to say to her. How was a Neek—a member of a species that gave up their individual names upon adulthood so they could become symbolically closer to a mythical planet—supposed to address an Ardulan? What did one say to someone whom her people worshipped as a god? What was a religious outcast supposed to do when a woman with not one but *multiple* Talents was stuck with her on a ship? Furthermore, how had she forgotten about the description of the Eld? If Emn really was Ardulan, if that fucking traveling planet did exist, she just...just...

Neek's thoughts continued to drift. It took Nicholas clearing his throat for her to realize that her posture had become rigid, her back ramrod straight and arms tight at her sides.

"Dry reading," Nicholas ventured. "Looks like yours is more interesting. What's it about?"

Neek shrugged her shoulders, picked up another tablet, and made an effort to stare at it. She shoved her emotions down, buried them under other repressed memories, and kept quiet.

Nicholas continued to fish. "Find the planet, by any chance? Or did you stumble upon a declaration of non-divinity?" Neek could feel Nicholas's pointed stare. "That'd be really convenient, because maybe then you'd stop acting like a doofus every time Emn was in the same room as you."

A growl bubbled up from Neek's throat despite her best efforts to squelch it. Nicholas always knew just the right buttons to push. "I have no fucking idea what to believe," she muttered. "I'm willing to accept that the Risalians tinkered around with some poor species and made very powerful weapons. Are they connected to a traveling planet that maybe shaped Neek civilization? Who knows. It would be nice to find out, sure. Nice to find out, then go back home, and rub it in everyone's smirking face if it doesn't exist, which, realistically, it probably does not."

"If you don't think Ardulum really exists, then *why* are we doing all this?"

Neek continued avoiding his eyes.

"Well?" Nicholas demanded. "If you say it out loud, it might actually help."

"I'm not talking about this anymore, Nicholas." Neek's voice was low and cold. It was enough to shut Nicholas up, but even after Neek raised her head, he was still staring at her, a look she couldn't place on his face.

"You can't avoid her forever."

"What am I supposed to say to her?" Her tone came out pleading instead of angry, but it was too late to stop the flood of words. "I don't know how to act." Neek swiped her knuckles across the pants of her baggy flight suit. "Mental guide, I could deal with. Protector, I can live with. Whatever I am now..." she trailed off and grabbed her pad again. "I just can't, Nick. Here. Read this." Neek tapped the tablet in her hand to bring up *The Book of the Uplifting*, scrolled to the paragraph on the Eld, and then handed it to Nicholas.

"Second of the holy books, huh?" he asked before silently scanning the page. When he finished, he put the pad down and looked appraisingly at Neek. "The Eld are the leaders, that much I know. Is there something else I am supposed to be getting out of this?"

Neek picked the pad back up and shut it off with a quick swipe. "*Many* Talents, Nicholas. As in, more than one."

"Yeah, but couldn't that just mean more than one because they each had one? So therefore, there were many Talents?"

"Maybe. But maybe not. I have to check the other editions. But if an eld can have more than one Talent..."

"Emn potentially being of the ruling caste isn't what this is about, Neek, and you know it." Nicholas brought his hands down and tilted his head. "Be reasonable. She's Emn. She's our Emn. Eld, Ardulan, or Risalian construct, treating her with deference and piety isn't going to help anything. *She* certainly doesn't know the protocol for Neek-Ardulan interactions. Why should you care?"

"Right," Neek muttered. "So, if the next wayward passenger we get on our ship is baby Jesus or Buddha or some other Terran deity, I'll be sure to remind you that protocol is irrelevant."

Nicholas rolled his eyes. "Fine. Then don't talk. Spend some time together. Get to know her as the adult she is, not the little kid we rescued. If she starts turning water into wine, call me." A smirk crept across his face as he stood, hunched, and opened the door to the hallway. "Emn said we should arrive at Risal in the next twenty minutes, assuming a Mmnnuggl pod doesn't try to take us out again. Your time in your cave here is almost up. Emn and I will be waiting for you in the cockpit when you're ready to face her or bow down in reverence. Whatever suits you."

Neek halfheartedly tossed a pad at Nicholas as the door slid shut behind him. After waiting a moment to make sure he wouldn't reappear, she picked up the pad with the Eld passage, took a deep breath, and swiped to the next page. She could do this. She could stay focused on their goal of finding the traveling planet. She just had to ignore the woman in the cockpit, the emotions that kept bubbling to the surface, and what all those Talent markings could mean if they ever landed on Ardulum.

Chapter 3: Mmnnuggl Pod, Risalian Space

We have become increasingly interested in the Terran who travels with the captive Risalian Ardulan. We have included select video of their interactions to date. Request guidance on how best to proceed.
—Tightband communication from the small Mmnnuggl pod *Bysspp*, to the Mmnnuggl president's office, Third Month of Arath, 26_15

WETNESS RAN ALONG her ear canal. Emn tilted her head, allowing several drops of maroon blood to trickle out. She checked the area where they fell, but just as before, the texture of the floor hid the blood from view. Relieved that there wouldn't be awkward conversations when Neek finally surfaced, Emn slid her mind from the interface, the pressure inside her skull waning.

They'd entered Risalian space only moments ago. While Emn wasn't looking forward to communicating with the Risalians, she did understand the reasoning. Besides, if the Risalians did have information on Ardulum, the crew might finally—*finally*—be able to leave the Charted Systems and find the planet from which her progenitors originated. They might find her genetic family, however distant, and maybe, just maybe, find a place where she wasn't hunted for her abilities.

"You have to tell her," Nicholas said. He pushed himself out of a lean and pointed to where Emn's blood had fallen. She'd been interfacing with the ship all the way through the wormhole and hadn't noticed Nicholas return to the cockpit. That meant Emn was getting a lecture, one way or the other. Annoyed, she tugged at the fabric across her chest, the sensation something she was still getting used to, and turned to look at Nicholas. She'd have much preferred a lecture from Neek.

Nicholas's eyebrow rose. "This is the fourth time I've seen you bleed from interfacing with the ship. If your physiology is so incompatible with it, then Neek needs to know. We need to find another ship."

Emn dabbed at her ear with a finger, ensuring the canal was clean, and then straightened the front of her dress. She'd already stopped the bleeding. The blood vessel breaks had been small—only minor capillaries affected—and healing was simple first-*don* stuff. Except, each time she synced with the ship, the pain was worse. What had started as a light buzzing during her time on the Mmnnuggl flagship *Llttrin*, during the Crippling War, was now a pressure that thumped between her skull and brain. It was ever-expanding, pulsed behind her eyes, crushed blood vessels, and had her leaking maroon from her ears and nose.

After sitting down against the black paneling, Emn looked at her lap. The dress, which she'd managed to keep mostly clean of blood, was tight in areas she'd not anticipated. It clung to her hips and chest, highlighting the most notable changes since her metamorphosis. It was... Could something be uncomfortable and yet comforting at the same time? She was an adult. There was no denying that, not with something so formfitting. Emn enjoyed the visual reminder of who she had become.

"For me to discuss any of this with Neek, she'd have to actually talk to me. Right after the Crippling War, I thought we had broken through that layer of self-doubt, or whatever makes Neek so rigid around me, but I guess not." Emn went to pull at the front of her dress again before catching herself.

Nicholas ran his hands through his thick hair and shook his head. "You're telepathically connected. You don't have to be in the same room to talk." Just as he had when she was in first *don*, Nicholas plopped beside her so she could lean into him. The reminder of their friendship helped ease the thumping in her head. She was forever grateful that Nicholas didn't seem at all uncomfortable with the changes she'd undergone.

"Do you think it looks all right?" Emn asked, looking down at the front of her dress.

Nicholas snorted. "You look like a woman in a dress, Emn. It fits well. Your chest looks normal, if that's what you're asking, although you'll crease the fabric if you keep pulling at it like that. If you want more specific feedback, there's a different person you should ask. I know you don't have a perpetually open connection, but even if she's closed down, you could still nudge her. It's good for her."

Emn returned the half smile, imagining how Neek would react if she just started chatting to her through their link about mundane things, like constellations or cellulose biometals, or if she actually asked about the dress...

As if Neek had been listening, the door abruptly slid open, and the room was filled with the distinctive sound of booted feet. Emn and Nicholas stood up.

Neek took a moment to stretch, reaching her hands up over her head and letting her sixteen fingers, eight per hand, brush the ceiling. This was the only room in the small Mmnnuggl pod where any of them could stand upright, and it was blissful to do so. Stretching pulled the fabric of the flight suit taut against Neek's chest and Emn let her eyes linger, careful to ensure the image did not leak across their bond. They needed Neek in the cockpit, captaining, not hiding in her room. She didn't need to know about Emn's burgeoning...*something*. Not yet, anyway. Still, Emn followed the tightly braided red-blonde hair to her narrow shoulders and then to her wide hips partially hidden in a baggy flight suit. Neek had her sleeves rolled up to her elbows, and Emn wrinkled her nose without meaning to. The lighting in the pod did not go well with Neek's olive-brown complexion. Realizing that she had probably stared for a bit too long, Emn walked back to the viewscreen.

"Looks like such a harmless planet from out here," Neek said as her arms fell to her sides. Currently filling the floor-to-ceiling viewscreen was Risal, its orange algae oceans and brown landmasses looming above them. Risal's two moons, the red Korin and white Rath, buffered the planet on either side. At their current position, the shadows from the sun overlapped Risal in two intersecting crescents, leaving a thin hourglass shape of lit land. Two cutters were in orbit around Korin, docked next to one another near the moon's north pole.

Emn knew more than she cared to about those moons. She had no firsthand memories, but being synced to the late Captain Ran's cutter had given her data on both. Rath was used as an andal plantation, although it was not a very successful one. Korin, in contrast...Korin was likely where she had been born. Emn probably had had siblings there, perhaps other genetic parents as well. They'd be dead, of course, like all the Risalian Ardulans, but that didn't make the moon any less oppressive.

Her focus was suddenly returned to the cockpit. Confused, Emn blinked, trying to clear her vision, and then realized what was happening. Her thoughts must have leaked. Now, instead of Korin, she was seeing herself through Neek's eyes, their connection taut. It was strange to see herself from the back—a woman in a knee-length, gray dress with shoulder straps and a flared hipline, tracing a finger over the moon's image. Her black hair held only hints of the red that shone in her youth, and the moonlight highlighted the dark veins that streaked across her translucent skin. Patterns emerged, if one looked long enough—and Neek was—patterns of geometric shapes bound tightly together, distorted and intersecting. Several words bounded across their link despite Neek's best efforts to rein them in. One in particular struck Emn as odd.

Beautiful.

Except, calling the markings such belied their daunting mythos and marginalized Neek's history. Emn tossed the word aside, conscious of its relevance but unwilling to call it to Neek's attention.

Emn chanced speaking, her mind caught in a spiral of the past. "How many Risalian Ardulans were at the Korin facility, do you think, at the end of the Crippling War? How many died there? One hundred? One thousand?" Korin could no longer be seen on the viewscreen, but the moon lingered in Emn's vision.

A bright, green light shot across the interface.

"Is that normal?" Nicholas asked as the light repeated. "Did we break the ship?"

Emn put her hands back on the interface, closing her eyes. Pressure raced into her head as soon as the connection reestablished. Blood vessels burst instantly, but Emn didn't bother to stem the flow. "It would appear our new signal identifier is not working. We have a priority communication from one of the cutters." She opened one eye, ignoring the blood threatening to drip from her nose, and looked at Neek. "It says they're glad we could make it and want to know when the rest of the delegates will be arriving." She paused and considered. "What's going on?"

Blood began to drip from Emn's nose before anyone could answer. She tried to discreetly catch it on her shoulder, but Neek pulled her forward, snatching Emn's hand from the panel and her consciousness from the interface. Momentarily disoriented, Emn wove into Neek's mind. Neek sighed, pulled a small square of cloth from her pocket, and gingerly wiped the affected area.

Soft cotton traced Emn's lips. Fingers brushed her cheeks. Neek's movements were surgical, but Emn's mind still wandered. Not wanting to create any additional tension between them, Emn pulled away and tried to focus on the current problem.

Neek, you've severed my connection. Emn winced as Neek persisted and brushed her nose bridge, checking for breaks.

You're the only one who can fly this thing, Emn. Hell, I can't even work the food printers without your help because of the intricate telepathic interface. I don't want you bleeding out in the cockpit.

Emn caught Neek's hand in hers. *Is this what it takes to get your attention?*

Neek pulled back as if stung. "I'm not avoiding you," she said out loud.

"Yes, you are," Nicholas said. The large cutter broke away from the moon and accelerated towards them. "Let's table that for a minute though. What sort of delegation do you think *they* think we're from?" He furrowed his brow. "We've been keeping up with the Galactic News Network broadcasts. The Risalians have been busy installing the new Markin and soliciting volunteers for sheriff forces. That's plenty to keep them busy. How could they have time for anything else?" He paused and considered. "You don't think the Nugels are sending diplomatic envoys to Risal, do you? That'd be...awfully nonviolent of them considering all the trouble they just went through to wipe out the Risalian Ardulans."

"It does seem really unlikely, but I don't think we should make assumptions about the Risalians. Not after this last month." Neek edged closer to the panel, keeping her distance from Emn. "If they think we're Nugels, maybe they'll be more open with us. Emn, would you send them a message that asks for an itinerary of the visit? Maybe that will give us some information."

Frustration rose in Emn, but she pushed it down. They needed to have a proper conversation about what had just transpired, but it'd have to wait. She reengaged with the ship, her eyes back to staring at the shiny, black paneling instead of Neek. "This would be an ideal opportunity to just shoot them," Emn muttered as she transcribed the message into the relay. "They've fired enough times on us without any reason for a warning shot to be well-deserved."

"No," Neek said abrasively. "We need information from them, remember? Shooting is not going to help us achieve that."

Emn waited for yet another reproach, or even for Neek to run away again. Instead, Neek scuffed her boots over the floor. When she did speak again, her tone was tempered. Hesitant.

"If you want to avoid interacting with the Risalians, the pod's logs are the only other option for finding coordinates."

Emn closed her eyes, catching some blood on the back of her hand as she did so. The logs. She'd tried repeatedly to access them. They were nestled somewhere near the life support systems, bundled in wires and cellulose and chips that took too long to untangle from the air compressors and heating. The concentration required to retrieve them brought her to her knees in pain each time she had tried. Of course, it was her own fault that Neek didn't know that, although Neek hadn't exactly been around to see.

Another green light shot across the panel.

"They're saying these are just preliminary negotiations, so they didn't prepare an agenda," Emn recited as the information relayed from the ship into her mind. "Now they're asking if we have anything specific we would like to address other than hemicellulose and the Ardulans."

"Genetic salvage operation?" Nicholas asked seemingly no one in particular. "I'd have thought the Risalian Ardulans were moot at this point. Also, who cares about hemicellulose anymore?"

Nicholas's words, while clearly unintentional, hurt more than the interface. Emn debated whether or not to mention it, when a proximity alarm chirped. After checking the message, Emn changed the view on the screen to aft. From the throat of the Risalian wormhole, three small Mmnnuggl pods and one large pod frigate emerged on a clear intercept course. The Risalian skiffs made no move to engage them.

Emn's frustration pushed warmth into her cheeks. As soon as they had left Craston, the Mmnnuggls began trailing them. She was tired of the constant Mmnnuggl pursuit. It had been easy enough to disable any pods before they could get a shot off, but when would they give up and let her get some rest?

"After us, or here for the meeting? Emn, could you disable them if needed?" Neek asked.

"If they were tailing us, they're just going to keep coming, Neek," Nicholas returned. "It's been weeks. We're never going to shake them in one of their own ships. Disabling them is accomplishing nothing."

Neek raised an eyebrow. "Are you advocating for shooting them?"

Nicholas kicked the wall. "No! Just...we need another strategy. Like, say, using the wormhole generator and leaving the Systems. Getting another ship. That sort of thing."

"I don't think any of that is necessary," Emn cut in. "Those pods seem to be expected." Emn pointed at the screen. The Risalian ships were now moving in tandem with the pods. The group changed heading and circled to Korin, the second cutter already disappearing behind the far side of the moon.

"We should probably follow them, if we don't want to seem out of place. Neek?" Emn didn't mention her desire to shoot at the pods. This entire situation was starting to mirror the Crippling War a little too closely.

"Neek, we should talk to the Risalians," Nicholas interjected. "We've come all the way here. This is our one chance with them. We shouldn't waste it. If they have coordinates, we can just pop them in the wormhole generator and go, maybe lose our Nugel tail, too."

Neek shook her head, although Emn could feel her desire to leave the Systems and ignore the whatever-it-was brewing behind Korin. She didn't blame her. They were in no place to get involved in another conflict.

"We'll play along for now," Neek declared. Her tone was crisp, but even Nicholas raised an eyebrow to Emn. He'd apparently caught the hesitancy, too. "I want to know why the Risalians are parleying with a species that slaughtered hundreds of unarmed civilian ships. Besides, I have reservations about the generator." This time, Neek's tone was serious. Their link tightened, as if Neek wanted to be certain Emn was listening. "With the connection problems Emn's been having, trying out a new piloting system might not be the best course of action."

Emn closed her eyes and let out a long breath. So, Neek did know, then, about her problems connecting—or perhaps she'd caught the edge of Emn's pain during her last interface. It didn't matter. Blood leaked from Emn's nose before she could catch it and hit the floor. Emn mentally cursed her body's poor timing.

"We can't go on this way, Emn."

Nicholas swallowed a laugh, and Emn bit back what she wanted to say. Instead, she edged the pod towards Korin and then turned to look Neek in the eyes.

"Do you have a suggestion for how to better deal with the issue between us?"

Neek held her hands out, her eyes landing on anything except Emn. "I meant the ship! The interface with the ship."

Nicholas winked at Emn.

Hoping that the issue would die where it stood, Emn sent, *I'm not a child anymore, Neek. I can define my own limits. We won't get far outside the Systems without using the generator or stumbling upon a new wormhole.*

That didn't garner any response, even an emotional one, although Neek's color was slowly normalizing. Instead, Neek focused on the viewscreen. As they rounded the far side of Korin, the Mmnnuggl pods came back into view, along with the Risalian cutters and skiffs. What Emn had not expected to see, however, were the other ships. Frigates, larger Mmnnuggl pods, galactic liners, and cutters, all massed behind the moon. Aside from the pods and Risalian ships, Emn didn't recognize any of the crafts. The scanners told her there were over one hundred ships present. Looking out the viewscreen, that seemed like an understatement.

"Xylnqs, Astorians, Wens, Nugels, and four others I can't hope to pronounce, but a few I recognize from the war." Emn dictated the names as they came through the interface. When she tried to dig deeper, however, her scans were rebuffed. Since some of the ships were Mmnnuggl as well, there had to be a way to reach their databases through the link in the small pod, but Emn was too exhausted to trace the connection.

"I don't think following was such a good idea. Where are they from?" Nicholas breathed. "If they're from outside the Systems, how did they get here? Why are the Risalians allowing this?"

"They're weaponized," Emn murmured. She didn't need a scan to tell her that—she could see the laser ports mounted to the ships. "All of them are, including the Risalian ships. That includes the Risalian transports."

"But *why*?" Nicholas asked. "The Crippling War is over. The Nugels lost. They should be heading back to the Alliance with their tails between their legs." He pointed to a Risalian transport in the upper-right corner of the screen. "There's no reason to weaponize anything. The war is *over*."

Neek wrapped her arms around her chest and shook her head. She walked to the viewscreen, let her fingers glide across the fleets, and then paused on a Risalian cutter.

"Emn, can you give us *any* additional information on the fleet?"

Reluctantly, Emn sank into the pod's computer. Fatigue batted at the edges of her mind, and she could feel a sticky wetness gathering in her inner ear. When she focused the scan, she reinforced it with a touch of her own energy.

This time, a travel log pinged back from a tiny Wen ship that floated just starboard of them. Hoping it would be enough to satisfy Neek, Emn read the entire script aloud. "I have a Wen travel log," she said through the exhausted haze that was settling over her mind. "Last stop before this, Wen homeworld of Querl. Before that, Xinar Hub. Before that, the Keft homeworld of—"

"Wait. Stop." Neek's hand was on Emn's shoulder a moment later. Her grip was uncomfortably tight. "You said Keft?"

"Yes," Emn confirmed. "I can't do any more, Neek. I'm exhausted."

The hand slid from Emn's shoulder, and suddenly Neek's mind was alight with excitement. "We have coordinates though, right? From the log?"

"Yes. Why?"

Neek clapped Nicholas on the back and grinned. "Because, as Nicholas has just seen, Keft is mentioned repeatedly in the Neek holy books. If it's a real place, home to a group of people who may have interacted with the Ardulans, then we have our first lead."

"It could be an asteroid, too," Nicholas added, but his tone was also laced with excitement. "Or a constellation or a dead planet, but you did say 'homeworld,' so—"

"I get it," Emn cut him off. She wanted to be excited, too, but she really needed to sit down.

Neek's eyes turned back to the viewscreen. The space around the small pod was now littered with ships, the Risalians well interspersed among them. Emn touched Neek's mind and felt the anticipation and, just behind that, crippling concern about the ships in front of them. When Neek spoke, her words were low, almost a whisper.

"Engage the generator, Emn. This, here, isn't what peace looks like. It's definitely not what treaty talks look like. If the Risalians are consorting with more aliens from outside the Systems, if something is brewing, I don't want to know about it. We did our part. Our war is over, and we need to move on. Let's get the hell out of here and find Ardulum."

Chapter 4: Research Station K47, Ardulum

We need to schedule a meeting immediately. A situation has arisen just outside of Risalian space that needs addressing. We can no longer afford to ignore the Alliance worlds. Inform the new head of Cell-Tal and bring the best linguist we have—and make sure xe speaks Mmnnuggl.

—Encrypted communication from the Science Sector of the Markin Council to the other council members, December 5th, 2060 CE

ARIK PUSHED THROUGH the andal forest, wisps of other consciousnesses pulling at his mind. A crashing sound followed him. Loud voices called his name. Patches of sunlight filtered through the dense canopy, but the light wasn't enough to keep him from stumbling over vegetation. Brightly colored birds flashed their plumage as they flew overhead, dodging in and out of the leaves and distracting Arik from the path below. He tripped, caught himself on the downed trunk of a spined palm tree, and leapt to his feet. Laughter filtered through the canopy. Arik increased his speed, trying to ignore the warmth that trickled across his wrists.

The slope increased, and the voices behind him grew labored. Arik altered his gait and grabbed nearby trees as leverage. A primate chittered somewhere near Arik's right. A half-eaten *bilaris* fruit hit his shoulder, its juices sticky and warm. Arik ducked when the primate called again and changed course, skittering along the side of the hill, away from the light. This trail would lead him to the oldest part of the andal preserve, towards the ancient groves. It was a sacred place. A safe place. Perhaps they would not follow.

Trunks thickened as the ground flattened. His pursuers fell behind, so Arik slowed, his footsteps landing softly on the dry leaf bed. This area of the grove was familiar to him, and he picked a path across the open understory with growing confidence. Just beyond lay a thicket where the oldest andal grew in tight clumps surrounded by rings of spined tangarana trees.

Arik avoided the tangarana, giving the spines a wide berth. When he finally spotted a game trail, he resumed running.

The path ahead was brighter. Arik looked up to see the canopy thinning, the trees decreasing in diameter. Another few meters, and he was in a new place. A plantation. His family's plantation. He picked his way around waist-high saplings, careful not to compact the ground near the trunks. He could no longer hear his pursuers, and when Arik looked over his shoulder, there was no forest to see. His family's land stretched to the horizon.

"Arik!"

Arik turned, surprised. His talther stood over him, smiling and holding out a watering bowl. Arik reached for the bowl.

"You're almost grown now, Arik. Another few weeks and you could be taller than me." His talther clasped Arik's shoulder, the linked black circles of zir marking visible just under zir sleeve. "Your mother, father, and I—we're so proud of you. Perhaps you will be of Science as well, like us." His talther shaded zir eyes and looked out across the fields. "Lot of work to do today. I'm glad you're here to help."

Arik poured the water from the bowl, careful to keep the stream to the channels cut into each mound of mulched earth. His toes curled into the rich soil, and he delighted in its buoyancy. If he did manifest of Science, he could stay here, on the plantation. The trees in this field, seeded from a Neek variety of slow-growing andal, had been planted just before he was born. He'd grown alongside them—these ruffled siblings— had played chasing games across their rows and hiding games amongst their foliage. Arik knew each sapling, had named each one within three hectares of where he now stood. A Science Talent could nurture these trees, grow them to adulthood. Arik could be a part of their lives for the rest of his. If he manifested another Talent, he'd almost certainly have to apprentice elsewhere. His parents could not afford to pay day laborers. Arik's saplings would die.

He looked for his talther, but the gatoi was nowhere to be seen. Zie'd probably gone to the cistern, Arik reasoned and then took careful, high steps over the mulch mounds in that direction. His pant leg snagged against something sharp, and Arik tripped, landing on the bowl.

His leg burned. What he'd assumed was simply an overlooked berry bush was in fact a tangarana sapling. It reached only to his knees, but its long, thin spines were adult-length, and several were embedded in his leg. Wincing, Arik removed the spines and tossed them at the tree's base. As if he had refused a gift, sheets of ants rained from its leaves, coating his calves. The tiny biting insects burrowed into his skin and crawled into his clothes, even his undergarments. Arik batted at the ants, screaming for his talther.

There was no one to hear him. Arik began to run again, ignoring the root areas of the saplings in his desperation. Someone's hands were grabbing him now, and Arik pulled and lunged from ripping fingers as the ants burrowed. Arik risked a look back over his shoulder. His eyes searched for what was grabbing at his arms, yanking at his feet, but he saw only the saplings and a steady stream of ants seething over the mulch.

"WAKE UP!"

Arik, startled, tripped over an exposed andal root, and fell onto his side. He screamed and shook his arms and legs, desperate to remove the insects. He tried to stand, but his foot was still wedged under the root. The ants took advantage of the situation. Arik watched, horrified, as rows of them streamed into the holes in his pants and into his pores, creating bumpy, moving lines inside his leg.

Water splashed across his face. Except, that didn't seem right. He hadn't made it to the cistern. Another spray of water hit his face. Arik put his hands down and gripped fistfuls of soil that turned to fabric at his touch. Black dots swam across Arik's vision before he saw that he was on a bed. His pant leg was partially rolled up, and there were small, red bumps along his skin. Not from ants, he realized, but needles. He wasn't in a forest—he was in a room. A sterile, silver room that was barely large enough for a bed, a sanitation chamber, and a table.

"You're awake," a deep voice said behind him. Arik turned to see a healer, the black circles prominent on his wrists as he jotted notes on a hard, plastic pad. The medic bent down and tapped Arik on the chin. "Open up. Let's see how your throat is healing."

Bewildered, Arik's mind raced between what appeared to be the dream he'd just been having and what he remembered from his Talent

Day as the healer probed his throat with a long, flat plastic stick. That was odd, too. Arik hadn't seen plastic without at least a partial cellulosic component in years. Where would the healer have gotten it? There wasn't a supplier anywhere on Ardulum that would stock such a useless tool.

"Looks normal," the healer said as he retracted the stick. "Normal for you, anyway." He made a quick note on his pad. "Already did the rest of the physical examination. You'll be allowed to stay awake unless you cause trouble." He straightened his long, white coat and pointed to the door. "This is your room. Just outside is the common area, where you are permitted to interact with the others. You are not permitted in another's room. You are not permitted to leave the common room unless accompanied by medical staff. You are not permitted to express any Talent, for any reason. Do you understand?"

Arik opened his mouth to ask what had happened to him, but only a tiny squeak came out. What was going on? Was he still dreaming? He pressed his fingertips against his throat, massaging his vocal chords before trying again. This time, he managed a short grunt followed by a wheezing sound.

The healer snorted. "You can't talk anymore, idiot. That's what happens with people like you. Genetic problem—weak chromosomes." The healer sighed. "Bad parenting, if you ask me. Never taught you to focus. Confused your body, making it think it could have all the Talents instead of focusing on one. Now look at you."

Arik looked. It took him a moment to realize he wasn't wearing a shirt—the interwoven, geometric lines on his skin were just that condensed. Shaking, Arik turned his wrists up. His Science markings were still there, but he could see the marks for Aggression and Hearth as well. Arik grabbed at his left pant leg and pulled it up, exposing new Mind markings.

All of them, he thought to himself, swallowing back the bile that rose in his throat. *All of them, and so many more besides. What am I?*

"You're defective," the healer said, dispassionately. "And you're broadcasting. Times past, the Eld would have outright terminated you, or sold you off as slave labor. Now—" The healer tapped his tablet against the wall. "—these new Eld think we might find a cure."

Arik was having a hard time unpacking his thoughts. Slaves weren't used on Ardulum. Where would they have been sold? No one was ever killed on Ardulum, not even the criminals. Arik wasn't even a criminal! His family had tended to andal plantations for generations, and while they held a great deal of land, they barely had enough liquid assets to eat regularly. They were solid sentients—law-abiding, hard-working sentients. They'd done nothing to deserve this, and neither had he.

Arik reached for the healer, questions tumbling in his head, but before his hand could touch fabric, the healer spun and backhanded Arik across the face.

"By order of the Eld, you are not to touch those without your condition. I am authorized to have you put down should you do so again. I have no space in my unit for troublemakers."

By order of the Eld? Arik's fists unclenched. He sat back down on the bed, stunned, as the healer left the small room. If he was here by Eld dictate, there was nothing he could do. The Eld were of the andal. Perhaps...perhaps *he* was not.

Arik's thoughts returned to his family. How long had he been unconscious? Where was he? Arik was supposed to have gone directly home after his ceremony. The next morning, he had been planning to perform a release treatment on the saplings, test his new Talent, and help his parents prepare the ground for the winter tree harvest. He was their only child. They *needed* him. He'd even promised the saplings he'd be there to watch them grow. They'd die without his care. His parents couldn't manage the entire plantation alone. He just...he couldn't be trapped. There had to be a way out. Surely a healer could take away some of the markings. They'd only just shown. They couldn't be permanent.

Help me! Arik screamed into his mind.

Come outside, an amused voice echoed back. *We can answer some of your questions.*

Arik froze. No one had spoken to him telepathically since he'd emerged from metamorphosis. All Ardulans were capable of it, even as adults, but no one actually *used* that skill. It was for children.

No need to be afraid, another voice soothed. *We've all been where you are. Just visited the Eld, I assume. Got a Talent, then a few more? Have markings all over your body?*

Arik looked down at his naked torso, felt heat rise in his cheeks, and looked around for something to wear. One shirt dangled from the edge of his bed, so he grabbed it and hastily pulled it on. Giggling wisped through his head.

Modest, isn't he? the first voice said.

Oh, hush, Kisak. When you first came here, you didn't leave your room for a week!

Waiketh spent the first night vomiting, a third voice chimed in smugly.

The mention of vomiting made Arik's stomach turn. He tried to ignore it. Instead, he got up and hesitantly moved to the door, placing both hands flat upon it. The voices in his head quieted, but he could feel the pressure of their presence in his mind, each a distinctive little weight in his consciousness. It reminded him of his first *don,* when his mother's mind was a constant assurance. That link had severed when he'd entered metamorphosis, and now having other Ardulans in his private thoughts felt wrong, like a violation.

As if they had all been listening in, the presences pulled back, leaving only the softest cluster of touches. Reassured, Arik slid open the door and walked into the common area.

Six smiling faces greeted him when he emerged. The other Ardulans lounged on tattered furniture, sprawled in various manners over arms of sofas, backs of recliners, and across the broad surfaces of plastic stools. All wore the same plain white pull-up pants and shirt that he wore, some with pant legs ripped shorter. On the exposed leg of a woman to his right, Arik saw a distorted likeness of his own leg markings, her translucent skin almost completely covered with geometric, black veins. Images entered his mind, each Ardulan sharing their own unique markings.

Come and have a seat, Arik, a voice called in his head. Arik looked from one face to another, unsure of whom had spoken to him. His eyes roamed over them until he caught the eyes of a stocky woman with long, black hair patting a cushion next to herself.

Arik walked towards the woman, watching the others as he went. Each time he made eye contact, pressure increased in his mind until he felt like the entire room was lounging not only in their seats, but on his brain as well. When he reached the woman, Arik knelt on the tattered, white cushion.

The woman leaned in. *I'm Waiketh, a second don. Came here ten years ago. I'm the most recent, next to you. Should be entering my second metamorphosis to third* don *any day now.*

Congratulations? Arik responded cautiously. Second metamorphosis was much more mental than physical, but surely she'd not have to undergo the change here. Her family should have been at her side, her friends, a trusted healer... She deserved the basics of sentient dignity, no matter how sick she was.

We are our own family in here, Arik, Waiketh sent. *We welcome you.* She gestured to the others. *We know you have a lot of questions, so we all gathered here to help answer them. We'd also like to ask you some questions, if you don't mind.* Her smile faded. *We don't get the news in here, you see. We're completely cut off from Ardulum and the rest of the Alliance.*

No news at all? Arik let his mouth hang agape. *Titha* were treated better than this—they weren't *animals,* for andal's sake!

Don't your family members tell you when they come to visit? he asked.

No visits, another voice said. Arik recognized it as Kisak, the first of the group to have spoken to him. A short, wide gatoi nodded in Arik's direction. Zir black hair was cropped closely to zir head, face deeply etched in wrinkles that highlighted the dark tint. *No visits—no visitors. Just us and the scientists.*

Waiketh tapped Arik on the arm and gave him a reassuring smile when he turned back to her. *Kisak is old and nearing the end of zir third don. Forgive zir temperament.*

Arik's thoughts went to his talther. The idea of zir dying alone in a plastic lab, away from the forests and the trees zie had worked with zir own parents, was incomprehensible. The gatoi sex was so rare that each was to be cherished—ones who decided to have children that much more. Arik had to look away from Kisak. He was too afraid he'd see his talther's face reflected back.

Waiketh's hand clasped his shoulder. *We're in a big lab. The scientists and healers won't give any answers, and no one who has tried to escape has ever come back. We're fed, clothed, and experimented on. That's all we know for certain.*

We don't even know what is wrong with us? Arik asked. He kept his head down, eyes on the floor.

What makes you so sure there is something wrong? Kisak spat back. Zie pointed to the ceiling. *They're afraid of us—the Eld are. We've more Talents than them, so they keep us locked up.*

Calm, Kisak, Waiketh soothed. To Arik, she added, *Conspiracies. Mind went a few years back, but the body keeps on going.*

Kisak stood angrily, launched a cushion at Waiketh, and stormed out of the common area. Arik watched zir go, unsure if he could help. To die in a place like this... Arik would be angry, too. To die without the opportunity to have children was that much worse.

The other Ardulans turned back to their private conversations or plastic tablets.

We have a lot of time to think in here, Waiketh explained when Arik looked at her. *It's hard to not use your Talents, especially since we have so many. Combine that with a small living space and the medicine we're all on, and, well, you can see how it might affect people.*

Kisak's wrinkled face hung in Arik's mind, zir age and isolation. On top of that was Waiketh's pending metamorphosis, alone, in their synthetic prison. Arik could feel the presence of the other Ardulans trying to reassure him, to comfort him. He didn't want it. He didn't want their despair, their hopelessness, their abandoned selves. He wouldn't just slouch like an old, tattered doll in an armchair.

I'm getting out of here, he whispered to himself, trying not to leak into the others' minds. A headache threatened, the presences in his mind suddenly overwhelming. Arik stood and headed back to his room. His footsteps began to feel heavy as he crossed the remaining floor and opened the door. His bed looked inviting. The nightmare of less than an hour before seemed distant, too, and not as threatening. He fell onto the bed face-first and closed his eyes.

Immediately, sounds of birdsong fluttered past. He felt a breeze play across his face, its coolness lifting the hairs on his arms. The bed was becoming firmer, slightly prickly. Arik opened his right eye and saw that he was once again lying on the forest floor instead of a bed, several blades of grass sticking into his nose.

With the headache extinguished but the fatigue still present, Arik decided he didn't care where he slept, as long as he slept. Unconcerned about his sudden change in venue, he closed his eyes, pillowed his head in the crook of one arm, and fell asleep.

Chapter 5: Outskirts of Alliance Space

Three hundred and fifteen ships spanning eleven Alliance worlds have massed near Risal, hiding just outside Alliance borders. Communicate to all Alliance territories—the Risalian Markin are willing to share their knowledge with us. Now is the time to break away from Ardulan rule. Now is the time to destroy the Ardulans!

—Communication from dissident Alliance fleet, Third Month of Arath, 26_15

"WE'RE IN ORBIT around an inhabited world," Emn said right before passing out.

"Damn it!" Neek and Nicholas both ran to her, but did not manage to catch her before her head hit the floor with a dull thud.

"Emn?" Nicholas helped ease the younger woman's head into Neek's lap. Maroon blood trickled from her ears and nose, and Neek cursed again. This is what she got for ignoring things, for ignoring *Emn*. The Ardulan was going to kill herself on this damned foolish mission, and it was going to be all Neek's fault, because she was too wrapped up in her own head to notice that Emn...that Emn... Argh!

"Go grab a scanner from the mess. We might be able to—"

"I'm fine." Emn's eyes fluttered open, and she groaned while pushing Neek's hands away from her face. "Really. Just a little overloaded. I borrowed some cellulose from the ship, and I'm fine now."

"Emn—" Nicholas began, but Neek cut him off.

"You are *not* fine. Why didn't you tell me what the generator would do to you?"

Emn sat up and turned to face Neek. She wiped the blood away with the back of her hand. When Neek held out a cloth, offering it to her, Emn didn't take it. Instead, she tilted her head, looking at Neek reproachfully. "Why didn't you ask?"

Just like a jab to the gut. Neek's *stuk* thinned, and she tried to discretely wipe it on the back of her pants. "Because I'm an idiot, okay?" she muttered.

Nicholas stood and offered Emn a boost, which she took. "That was almost an apology," he said, smirking at Neek. "Careful. You'll set a dangerous precedent."

"Could we focus back on space?" Neek asked. Privately, mostly so Nicholas wouldn't rib her, Neek asked Emn, *Are you sure you are okay?*

The response that came back had far more bite than Neek expected. *No, I'm not, but it has nothing to do with the generator. Let's figure out where we are and you and I can talk later?* Emn's tone lightened and turned delicate. *Please?*

Neek was still debating how to respond when a blue and white planet swam into focus on the viewscreen. Neek hadn't expected the generator to be so...instantaneous. She stood, mouth agape, as the planet grew steadily larger across the viewscreen. Nicholas stood next to her, shifting from one foot to the other with nervous energy. Her *stuk* was threatening a dance of its own on her fingertips, so Neek shoved her hands into her pockets. The last thing they needed was more bodily fluid on that ridiculous floor.

On the viewscreen, a silver space station hung just between the planet and its first moon. It was an ungainly thing, with ramps, ports, and what looked like protruding habitat spheres attached to its cubed surface. The station was slowly spinning, although its rotation was not uniform as the entire structure shifted between axes every few minutes. A handful of ships, mostly of the same design, were either docked, or in the process of docking or departing.

"Any chance..." Neek began, her voice slightly shrill. "Any chance that this is Ardulum?"

"How would we know if it was?" Nicholas inquired. "Does it *look* like Ardulum? From an old painting or something, maybe?" He pointed to one of the small, star-shaped skiffs passing in front of the pod's view. "We could just ask."

"That's probably better than me asking the ship." Emn turned to the interface and swayed, her legs threatening to give way.

Cursing her own uselessness, Neek steadied Emn with an arm around her waist. Neek pulled out a raw andal twig from her pocket, the remains of their supply, and handed to Emn. She'd meant to cook it this morning, offer it as a sort of peace gesture between them, but they'd run out of fuel for the portable cookstove Chen had given them. Now, all she had was a tiny, gnarled stick of springwood that Emn would have to gnaw on to eat. It wasn't exactly the reconciliation Neek had intended.

Emn took the andal, gave Neek a tired smile, and leaned into her, taking advantage of the support she provided. "Thank you," she said lightly as she bit into the twig and began to chew. "All I know is that we are in a solar system, and the planet does have two moons, so it seems a little unlikely this is Ardulum. It must just be Keft like the coordinates said."

Emn's color was starting to return as she swallowed, but she stayed leaning heavily against Neek's side. Unsure of what else to do, Neek moistened the cloth with her *stuk* and wiped dried blood from Emn's arms. She would let Emn clean her own face this time. The images that had tumbled between them from Emn's broken nose still lingered and didn't need any encouragement.

"We should at least land." Nicholas assessed Emn. "We could get some fast print, maybe get off the ship for a while. Take a break. Maybe they know where we could look next."

A break seemingly appealed to Emn, too. Relief washed into Neek's mind as she finished wiping the first arm, folded the cloth inside out, and moved on to Emn's right. There was more texture to Emn's skin than Neek had anticipated, each dark vein embossed on the surface. Her fingers strayed without her realizing, and Neek brushed a thumb across the inside of Emn's wrist, tracing the braided circles. Emn's pulse quickened, the beat strong under Neek's thumb. Realizing what she was doing, Neek brought the cloth back between them, as if nothing had happened.

"Would you mind?" Emn asked. She flipped her arm, exposing her wrist, and Neek hastily resumed cleaning. "It would be a nice break from the travesty of Nugel architecture." *And I don't mind your touch.*

"Done," Neek said hurriedly. She steadied Emn, shoved the cloth into her pocket, and backed away to the wall. It was suddenly uncomfortably warm in the cockpit.

"I agree," Nicholas said. "What do you, say, Captain?" He saluted.

Neek winced despite Nicholas's obvious attempt to lighten the atmosphere. The title cut too close on several counts. Yorden was—had been—a captain. Neek didn't have the temperament or the experience for such a job, although she and Yorden had certainly joked about her inheriting the *Pledge* one day. No, she was a would-be Heaven Guard pilot, currently useless on a ship she couldn't even fly. She was passably decent with a knife and gun, only one of which she had with her on the pod. That was it. She certainly was not qualified to be in charge of this operation.

"Could we hold off on the captain title for a while?" Neek tugged at the right pocket of her flight suit, managing to avoid everyone's eyes. "I just...I can't. Yorden...and Emn..."

Emn reached for her hand, but Neek flinched away. There didn't need to be so much damn touching, especially with soft cloths and women who filled out dresses a little too well. This was why she needed to be in her room. Alone. She was turning into a jabbering idiot.

Nicholas leaned against the black panel and shook his head. "Christ, Neek," he muttered. "You've got to get this figured out."

"Neek?" Emn asked. "What do you want to do?"

"Whether or not the populace has any knowledge of Ardulum is questionable, but I think—" Neek cast a glance at Nicholas. "—that we could all use a break. A real break, on solid ground. We need to relax."

Relax. She hadn't done that since the Neek government quarantined them on the beaches of her home province. Memories drifted to the forefront of her thoughts. Nicholas and Emn played in the surf. Yorden debated upgrades to a ship that was to be blown apart hours after leaving her homeworld. A smile threatened. As horrible as it had been to visit Neek after such a long time away and not even get to see her family, to be tormented by Heaven Guard trainees and their settee drills, to watch the *Pledge* disintegrate around her, that time was the closest Neek had come to happiness in...well, longer than she cared to admit. Maybe there'd be something similar on the planet—a resort, a beach...hell, even a bar. They could sit together, talk about something other than Mmnnuggl schematics and Ardulan folktales. Maybe Nicholas could wander off to join whatever was the equivalent of Journey youths in the Alliance, and she and Emn could—

A small, green light began to blink on the panel. Emn brought one hand back to the interface and frowned. "We're being hailed. There is a ship just out of our current field of view requesting a visual connection. I'll put them on audio so you can talk to them, Captain. I mean, Neek. Sorry."

Fuck. They couldn't keep walking on eggshells. Neek ran her hands down her crumpled flight suit, pulling out a crease in the leg and hastily wiping off the excess *stuk* onto her pants. Attempting to hide her emotions on her clothes was futile, but that didn't keep her from trying.

Neek straightened, fingertips dry for the moment. "A standard greeting is a good place to start."

"Doesn't that require a ship name?" Nicholas whispered to her. "*Captain.*"

"Audio is on," Emn responded.

Neek managed a seething glare at Nicholas after the comm clicked. "Greetings and good journey to you, fellow travelers. We of the..." She glanced around quickly from Emn to Nicholas, neither of whom offered any help. "Of the...tramp ship *Yorden Kuebrich*," Neek sputtered, "from the planets Earth and Neek, wish you the best of luck in your chosen endeavors." After another pause, she nodded to Emn to cut the audio. Nicholas slapped her on the back.

"Nice name," he said enthusiastically. "I think Yorden would appreciate the honor of having a stolen ship named after him."

"That's what I was thinking. Glory seekers or renegades, Yorden would have enjoyed both. He never forgave the Systems for their rotten peace treaties." Neek turned back to the console as the unknown ship moved into view. It had a long, bottlenose shape with what appeared to be thrusters on both the bow and stern, and the paint looked to be a middling peach color.

"They're not powering any type of weapon that the ship can recognize," Emn said. "That's a good sign. Do you think we should—"

A burst of static came through the ship's speakers. A definitively masculine voice—at least by Charted Systems standards—responded, the tone and inflection identical to Neek's.

"Greetings, *Yorden Kuebrich*. We hope you will forgive the intrusion."

"Intrusion?" Neek asked, turning to Emn. "What intrusion?"

"They accessed the ship's database," Emn said, opening her eyes. "Downloaded all the culture files as well as ship schematics." She blinked rapidly and then shook her head. "I tried to block them, but they had already pulled all the system files. They know how to work this technology better than I do."

"And no doubt think we're Nugels," Nicholas added sourly.

"Tramp?" came the voice again over the speakers. "Please confirm that this language is acceptable for communication. We are familiar with your ship's architecture but not your planets of origin. We once again apologize for the intrusion and hope we have not offended you in any way."

"Guess that answers that question," Nicholas murmured.

"Audio back on."

"No apologies are necessary, friend," Neek said. "We were just a little startled. May we ask the name of your species and how we might refer to you?"

"I am Captain Effin, and my vessel, *Elkrade*, is a tramp ship by your classification system. We work mostly in small-scale, interstellar trade. Our people are the Keft, and you are in orbit around our planet, on the very edges of Alliance space. Some might say just outside Alliance space." Effin made a noise that sounded between a throat clearing and a cough. "We run supplies between the space station you see in front of you and the one on the opposite side of the moon."

"Would it be possible to visit your planet?" Neek asked. "We'd like to meet some of your people, maybe get something to eat, and stretch our legs."

"Certainly," Effin responded cheerfully. "We don't get many visitors to Keft, but I'll send you coordinates to the visitor landing pad and customs office. Tourists are always welcome." He paused, and Neek heard a soft clicking in the background.

"We just received the coordinates," Emn whispered.

"As much as you want to be planetside," Effin continued, "you might consider instead visiting one of the space stations. Our planet is not particularly picturesque. The ecosystem collapsed some time ago due to poor farming practices."

Neek couldn't do another space station. They'd been at Craston far too long, and the smell of porous biometal and Oorin respirator fumes still clung to her clothes. An ugly planet was still a planet. "We'd like to visit Keft first, if that is all right. We can discuss the stations when we are planetside."

"Your choice," Effin responded. "Have a nice trip."

Emn brought a hand away from the panel and looked from Neek to Nicholas and then back again. A smile crept up to her face as she said, "They terminated the connection. Orders, *Captain*?"

Neek bristled. "Fine!" she seethed, giving up what was obviously a losing battle. "I'm the captain." She took two long steps to the door and then turned back around. Nicholas was doing his best to suppress a smirk, and Emn, while smiling, looked altogether too innocent. Neek wondered if she had imagined Emn's eyes quickly darting back up to her face, but she made a point not to confirm that telepathically.

"Someone...Nicholas, come get me when we've landed, all right? I'm going to go...just...yeah." She stepped out the door, hunched, and walked briskly to her room, ignoring the excited chatter that followed her from the cockpit.

Keft. Had Ardulum really come here? She hadn't really registered what Captain Effin had said, but now his words repeated in her head. A dead ecosystem. Poor farming practices. Neek slid open the door to her room, stepped over a mound of data pads, and leaned against the wall. In the stillness of her quarters, she let her mind wander to the eerie similarities to her homeworld, and what that could mean for the reality of Ardulum.

Chapter 6: Mmnn, Ggllot

We will serve the Ardulans no longer. Send a message to the Alliance. Those that wish to join us can meet here in Mmnn. It is time to unite and be our own lords.
 —Intra-planet communication from Mmnnuggl dissidents, Third Month of Arath, 26_15

JANU FRUIT JUICE and bits of pulp slid down the side of Ekimet's head and onto the paved footpath. The Mmnnuggl youth responsible, a secondary female just past puberty, chittered from the other side of the street. The purple-black sphere, which levitated right around the height of Ekimet's wide hips, spun counterclockwise and wildly spouted a colorful assortment of insults from the lateral opening of her mouth before zipping back into traffic.

It wasn't worth responding. It never was. Ekimet loosed zir long, black hair from its bun and pulled the *janu* flesh from the strands. The blue juice stained zir translucent skin and left a rotten smell. Ekimet had never been physically attacked before—not in public, anyway—but zie supposed it was the logical next step in Mmnnuggl harassment. Ekimet had been on Ggllot, the Mmnnuggl homeworld, for nearly three years, and in that time, the populace had progressed from abrasive disinterest in zir to active harassment. Ekimet had known the risks when accepting the assignment, knew the Mmnnuggls thought little of the gatoi sex. Where the Eld dictated, however, one followed. The Eld were of the andal. Ekimet would fulfill zir duties as diplomatic envoy, no matter the humiliation.

Ekimet rebound zir hair and moved to the noisy street corner just outside the capitol building. Zie waited for the rushing glob of Mmnnuggls to pass before entering the street.

Ekimet still wasn't used to the aesthetics of the planet. Here in the capital city, huge spherical buildings of pale green and dark purple hovered centimeters off the ground, tethered to their positions by a unique blend of gravimetric forces and cellulosic engineering. Residential spheres sat in tight rows on the outskirts, each individual dwelling surrounded by a narrow moat of green water. Even with all the infrastructure, however, the city was not overly large. A twenty-minute brisk walk could take a biped out of the main commerce division and into plantations of *janu*, the cultivated, golden-leaved tree species native to Ggllot whose oval fruit burst from the branches twice a season. Beyond the trees lay endless hilled pastures of grass that were perfect for grazing *titha*, a ruminant prized for its meat and thick leather hide. Even a year ago, there would have been second-*don* Science Talents working the fields on apprenticeships, learning about soil and growing conditions for non-andal species. Now there wasn't a biped to be seen for kilometers, and the fields stank of negligence.

Ekimet covered zir nose as zie walked across the street. In the capital city of Mmnn, the stench of the overripe *janu* trees, left fallow in the fields past what Ekimet considered a reasonable harvest date, hung right at biped nose level. The smell, something in between cooked wet cloth and kneecap sweat, stuck to Ekimet's clothes like *titha* dung.

Ekimet jogged the few, remaining blocks—all mercifully on an unbroken footpath put in for the convenience of visiting bipeds—to the short landing strip behind the main city communications building. Here, there was no masking the smell of the *janu* trees, their low-hanging branches swaying slowly, golden leaves dripping foul, gooey sap onto the edges of the tarmac. Ekimet moved to the small strip where the trees had been cleared, and zie scanned for the Ardulan governmental skiff that would bring zir new assistant.

The skies were clear. Ekimet frowned and dug zir toe into the seam between the landing strip and the loose, red soil, flicking a few bits onto the tarmac. High-ranking or low-ranking, as long as the Eld sent a male or female Ardulan, Ekimet could make it work. Another gatoi, however, would spell disaster for diplomatic relations. The Mmnnuggls, as with the other sentients of the Alliance, reproduced in binary or quad systems. Ekimet's presence was meant to have been an honor for the Mmnnuggls, but it seemed cultural mores traveled poorly across space. Ekimet was ignored at governmental banquets. Ekimet was not consulted when new trade deals were being established. Ekimet's seminars—the ones zie painstakingly put together on Ardulan culture, andal evolution, and Mmnnuggl-Ardulan history—all went unattended.

A familiar, high-pitched whine filled the air, startling Ekimet. A quick glance skyward confirmed the presence of a stellar skiff. The delicate, triangular ship cut its thrusters and drifted gently to the tarmac with only three short stabilizer bursts to steady its descent. Its wooden frame groaned as it came to rest on the planet's surface. When its glowing halo of heat evaporated, Ekimet was able to make out etched andal tree designs across the bow, the curly bark unmistakable. The ship's name was carved on the stern, the letters cut to look like thin andal branches placed tightly together. *Renewal*. It was a prophetic title. Ekimet hoped that the Ardulans inside lived up to the stylized name.

The *Renewal*'s main hangar opened, and her captain stepped into the bright light of the Mmnnuggl city. Ekimet smiled appreciatively at her thicker build and feminine hips. A female was likely to do well on Ggllot. Hopefully the passenger also identified as such.

"Sister," Ekimet began, erring on the side of formality as zie tried to subtly peer inside the *Renewal* to catch a glimpse of zir new assistant. "Welcome to Ggllot. I am Ekimet, diplomacy Hearth of the second *don*."

The captain flashed Ekimet another bright smile. "I've heard such things about you, Ekimet," she said. "We're from the same province, you know." She flashed Ekimet her ID badge. "I'm really excited for this assignment, and to meet you, of course."

Ekimet blinked. "This...assignment?"

Her grin broadened. "Yes, the assignment to assist you. The orders came down through the Eld this morning. I barely had time to pack before the skiff dock called me for departure." She looked up at the sky and then turned slowly around in a circle. "The Mmnnuggls have some crazy architecture. They're brilliant engineers—did you know that? How they get those huge buildings to stay put *while* hovering...well...I know you probably don't like calculations, but the math is *incredible!*"

Ekimet's jaw hung agape. Was this someone's idea of a joke? What was Ekimet going to do with a *Mind* Talent? Calculus? Zie needed someone with poise, with tact. This—this *pilot* was simply not going to do.

The woman caught Ekimet's facial expression and blushed. "Sorry," she said, her tone abashed. "I haven't been off-world before. However, I have a lot of experience in xenocultural manipulation. The Eld did get your messages. I specialized in cultural discord alleviation at the Mind Academy on Ardulum, with a minor in Mmnnuggl studies. I'm up to speed and ready to help." She paused, considered her words, and then smacked her forehead with the flat of her hand. "Oh, sorry. My name is Miketh. I'm third *don*."

"It's...a pleasure, Miketh," Ekimet stammered, still processing the information. Ekimet managed a partial smile. At least she was female. "It does seem like your background is applicable. Would you like to grab your pack, and I'll show you to the residential spheres?"

After jogging back inside, Miketh returned carrying two small bags, one slung over each shoulder. They were woven of beaten andal bark, standard issue for interstellar travel, and neither looked particularly full. Ekimet reconsidered this pilot's usefulness. *They might as well have sent me a Science Talent. Rational thinking—rational packing. No room for fun or creativity. No room for passion.* Zir uncle was a Science Talent, forever tending andal plantations, bogged down in the minutia of farm work. If Miketh was anything akin to him... Well, at least she had the advantage of having a clearly curvy figure. The Mmnnuggls would take a female much more seriously than a gatoi.

"Ready," Miketh pronounced when she reached Ekimet's side. "I memorized the city layout on the trip over. I know the way but have a tendency to gawk. Keep me from running into something, would you?"

Ekimet nodded and set a brisk pace off the tarmac and into the west side of the city where the residential spheres hovered. "It'll take about ten minutes," Ekimet said as they reached the first intersection. Zie had to hold an arm out to prevent Miketh from stepping right into oncoming Mmnnuggl traffic. A trill of high-pitched whistles sounded from the commuting spheres, warning the foreigner of her peril.

"Doesn't smell so bad away from the landing platform," Miketh commented as she scanned the multitude of large hovering buildings. "The books don't really do a great job of explaining just how awful the smell of rotting *janu* fruit can be."

"It takes some getting used to," Ekimet replied sympathetically. Zie grabbed Miketh by the front of her flight suit and tugged her across the street during a break in the traffic. Miketh followed, tripping over the uneven surface as she focused her attention on the architecture rather than down at her feet.

"I don't really understand why we bother with the Mmnnuggl cultivation anymore." Miketh straightened her clothes after Ekimet released her and quickened her stride to keep up with Ekimet's brisk pace. "We got what we wanted. The Risalian toys are all dead. Why take the time to deal with this headache?" She sniffed. "They're not of Ardulum, and andal can't grow here. They have a large star fleet. That's it. If we aren't going to war with another species anytime soon, our presence here seems superfluous."

Rational. Always so rational, Mind Talents. How was zie going to explain the delicacy of their current diplomatic ties? The Eld were invested in Ggllot and the Alliance for reasons far outside seeding and genetic resources, but if the rulers of Ardulum had not seen fit to explain the details to Miketh, Ekimet wasn't certain zie should, either. Still, the importance should have been apparent. A gatoi would not have been sent to an unstable world to mediate simple political unrest.

Ekimet led them down a steep slab of pavement to an underground tunnel. The ceiling was low, and the two Ardulans had to stoop to continue walking. The dim, green lighting made it difficult to see too far ahead, but Ekimet knew the way. They continued down the tunnel in silence for several minutes, Ekimet unsure how best to continue the conversation. As they reached the first T-junction and Ekimet veered them to the right, a peculiar sound began to build. It was soft at first, a gentle hum that grew to a buzzing after another few moments of walking.

"What's that noise?" Miketh asked, tilting her head to the side when she finally heard it. The buzzing was causing slight vibrations in the tunnel walls, and Ekimet's teeth started to chatter.

"Don't know," zie replied. Ekimet reached back and gently grabbed the sleeve of Miketh's flight suit, pulling her along as they broke into a jog. Zie caught sight of a row of spheres ahead, but the group turned a corner and was gone a moment later. "I don't like it. It isn't normal. I suggest we get out of the tunnel and into the open as quickly as possible."

The tunnel sloped down and the ceiling height rose momentarily, allowing Ekimet and Miketh a brief respite from their bent postures. Five more spheres zipped past them, clipping Ekimet at the knees before turning right and out of sight. With a deep breath and a hand on Miketh's shoulder, Ekimet led her to the middle of the intersection and turned towards the noise.

"Andal save us," Ekimet murmured under zir breath as zir guiding hand turned into a death grip. Here, where the main tunnel for the business district intersected the tunnel for the habitation district, Mmnnuggls swarmed. The buzzing had turned into a vibrating roar with the agitated shaking of nearly a hundred Mmnnuggls of various ages stacked three high throughout the intersection.

The Mmnnuggls were throbbing in agitation and still more were arriving, blocking off the way they'd come. Graffiti covered the dark walls of the tunnels—splotchy, purple writing that dripped into viscous pools on the floor. It looked like Mmnnuggl blood. It *smelled* like Mmnnuggl blood. Ekimet couldn't see any bodies anywhere, but that didn't mean anything.

"They're displeased. We need to leave. *Now.*"

"I think displeasure might be too gentle of a word for this mob," Miketh responded, bringing her hands to her ears in a likely ineffectual attempt to block the sounds. "What are they so unhappy about, specifically?"

"Any number of things." Ekimet surveyed the crowd for the best route of escape. "They don't like how the Charted Systems conflict ended. They wanted the Risalians wiped out along with the Ardulans. They see the Risalians as the architects of the entire problem. To add to that, a month ago, someone got information about a captured Risalian Ardulan being brought back to the Alliance for testing, along with some inconsequential Terran. They don't like that they missed one, and that the Eld haven't sent reinforcements to finish everything off."

Miketh nodded gravely. "The Eld briefed me on the flare situation before I left. I'll bet the Mmnnuggls want to tear that altered creature apart. Disgusting thing—I can't blame them for that." She shivered. "Why we sold defective stock to the Risalians in the first place is beyond my understanding."

A high-pitched shriek went up from somewhere in the middle of the crowd. A Mmnnuggl, slightly smaller than average and with only one ear, rose up and began to twitter loudly. It took Ekimet a moment to realize that what zie thought was a trick of the light reflecting strangely off the top of the Mmnnuggl was actually the top half of a separate Mmnnuggl perched on the first. It was wearing half of another Mmnnuggl for a *hat*. Ekimet turned aside and vomited.

"Looks like they've got a ringleader," Miketh commented, her voice a pitch higher than Ekimet remembered. She grabbed Ekimet's hand and tugged. "Let's move while they're distracted."

Ekimet ignored her. Zie straightened instead and tried to listen to the speech, hoping to catch the purpose of the gathering and perhaps the supposed crime of the victim.

"Today I speak to you, fellow Mmnnuggls. I am Oorpp, who has freed you from our president's poor decisions. No more shall we listen to these sycophants. There will be no more mercy for those who bow to the Eld of Ardulum!" The twittering Mmnnuggl rotated forward. The half-Mmnnuggl slid off his round body and cracked on impact with the floor. Purple blood, thick and partially congealed, streaked across the shiny, purple-black surface of Oorpp's body. He twittered quickly, the words running into each other. Ekimet had to strain to understand.

"The Eld have forgotten Ggllot the Ardulans use us Mmnnuggls for their technology without giving anything in return the Eld do not lead the Eld do not help the Eld must be removed and Ggllot taken from Ardulan rule death to the Ardulans."

They were treasonous words. Murderous words. Coup d'état. Ekimet's mouth fell open. The Eld were selected by the andal. No matter how strange their orders, no matter the outcomes, their removal was not an option. Unseating the Ardulan government—or the Mmnnuggl government, for that matter—simply didn't make sense.

Miketh tugged at Ekimet's hand again. "He's speaking very quickly," she whispered, eyes wide. "But is he...is he talking about *us*?"

Ekimet nodded and began trying to scoot along the concrete edges of the intersection, hoping to reach their exit while the Mmnnuggls were still occupied. More had filled in the passage behind them. The only route left was forward.

"This has been a long time coming," Ekimet whispered as they progressed. "I've warned the Eld, many times in fact, but you're the first help they've sent. A little too late, I think." Ekimet bumped into a sphere and rammed a hand into the wall to prevent falling. The Mmnnuggl beeped, irritated, but did not turn around. "I'll explain once we get out."

Miketh nodded. They kept their right shoulders to the wall as they wove through, leaning away only to sidestep obstacles. Their destination, the second right exit of the intersection, was quickly filling with more Mmnnuggls. The spheres ranged in size from twice to three times the size of Ekimet's head, packed tightly together. Still, Ekimet could make out a few small spaces narrow enough for bipeds to pass through. Ekimet pointed to an opening between two Mmnnuggls just off the wall.

"Over there," zie yelled above the increasing din. "That's the exit."

Miketh nodded and released Ekimet's hand, preparing to push apart a small pool of Mmnnuggls that was directly in her path.

The intersection went quiet. Oorpp stopped his fast-paced twittering, and the other Mmnnuggls rotated, simultaneously, to face the Ardulans. Ekimet and Miketh stopped walking.

"Perhaps our Ardulan diplomat can address these concerns," Oorpp said quietly. He spoke cleanly now, without accent, in High Uklam, the formal language of Ardulum. That did not bode well. Ekimet hadn't heard High Uklam on Ggllot since the last Eld visit.

"He seems to be so very well educated in other matters. We'd appreciate his thoughts on the issues presented."

Ekimet's face reddened with anger, the blood a deep maroon beneath zir translucent skin. "I am not male," zie said loudly, turning towards Oorpp. "Your perpetual attempts to shame my sex do nothing to endear me to your cause."

"No?" Oorpp responded, his tone falsely apologetic. "How rude of me." He swiveled around completely and then rushed towards Ekimet, stopping two meters before zir and hovering right at face height. "I do have questions though. Tell me—why allow so many Mmnnuggls to perish in a war fought for you, when their deaths were so easily preventable? We know what your species is capable of—the powers you possess." Oorpp turned back and addressed the crowd. "Why worship gods who refuse to use their powers to help those who help them? We rid the Charted Systems of *their* mistakes, and *we* are the ones that died!" Oorpp whistled a low, wavering note. "Yet, our *janu* fruit remains unharvested. Our ships unrepaired. The families who lost fathers and mothers uncompensated. Meanwhile you, you *Hearth*, you speak of manners and formalities. You are *worthless!*"

The buzzing began again, building until it felt like the concrete walls were beginning to shake. The Mmnnuggls started to rise higher despite the crowded area, individuals stacking in even higher columns and surrounding Ekimet and Miketh, preventing their escape.

"We have to get out of here!" Miketh yelled. "Do you have any weapons?"

"Haven't got anything useful," Ekimet yelled back. The Mmnnuggl columns shoved the two Ardulans, forcing them back-to-back. Ekimet heard Miketh mutter some calculations under her breath, after which she swung one of her packs at the nearest column. It connected with a loud smack and pushed the middle Mmnnuggl out of the column, causing the entire structure to topple onto the ground.

"Why don't we talk about this calmly?" Ekimet shouted into the crowd in the direction zie had last seen Oorpp. "If you have problems, I can take them to the Eld. Your concerns will be heard!"

Smack—Miketh's bag disrupted another column. Mmnnuggls fell towards Ekimet. One hit the ground at a bad angle, rolled to a stop until one ear was sticking directly towards the ceiling, and then remained still. Another hit zir in the side of the head. The jolt caused Ekimet to lose balance, and zie grabbed Miketh's shoulder for stability. Miketh was already coiling for another hit and sprung away from Ekimet's grasp. Ekimet fell heavily into a stack of Mmnnuggls and toppled it, their hard, round bodies bruising Ekimet's ribcage and hips on impact. A moment later, zie felt a telltale deflation under zir hip as a Mmnnuggl collapsed in on its hollow form, oozing purple entrails onto the pavement.

"Ekimet!" Miketh yelled over the screeching. Her last swing had gone wide as the Mmnnuggls adapted their column construction to her tactics and gave her pack a wider berth. Five additional columns approached and surrounded Miketh, cutting her off from Ekimet and closing in so tightly that she could not break free.

"Ekimet!" Miketh screamed again. "What do we do? Talk to them! Offer them new *titha*, or a case of high-speed cellulose fibers. Anything!"

Ekimet's head felt fuzzy, and zie couldn't seem to respond. As zie tried to get zir bearings, Mmnnuggls sat on all of zir appendages. Zie felt the ichor of the crushed Mmnnuggl absorbing into zir clothes. It was simultaneously painful and disgusting, and Ekimet had no idea what to do. Zie was no Aggression Talent. Zie had no weapons or aptitude for violence, and attempting to fight back was only killing Mmnnuggls, which certainly wasn't helping the situation. Although there was no denying its effectiveness, violence was not a preferred method of social change. There was really nothing left to do except see what the Mmnnuggls wanted. Perhaps if their demands were met, peace could be restored.

Miketh's screams tapered to whimpers and then finally died out altogether. The vibrations continued, rattling Ekimet's bones and increasing the pounding in zir head. A shrill tone began to sound from a Mmnnuggl next to Ekimet and slowly raised in pitch until Ekimet could no longer hear the note but felt the pain of it in zir ears. Another Mmnnuggl joined, and then another, their voices melding into a cacophony of stabbing pain.

Ekimet felt a popping in both ears and then the warm flow of blood down the sides of zir head. There was silence then—blissful, soft silence despite the continued vibrations—until a large Mmnnuggl accelerated directly into Ekimet's forehead. Then, there was only darkness.

Chapter 7: Eld Palace, Ardulum

I warned you about Risal. I warned you about Ggllot. This situation is entirely your fault, and you need to find a way to rectify it, or Ardulum will rectify it for you.
—Personal communication from Advisor Corccinth to the Eld of Ardulum, Third Month of Arath, 26_15

HER PALM FLAT against the plywood, Corccinth felt the wall move. Even through the casing, she could sense the andal roots that made up the primary structure of the Eld Palace stirring. Coming to life, it seemed—except, all the roots that made up the palace were already alive and attached to living trees. Something now made them fidget and push against their bindings. In time—perhaps a day, perhaps a week—the palace would split apart so the andal could focus on its goal. A few small roots had already meandered up through gaps in the plywood.

"Ardulum will move soon," Corccinth said blandly. She gave a twisting root a tap, imagining where the first large fissure in the plywood would begin, and moved from the wall towards the Eld. She'd not been in the Talent Chamber in years, as most of her meetings with the Eld were held in the flare apartment—part of a suite of specialized rooms within the center of the palace. Corccinth looked up as she walked, hoping to get the breathtaking view of the sky between domed andal branches and the cellulose-infused glass between them, but instead saw the dark carvings that loomed over the thrones. They were as tacky as she remembered.

Frowning, Corccinth sidestepped to get a better view of the ceiling and kicked over a small wood pot. It was empty, mercifully, of the synthetic mucus, but half-filled ones just like it were scattered across the floor. Refilling the vessels should have taken less than one night. She'd had that job once, when she was barely a second *don*. Quality of service to the Eld had clearly declined, although with their current missteps, they probably deserved a wet hemline now and again.

"The move will occur within the next month, I think," Adzeek, the male eld, said. He smiled and then followed Corccinth's eyes to the ceiling. "The andal is beautiful this time of year. We thought you might enjoy meeting in this room." He scratched his nose and looked briefly to Savath, the gatoi eld. "I assume you received the paperwork on the new flare, Advisor Corccinth?"

Corccinth stepped over another pot and released the fabric of her brown pants so that the hems once again brushed the floor. "I did, although I still would prefer if you let me do the transport. They're so *young*."

"He's fine, Corccinth," Savath soothed. Zie moved from zir throne and sat on the floor, motioning for Corccinth to join zir. "The day's report will be at your apartment by the time you leave this meeting. He woke up, he met the others, and he is adjusting. We put him in K47, as you requested."

Corccinth grumbled unintelligibly. It was the nicer of the facilities, if not the hardest to escape from—but escape *was* the goal, after all. The ones that managed it only did so through controlling their Talents, which meant they could be integrated back into society as upstanding citizens, if somewhat hidden. She'd need to make an appointment to visit Thannon to check the gap in the land mass that allowed ships to access the deeper ocean, and thereby the facility. K47 hadn't had a successful flare escape in almost a year, and if the land gap was filling in, that was likely the cause. That none of the flares at K47 had the drive to escape, had no ability to focus and really *plot*...that she didn't want to consider. There were always a few who had the motivation and the will to push past the barriers and find her. Learn from her. Reenter society and practice control. K47 was just...just having a dry stretch.

"What about Ggllot?" Corccinth asked, changing the subject. Her mind didn't need to dally in Thannon. "What about Ekimet?"

"What *about* Ggllot?" Adzeek returned. His tone took on an edge. "You knew the possibilities when you suggested your grandchild for the position. Zie is the best diplomat we have, but Ggllot is lost. Ekimet's presence there buys Ardulum the time it needs to prepare for the move."

Corccinth breathed out, forcing air loudly through her pierced nose. This wasn't why she had asked for a meeting, but it was not a topic she was willing to let go. "Ekimet is not a bargaining piece. I lost my tochter to your political overreach. I'll not lose my grandtochter. I will have Ekimet back." Corccinth spat onto the wood floor, the phlegm landing a handspan from Savath's knee. "Send a rescue mission."

Asth, the female eld, shifted uncomfortably in her chair. "Corccinth, you are invaluable to us. Your advice to the Eld...you are irreplaceable. We have overstepped many times at your request, but this...you know we cannot do this. Ardulum could request a move tomorrow. There is no time. Perhaps after the move—"

"Perhaps after the move, Ekimet will be *dead*."

"Corccinth—"

"No." Corccinth's voice lowered, became calm and dangerous. "I do not believe you speak for Ardulum on this. Ekimet is gatoi. Ekimet is Savath's dearest friend. Ekimet will advise you in my place when I die. I have trained Ekimet from the time zie was born to be an advocate for the flares, and now, now you have a Risalian-bred flare bumbling about the galaxy, who will eventually come looking for us, and you want to rid yourself of a diplomat who could work with her? Ease her into our life? Keep her from melting the planet into cellulosic mush?" Corccinth tugged at the sleeves of her shirt and hissed through clenched teeth. "You ask it. You ask Ardulum if that is what it wants! *You ask it!*"

Savath looked first to Asth and then Adzeek. Their shared sheepish expressions only made Corccinth's face warmer. She balled her fists, ready to let loose a string of curses, when Savath spoke.

"Peace, dear one. We will ask." In her mind, the gatoi's voice added, *I have asked already, privately, but received no response. Prepare yourself for the possibility that Ardulum...that Ardulum does not work on a scale of individual lives.*

Ardulum isn't cruel, she returned. *And Ardulum is always pragmatic. Ask again. I will wait.* She humphed and sat cross-legged on the floor.

Roots just underneath the floorboards stretched, and Corccinth felt the wood at her backside ripple. The walls, the floors, even the roots in the ceiling, twisted in their casings. A week seemed generous. Ardulum could move tonight, even. It was ready for something, clearly.

Savath's eyes flew open. "The move," Savath stammered, bringing Corccinth's attention back to the Eld. The gatoi tried to get to zir feet but became tangled in the bottom of zir robe and fell clumsily back to the floor. Asth and Adzeek knelt to help the gatoi, but Savath slid zir hands under zir trembling legs.

When zie spoke again, Savath's voice was soft and hesitant. "You've worked so hard, Corccinth, to reintegrate the flares, but...there's...are too many of them. Ardulum assures me that Ekimet is not forgotten, but the planet has officially made the request. The flare population has become too unmanageable. Ardulum can't move, even with our guidance, with so many on-planet. We have to..." Savath trailed off. Corccinth read the panic. Absorbed it. Knew what was coming before it was said, but that didn't draw the pain from the words.

"They're to be culled."

Ardulum's reassurance regarding Ekimet washed from Corccinth's mind. A cold rage ran down her spine. "How many?" she asked.

Asth responded. "Not the ones in towns. The escapees you mentor are not the issue, as we had hoped they would not be. Their minds are ordered enough for Ardulum to deal with. It is the wild ones still in the containment facilities. Even with the precautions we have taken, their collective telepathy is too much for Ardulum. It can't block their voices."

Slowly, Corccinth stood. She steadied her breathing and tried to will some warmth back into her gnarled fingers. The hair that fell about her face was thin, white, and reminded her of how far she had come—with the flares, with their training, and with the Eld. And yet, she hadn't done enough. All that work, all those years encouraging and finding and training, and still this was going to happen. She shouldn't have been surprised.

"Don't think I am unaware of history or protocol," she said to Adzeek, whose wary stare grated. "You look at me as if you expect me to disintegrate you."

Savath struggled to zir knees. "The Markin of Risal found an alternative method for control in the Charted Systems. We could inquire—"

"No!" Corccinth's foot stomp was so emphatic that Savath fell back. "That supposed act of mercy led to war with the Charted Systems and the loss of both my child and now perhaps my grandchild. The cull must be done." Her voice softened. "It must be done."

Asth stepped away from Savath and took Corccinth's left hand. Her skin was weathered, like Corccinth's, but warm. She smelled strongly of cinnamon, and Corccinth had to pull back her sense of smell in order to remain focused. "With your blessing, then, we will proceed."

Corccinth nodded, almost imperceptibly. "I know the strength of a flare mind all too well. They are always a gamble, even the ones that can focus. Even the ones that accept training. I have done as much as I could reasonably do. We all have." She was whispering now, unsure if her voice was loud enough for all three elds to hear. "But..." Her mind flitted through ideas, still desperate for some other answer she had overlooked. Desperate for one last chance. "Perhaps...slowly. Give them time...as much time as we can. There could be one planning to break out even now. Gather the younger ones, the spirited ones, and put them together. Maybe...there's still a few in there who can be a part of society."

Savath was up again and now took her other hand. Zir skin was cooler than Asth's, but the dual support kept Corccinth from collapsing onto the floor. Her legs were suddenly too unsteady. Though she felt cold, she was sweating, and her makeup was starting to clump on her skin.

"We'll move them to K47," Savath said. "It's the largest facility. We can fit more in—give them a longer interval to break free."

Corccinth nodded. The Talent Chamber became blurry. Her eyes refused to focus. "I'll move my entire surveillance team to Thannon. Increase the testing intervals and any other stressors you have there. It might push some of them far enough. Any that break out, we will guide to the palace. That way, they can be tested immediately and hopefully put back into the population—with training, of course."

Savath's grip tightened, but not uncomfortably so. "We'll start the culling tonight, Corccinth. The stressors will be increased immediately."

She nodded, eyes still refusing to focus. *Please help some of them find their way to me,* she said in a silent prayer to the andal. *I've worked so hard to train the ones that have shown an ability to focus their Talents. Please, there are over four thousand flares in the containment facilities around Ardulum. Please, don't let all of their lives be sacrificed for this move.*

Chapter 8: Keft

The Markin Council of Risal formally invites the ruling heads from each inhabited planet of the Charted Systems to join us at Raleigh, the capital of Risal, as soon as possible. A delegation from the Alliance—a group of neighboring systems—has entered into treaty talks. A common enemy threatens us all, and a strong bond now could ensure the safety of the Charted Systems for centuries to come.
—Broadband communication from the Markin Council to the Charted Systems, December 12th, 2060 CE

THE DOOR TO the pod opened with a blast of warm, damp air. It hit Neek in the face, carrying with it the smell of rotting vegetation and decay.

They had landed on a paved platform with several short, glass buildings situated around its perimeter. Completely unhindered by other buildings or foliage, the flat landscape stretched for kilometers until it reached the horizon. Neek would have taken it for agricultural land, except there were no crops that she could distinguish. The ground was mossy green outside the platform, and if Neek squinted, she could make out small shrubs in the distance. Otherwise, the terrain appeared empty.

"That is *the* most disgusting smell," Nicholas sputtered as he stepped from the ship and stood beside Neek. "Like decaying plant matter. I can't even see where it would be coming from."

Emn took a step onto the exit ramp and inhaled deeply. The spotty pressure in Neek's mind that came from Emn's connection to the ship shifted, became lighter. Emn touched down onto the platform and did a small spin on one foot, the folds of her dress flaring in the breeze. Neek looked away from the dried maroon spots on the hem.

"I like it," Emn said, taking another deep breath. "It's almost like a perfume, maybe. Strong, but nice."

Nicholas pulled the collar of his flight suit up over his nose and turned back to look at her. "You have got to be kidding," he said, his voice muffled by the fabric. "It's *vile.*"

Neek scanned the area again. Emn had landed them next to another bottle-nosed ship—all soft blue curves with a greenish tint—but its pilot was nowhere to be seen. She could feel the heat still radiating from the engines, so they couldn't be far. Neek had to stop herself from running her fingertips over the cellulose weave in the biometal of the ship. A shape like that, with a dense enough component of cellulose to be visible even from a distance, indicated speed and agility. It'd be amazing to pilot, and Neek let her mind wander into that possibility for a luxurious moment.

"We should probably try to find someone," Nicholas suggested. Neek dropped out of her daydream. A concrete path led from the landing strip to the stretch of single-story glass buildings, the second one of which was labeled in a script she couldn't read, the words carved onto a swinging wood sign.

"We could start there, I suppose," she said, pointing. "At least it has a label. Maybe they have a map or a restaurant. I think we could all use a solid meal that didn't come from a Nugel printer."

"Excellent idea," Nicholas agreed. He clapped Neek on the back and jogged ahead, slipping into the building and disappearing from view.

"Wait, Nicholas!" Neek called out. She began to quicken her pace, but Emn's hand landed on her arm, pulling her back.

"Could we just slow down for a minute?" Emn asked as Neek turned to face her. "We haven't been alone since the end of the war." The memory of their embrace, of Neek's promise, of the cascade of emotions that led to that moment, crowded Neek's memory. "I'm not asking for anything from you, Neek, except maybe to stop avoiding me. Could we work on that?"

Neek looked away. She didn't have any words of her own to offer, and she wasn't ready to use the words that she suspected Emn wanted to hear. Instead, hoping it would be enough, she slowed and walked next to Emn down the path, letting the silence drift between them.

Emn stayed close to her, their shoulders occasionally touching. A persistent breeze blew green pollen across their path, coating their clothes and skin. Neek's *stuk* began to flow as her body tried to clear blocked pores, and a walk that should have been leisurely became sticky and uncomfortable. The stillness of the landscape didn't help, either.

There were no bird calls, no engine whines, and no distant rumbles of thunder. Even the breeze produced no sound as it lifted the pollen from the ground and spread it across the horizon.

Neek had seen a landscape like this once before. The entire scene was eerily familiar. On her twelfth birthday, her name day, her brother had snuck her out of her party and onto her family's land skiff. They'd woven through native andal forests, new plantations, swampland, and trillium fields, before emerging into a mossy clearing. It'd looked just like this—barren of larger life. No bird song. No animal tracks. No vegetation, save the moss. No trees. He'd found it during survey class, he'd told her. He'd reported it. He'd been told to forget it existed.

Neek shook off the memory as she and Emn reached the door. It pushed in easily, glass gliding towards the wall. A cool gust of air met them as they stepped in. The building's layout was entirely open, the space segmented only by rows of display plinths encased in transparent crystal.

"It's a museum." Nicholas said from several rows away. He moved towards the nearest plinth and squinted through the case. "This one has a miniature model of the planet with a bunch of ships speeding around." He motioned to Neek. "Pretty cool. Come see."

"There's a plaque, too." Emn moved to the opposite side of the plinth. "This one is labeled 'Keft, twenty-five years before the Collapse.' There's a Common translation at the very bottom."

Neek stood next to Emn and read the inscription. "A monument, maybe?" she said when she looked up and peered at the display.

It was a cityscape of some form, but Neek had seen no skyscrapers or zipping spacecrafts on their approach, which confused her even more. Nicholas put a finger to the glass case and a tiny model skiff flew up to meet him. He chuckled in amusement and traced his finger around tall, glass buildings while Emn did the same with one of her own. Their fingers hit near the top as the ships they were trailing sped past one another. Emn's ship, which appeared to be made from wood, dove sharply towards the ground. Just as it was about to hit, the ship flattened its course, turned belly-up, and began to wind around a bulbous, glass building.

"Show-off," Nicholas snickered.

Emn bowed. "I learned from the best, you know—she's the only pilot in the Heaven Guard to find an Ardulan."

Neek humphed at the reference to her past. Emn grinned. She put her hand on Neek's arm, squeezed, and then moved to the next plinth.

"Neek, come check this one out." Nicholas had slid over several rows and was pointing to a short, wide plinth. "This one shows the traditional forests of Keft. Totally different from the outside."

The living diorama in this display was breathtaking. Featured was a forest with little undergrowth, the trees so old and large that their canopies shaded most of the floor. Brightly colored birds flew overhead, their songs audible through the case. Neek studied the trees, following the roots from stem to crown, remembering the times when she had visited her uncle's home—only a few kilometers from her parents' house—near a small patch of old-growth forest. There was no similarity in the trees between the two worlds, but the red and green leaf-littered ground was close enough to remind her of the Neek homeworld.

Actually, some of the trees did look familiar. Neek put her hands on the sides of the crystal, getting her face as close as she could. Her *stuk*, instead of sticking her fingertips to the surface, gelled upon contact, preventing the *stuk* from dripping down the sides of the case. In the far-right corner of the forest stood a tall, thick tree, its crown dominating the canopy. Neek followed its limbs to the trunk, to the curly, black bark growing there. She shivered.

"Hey, Emn?" Neek asked warily. "Look over here and tell me if you see what I do."

"What is it, Neek?" Nicholas pressed his nose against the crystal. "What are we looking at?"

"I see it," Emn said. "It...looks like an andal tree."

Neek pulled her finger off the crystal, noting as she did so that her *stuk* mark slowly dissolved until it was no longer visible. As she turned, her eyes caught another display. The next plinth over showed another forest. Instead of multiple tree species, however, Neek saw only andal. The trees were shorter, with epicormic shoots and yellowing leaves. The crowns were lopsided and sparse. The undergrowth looked like a nightmare, with ferns and bushes sprouting chest-high throughout the diorama. Now Neek was *certain* it was andal. She'd seen the same decline on her homeworld in the plantation trees and in the sapling stock she and Yorden had occasionally hauled for the Risalian Markin. In the places her brother had taken her to, in secret.

Nicholas followed Neek's gaze and ran over to the plaque. "Keft, seventy-five years before Collapse. Plantation farming." He stuck his hands in his flight suit pockets and pursed his lips. "What do you think happened?"

"A traveling planet happened."

Neek jerked around, startled. A biped with short, red hair, deep brown skin, and a thin, willowy frame jogged from the doorway and joined them at the plinth. His long, yellow shirt and black pants were green with pollen dust, and he hastily batted at them, sending particulate into the air. He could have been a Terran or a Neek or an Ardulan, so nondescript was his appearance.

"I'm Effin. We spoke earlier. Sorry it took me so long to join you. I didn't realize our customs officer was out, and I had to drop the family and our ship off at Tig Station—our local hub—first and snag a rental. Nothing for them to do here while we chat except gawk at off-worlders. You're our first visitors in years. We used to get more—even a few from the Systems, which is why there's Common on the plaques. I can give you the quick version of the tour if you'd like, although it looks like you've already made your way around." He paused and studied each of them in turn. "I'd also love to know why you don't look anything like Mmnnuggls."

"A...a traveling planet," Neek finally managed. It was supposed to have been a question. There was a hand in hers, gripping tightly. Neek hadn't even felt Emn move next to her, so overwhelmed was she by the question bubbling in her mind. The comfort was welcome.

"I'm Nicholas St. John." Nicholas pushed forward and held his hands out, palms up. "I'm a Terran from Earth, in the Charted Systems." He pointed first to Neek and then Emn. "Our captain is Neek, from a planet of the same name, also in the Systems, and Emn is... Emn was born on Risal. We got the ship from Nugels, but they gave it to us. It's legal," he added awkwardly.

Neek struggled to form words, ignoring the introductions entirely. "Effin, the planet—did it have a name? Could you describe it?"

He shook his head and leaned on the crystal casing. "It's a pleasure to meet you, but I'm afraid we have no pictures. We've got an image or two of it in one of these, but I'm afraid the name was scrubbed from the databases." He pointed to the weeping trees, his finger leaving a wet trail in its wake. "A planet arrives in your solar system unannounced, and it throws all kinds of things out of balance. We were a younger civilization back then, easily influenced. The aliens were really interested in our keft tree—the one you see in here surrounded by the spined liana—named after our homeworld. They taught us monoculture farming, made some genetic upgrades." Effin spat on the floor. "What you see outside is the result. When things got bad, they left. Just like that. We've had to abandon the planet for the most part. The food web is almost entirely gone."

Neek, his fingers, Emn sent, but Neek had already noticed. As Effin became more agitated, beads of what Neek thought were sweat had burst from his fingertips. Now, small drops of what looked and smelled exactly like *stuk* hit the floor in a silent rain, dripping around Effin's long, purple talons.

"You...you don't happen to know where the planet went, do you?" Neek managed to choke out the words while her brain processed the coincidences around them. What had been amusing to consider on the pod was now far too real. Tree decline. Traveling planets. Monoculture plantations of andal. So much *stuk*. Effin only marginally resembled a Neek, in the way most bipeds she'd encountered had the same basic construction, but *stuk* was a feature she had never before encountered on another species.

"It was decades ago. No one knows, and I doubt anyone cares." Effin held out a hand to Neek, and she quickly counted the fingers—eight per hand. Just like a Neek. "You all right, Captain Neek? You look pale."

She wouldn't be all right for a long time, of that Neek was certain. "Just need some air. Give me a minute." Neek let Emn lead her back outside. The sun was beginning to set, sending purple light across the landscape. Emn's grip was firm, and Neek tried to ground herself in the tactile sensation. There could be other traveling planets, right? Couldn't others have unlocked that sort of technology? Maybe she had misidentified the tree? Maybe lots of species secreted mucus? Maybe...maybe she'd just been wrong.

They stopped just outside the door. Neek tightened her grip on Emn's hand, though what she really wanted was to let her forehead rest on Emn's shoulder. She tried to sort the possibilities but kept coming to the same conclusion.

"It's real," she murmured, her eyes to the ground. "It's fucking real."

Emn's arms were around her then, and Neek drowned in the embrace. She pressed into the hot skin of Emn's neck, inhaling the smell of andal and soap. Neek's emotions drifted, desperately searching for an anchor. Emn's hands were on her back, fingers smoothing over the flight suit's fabric, holding Neek to her. Neek tried to surface.

"There are still a lot of questions," Emn whispered into her ear.

"So, are we going to talk about the weirdness here?" Nicholas asked, breaking through the questions swirling in Neek's head. She jerked out of Emn's arms and shoved her hands into her pockets, turning her burning face away from Nicholas and Effin for a moment.

Nicholas pointed to Neek's pocket. Momentarily confused, Neek pulled her left hand out and held it up. "What?"

"Red hair, sixteen fingers, and empathic mucus production all on bipeds of a similar height. No one thinks that is a strange coincidence?"

Neek glared at Nicholas as Effin barked a laugh. "Tact," she whispered. The breeze tossed her words, but she was certain Nicholas had heard.

"Weird," he whispered back. "Don't pretend it's not."

"You secrete empathic mucus as well?" Effin's expression turned quizzical. "It's not outside the realm of possibility, but still. Not all my people have this number of fingers, or this shade of hair, but we all secrete the mucus."

Neek offered her hand to Effin. He ran his own slippery fingertips over hers, his talons scraping her skin. Her *stuk* had gelled from being in close contact with Emn, but it thinned as Effin's mixed in. A muddied consciousness skirted Neek's mind and then slipped away when Effin stepped back, surprised.

"Nicholas was telling me you also grow keft, although he called it andal, on your homeworld. How interesting. As to our appearance... Convergent evolution? While common, the red hair color is not ubiquitous. It's mostly in the working class, not so much in the ruling class." He pointed inside the building. "I can't explain the trees though, not at all, and certainly not the mucus. We have nothing else in common otherwise, unless you count legs and arms."

She hadn't expected their visit to bring up questions of her own heritage. Neek ran through the people she had known on her homeworld, the families that had red hair, those that didn't, and where they stood on the social ladder. There were only a few old family lines left, characterized by the red-tinted eyes, pale hair, and bone-white skin that Neek had always assumed was a result of inbreeding. Now, she wasn't so sure.

"You wouldn't happen to have a genome sequencer available, would you?" Neek asked. "There are a lot of questions here that could be answered pretty quickly."

Effin brightened. "Solid idea. The rental has one in the med bay. Let's go get it." Effin jogged ahead to the landing platform awash with green pollen and ducked into the bottle-nosed ship. Neek's boots slipped as she followed, little green clouds puffing up with each step. Their Mmnnuggl pod now had an inadvertent sheen as well, glistening green in the sunset, the pollen sticking to the sphere in pyramidal clumps.

"Here," Effin said, walking back down the ramp and handing the small, spherical device to Neek. It was warm in Neek's hand and thick with cellulose weave. She turned it over, admiring the craftship.

"Go ahead and scrape your skin with the edge there," Effin prodded. "I already did mine, and I uploaded your language database as well. Results will read over the front display." Neek allowed herself one more appreciative glance at Effin's ship, which the Keft noticed. He grinned. "She's a beauty, isn't she? The rental company just had the detailing upgraded with the new tech from the Alliance."

Neek whistled. "She's amazing. I'd love to get my hands on one. Would love to ditch this junk too, while I'm at it." She pointed at the stolen Mmnnuggl pod and then pressed the disc's edge into her palm, dragging it over the surface. A thin layer of *stuk* impeded the device before it finally found purchase near the center of her palm. Moments later, the machine beeped, and Neek handed it back to Effin.

"Here," she said. "You're likely a better interpreter than I am."

Effin laughed. "If it's a trade you're after, there's a space hub about sixty light-years from here in the Xinar System. They have a shipyard and don't ask a lot of questions. Mmnnuggl tech is always in demand." He tossed the analyzer into the air and caught it. "As for this, it is a consumer-grade genetics tool. A *titha* could use it. Look."

He held up the analyzer so that everyone could see. Across its surface, in bright green letters, it read:

SPECIES 1: KERR SUBTYPE B
SPECIES 2: KERR SUBTYPE UNKNOWN
GENETIC MATCH: PROBABLE SUBSPECIES, GENETICALLY COMPATIBLE

"Shit," Nicholas breathed.

Effin turned the screen around. "Let's just see..." His sentence hung, unfinished. "Well, that is definitely interesting." He looked up at Neek and smiled widely. "Nice to meet you, cousin."

Chapter 9: Mmnn, Ggllot

The Mmnnuggl population has ceased to be of use. Terminate our contracts immediately. Do not evacuate personnel—the risk of additional hostages is too great. Our time with the Alliance is nearing its conclusion.
—Encrypted communication from the Eld Council to the Aggression Force Leader, Third Month of Arath, 26_15

THE TREES WERE dead. Ekimet sat in the remains of an andal forest, the charred, black trunks stark against the once-green landscape. Across from zir sat Corccinth, zir maternal grandmother. The third-*don* woman dug through the ashen ground, pulling mushrooms to the surface and placing them into the bark bag on her hip. They came to the controlled burns every spring, when the rains brought mushrooms from the duff and a skilled hand could locate the edible fungi with little effort.

"You're going, then?" she asked Ekimet as she pulled a pocked, triangular mushroom from the ground. "Big opportunity, Ggllot. The Eld require a steady hand there."

Ekimet squinted in the hazy sunlight. Zie had never spoken to zir grandmother about zir Ggllot assignment. Zie had never spoken to anyone about it, save the Eld themselves. No one was to know about Ekimet's placement—on that the Eld had been quite clear.

This wasn't real. Zir surroundings were too sharp to be a dream, yet Ekimet's inability to ascertain the time of day or zir location did indicate a level of unconsciousness. Curious, zie decided to play along.

"You're the one who suggested I pursue diplomacy in the first place, Granny. Do you remember? You had me signed up for international relations training before I even finished my Talent training at the Eld Palace. You made it a point to tell me state secrets at our tea parties. Are you surprised that I chose this path?"

It hadn't been what Ekimet had wanted, not at first. Over the course of the first year, however, Ekimet had found things zie enjoyed. Languages, for one, came naturally to zir, as did conflict resolution. The courses in species history—especially the history of seeded-world species—were particularly interesting. A placement on Ggllot, however, had been unexpected. There were many better qualified Hearths for the position—even more better qualified gatois, if a gesture of respect was what the Eld were after.

Corccinth wiped sweat from her brow, cakey, white makeup rubbing onto the back of her hand. She set her bag down and moved to her knees so she could look Ekimet in the eyes. "There are things for you to do there, Ekimet." She smacked zir ears with her palms. Ekimet shrank back, confused, as zir ears began to ring. "Pay attention, Ekimet!"

EKIMET AWOKE WITH two blazing earaches. Bright sunlight poured in through the open window near the bed the Hearth lay on, creating an uncomfortable amount of heat on the blankets. Zie shook zir head several times, trying to clear the remains of the dream. Ekimet had not seen zir grandmother in years. What would have brought old Corccinth to the front of zir consciousness now?

When Ekimet was reasonably certain zie was awake, zie looked around. Zie was surprised to find zirself on a biped bed and wondered if zie and Miketh had left Ggllot and, if so, how the Mmnnuggls had managed to get them off-world without inciting a riot.

The room certainly indicated an Ardulan presence. Unfortunately, the smell of the rotting *janu* fruit was faint but still present, indicating they were likely near the city center of the Ggllot capital. Had they been sequestered away in the countryside, the smell would have been overwhelming. Had they been back on Ardulum, it would have been blissfully absent.

The ostentatiousness of the room, however, was confusing to Ekimet. The bed, wide enough to fit three adult Ardulans, was ornately carved and inlaid with dark andal heartwood. The floor appeared to be highly polished andal as well, an artistic blend of heart and sapwood forming the geometric patterns of each Talent marking. Shimmering tables and chairs, all carved from lone andal trees and embedded with diamonds were artfully arranged throughout the room. There were woven andal bark writing sheets and *titha* blood pens on the sole desk, and diamond glasses filled with an unknown liquid sat on the dining table. Ekimet was particularly interested in the steaming metal pot placed squarely between the two goblets, the smell of seasoned and cooked andal twigs rising from beneath the lid.

Zie glanced over zir shoulder and was surprised to find Miketh lying next to zir on the bed. Ekimet nudged her, attempting to rouse her from sleep. Miketh made no sound but her eyes flew open at Ekimet's touch, her mouth dropping open as she too surveyed their room.

Ekimet watched Miketh for a moment and then swung zir legs off the edge of the bed, feet smacking onto the cool wood floor. Except there wasn't a smack. Confused, Ekimet stood and experimentally tapped zir left foot against the wood. Soundless. That was strange. Andal floors squeaked—it was one of their features.

Miketh's hand clasped Ekimet's shoulder. Zie spun around to see Miketh's wide eyes, her lips moving but no sound coming from them. Ekimet tried to respond, felt the vibrations in zir throat from the effort of speaking, but could hear nothing. There were no sounds at all—not from birds or wind outside, nor from either of the Ardulans.

Ekimet noticed, then, the fine trail of dried blood that framed either side of Miketh's face. Zie took Miketh's chin gently in hand and turned her head to the right, tracing the origin point back to her inner ear. Reaching up and patting zir own cheek, Ekimet confirmed the presence of blood.

The sounds the Mmnnuggls made, Miketh sent into Ekimet's mind. *Ruptured our ear drums.* She shrugged her shoulders to indicate that it was a question, not a statement.

Ekimet shrugged back. *We need a Science Talent—someone with healing.*

Miketh nodded her assent. She looked around the room again, scanning the contents, before pointing at the writing sheets. *No computer, just paper.* She took several quick, fluid strides to the door and tried to open it. Unsurprisingly, it was locked.

We're prisoners, Ekimet sent. *Best to wait and see what they want with us.*

Miketh frowned. *Or we could try to escape.* She pointed at the window. Together, the two walked over and peered over the ledge. Much to Ekimet's dismay, the ground was barely visible from their height. Further obstructing their view were thin wisps of white clouds floating several stories below. Escape via window was clearly not an option.

Ekimet tapped Miketh's shoulder and pointed at the paper and pen. *Eventually, they'll have to see us. Since they've provided a means of communication, I say we use it.*

Miketh nodded in assent. The Ardulans strode back across the room, the floor still cool under their bare feet, and sat at opposite ends of the writing desk. Ekimet took the blood pen and began to scratch out characters in High Uklam.

Oorpp et al.,

We, your Ardulan compatriots, request information as to our capture and containment. While you clearly articulated your disdain for the current political climate, my companion and I are unable to adequately address your concerns while sequestered. In addition, we appear to have suffered some physical injuries during your rally, which should be seen by a Science Talent as soon as possible.

We request that you inform us, via writing as our hearing is currently impaired, of your needs so that we may relay them to our government. We would also request some form of communication device to achieve the aforementioned goal, as well as to secure an appointment with a healer.

Respectfully yours,
Ekimet, second-don Hearth, diplomat
Miketh, third-don Mind, pilot and xenoculturalist

Ekimet handed the finished letter off to Miketh, who quickly scanned the text. When she finished, Miketh placed the paper gently down onto the table and looked up at Ekimet. The Hearth Talent could tell she was doing her best not to laugh, but the corners of her mouth kept twitching.

Perhaps this is not the best...tone to take, Miketh suggested. *I don't think fancy language is going to win them over.*

Ekimet gave her a miffed look. Zie rolled the blood pen across the table and slid a fresh sheet towards Miketh, indicating that she should write a letter as well. Miketh accepted both tools and sat back in the wood chair, tapping the pen on the edge of the desk and contemplating for several moments. Ekimet watched silently, amused.

It should be short and to the point, I think. No flowery words—no niceties. Ggllot is under Ardulan rule. Kidnapping diplomats is generally not a negotiable offense. Miketh puffed her cheeks in mild agitation before leaning forward and settling over the paper. She quickly scratched some words down, using High Uklam like Ekimet, but spent far less time on the script.

Your actions towards us are unacceptable. There will not be enough left of your little, round bodies for the Eld to investigate if we are not immediately released. Consider your actions carefully, or consider how fast a Mind Talent can find weaknesses in squishy, inflated objects. Your choice.

Ekimet read the short note and raised an eyebrow. *Very...to the point,* zie sent. *We can give them both, perhaps.*

Miketh opened her mouth to respond but was cut off when shadows spilled across the floor. They both turned to see that the door was open. Three Mmnnuggls floated inside, stacked in a column and rotating slowly.

The Mmnnuggls stopped one meter from the Ardulans and separated, expanding outwards to encase them in a triangle formation. Ekimet held out the papers. The Mmnnuggl in front of Ekimet moved forward until its front just touched the first piece of paper. Their long, vertical mouth opened and began to suck in air at an alarming rate. The papers ripped out of Ekimet's hand and disappeared inside the Mmnnuggl. The mouth slit closed quickly, shutting off its "vacuum" and leaving Ekimet wondering if the sphere had eaten the papers, or if this was some new form of processing written information that Ekimet had never heard of.

A second Mmnnuggl floated towards the Ardulans as the first backed away. This one got closer to Miketh, and its slow approach caused her to back up against the Hearth, who placed a reassuring hand on her arm. Again, this one's mouth slit opened, although instead of creating a vacuum, a wet, sticky wad of paper shot out of the opening and promptly stuck to the front of Miketh's flight suit.

A shudder ran through Miketh as her disgust seeped into Ekimet's mind. The expulsion of the wet paper mixing with the faint odor of the *janu* fruit turned Ekimet's stomach as well.

Slowly, as if unsure what she should do, Miketh peeled the paper from her front and straightened it out. The script was faint and black, but—looking over her shoulder—Ekimet could make out that the lettering was also High Uklam.

Miketh took a moment to read the paper and then handed it to Ekimet, the edges tearing in the transfer as they stuck to her fingers. Ekimet held the paper as far away from zirself as possible and read the text.

You are our prisoners. All communication panels within this room have been disabled. Your personal auditory sensors have been disabled. The Mmnnuggl government is now under our control. Oorpp wears the late president and has taken control of her office.

You two will have no more interaction with Ardulum, and the Mmnnuggls are breaking their ties to your homeworld. We will no longer serve a species that does not fulfill its promises. You are not gods—you are merely magicians. If your Eld choose to ransom you, you will be released. If not, you will be killed. Until such time as a response is received from your homeworld, you will not be harmed. This room was designed solely for the visiting Eld. You will be comfortable. Food will be brought at regular intervals. Do not make us regret our decision to keep you alive.

Ekimet folded the now dry and crusty paper in half and nodded to the nearest Mmnnuggl. Zie didn't recognize these three from the mob, but judging from their nervous rotations, the idea of incarcerating Ardulans, even in what was undoubtedly the nicest facility on Ggllot, was probably unpalatable to them. That potentially meant that these particular Mmnnuggls would be easier to negotiate with.

"What ransom are you demanding? Currency? Ships? Raw goods? Miketh and I might be able to meet your request without involving the Eld." Ekimet hoped zir words were loud enough. Speaking without hearing was surprisingly unsettling

The Mmnnuggls were still for several seconds, contemplating a response. Without any warning, another wad of paper shot out and hit Ekimet's forehead.

Your offer has been considered and rejected. Material goods are not of interest. Our ships are superior to yours. We will trade your lives only for other Ardulans. Your species has precedent for this with the Risalians.

Miketh covered her mouth with her hand. *They want flares? Of all the stupid demands! They're better off with us.*

I would prefer to not encourage that line of thinking, Ekimet responded sourly. It was nice to know, however, what the catalyst was for all of this. The Risalians' success with reversing many of the safeguards genetically integrated into the flares they were sold was admirable, if ultimately responsible for the recent war in the Charted Systems. Corccinth had served her entire adult life on the Eld's advisory panel for flare studies. Ekimet was very well versed in the politics of the subject.

Out loud and as best zie could, Ekimet said, "We appreciate your sharing of information. We hope you receive the outcome you most desire in this matter, and thank you for your accommodation."

That seemed to please the Mmnnuggls. They restacked and backed out of the door, rotating laterally. When the door shut, Miketh turned to face Ekimet, a look of irritation on her face.

I have no idea what to think of this situation, she sent. *The Eld are likely to consent, and we are very well taken care of prisoners. Escape, at this point, might be counterproductive.*

Ekimet nodded. There hadn't been any new breakthroughs in flare research in almost half a century. The population in the detention centers was overflowing. *A few flares in exchange for us shouldn't be hard to accomplish.*

Zie walked over to the large bay window and peered down, attempting to estimate how many meters they were off the ground. One hundred? Four hundred? The Eld suite was housed in the governmental sphere, not far from where the mob had captured them. Ekimet couldn't quite remember where in the sphere the suite was supposed to be, but knew they couldn't be more than several floors from the governmental head offices.

Clever, Miketh sent, joining Ekimet at the window. *Keeping us close to the president's office. Who'd think to look here, if they were looking at all?*

Ekimet nodded, glad that Miketh had a better memory for schematics than zie did.

I bet cleaning staff have to come in here all the time, Miketh continued. *They have to keep fresh andal going in on the off chance the Eld do show up. No suspicion will be raised when Mmnnuggls keep coming and going, although I do wonder how they got us in here with no one seeing.*

Ekimet shrugged. After months of struggling with an unwilling populace and being constantly bullied about zir sex, Ekimet didn't mind the forced vacation. Looking around the room, zie noticed the bookshelves, the wall console that controlled the door, and again, the still-steaming pot of andal. There were definitely far worse ways to spend time as a captive, Ekimet thought as zie settled down into a plush chair and popped a fresh andal twig into zir mouth. Zie grabbed a book at random from a shelf behind zir head and opened to the middle, skimming the pages.

Miketh plucked the book from Ekimet's hands and gave her counterpart a sharp look. *Now isn't the time for reading,* she said, placing the book back on the shelf. She took hold of Ekimet's sleeve, pulled zir back over to the table and chairs, and gently pushed zir to sit.

What would you prefer? Ekimet asked, amused. *I can recite all ninety-seven Ardulan subspecies in alphabetical order, and I can peel a* janu *fruit in under ten seconds. Either of those sound appealing?*

I want a contingency plan, Miketh returned. *Posh or not, if the situation changes, we have to be ready.*

With a long sigh, Ekimet nodded. *All right, let's plan. Can we keep our potential escape to the higher floors of this building, by any chance? The farther away we can stay from the smell of* janu *fruit, the better.*

Chapter 10: Xinar Hub, Xinar System

What do you think? Worth investigating? I've never been outside the Alliance before. Maybe the Mmnnuggls and these Risalians have something interesting to say.
—Shortband communication from Effin M'yin Erl to his husband, Krell M'yin Erl, Third Month of Arath, 26_15

NICHOLAS TRAILED BEHIND Neek, Emn behind him, as Neek wove her way through aisles of rusting, dilapidated ships. As much as he might have thought that Effin had oversold Xinar Station as a high-end tourist mall when it was really more of a flea market, he knew better than to say anything about it. Neek was smiling and giddy with joy for the first time in weeks, which meant she wasn't being awkward with Emn or acting like a complete nutjob. It was a welcome change.

Besides, the shipyard was interesting. He'd studied old ships, of course, in secondary school history classes and in his elective electronics class. He'd even taken advanced placement exams in biometal engineering to prepare for his Youth Journey aboard a starship. That he'd ended up on one of Earth's first shuttles—a ship so old it was mostly plastic and plain metal—had always been frustrating.

Here, however...here he could put his education to use. At least one hundred ships were scattered across the warehouse floor, none new and all in various stages of disrepair. The last hour had been like a historical tour of space travel, with ship parts ranging from dilapidated wood frames to gleaming cellulosic plating, and everything in between. There were metals here he had never seen before and cellulose weaves varying from almost nonexistent to over eighty percent of the craft. He'd even seen some of the rare transition biometals, like the failed galactoglucomannan and xylan hemicellulose interweaves. Their use had been pretty short-lived in the Systems, since cellulose was such a better conductor. They'd been a step in the right direction though, and it was neat to get to run his hands over a piece of technological history.

"What about that one?" Neek asked the transparent, gelatinous mass that was their sales representative. She pointed to what looked like a skiff soldered directly to another of the same model, both in desperate need of paint, shielding, and probably an engine. The external plating looked old and flat. Nicholas guessed petrochemical base, but couldn't be sure unless he actually touched it.

"Half," the blob wheezed through a frayed, yellow stalk near the apex of its mass.

Neek frowned and resumed walking.

"What was wrong with that one?" Nicholas called out, careful to keep his tone neutral.

Neek waved her hand dismissively. "Economics, Nick. The *Kuebrich* is worth twice that, and they already said they won't pay the difference. I have never been in a position where I have too much capital, and I intend to— Oooh!" Neek took a sharp right. Nicholas sighed, tossing a small smile back at Emn as they ducked under the wing of another ship and followed Neek past a row of four Mmnnuggl pods so old that they had started to gray.

"This one," Neek breathed. She stopped and touched one finger gingerly to the peeling paint on an acorn-shaped ship reminiscent of Effin's vehicle. As Neek silently walked around it, prodding here and there and muttering pleased sounds, Nicholas studied the design. It did look surprisingly like Effin's, the longer he stared at it. The angles were the same, and the surface had a similar weave. Maybe an older model? Maybe Neek just liked curved ships.

He reached out and peeled back a layer of paint. Underneath, the metal glistened in the overhead lighting. He licked his thumb and pressed it to the surface, pleased when the touch came back warm and tingly. "Cellulose-based," he called out to Neek, though she likely already knew. "Should have speed and a decent computing system."

The salesblob spoke before Nicholas could continue his observations. "Saaaame," they wheezed through their stalk. "Works. New motor."

Nicholas sincerely hoped "motor" was just a bad translation of "engine."

"Paint upgrade okay. Facility here," Salesblob added.

"Can we see inside?" Neek asked, her voice hushed as she danced slightly on her toes.

Salesblob vibrated and then pitched forward. They elongated their stalk to what Nicholas found an alarming height, jiggled their transparent body, and then whacked the side of the ship. An oval plank extended down, the edge just above the floor.

"Fantastic!" Neek took several long steps and was inside the ship before Nicholas could ask about details. Salesblob followed closely behind.

Nicholas felt a hand on his back and turned to see Emn grinning. "Come on," she said as she moved past him and up the plank. "I want to check out the interface. It would be great if I didn't have to be the sole pilot. Or a pilot at all, really."

Nodding, Nicholas followed her up. Despite its apparent smoothness, the metal was textured under his bare feet, providing ample traction. It was warm, too, which surprised him. Cellulose in the hull made sense. Cellulose in the ramp just seemed wasteful.

"Do you think the pointy bit is a gun, or part of the cockpit?" he asked as they followed the sound of Neek's excited voice through a circular entry room and into a corridor.

Emn shrugged. "It'd be a waste of space for a cockpit, I would think. How badly do you want to know?" She tapped a finger against a wall as she walked past. "Effin gave me a small piece of andal on Keft, so I can take a peek if you want."

"No, it's fine. Maybe we can check it out later if Neek decides it's the one she wants." They rounded a tight corner, and Nicholas had to stop abruptly to avoid hitting their sales rep. The blob, whose name and gender they still didn't know, was standing in the round doorway. Through their body, Nicholas could make out a distorted outline of Neek bent over a computer interface.

"You okay, Neek?" he called out, unsure how to politely maneuver around the blob.

"Just checking the databases," she called back, not looking up. "Interestingly, it has a Neek language option, which is making things easier."

Nicholas wasn't sure how to respond to that, so he decided against saying anything. Instead, he prodded Emn's leg with his toe. When she looked over, he shrugged his shoulders and put his hand on the wall next to his face. "Maybe you should check it out," he whispered. "Just in case."

Neek called out again. "Hey, Emn, could you come over here and see if you can help me find the navigation controls?"

"That almost sounds like the old Neek," Emn whispered to Nicholas as she squeezed past Salesblob. Although they shifted a bit to let her pass, her hips still pushed into their form, indenting the side of their body.

Not wanting to be stuck in the hall, Nicholas squeezed past behind her, avoiding the blob entirely. Once inside the cockpit, he realized why Neek was taking her time with the interface. On first glance, the interior looked flawless. The ceiling was high and arched, and the three separate chairs, complete with shoulder harnesses, were designed for bipeds. The walls had been painted a soothing yellow, and the upholstery on the chair cushioning was a somehow not-blinding lime green. The colors should have been hideous but, combined with the paler yellow of the interface console, were more comforting than anything else. Someone had customized the interior, he realized. Someone probably with money and a lot of time on their hands.

"—Keft." The last of Emn's sentence caught his attention. She was standing next to Neek at the interface, pointing to some scrolling text he couldn't make out. "The indents here, next to your hand, Neek, are a fingertip interface. Ship says they need a conductive gel to work, but since it's Keft-made, maybe your *stuk* will do the trick."

Neek backed from the console and looked wary. "This isn't a telepathic interface, is it?" she asked. "I can't deal with anything else in my head right now."

"I didn't realize my presence was so problematic," Emn returned. Her tone sounded serious, but Nicholas thought he caught a hint of humor. Neek apparently missed it.

"Emn, that's not what I meant!" Her face reddened.

The younger woman took Neek's hand and placed it back on the panel, aligning her fingertips with the depressions. "I know, Neek. I'm only joking. Here." She tapped the area next to Neek's fingers, and the interface lit up. "You command with one hand—drive with the other using gentle movements from your fingertips. Sort of like the *Pledge*, except this system was intentionally designed to be complex."

"Complex, or intuitive?" Nicholas asked. He stepped closer and watched Neek scroll through menu options, or what he assumed were menu options due to their layout. He probably should have studied more of the Neek language when he was trapped there with the crew several weeks back.

"I like it," Neek said finally. She turned back to the blob. "Let's take a quick tour of the rest, then talk paint. Also—" She narrowed her eyes and rapped her knuckles against the nearby wall. "—I want to negotiate overage. Our pod is in perfect working order and spotless. This skiff is obviously older. Let's talk about some ways to make up the difference."

SEVERAL HOURS LATER, Nicholas found himself staring at a magenta skiff with white piping and the name *Scarlet Lucidity* scrawled across its hull, while Neek carried two large sacks—one of clothes and one of foodstuffs—into the ship. Emn elbowed him in the ribs and chuckled.

"Relax, Nicholas. It really was the better color option. The green was hideous."

"No," said Nicholas resolutely. "The better color option was to leave it the color it was. Another possibility would have been to cover it in dirt." He shuddered and smacked his hand against the hull. "Seriously? Neon-colored clothes, fine. I can get onboard with that. But a ship? Are we trying to stand out everywhere we go?"

"All packed," Neek called as she descended the plank and rejoined Nicholas and Emn. "Blob said we could leave the ship here for a bit if we want to look around. Any interest?"

Nicholas tore his eyes from the grotesque paint and rubbed his forehead with his palm. Since they had no new coordinates to try, poking around a space hub seemed as reasonable a plan as any. If it kept Neek in a good mood, all the better. He did not mention the paint.

"Sounds great," Emn said.

Nicholas nodded in agreement. "I'd really like some fast print," he added as they made their way to the exit and into the main plaza. "Could we make that a priority?"

"Agreed," Neek yelled over the sudden din. Outside the shipyard, the noise was staggering. The hub was only the length of a Risalian cutter, but Nicholas wasn't able to get an accurate count of the number of levels it had. Some shops, like the shipyard, were housed in pods just off the main core. Mostly, from what he had seen when they first landed, the shops were smaller and similar to the ones on Craston.

There was nothing dim or quiet about this spaceport, however. Weaving in and out of the masses as he tried his best to follow Neek and Emn, Nicholas saw more species than he could keep track of. Most were bipeds and quadrupeds, but there were Mmnnuggls too, a number of phase-shifting beings, and at least three types of gelatinous creatures that may or may not have been the same species as Salesblob. Some beings were sticky when he brushed past, most had significant body odors, and he was certain at least one had gotten grabby with his posterior.

"To the right!" Emn shouted as she stood on her toes to get a better view. "I see a glowing cellulose image and something next to it that looks like a very short, fat Yorden. Could be food." She took Neek's hand and the lead, pushed through a group of tall quadrupeds, and sidestepped two bubbling puddles before stopping at the entrance to a small shop.

Nicholas peered inside. A Terran man—except as far as Nicholas knew, Terrans did not generally have purple hair—winked at him from the back. Nicholas cleared his throat and looked away. The interior of the restaurant was brightly lit, with seven print stalls in a row and a dozen round tables at varying heights. Only a few were occupied, which meant either the print quality was low, or it was not a standard eating interval.

"Want to try it?" Neek asked. "I don't how we'll read the menu."

"Don't care," Nicholas responded. "At this point, I could eat anything. I just hope they take diamond rounds. I know we only have the few Chen gave us." He led the way to the first empty printer and stared at a scrolling, anthropomorphized cellulose chain as it wound around the screen. Its mouth gobbled glucose molecules as it went, increasing in length until it filled the screen completely and the image restarted.

Too hungry to be amused, Nicholas tapped the screen. The moving chain broke apart into six different stylized chemical structures, each with a number of diamond rounds and what Nicholas thought might be sapphires under the picture. He studied his options and then tapped the second down on the left.

"No chlorines on this one," he said. "Probably won't kill me—at least not directly."

Neek fed the required number of rounds into a slot in the top, and a whirl of cellulose spun into motion in a clear tube just to the right of the machine. After a few seconds, the whirring stopped and a door to the

0

0

0

0

0

0

tube opened, revealing a flat slab of something fluffy and yellow, perforated into four parts.

"Classic perf," Nicholas said. He picked up the slab, which was denser than he had anticipated, and pointed to an empty table. "I'll hold the table. See you two in a minute."

"So, YOU THINK it's just the Keft and the Neek, then?" Nicholas asked between bites. He'd broken his meal across the perforations and given half to Neek to try. He'd already had half of hers, which tasted slightly worse than corrugated cardboard. Emn had flat out refused all of it.

"Enough, Nicholas," Neek responded in a weary tone. She grimaced at her remaining slice of perf and then took a large bite, chewing and swallowing quickly. "It was nice of Captain Effin to let us keep the analyzer, but we need to consult an actual geneticist before we get too worked up about the results."

Nicholas wiped his hand on his leg, sending crumbs everywhere. "It'd be nice to talk about it at least a little," he said, mouth full of perf. "Especially since the fingers and hair thing isn't consistent across either the Neek or Keft populations, but the *stuk* thing is."

"Do you want my suspicions," Neek asked, giving up on her remaining piece and pushing it away, "or do you want facts?"

Nicholas grinned at Emn. "When have facts bothered any of you? Let's go for suspicions."

Neek eyed the perf, pulled it back in, and took a tentative bite, considering. "The older family lines, the ones with the well-charted genealogies, have three fingers and don't manifest any shade of red in their hair. At this point—" She looked apologetically at Emn. "—I suspect some form of interbreeding when the Ardulans came. It would work with the Keft double phenotype system as well. I think the Ardulans must target genetically compatible species, though how they do that I have no idea. They target them, interbreed, and plant andal—or change the genetically similar andal already on-world." She frowned. "They genetically conquer both the land and the people."

"You think empathic mucus is the link?" Emn wrinkled her nose and pushed away the small piece of perf Nicholas offered her. "Like it is some kind of marker?"

Neek shrugged. "Maybe. It's just a hypothesis."

"So the Ardulans and Neek are genetically compatible." Nicholas tried desperately to suppress his grin. "Subspecies can totally interbreed. That's...interesting. Right? Useful information?" Although he was staring at Neek for her reaction, he caught Emn suppressing a smile from the corner of his eye.

Neek missed the implication entirely. "I wonder if the *stuk* helps with interbreeding with genetically distinct individuals. I suppose I'm making an assumption that Ardulans have *stuk,* which, considering Emn doesn't have any, might be a leap."

"Yeah." Nicholas rolled his eyes. "That's exactly what I meant." He leaned over and poked Neek in the shoulder. "So we're looking for a planet of conquerors?"

Neek nodded absentmindedly as she finished the perf Nicholas had given her. "It also means there is almost certainly a 'there' to find," she muttered. Standing from her chair, she brushed the crumbs from her lap and inclined her head towards the exit. "Want to get moving?"

"Are we in a hurry?" Nicholas stood as well and the three moved back out into the throng of beings. He preferred the quietness of the print shop but knew there was little chance of Ardulum's coordinates dropping into their laps while they sat around and crunched on bland food.

"No, but I see another neon ship sign. I wouldn't mind checking it out, especially if it is a travelers' pub. We could use some practical Alliance guidance."

Together, the three bumped and jostled their way across the hub to what appeared to be a bustling entertainment hall. A tall biped—several heads taller than Nicholas—stood to the side of the door and checked the wrists of those entering. Checked the wrists of those that had them, anyway. Nicholas watched one potential patron have her hind right hoof lifted up and prodded before being allowed entrance.

"How are we supposed to get in?" Emn asked. She wrapped her bare arms around her chest, and Nicholas wondered if she was suddenly feeling self-conscious about the markings all over her body.

"Try," Neek responded absently. Nicholas followed her gaze past the bouncer to the main stage area. Inside, a raised circular platform sat in the middle of the room. Beings sprawled across cushions, water tanks, chairs, and bales of grass, sipping drinks and chatting over the music.

"*Why* are we going in?" Nicholas asked. He came up behind Neek and put a hand on her elbow. A thick quadruped pulled the drummer from the stage by its teeth and a band of golden spheres—maybe Mmnnuggls?—began to play levitating woodwind instruments.

"We are going in because these are our people," Neek responded. "Look at them! Dirty. Carousing. It might not be a pub, but it is the next best thing. We should be able to ask some questions once we get inside."

Neek began to push towards the bouncer, but Nicholas stepped in front of her, his hands held up to his chest, palms out. "Neek, whoa. Hold on, please." When Neek glared instead of pushing him out of the way, he raised his voice so that it would carry. "We could ask questions anywhere. We could find a nice restaurant where they serve cooked food on glass plates. We could talk to people at a museum, or whatever passes for that here. This—" He pointed at the interior of the entertainment establishment. "—is not our only option. It is likely the loudest option, and the dirtiest, but not the only one."

"I didn't realize you had extensive experience in reputable versus disreputable establishments!" Neek yelled back over the noise. She moved to the side and strode past him. "I'm going in. Stay out here if you like. Same deal with you, Emn."

Neek took another two steps and then turned back and looked at the younger woman, her face conflicted. "Sorry. I meant you're welcome to come in, or stay here. Whatever you want."

A barking laugh drowned out Emn's answer. Nicholas saw the musicians turn their attention to the far corner of the room. One of the instruments clattered to the platform. The other performers fumbled the rhythm, and the music fell apart into a chorus of laughter from the audience. Another glass went sailing across the crowd.

Nicholas looked back to ask Neek what she thought was going on, but instead watched her gracefully sidestep the bouncer, who was busy arguing with a pair of Mmnnuggls adorned in bright lilac paint. The closest one rotated to face Nicholas, tilted ten degrees left, and then turned back to the bouncer.

"Neek!" he hissed after her, hoping his voice was both somehow loud enough for her to hear, yet soft enough that she wouldn't get caught. When she failed to turn around, Nicholas looked to Emn.

"Can you call her back?" he asked, unsure whether or not to follow. "There is no way we're getting past the bouncer."

Emn frowned, and her eyes unfocused. "She's not listening. She's already started talking with another of those blob beings. I think—"

Emn's pocket chirped.

She shook her head at Nicholas's questioning look and reached into the pocket on her dress. From inside, she pulled out a flat, metallic disc the size of her palm.

"Remote to the *Scarlet Lucidity*," Emn said, staring at the disc. Little, red lights illuminated the circumference. "Neek asked me to hold it when she was signing the purchasing papers and filling out the name registry for the ship. I forgot to give it back."

Nicholas poked the device. It was warm to his touch and vibrating ever so slightly. Another chirp sounded. "What's wrong with it?" he asked.

"Nothing. I think it..." Emn flipped it over and then held it between her thumb and first finger. She squinted, bringing the disc closer to her face. Nicholas had to suppress a laugh.

"That help?" he asked.

His question went unanswered, but Nicholas didn't press. The color was gone from Emn's face. Her hands began to shake. The disc fell to the ground, and while Nicholas scrambled to pick it up—not wanting to think about the repercussions should it be crushed or lost—Emn stood still and straight, her focused gaze unblinking.

"Emn?" Nicholas asked. The disc was firmly back in his hands, but the lights had gone out.

"It's a communication," Emn said slowly, the words sounding thick on her tongue. She turned her head towards the bar where Neek had disappeared and then looked back to Nicholas. The din of the spaceport quieted, as if every being were listening to Emn's next words. "It's a message from the Eld of Ardulum."

Chapter 11: Research Station K47, Ardulum

Cultures destroyed, famine, ecological ruin! The Ardulans take what is not theirs, rule what they cannot take. Throw off the yoke of your oppressors, beings of the Charted Systems! Do not fall prey once again to a species of fools.
  —Excerpt from a broadband conference to the Charted Systems from just outside Risal, December 14th, 2061 CE

ARIK THRASHED AGAINST the plastic strips that held his arms loosely above his head, strapped to the *titha* wool pad.

The guard had led him from the commons without a word before his first meal had been served. They'd walked only a few meters down a corridor before entering a pale blue room with pads lined evenly across the floor. One of the others, the male whose room was right next to Arik's, had been strapped into the far-right pad, unmoving.

That image had been enough to send Arik into a panic. He knew what was coming. Kisak, Waiketh...they'd all shared images with him of the testing. He'd seen this room a dozen times in fragmented minds and fevered dreams that bled into his andal forests and saplings. He didn't want this. He didn't deserve this. He needed help. If he could only get away and get someone to *listen*—

Additional guards had been called. It'd taken three to calm Arik's thrashing and get him to lie on the pad and a fourth to strap him down.

The plastic ties cut Arik's skin and were now stained maroon from his blood. He barely registered the pain anymore.

"Does it give you a sense of control to further desecrate your body?"

The small room was empty now save for Arik, the unconscious man, and a tall gatoi healer. Arik stilled. A gatoi, in this place. He couldn't imagine what would possess the Eld to assign a gatoi to a prison. Had zie done something to offend the Eld? Perhaps committed some crime and this was zir punishment?

"Bit of sense still left then. That's good to see." The healer pulled a plastic tablet from zir pocket and began to type on the glass screen. "Tell me—telepathically, of course—how your markings feel at this exact moment."

The question sounded in Arik's head as well. The tone was crisp, but Arik's mind rearranged the words, made them come out of his talther's mouth instead. Moisture collected in Arik's eyes, and he blinked it back, determined not to cry.

"Did you hear me, Arik?"

Arik nodded. His torso wasn't strapped to the pad. He could flip himself over, possibly crash into the gatoi, and take zir out near the legs, but then how would he get himself undone from the restraints? And how could he willfully injure a gatoi?

"I'm waiting, Arik."

They're still tender, Arik managed to send. The image of his talther was superimposing itself on the healer. The gatoi's hair darkened to near black, zir skin weathered to olive. The white lab coat melted into thick hide boots and a loose tunic, belted at the waist.

"And have you been expressing your Talents?"

No, mir, Arik responded, falling into formal address. He had to keep mental distance from the mirage above him. That wasn't his talther. He was a prisoner. He had to get it together!

"Has anyone else been using their Talents?" The healer knelt and gently brushed hair from Arik's forehead. "Come now, Rik, you can tell me. Afterwards, we'll go see the saplings. How does that sound?"

It sounded perfect. Arik melted into the comfort of the words and the familiarity of the pet name his talther had given him. *I haven't been here long enough to see what the others do,* he responded truthfully. *I still don't really understand what is going on. Why did this happen, talther?*

A disappointed look crossed his talther's face. "Because my chromosomes are likely weak, as well as your mother's and father's, I suppose. We'll be sure not to have any more children. We don't need to be seeding more recessive genes into future generations."

The moisture was back in Arik's eyes. *You're not faulty!* he cried into the gatoi's mind. *I love all three of you!*

"Do you now?" His talther stood and walked to a small, metal cabinet secured to the wall. From inside, zie took a vial of teardrop-shaped pills of varying colors and shook half the contents onto the palm of zir hand. "Do you know much about genetics, Arik?"

No, Arik responded as his talther knelt back down and clenched the pills in zir fist.

"Turns out, neither do we." Zie pushed a finger and thumb into Arik's cheeks. Arik opened his mouth obediently. "We learn a lot, though, from seeing how flares respond to various drugs designed to mimic natural hormones. You're new, so we don't have any data on you yet." Arik's talther dropped the handful of pills into Arik's mouth. Arik gagged momentarily before turning his head and swallowing.

A familiar flush emerged on Arik's face. The smell of overcooked andal assaulted his nose. Andal help him, it was like reliving his Talent Day, with all the horror that came with it. His skin burned, felt too tight and then too loose. Again, Arik pulled against his bonds, but the plastic just cut deeper.

The image of his talther faded, replaced by the healer. Arik's mind cleared of the fogginess he'd not realized had settled as muscles began to sporadically seize. He screamed silently in pain, unable to massage the cramps that set off across his body.

"We just need to get you caught up," the healer said. Zie moved to push another piece of hair from Arik's head, but Arik lifted his chin and snapped at the gatoi without thinking. He couldn't handle any more touch or deception. A muscle in his forehead bunched, and Arik slammed his head against the wool pad, desperately searching for release.

"We need you conscious to gather the data, unfortunately." The gatoi stood and walked to the door. "I'll be back to check on you in half an hour. Until then, try to breathe deeply. The male in the corner gave himself a heart attack late last night. What a waste of research. You do appreciate research, don't you, Arik? Weren't you supposed to be of Science?"

Double spasms in his legs caused Arik to arch, and he screamed obscenities into the healer's mind. The healer merely shook zir head, as if Arik was a galactic disappointment, and walked from the room.

Almost twenty minutes passed before Arik blacked out from the pain.

Chapter 12: Mmnn, Ggllot

We will not let this transgression stand. The Charted Systems would wage war on Ardulum. We shall wage war in return.
—Broadband communication from the Neek Religion Council to the Charted Systems WorldBand, December 15th, 2060 CE

THEY JUST HAD a rally this morning. What could they possibly be up to now? Ekimet leaned against the tall window and stared down. Zie had to squint to make out faint black lines streaking across the ground, the wavy formations indicative of Mmnnuggls in a highly agitated state.

You're making a pretty big assumption, Miketh countered. *Maybe they're just looting.*

Ekimet turned to stare at her. *Looting? Just because a species has advanced ships and weaponry does not make it inherently warmongering and destructive.* Zie turned back to the window. *See? They're in straight lines again, stacked evenly, with wide rows in-between. It's another rally. I bet someone is speaking—just trying to stir things up. That means not everyone is on their side.*

Miketh lifted her hand, pointing as she counted. *Twenty-seven, thirty-three...if we do some extrapolation where Mmnnuggls form chains of six, and there are twelve hundred forty-five chains I can count...Ekimet, that is a lot of Mmnnuggls. Mmnn isn't a large city, capital or not. That is a significant percentage of the population. That would be enough to do serious damage to the Alliance, if they wanted.*

Ekimet scoffed. *They just want some freedom. Even subspecies shed the guidance of Ardulum after a time. It's a natural course of action. You can see their passion from here.*

I'd rather hear *it.* Miketh moved to the small table near where she had been reading, picked up her book, and tossed it across the room. It hit the wall-mounted—and currently defunct—communications panel and slid silently to the floor. *We've been in this stupid room for ages. You even saw that Ardulan stellar skiff take off right in front of this building, probably taking the last of the Ardulan fruit pickers or tourists or whoever else was dumb enough to come to this planet. The Ardulans that weren't valuable enough to hold hostage.* She looked pointedly at Ekimet, who coughed. *It wasn't the royal Eld skiff that docks here—it was a passenger ship.* She pursed her lips and looked at the ceiling. *The Eld aren't negotiating, Ekimet. This planet has been abandoned, and so have we.*

Ekimet had seen the ship and still couldn't explain it. If the matter were as simple as a trade for flares, it would have been over and done with inside a week. This...this had to be much more encompassing. If zie had access to a communications panel, zie would have called zir grandmother. Whatever the Eld were playing at, Ekimet couldn't help without more information.

The Eld would be hard-pressed to abandon a planet in the Alliance altogether, Ekimet sent. *The only time we abandon planets is when Ardulum wants to seed and has to move. We've been in the center of the Alliance for a century.* Ekimet paused to consider. Seeding was a possibility zie had not considered before. *What would make the Eld move now? We deal with petty species conflicts all the time. A loss of faith is not uncommon, and the andal is doing well.*

Miketh sat in a huff. *You're the diplomat. You tell me.*

Frustrated, Ekimet left the window and sat down behind Miketh, leaning against her back for support. *If we are abandoned, then the Mmnnuggls don't know it yet. Otherwise, we'd be dead. If the Eld were mounting a rescue mission for us, we'd be back on Ardulum by now.*

Which means we've been left as fodder to keep the Mmnnuggls from suspecting something is up. Miketh pressed back against Ekimet, and zie felt her shoulders slump. *The Eld purge everything before a move. Why not keep things as smooth as possible?*

Because that was too simplistic. Because the Eld were of the andal, and the andal's motivations weren't linear. Because the Mmnnuggls weren't kept in the Alliance just for their ships and fruit trees. Except, Ekimet couldn't talk about any of that to Miketh, not without the Eld's approval. Zie tried to think of a response, but was interrupted when a low thrumming began to shake the building.

Is something exploding? Miketh asked, alarmed, as she followed Ekimet back to the window.

Zie shook zir head and pointed to a dark cluster near the far-left corner. *No, that's cheering.* The vibration faded, and the Mmnnuggl cluster slowly dispersed into rows and then into individual dots.

Finally, Miketh said. *I think now would be an excellent time to try one of our escape plans.* She paced across the width of the room. *If you wanted to try to override the communications interface, we should do it now. I bet most of the Mmnnuggls in the area were at that rally. They'll be distracted, not focused on their jobs. They might not notice the tinkering.* She paused, considering her words. *Or they might and then take out their frustrations on us.* She turned back to the interface and ran her fingertips over the smooth surface. *I've never used Mmnnuggl technology before. I understand the principles behind it, but have no experience with it. I know we discussed connecting with it telepathically, but really, a Science Talent would be better suited for the task.*

Well, we don't have one, Ekimet said flatly. *Just do your best.*

Miketh nodded, closed her eyes, and sank into the interface. *Some plastic tubing. Silicone and diamond wiring. Cellulose films and interwoven fibers. A few things that look hemicellulose-based—who uses that anymore? Talk about dead technologies.* Miketh continued to scan the panel and sent images to Ekimet. *Other things I don't recognize at all. Our best bet may be to just start pulling things and hoping for a short.*

If we are going to do that, why don't we just smash the panel with a chair? Ekimet asked, irritated. Zie pushed past Miketh's inventory and took a long look at what she was seeing. *Why don't you try that silver, round thing over there? It looks important.*

Miketh's irritation rose as well. *Ekimet, I'm not a Science Talent. I can't connect with computers.* She opened her eyes and glared disapprovingly. *Do you even understand how Talents work? I can view, same as any Ardulan, but manipulation requires a level of understanding of the system that I do not possess—an intrinsic knowledge, the same way you understand how best to not irritate other species or I fly ships.*

Miketh, Ekimet said urgently, ignoring her jab. *There is a charge building in the films. Disconnect before—*

The jolt caught them both. It blazed through Miketh's mind and then Ekimet's, taking advantage of their link. There was a cold pain, and for a moment, Ekimet thought zie had lost zir eyesight as well. Pressure pulsed at the base of zir skull, and Ekimet fell to the floor, clutching zir head.

Bad idea, apparently, Miketh managed to send between gasps. *Looks like they thought we might pry.*

Ekimet rubbed zir temples as the pain and pressure began to fade. *I don't know what else to suggest. That's the only panel I've seen in this room.*

Miketh stood and ran her fingers around the door seam again. As she neared the right side, the door slid open and a stack of six Mmnnuggls burst through. The tower knocked Miketh onto her back and then moved to the center of the room, where each individual sphere began to rotate in a different direction. They didn't bother to close the door.

They aren't happy, Ekimet said, backing into the main dining table. Miketh, trying to regain her wind, stumbled over to Ekimet and watched the spinning Mmnnuggls with wide eyes.

Are they just going to spin? Or will they actually chastise us at some point?

As if the Mmnnuggls had been considering the same thing, the tower stopped rotating and stilled. The second from the top opened her mouth and began to speak. Ekimet quickly realized that the one talking had no idea Miketh and zie couldn't hear a word. The Mmnnuggl continued for several long minutes before her mouth closed and the column began to rock slowly back and forth in anticipation of a response.

Miketh turned to Ekimet. *Can you tell them we didn't do anything? I didn't touch anything in that computer!*

Ekimet looked back at the table, searching for paper and a blood pen. *What did we do with the writing implements?* zie asked frantically. *Want to try to write again?*

I think now would be an excellent time for diplomacy, Miketh countered. *Use your charms to get us out of here.*

It isn't that easy. Those aren't our guards. Look at the red tint at the top of the ears. They're young—youths, more than likely. They're angry. If they're part of the protestors from the street, we're in trouble. Ekimet bent down and saw the paper and pen on the floor. Zie grabbed both and held them out to the Mmnnuggl tower, hoping they understood.

The tower moved closer to Ekimet until it was centimeters from zir face. The Mmnnuggls began to shudder against one another. The mouth of the second Mmnnuggl opened, and a wad of wet paper shot out, hitting Ekimet in the throat.

Ekimet did not care for this manner of communication at all. Delicately, zie took the paper and unfolded it. The text was in their native language, a series of tiny black dots, spread in rows and columns over the page. Ekimet hastily translated for Miketh.

No more Ardulan rule. You have abandoned us. Made promises you didn't keep. We are done. The treaty with Ardulum is severed. The Alliance is severed. Ardulans will be no more.

That is not good, Miketh sent. *Write back. Try to calm them down. We don't need to die thanks to rioting youth. I'm sure the Mmnnuggl government has a much more public death planned for us. Hopefully a death that is a few days away.*

Ekimet considered what to write. There were a lot of nuances to Mmnnuggl conversation. Words had many more meanings when one was angry than when one was happy. Zie had to be sure zie selected the best options to save their lives. Either that, or find a way to calm the Mmnnuggls down, perhaps even by force.

Force, actually, wasn't a terrible idea. In general, they weren't supposed to use Talents on the Alliance populace. If the Mmnnuggls were out of the Alliance, however, there was no moral ambiguity to the situation. Ekimet was free to use any tools at zir disposal.

Zie mentally reached out to the tower, making sure to connect with each individual Mmnnuggl. When zie was confident in the link, Ekimet sent feelings of calmness, of sleepiness. Zie sent images of young *janu* tree plantations with purple blossoms swaying slowly in the breeze, of *titha* drinking near a stream. Pastoral images were calming to most Mmnnuggls, and the effects were immediate. The column began to break apart and bob independently from one another. Sluggishly, each Mmnnuggl lowered completely to the ground and rolled in a tight circle, a sign of contentment.

What did you do?! Miketh asked, shocked.

I picked some images I saw on a Mmnnuggl children's program meant to put babies to sleep and sent them. I think as long as I keep feeding the images, they'll stay like that. Mmnnuggls aren't used to our telepathic strength. They're more on par with the Neek. Connecting to us tends to overwhelm their systems, if I remember my subspecies and alien biology classes correctly.

Miketh squeezed Ekimet's shoulder and grinned. *Just hold them like that as long as you can. I have an idea about getting us out of this building.* She moved to the other end of the table and dumped the remains of the andal from the bowl, being careful to keep the whitish sugar juice from running out.

What are you doing? Ekimet asked. A headache was starting to build, the strain of maintaining visions for six separate Mmnnuggls proving more difficult than zie had expected.

Making disguises, she responded. *On my way here, I read an immigration report on Ggllot. It gets a decent number of Keft every year who come for work.* Miketh went to the window and pushed one of the panes open. Using the edge of one of the books, she scraped soft bird droppings from the window and returned to the andal bowl, where she mixed the droppings with the remaining juice.

After a few moments of stirring, Miketh walked back to Ekimet and showed zir the resulting thick, brownish paste. *Not much difference between the subspecies and us. If we just cover up our Talent markings and keep our hands shoved in our pockets, it might be enough unless they take a* really *close look. Here.* She pulled down the sleeve of Ekimet's left shoulder and applied a thick layer of paste over the four aligned hexagons that showed just under zir skin. Ekimet was pleased that it smelled more like the andal than the bird leavings and blended in well with their skin tones. When she finished, Miketh pulled her left pant leg up and repeated the process on the back of her calf, on a pinwheel spiral of three equilateral triangles.

Just in case they check, she added. *And now, finished.* She set the bowl on the table. *What is your range with this? Can we get down the hallway before you release them?*

I don't know. I've never tested range before. Ekimet took a short step towards the door and then another. The Mmnnuggls continued their slow circles. *I am not confident in my ability to hold them here. We need a better way to keep them from following us.*

Miketh looked around. *Would you say you are fundamentally opposed to violence?*

Ekimet was startled by the question and almost broke zir contact with the Mmnnuggls. *They're prone, Miketh. We can't just attack them. Besides, they're juveniles. You wouldn't hit a first don, would you, no matter how bad the temper tantrum?*

Miketh sighed and took several long steps over to an andal chair. *Fine, we'll do things the hard way.* She studied the chair and picked it up, turning it around, and prodded its joinery with a finger. *Found one!* Grinning, Miketh grabbed the chair by its back, lifted it above her head, and smashed it against the table. The rear back leg splintered in half, and a shower of andal fragments fell to the floor.

I don't think you picked the right joint, Ekimet commented. *The leg dowel is still in the base.*

I don't want the whole leg. I want some small shards, which I got. Properly glued wood is stronger at a glue joint than elsewhere. Didn't you take the remedial andal course after your metamorphosis?

Ekimet decided not to comment. Arguing with Miketh and pacifying the Mmnnuggls was both tiring and wearing on zir patience. Instead, zie watched Miketh rip the waistband of her pants and remove the rubber insert that kept the garment on her hips. She shoved the band and a handful of andal pieces into her pocket and then rolled the top of her pants down in an effort to tighten the fabric around her hips. *Let's go. Keep hold of them as long as you can. I'll take care of any that question us.*

There is a landing pad on the roof of this building. The royal transport is usually there for the Eld. It would be our fastest way off-world, if you think you want to try going up instead of down where we might be able to walk to a spaceport. Ekimet paused at the door, checking zir connection to the Mmnnuggls. It was still strong, but once they were out of sight, zie wasn't sure what would happen.

Sounds good. Lead on.

Just remember to walk with purpose. We're Keft. We belong here. Their embassy suites are on the same floor as ours. Nothing about this is strange. Miketh straightened her back and shoved her hands into her pockets. Ekimet followed suit. The two walked at a leisurely pace down the corridor and had to hunch over as they ascended the ramp to the next level. None of the other floors were designed for bipeds, and Ekimet wondered if the Eld themselves had to hunch to get to their spaceships, or if they were perhaps loaded through the window in the room.

Everyone must still be dispersing from the rally, Miketh muttered as they continued to ascend. She turned back to Ekimet. *Do you still have a hold on the group?*

Yes, but not as much as I did. Another level and it will be gone. We have five more levels before we reach the roof.

Miketh quickened her pace. *Let's hope they're young enough to try to pursue us themselves, instead of contacting the authorities. I don't think we could realistically take on an entire squad.*

Not with a splinter slingshot, anyway, Ekimet retorted. Not wanting to cause ill will, zie patted Miketh on the shoulder. *Neat idea though.*

You work with what you've got.

The two rounded the crest of another floor and Ekimet stopped. *I've lost them. I suggest we run.*

Miketh nodded in agreement and grabbed Ekimet's hand. Together they bolted up the winding ramp, Ekimet paying close attention to every interface they passed to see if a green light had lit to indicate a priority communication.

They finally reached the top floor and paused for breath. Ekimet gave a gentle push to the roof door and was pleased when it swung open.

Miketh pulled the band and an andal shard from her pocket and slowly moved onto the roof. Ekimet was about to follow when a flash of green caught zir eye. Zie turned towards the light, only to glance back at the sight of round bodies tumbling, silently, to the ground. Ekimet wanted to confirm the Mmnnuggls were incapacitated, but rapidly scrolling text had appeared on the panel beside zir. Ekimet scanned the text, confirming zir suspicion.

We have a problem, Ekimet sent.

There's a ship—now without guards—so I don't think we have too much of a problem. It is definitely the royal skiff too, the reinforced one, and no one ever bothered to lock it, because who would steal the Eld's personal skiff? Miketh sent Ekimet her view of the ship's cockpit, which she was already sitting in. *I'm interfaced and ready. If you get onboard, we can go.*

Hold on. Ekimet read until the text ended and restarted from the beginning. Hoping zie had caught it all, Ekimet ran to the ship and shut the boarding ramp door.

I'm ready, zie said. *You need to take us back to Ardulum the fastest way possible.* Ekimet strapped into one of the large, cushioned Eld chairs just outside the cockpit and watched the view change as Miketh left the roof. She ignored the warning hails that flashed across the communications relay as startled Mmnnuggl pilots, patrolling the ground, realized something was wrong.

The stellar skiff left Ggllot's atmosphere. Ekimet watched the computer readouts. Two of the smaller Mmnnuggl pods had rallied to pursue them. They were lucky none of the larger ones had, but with so many individuals in attendance at the demonstration, it was no wonder more pilots hadn't joined the chase.

They don't react very quickly to surprises, Miketh said, amused. She set the generator and then reached over and patted Ekimet on the thigh. *Relax. Neither of us can use the weapons, but this ship has excellent armor plating. Even with their tech, we have a head start. They can't hurt us enough to matter.*

Ekimet pointed to one of zir ears with a dour expression.

You know what I meant, Miketh returned. The skiff jostled and several small indicators lit up on the panel in front of Miketh. She pointed at them and grinned. *See? They're trying their best, but we'll be far enough from Ggllot to use the hyperdrive in another minute.*

Ekimet counted another seven small shudders before the telltale stillness of the generator took over. The Mmnnuggl ships faded from view.

Miketh reclined in her chair and closed her eyes. *Just going to relax for a few moments until we arrive.*

Ekimet shook her shoulder. *Don't. I know why the Eld never sent anyone for us,* zie said as the familiar constellations of the Ardulan sky slid onto the viewscreen. *It was on the comm panel back on Ggllot. The planet just declared war on Ardulum. They've got a dozen worlds with them, most of them the outlying systems that we haven't interacted with in decades, systems that probably didn't even realize that Ardulum was running the Alliance.*

Ekimet could feel Miketh's displeasure at the word "war." *Sounds like the most uncivilized of species then,* she spat. *What do they hope to accomplish? We're technologically superior in every way. War would only end in their own total destruction.*

Funny, Ekimet said, pushing back into the soft chair and closing zir eyes. *Because it's our total destruction that they're after. And Miketh...they were talking about a flare.*

So? Miketh turned around to look directly at Ekimet. *I just put in a call to the Eld, and we've already been granted an audience. We should be landing in about five minutes on the pad near the palace. I'm sure they'll care about the Mmnnuggl rebellion, but why should they care about a defective Ardulan?*

How much could zie share? Certainly the information in the Mmnnuggl communication wasn't privileged. Miketh could draw her own conclusions. *The communication said this flare was trained. That she is a remainder of the Risalian Experiments. She is the one who ended the Crippling War in the Systems and dismantled the Mmnnuggl fleets. They seem to think she is more powerful than the Eld. They think she can destroy our whole planet, Miketh.* That was bordering on hyperbole, but the Mmnnuggls did love big writing.

Miketh turned back to the viewscreen and watched the andal treetops come into view. The ship slowed its descent and rotated to port, aligning with the landing pad that was still too far away to see. *Do they control her?* she asked, considering. *Is she somehow their prisoner?*

They said they were going to recover her, whatever that means. They'd never manage it. The Eld would wipe out the entire species before they'd let the flare be controlled by the Mmnnuggls. If that was the Mmnnuggls' plan, Ekimet doubted the conflict would last half a year.

Miketh nodded. The ship trembled as it made contact with the ground, and Ekimet felt the gentle hum of the engine subside. *Well,* she said as she stood and pushed the door open. The wet, green smell of the forest rushed into the ship, and Miketh inhaled deeply. *I'm sure the Eld will know what to do. Let's go see them.*

Chapter 13: Xinar Hub, Xinar System

The Eld have called for the next relocation. Transfer all remaining flares to the Thannon Facility and finish any hanging research.
—Communication from the Office of Eld Conveyance to all abnormality research facilities, Third Month of Arath, 26_15

FLUTTERING SILENCE HUNG in the cockpit.

Neek had heard Emn's wordless call, hadn't asked questions when Emn had taken her hand and pulled her through the crowds of people back to the *Scarlet Lucidity*. They'd stayed quiet through ship traffic, Neek unable to enjoy the ease with which the *Lucidity* dodged cluttered spacelanes. Now that they were in open space, drifting between systems, she could only stare at the text on the viewscreen, reading and rereading words from gods she'd sworn didn't exist. Couldn't exist.

She'd been wrong.

Ardulum. Neek screamed it in her head. The word reverberated, echoed from Emn's mind and crashed back into Neek's, deafening despite the aural silence. *Ardulum. We found Ardulum.*

A patchwork of images began to form behind Neek's eyes as she lost what small grip she had over their telepathic connection. There was Emn's mother—wild-eyed with matted, red hair, smiling in her mesh cage. Next to that image was one of a crimson settee, a gold and green robe laid across the bow. Then came an image of Neek's uncle—the high priest of her homeworld—and then Risalians, one face rising above the others. Captain Ran, pulling Emn off the *Pledge*. Captain Ran, taking Emn from the Neek homeworld. Captain Ran, crumpled and crispy, yellow tunic charred to brown inside the scorched hull of a Risalian cutter.

Neek focused, brought her eyes to a green pair that was already looking at her. She let her mind slip into Emn's and found an image of herself—hair loose from its braid and floating in a halo around her face. A baggy flight suit tucked sloppily into mid-calf utility boots. She looked unkempt, shocked, lost...

"Can you read the message to us?" Nicholas chanced. "Or can the computer do a Common translation?"

The message had come through in the Keft language, with only the correspondent's name written in Common. The *Lucidity*'s computer had translated it into Neek. She'd forgotten no one could read it except for her, and she didn't trust herself to read it out loud. With shaking hands, Neek pulled a rolled-up tablet from her pants pocket. She glanced up at the screen a few times as she typed, her fingers sliding over the film and slipping with every few taps. It was Emn's hand on her arm that finally steadied Neek's typing. Eventually, Neek handed the *stuk*-covered film to Nicholas, who read it aloud.

> *FROM: ELD TRIARCHY, ARDULUM*
> *TO: ALL ALLIANCE CITIZENS*
>
> *THE ELD HAVE VOTED TO SUSPEND DIPLOMATIC RELATIONS WITH THE MMNNUGGL PEOPLE. EFFECTIVE IMMEDIATELY, ALL AID, INTERNSHIPS, AND OPERATIONS WILL CEASE. DEPLOYED ARDULANS SHOULD RETURN TO THE BELOW COORDINATES FOR DEBRIEFING AND REASSIGNMENT.*

"Nice of them to provide coordinates." Nicholas bit his lower lip as his eyes narrowed. Neek took a step back. Yorden had used that same facial expression. Watching it on Nicholas, now, dredged up more memories. Neek's mind spiraled. It was the look Yorden had given her the first time they'd met, in the alley behind a bar on Mars. She was broke. Drunk. He'd beaten her in her final round of blackjack, taking the last of her diamonds. She'd screamed at him and thrown a mashed wad of perf at his head. Yorden hadn't ducked. Instead, he'd hired her, given her a job piloting a Terran tramp so old it was damn near impossible to fly. No one could fly it, in fact, after his last round of upgrades. No one except her. It was the look he'd had when they'd found Emn's chrysalis on the burned Risalian cutter, when the theology of the Neek people had fallen down around her.

Damn Yorden for not being here to see this. They needed a captain—a real one. What the hell were they going to do?

"Neek." Nicholas's hand landed on her shoulder. She looked at him, his face once again youthful, the traces of Yorden gone. "Neek, can you ask the computer about the Alliance? I think we need more information."

Neek nodded. She sat down on the thick padding of the captain's chair and queried the computer. It was so hard to focus. She could probably see what Emn was thinking if she made the effort, but there didn't seem to be any space in her head for someone else's thoughts.

"The Alliance is a planetary conglomerate under a solitary rule," Neek read in a monotone. The words barely registered. "Actual membership changes yearly. Application process is not rigorous. The ruling body—" She swallowed, clinched her eyes shut, and then opened them, rereading the information before saying it out loud. "The ruling body is Ardulum."

Emn was next to her, standing so close to the chair that her dress brushed Neek's arm. Emn's hand slid over leather and velour, searching, and found Neek's fingers. Neek's hand was slippery from *stuk*, but Emn was not deterred. Neek held tightly, unsure if she could let go.

"I don't like how the information is stacking up," Nicholas said. He shoved his hands into his flight suit pockets. "We've got a traveling planet with questionable intentions, a bunch of beach balls that hate the Charted Systems, and now it looks like an actual planet, named Ardulum, is cutting ties with the Nugels." From a brown bag in the corner of the cockpit, Nicholas pulled out a *bilaris* fruit and began peeling it. "This shitstorm sounds worse than the one we left."

That jogged Neek's memory. She queried the computer again, inputting the species names from the ships that had been massing near Korin. Xylnqs—full Alliance membership. Astorians—full Alliance membership. Wens—full Alliance membership. They hadn't left the conflict behind, it seemed. Rather, they'd wandered into the heart of it.

More information followed, the computer database proving more extensive than Neek had anticipated. This time, she narrated out loud. "The Alliance is made up of twenty-seven distinct planets within fifteen systems, at least four of which Emn named near Korin before we left."

That was more than enough. Neek exited the screen. Emn's grip tightened as apprehension mixed with hesitant anticipation and she asked, "If the Nugels have been kicked from the Alliance, then these other species—"

"Do you think they're in league with the Risalians?" Nicholas asked, cutting her off.

"No." Emn's response was curt. "The Risalians worked alone. They might be in discussions now, but their actions were entirely their own in the Crippling War." Her tone turned bitter. "They valued 'sentient' life, remember? They would not have willingly let so many people be slaughtered."

Nicholas handed the fruit to Neek, half-peeled. It bobbed across her vision, an abstraction in the face of so much cold information. When she didn't take it, he lobbed it back towards the bag and then leaned against the console.

An indignant chirp sounded from Nicholas's backside.

"I didn't touch anything!" Nicholas hopped forward, jittery in the apprehensive atmosphere of the cockpit.

"It's fine, Nicholas." Her words weren't as soothing as she'd hoped, but Neek couldn't find any emotion to spare. She released Emn's hand and turned the viewscreen back on. Neek text scrolled across the bottom.

"Of course," she muttered. When Emn questioningly tugged at her mind, Neek continued, louder. "We are being flanked by three Nugel pods. The big ones. They're not firing, just keeping a constant distance." She paused and then added, "And they're towing us with some sort of field. It's not mechanical. The ship doesn't know what to do with it." Neek sat back in her chair, letting the stuffing pillow her head. "I can't with this right now. Emn, could you disable them? There's a tactical console on the opposite wall. In the meantime, I'll set coordinates for halfway to Ardulum in the generator. That should give us some breathing space."

You're not alone in this, Neek. Emn gripped her hand again, squeezed, and then moved to the far chair. The viewscreen switched to space and showed one of the Mmnnuggl pods hovering in front of them, a blue-green beam extending towards the *Lucidity*.

Emn rested her right hand on the console and closed her eyes. There was a click in Neek's mind—Emn's connection to her still taut—and ship systems leaked across their bond. Neek remembered the vivid details of Emn's annihilation of the Mmnnuggl forces during the Crippling War, the ease with which the younger woman had disabled Risalian lasers. The memories weren't helping Neek's state. At least for a little while, she wanted things to stop being so damn complicated. Needed something simple. A respite, so they could take the time to process the new information. And, she needed to talk to Emn. Really talk to her, not this flitting around business that Nicholas kept ribbing her about. It was time to start dealing with things.

The corners of Emn's mouth turned town, and her eyes opened. "I— I can't do anything," she stuttered. She turned to Neek, brows furrowed. "I can't touch the beam. It's reinforced with biological material that I can't see. The computer sensors say its xylan. I don't know what that is."

"It's a type of hemicellulose," Nicholas offered. He stood upright and walked to Emn. "Comes from xylose—another wood sugar—but it's old tech. The speed it gives is substandard at best."

Emn shook her head. "That isn't an old ship. You can see the sheen of the new reflective coating from here. The computer lists the xylan interweave at eighty percent. That's too high for old tech."

"It'd be stupid to make a new ship with xylan though." Nicholas crossed his arms, his tone agitated. "Nugels are smarter than that. Come on."

Neek exhaled slowly. The gravity of the words spinning through the cockpit weighed her down. Xylan made a lot of sense, if you looked at the context of the situation. It made terrifying sense.

"Emn," Neek said in a low tone. "Would you please fire our ship laser directly at their tractor beam?"

Emn's eyebrow rose, but she turned back to the console. Purple light shot from the *Lucidity* towards the pod in front of them. It connected, but, after a pause, their laser beam broke apart.

"That...they didn't even try to evade, Captain. I don't understand what is going on. They're not powering weapons, either."

"Target another one. Any one. This time, aim for their engines."

"Neek, what are you getting at?" Nicholas asked. Neek held her hands up, hoping to forestall more questions.

"They raised shields in that area." Frustration leaked from Emn. "The shot was deflected, and even when I cascade a breakage in the disordered areas of the cellulose in our beam, it doesn't affect the xylan."

"Try navigation. Hell, try any of their systems. See what you can hit."

Another pause before Emn shook her head. "Deflected on all counts and...and they're *leaving*." The pod in front of them edged to port and then disappeared entirely from view. Neek moved back to the pilot's console and tracked the ships through the computer. The pods rejoined formation, coasted for a long minute, and then engaged their generator. A moment later, they were gone.

Again, silence descended in the cockpit. Neek let it stretch, let her mind process the details. What were their options? Return to the Systems on the brink of another war? Continue to a planet that was, what? About to be overthrown?

"Neek," Nicholas prodded gently. "What are you thinking?"

"I think that Emn—" Neek said as she stood. "That you had best make a call to Ardulum. Now." She gestured over her shoulder to Nicholas as she moved towards the door. "Hemicellulose ships are a brilliant idea, if you're fighting an Ardulan. We were tested. We failed. An Alliance coup is brewing, and the Nugels just figured out that an Ardulan without cellulose is no different than anyone else, even if that Ardulan is you. We need help, and so does Ardulum."

Chapter 14: Research Station K47, Ardulum

To possess a Talent is a gift. To possess two is a blessing. To possess all is to teeter on the precipice of insanity.
—Excerpt from *The Book of the Uplifting*, supplemental material

ARIK SAT UP and opened his eyes to absolute blackness. There had been no dreams this time, for which he was grateful, but some escape from this new reality and his aching muscles would have been nice. It was hard not to think about work that needed to be done at home, how his parents were managing without him. How his saplings were managing without his care. Did his parents know this was a possibility, that their son might never return from the Eld Palace? Had they prepared for it, secretly, whispered about it to third *dons* who had lost their own children? Would they look for him? Mourn him? Replace him?

Cautiously, Arik moved his shaking legs off the bed and felt for the floor. It was cool on his bare toes. Slowly, taking time to remember the layout of his room, Arik edged to the door. He pushed it outward and was relieved to see two little lights on at opposite ends of the common room. Company was what he needed right now.

You're up early. Waiketh's mental voice greeted him from the closer of the two lights. *It's usually just Kisak and me up at this hour.*

Guards aren't even up this early, Kisak added, shaking zir head. *Gives one a certain freedom. A certain time to think without our benevolent overlords listening in.*

Arik stopped and stared at the outline of Kisak. *Wait*, he responded, feeling suddenly very trapped. *They're listening to us?*

Waiketh chuckled. *I doubt they're that bored, dear. No one cares what we think.*

Like you know, Kisak shot back. *They're listening to our every word. Deciding who would make the best new toy for their Science Talents.*

Arik's heart sank. Science Talents. He was supposed to have been a Science Talent. He wondered briefly if one of his apprenticeships would have been here, working with these people. If he would have been the one doing the experiments. Maybe he would have uncovered the cure. Maybe he would have been famous—the youngest Science Talent on Ardulum to receive the rank of Master of Science. Maybe he would have just stayed at home, studied andal farming and inherited his family's land one day. Watched his saplings grow to maturity.

You're a moron, and you're broadcasting. Didn't your parents teach you anything during your first don?

Arik spun around to face Kisak, angry at the intrusion, but his rage dispersed when he made eye contact. The dark purple bags under the gatoi's eyes were deepened in the dim light, zir body slumped with age and confinement. It wasn't Kisak's fault, Arik reminded himself. It wasn't any of their faults. Getting angry at each other wouldn't help anything.

I wonder if they miss me, Arik asked across the shared link. *I wonder if they knew, about me. That this was inside me.*

Doubt it. On both accounts. Kisak yawned and plodded towards zir room. Arik scowled after him. Of course his parents missed him. They had to be sick with worry.

Time for breakfast, Waiketh sent merrily. *The ninth day is always* titha *bacon. Delicious.*

That was disgusting. Disgusting and confusing. Arik swallowed and wrinkled his nose. *Why would you eat a* titha? he asked. *We don't have the right enzymes for meat digestion, do we?*

What do you think would happen if they gave us andal, in any form? Kisak snorted and gestured towards the long, plastic table in the middle of the room. For the first time, Arik really looked at his surroundings. Everything was either metal or plastic—the tables, the chairs, the floor, and the walls. There were fabrics covering some furniture, but upon closer inspection, Arik realized they were synthetic. There wasn't a single organic substance in the room, other than the Ardulans themselves.

What are they so afraid of? Arik sent to no one in particular.

Us, Kisak responded. Zie slammed zir door shut and Arik heard a thump from inside the room.

We have a lot of Talents. Waiketh gestured for Arik to come sit next to her on the couch. *If they gave us andal, think of what we could do. Potentially, I mean. If we had training.*

But we don't, Arik sent as he sat down, *and that still doesn't explain why we can't have wood furniture. There are trees other than andal they could make it from if they thought we would try to chew on the furniture.*

Waiketh shrugged. *I don't know what to tell you, Arik. This is just the way it is. Play by the rules, and it isn't too bad. You're young. Maybe they'll find a cure while you're alive. It's something to look forward to, at least.*

Saplings swayed in Arik's mind. *What about escape? Anyone ever try it?*

No. Not in my memory.

Impossible, Kisak added from zir room. *Too many guards—too much we don't know about the building and layout.*

Arik threw his head back and stared at the white ceiling. *This is stupid,* he said. *There has to be an option. I refuse to just sit around and wait to die.*

I prefer to sit around and wait for breakfast. Waiketh nudged him. He straightened and saw two guards enter the main room bearing plastic bags filled with steaming flesh. Upon reaching the table, they threw the bags onto the top and walked back out, the door pulling closed tightly behind them.

Fantastic! Waiketh's voice was giddy in Arik's head. She reached for a bag, turning it upside down and dumping its wet contents onto the table. Arik watched the rivulets of blood and some type of meat juice he didn't want to think about run over the side and down the table legs, collecting in small pools on the floor, and swallowed bile.

Try some, Waiketh prodded, ripping out a chunk of flesh with her mouth and handing it to Arik. *It will make you queasy at first, but you'll get used to it.*

This time, Arik did vomit. He missed Waiketh by only a few centimeters, but the bile hit the tabletop and the bag, dripping slowly down the side and joining the other fluids.

Way to ruin breakfast for the rest of us, Kisak muttered. *Grow up.*

It's fine, Waiketh countered. *It only hit the bag. The rest of them will never know.* That thought made the bile rise in Arik again, and he had to work to contain himself.

I can't eat that, he sputtered. *I just can't.*

You will, Waiketh returned, taking another bite, *when you get hungry enough. Just wait.*

Kisak stomped from zir room, pulled the remaining meat from Waiketh's hand, and took a large bite. *Share the vomit-free stuff. Second-don puke tastes terrible. I got stuck with the stuff you ruined, Waiketh, on your first day here. Remember?*

Waiketh blushed. *All too well. At least I'm not the youngest here anymore.*

Arik watched in silence as Kisak finished the remaining meat in zir hand and wiped the sticky juice on zir shirt. *Not a bad breakfast, as far as they go,* zie said. *Ninth day food is usually decent. It's the tenth day you have to watch out for. End of the week is always leftovers.*

Leftover and discarded, Arik thought to himself bitterly. *Just like us.*

ARIK WASN'T SURE how anyone tracked time in here. After breakfast, he'd lain on the couch and stared aimlessly at the ceiling, trying to structure his thoughts. He counted sapling rows, went over seed bank contents, made up new watering schedules... He could hear the rest of his companions moving about and caught snippets of their conversations with one another in his mind. Lunch came, and he didn't even go to look. He was going to have to get a lot hungrier before he would eat meat, of that he was certain. He was also certain that he would kill himself if he had to stay here for years. Life was useless in a place like this, worth nothing. There were plenty of objects he could kill himself with, too—plastic edges, hooks, and screws were everywhere. It wouldn't be too hard to ram into one. Maybe bash his head into a wall seam and fall onto something sharp for good measure. He could probably sharpen a table leg using the gritty tiling on his bath floor...

The door to the common room opened. Arik tilted his head to the right and made out a third-*don* Hearth female, followed by a large group of other Ardulans. That didn't seem right. Arik sat up and squinted. They weren't just Ardulans—they were more leftovers, like the rest of them, both second and third *dons*, spanning every sex. He started to count but lost track at thirty-five, when the room became too congested to see anything. Although many had sat on the floor, Arik doubted they would all have room to sleep lying down.

"You're here from now on," the Hearth said as she pushed the last one in and backed out of the door. "Figure it out. No dinner. We didn't get the final shipment today."

The door slammed shut, and Arik covered his ears. There was a buzzing in his head, and it took him a moment to realize that it was the sound of several dozen conversations happening simultaneously without a care for who overheard.

Welcome, Arik heard Waiketh yell over the mental din. The buzz calmed to a whisper and then died completely. *This is unexpected, but you are most welcome. We've never had this many transfers before. Could one of you tell me what you know?*

I can tell you we didn't all come from the same place, someone responded. *I was shoved onto a skiff with a bunch of these guys already on it. The rest of my group didn't end up onboard though. No idea where they are.*

Same, said another. *Myself and Tik over there came from the southern hemisphere, originally. Assuming we're in the north now, since I felt the weather change in transit.*

We sleeping on the floor? asked a third.

Unfortunately, yes, Waiketh responded. *There aren't any empty chambers, and there are forty-seven of you. Add that to the six of us already here, and you can see that we're suddenly very tight on space.*

The beds we do have are narrow, Kisak added. *So don't suggest sharing.*

The buzzing began to increase in Arik's head again as the new arrivals resumed their discussion. The whole situation was getting more ridiculous by the minute, and Arik was losing patience.

Does anyone here actually know what's wrong with us?! he yelled into the din.

A flood of responses filled his head.

Defective.

Mutated.

Archaic.

Who cares?

It matters! he continued. *If everyone has a different opinion, that means there is no consensus. So how are we supposed to get better if we don't know what is wrong in the first place?*

Waiketh came over to him and put a hand on his shoulder. *Calm down, Arik,* she said. *There is nothing you can do about your present situation. Just accept it.*

No! Arik yelled. Drought was something you accepted. Market prices were something you accepted. Genetic drift could be dealt with. He pulled his shoulder away and squeezed past the crowd to the main door. *We have a right to know why we are being held. We are citizens of Ardulum! We're not some lower subspecies, and we haven't devolved into a primordial goo. We deserve answers. We deserve healers.*

Arik wrapped his fingers around the handle. Slowly, he twisted the knob. The cool plastic turned easily, and the door swung open, revealing a dimly lit, long and empty corridor stretching before him. Arik blinked in surprise. Were the guards so confident in their control that they didn't even lock doors? Or was this some type of test to see who could follow rules, and who was going to get a mouthful of pills?

He didn't care. *I'm going to go find those answers,* he sent as loudly as he could. *Anyone want to come with me?*

Silence.

Arik waited two breaths and then three. Finally, a grumpy voice spoke up.

I'll come. Why not? Going to die soon anyway. Kisak pushed zir way to the front and looked Arik up and down. *You know this is the last thing we will ever do, right?*

Arik narrowed his eyes. *I'd rather die fighting than from an experimental injection. I'm not an animal.* He held out a hand to Kisak. *You deserve better, too.*

The murmuring began again in the back of Arik's head. People were discussing what he said; some were just making fun of him. Arik didn't have time to wait for them. His window of opportunity was small.

Have you ever even checked this door to see if it is locked? Arik asked Kisak when the gatoi took his hand.

Kisak shrugged. *I haven't. Someone has at some point, no doubt. Probably got shot. Probably why no one does it anymore.*

Three hands rose into the air. *Us—we're coming.*

Three second *dons*, young second *dons* judging by their appearance, came forward. The two females had the large eyes and heavy build common to the peoples of the coastal southern hemisphere. The male was tall and lean, and he had the fewest markings of any of the captives Arik had yet seen.

I'm Kallik, and this is my sister, Ukie. We're coming with you.

I'm Tik, the male added. *We should go. Who knows when the guards will next make rounds.*

Arik nodded and blocked out the rest of the mental chatter. *I'm Arik, and this is Kisak. Did any of you get a look at the layout when they brought you in? Any idea where an exit might be?*

We went through a lot of corridors, Kallik responded as she and her sister moved to the hall. *We're underground—that much I know.*

Near the water, too, her sister added. *You can smell it in the air, even down here.*

Kisak snorted. *So if we try to escape, we drown. Perfect.*

Quiet. Arik gestured for the rest to move to the hall. When they were all out, he waved to the Ardulans still inside and received a slow, sad wave from Waiketh in return. *We'll be fine,* he told her as he shut the door firmly. *You'll see.*

Kisak laughed inside his mind, but held tightly to Arik's hand. *We will* not *be fine. But I don't mind going out in a blaze of glory. Let's go. Your show, Arik. Lead on.*

Right. Navigating halls couldn't be as hard as navigating plantation rows. At least here vines didn't catch your every step and threaten to pull you down into brambles. Of course, you didn't tend to get pursued in plantations, either.

Arik moved with soft steps down the corridor. The others fell in behind him. They walked cautiously down a narrow, plastic hallway that fed into another and then another. Everything was bare and white, lacking any type of panel or interface. There were doors spaced sporadically throughout, but each one they tried was locked.

Where are all the scientists? Tik asked as they continued down another hall. *You'd think there would be someone about. Especially after bringing us all in like that.*

If I worked here, I'd spend my evenings taking long baths to wash off the guilt, Kisak said. *Then I would go have sex with a Mmnnuggl, because I'd obviously have no soul.* Kisak broke away from Arik and ran zir hand across the unbroken wall. *We're getting nowhere.*

They have souls, Kisak, Tik responded acerbically. *Maybe just little ones. Potentially other areas of their anatomy are smaller as well. It's hard to say.*

Arik was about to tell everyone to be quiet again when Ukie stopped, causing her sister to walk right into her back. Arik began to ask what was wrong, but paused and stopped in his tracks. He followed Ukie's line of sight and saw a brown-clad elbow and shoulder poking around the next corner. The hallway was different in this area of the station, too. Plastic had transitioned to metal, and communication panels now dotted the walls. They were near the laboratories, Arik reasoned. Possibly the staff quarters. The Eld wouldn't force everyone to live in cellulosic isolation. They'd never get any work done.

The figure disappeared around the corner. Their footsteps echoed faintly back towards the escapees. They could progress no further without discussion. *Decision time,* Arik sent. *What do we do with guards we see? Anyone know anything about hand-to-hand combat?*

Don't tuck your thumb. Don't get into fights with armed guards and crazy scientists in laboratories. Kisak chuckled. *Whatever you decide to do, I'm too old for antics. I'll be back here, waiting until you've cleared the way.*

Tik glared at Kisak. *You're useless.*

We'll all help, Arik said. *Let's just try to knock them out. Quietly, if possible. Maybe see if they have some keys or identity card we can swipe.*

Kisak leaned heavily against the wall. *Look at yourselves! You're covered from head to toe in those stupid black marks. Everyone who sees you will know you. You leave people beaten but unconscious, they will eventually wake up. Someone will find them. Then, they will start looking for us.*

So, what do you suggest? Ukie asked. *We have to get past a lot of people. We need a good way to do it.*

Just kill them, Kisak said firmly. *We're all going to be executed. It isn't like there will be some form of leniency. Do what you need to do. You can bet that they will, once they see us.*

Arik swallowed and considered his options. He didn't like the idea of killing other Ardulans, even ones that were keeping them prisoner. Kisak had a point, however. Being merciful wouldn't get them released. It wouldn't get them pardoned—or healed, if that was what they needed. It certainly wouldn't get him back to his saplings.

I'd like to suggest a different idea. Kallik moved to the front and held out her hands. *How many Talents would you say we each possess?* She pointed to the inside of her right wrist. *Science.* She lifted her shirt and turned her right side towards the group. *Aggression.* She pulled her shirt down and then tugged on her left sleeve, exposing her shoulder. *Hearth, and of course, Mind.* Kallik straightened her shirt and exposed her left calf. *But what about the rest?* She pulled up her right sleeve and held out her forearm. Polygons and triangles massed and intersected across the flesh, each black line slightly raised and stark against her pale skin.

Curious, Arik pulled up his own shirtsleeve and compared his arm to hers. He already knew he had the markings for the four Talents—he had checked that when he'd first arrived. But, the marks on his arm—six circles, all the same circumference and all interwoven—were completely different from Kallik's.

Mine are different, too, Tik said. *What does that mean?*

That we shouldn't have to bludgeon people to death, Kallik responded. *They're afraid of us, otherwise they wouldn't lock us up. I think it is time to find out why.* She pointed to a silver screen on the opposite wall—the first interface Arik has seen since leaving the communal room, and the first biometal he'd seen since arriving at the facility. Unlike the rest of the molded plastic walls, it shimmered and hummed faintly.

Communications panel, Kallik said.

Arik nodded. In fact, the more he looked at it, the more unusual it seemed. Every communication strip he'd ever used had looked like an opaque sheet—easy to bend and curl and completely unremarkable. This one was swimming with shiny, little zigzagging things that seemed to be glowing, giving the panel a rigid, gem-like look.

We're not allowed biometals. Or andal. Or cellulose of any kind. I manifested as a Hearth Talent, before things went crazy. I spent my whole life on communication panels. So... Kallik reached out and put her hand on the panel, smiling.

Be careful! Ukie warned. Arik had wanted to say the same thing, but found he was far more interested in what was happening to Kallik. At her touch, the panel stopped shimmering. Arik moved closer and could see millions of cellulose strands hovering before it, dancing in the hall light.

I'm...seeing crystalline cellulose, Tik said. *That shouldn't be possible.*

If we can see it, Kallik said, grinning, *I bet we can move it.* She flicked her thumb and sent a mental command, broad enough for them all to hear. Arik watched, fascinated, as the cellulose responded, swarming around her hand. More strands followed. Bits of metal began to flake to the floor, loose without their cellulosic matrix.

If we leave holes in walls, someone is going to realize what we are doing, Arik sent.

Doesn't matter, she responded. *Watch.* She brought the strands together, weaving them into a tight cord. Bonds formed and energy pulsed into Kallik. With that energy, she widened her reach. More cellulose came to her, the cascade broadening quickly as the wall buckled. Kallik began to glow.

I think we're going to be just fine, she said. *Anyone else want to give this a try?*

Chapter 15: Eld Palace, Ardulum

Those inhabitants wishing to help end the Ardulan threat are invited to mass with the Risalian and Alliance fleets at Korin. Battle training and ship weapon outfitting will be provided to all who attend, regardless of experience level. Together with our allies, we will crush the Ardulans and return an everlasting peace to the Charted Systems. They took from us our innocence, and in return, we will take their lives.
—Broadband communication from the Markin Council to the Charted Systems, December 16th, 2060 CE

THE ELD SAT before Ekimet, looming on their intricately carved wooden thrones. Ekimet shifted on the coarse andal mat, bumping into Miketh's leg. The limb twitched, but Miketh remained rigidly straight, eyes fixed ahead on the male eld of Hearth and Mind and on the female eld of Mind and Aggression. The third throne sat empty, the gatoi eld— Ekimet's childhood friend—mysteriously absent. Ekimet wanted to inquire, but knew it would seem out of place to Miketh. Ardulans did not ask the Eld questions, and certainly did not question their attendance at meetings. Disappointed in losing the chance to at least share a smile with Savath, Ekimet settled back down and awaited instructions. Surely they would find each other later, after the debriefing. Ekimet desperately needed a friendly face.

They were in a small room just off the throne room, which Ekimet recognized as the Talent Chamber from zir ceremony almost exactly ten years ago. Nothing had changed, not even the andal bark mats upon which zie and Miketh knelt, the weave just as coarse as it had been the day Ekimet received zir Talent. Of course, zie had had other meetings here too, over the years, but those had never utilized the thrones, kneeling, or any type of ceremony. They also seldom took place during the day, and this was the first time zie had seen the entire collection of anointment oil spread across the floor. If there were any unusual noises about, Ekimet couldn't hear them. Zie and Miketh had gone straight to the Eld, as they'd been instructed. The healer could wait.

Of course we are glad you could return to us. We will have you see a healer after this meeting has adjourned. Asth smiled slightly, and Ekimet shivered. Zie had not spent a great deal of time with Asth over the years, but the woman's chilling presence still set Ekimet on edge. *You understand that recovering you was not a possibility. Not with the current political climate on Ggllot and the move so close.*

Your information is useful. Adzeek patted the arm of his throne twice. *You are to be commended.*

So, what are you going to do? Miketh blurted. She shrugged off Ekimet's cautionary hand. *The Mmnnuggls will follow us no matter where we move.*

I do not like the idea of a flare helping them, Ekimet added softly. Being aggressive would not get them anywhere with Adzeek. *We cannot have Ardulans fighting Ardulans, no matter how damaged they are. Your guidance is desperately needed, my Eld.* Zie also wanted to ask about zir grandmother, but now seemed not the time.

Asth turned to Adzeek and stared for several seconds. When she turned back, there was a jovial look on her face. Any hope Ekimet had had for the Eld taking the threat seriously evaporated.

The flare will come to us. We have dreamt it. The Mmnnuggls will be unsuccessful in their attempts. Her expression turned smug. *We are unconcerned about Mmnnuggl aggression on Ardulum at this time.*

We have need of you again, Ekimet and Miketh. Will you serve? Adzeek offered both hands, palms down, out to Ekimet. Asth did the same to Miketh.

Hesitantly, Ekimet laid zir own hands on top of Adzeek's. Zie would have much preferred to lay out a plan instead of blindly following, but there was something going on behind the scenes that even zie wasn't privy to. It would be vitally important to reconnect with Savath after this meeting. *We are always in your service,* Ekimet said.

Approval radiated from the elds' minds. *Tomorrow, once your hearing is restored, you are to travel to the Charted Systems. The coordinates of a planet called Neek have already been entered into the ship's computer.*

Ekimet pulled back. Leaving so soon? No chance to connect with family? And...the Charted Systems? Were the Eld joking? What possible reason could they have for returning there, now that the Risalian flares were dead?

Ekimet tried to sound a reasonable excuse. *I am not well-versed in Neek culture. I have only studied the subspecies of the Alliance.*

I barely remember them from training, Miketh added. *Why would they side with us? When was their homeworld seeded?*

Adzeek waved his hands from side to side. *Your lack of knowledge on this species is inconsequential. They view us favorably and will no doubt assist us. You will build there—build and train a defense force. We agree that the Mmnnuggls will not leave Ardulum alone. They are a species of technology. Conflicts must be decided with power, leaving only the victors and the defeated.*

We are uninterested, however, Asth cut in, *on having conflict near Ardulum. Our andal is weak and must be protected.*

If the andal is so weak, why move? Miketh asked. *The change in environment will not help.*

Adzeek reached across Asth and smacked one of Miketh's hands. *It is not your place to question.*

Miketh bowed her head and brought her hands to her sides, muttering, *There's no strategy!* across her link to Ekimet.

We have decided the battle will be near Neek. We have prepared a small fleet to draw the Mmnnuggl forces there. Regardless of the outcome, those who remain on our planet will be safe.

Ekimet did not like where the conversation was going. *What is it you require of us on Neek, Eld?*

We will have forces in space, but none on the planet Neek. You and Miketh will be in charge of the populace. You will keep them focused. Asth stood from her throne, walked over to Ekimet, and took zir hands tightly in her own. Ekimet wanted to pull away, to wipe the coldness from zir palms, but stayed still. *You will work within their belief structure. You will comply with their religious leaders. You will lead, but you will not usurp.*

Miketh rubbed her forehead. *If the Ardulan forces fail, we will die.*

Adzeek stood, reached out, and tipped Miketh's chin up so they were once again eye to eye. *You died on Ggllot. We have informed your family as such.*

Ekimet felt Miketh's rage. It mirrored in zir, reverberated, and then lay flat. Savath would have an explanation, if not a mitigation. Until then, there was nothing to do but consent. The Eld were their leaders. The Eld were of the andal. They had no choice.

We will perform to your expectations, zie managed to stutter, hands still encased in Asth's icy grip. *No harm shall come to Ardulum. The andal will remain safe.*

Adzeek and Asth smiled broadly. They gestured to the door, where a healer waited. *Your appointment is ready. Tomorrow, you leave. The fleet will remain in contact with you, but you are to speak to no one else.*

Understood, Ekimet said.

SOMETIMES, IT IS really hard to be an Ardulan, Miketh said as they trailed after the healer.

It sounds harder to be a Neek, Ekimet retorted. They entered a small laboratory sectioned off from the kitchens, containing six small wood beds. Zie lay down on one and closed zir eyes. *Especially once the warships begin to arrive. This wasn't how I planned on spending my birthday.*

I thought it was sometime soon. Ekimet opened zir eyes, looking up. A soothing calm filtered across Ekimet's mind as Savath entered. Golden robes billowed behind the gatoi eld. Zie had zir long, dark red hair braided and wrapped around zir head, a style that Ekimet recognized from zir own childhood. Ekimet had even braided Savath's hair into this style on more than one occasion during zir first *don*, before Savath had ascended to Eld and become of Science and Hearth. Back when Savath had been a mentor, a confidant, and Ekimet's closest friend.

Savath brought wisps of emotion with zir, the flavor of which Ekimet could not readily discern. It didn't matter. Zir presence was enough. *Happy birthday, Ekimet. I've missed your friendship during these troubling times.*

Savath— Ekimet began, urgently, but the gatoi eld cut zir off.

Be at peace, Ekimet, Savath sent. *The healing must be done, and then I must leave. We haven't much time, you and I.* A cool, damp hand covered Ekimet's mouth and zie started—a moment of panic before reminding zirself that there was nowhere to run to. That zie was safer in Savath's hands than any other's.

Zir hand was covered in the synthetic mucus used for Talent Naming. Zie, however, was no doubt using it to boost zir healing ability. The mucus turned warm, and then Ekimet's inner ears began to itch. The itching turned to burning, and zie had to work to keep a mental scream from leaking to Miketh.

Almost finished, Savath soothed. There was a pinch and what felt like ripping before a low buzzing began in Ekimet's ears. The buzzing slowly faded into the mechanical white noise of the laboratory, leaving only a dull ache behind.

"You're done," Savath said, helping Ekimet to a sitting position. Ekimet steadied zirself on Savath's arm, stealing a moment of kinship. No words came from Savath, but Ekimet felt a mental embrace before the eld pulled away and moved to Miketh.

She lay on her bed with her eyes squeezed shut, breathing heavily. Perhaps Ekimet hadn't done as well at sealing zir emotions as zie thought. Uninterested in watching the operation on Miketh, Ekimet looked around. The wood walls were lined with shelves of glass beakers and flasks. Expensive looking machines hummed on the countertops, and in the nearest corner sat a small andal sapling in a pot.

Ekimet hopped from the bed and walked to the potted andal. Zie ran a finger down the middle of a fat leaf, and it curled in response around zir fingertip. Moved by the gesture, Ekimet reached out with zir mind and tried to get a feeling from the sapling. Some of the varieties had a wispy consciousness about them, although only the Eld could really communicate with the andal on any significant level.

The sapling responded to Ekimet's prod by filling zir head with a rolling wave of fog. It felt damp but warm, as if the andal was happy to see Ekimet but unable to elaborate.

"This one is a new variety," Savath said, coming up behind Ekimet and brushing Ekimet's back with zir hand. "The scientists in this lab are working on lower lignin contents so there is more cellulose per cubic meter. It should help the resource go further."

"That would explain why it looks crooked," Miketh added, joining them. "Without lignin, how will it stay upright?"

"We're actually considering growing the andal on scaffolding, to alleviate that issue." Ekimet raised an eyebrow. That sounded like a horrible idea, but what did zie know about farming? Ekimet looked up at the skylight and tried to imagine living life inside a lab, with only the faintest glimmer of sunlight. It was almost akin to being raised gatoi— treasured but confined within the Eld Palace. A constant reminder of preciousness.

The glass dimmed. Ekimet hoped to check the height of the sun to determine how far into the day it was. When no light returned after several seconds, zie squinted, trying to determine if something might be clouding the view. Was there a blind that was pulled down at sporadic intervals? Maybe low-lignin andal couldn't tolerate too much sun.

After another moment, a shape became clear. It was a bird, and it was headed directly for the window. Savath grabbed Ekimet and threw them to the floor, covering Ekimet's body with zir own. The glass shattered and rained down, bits scratching the back of Ekimet's exposed neck. The bird screeched as it dove and struck the top of the sapling, snapping the main stem in half. The bird and the broken-off andal hit Miketh squarely in the chest, knocking her back against the wall.

Indistinct sounds blared inside Ekimet's mind as Savath rolled off and helped Ekimet sit up. A large piece of glass stuck out of Savath's back, maroon blood staining the robe.

Are you all right? the eld asked. Ekimet nodded, tried to reach around Savath to assess the damage, but Savath gently brought Ekimet's arms down.

"It is as it should be, Ekimet," Savath said. "When Ardulum speaks, we all must listen." Zie kissed Ekimet lightly on the cheek and then stood. "It is your own injuries I am concerned with. Yours and Miketh's."

Ekimet's mouth snapped open and shut several times. Of course Savath could heal zirself. Zie was of Science. Still, the glass had to be excruciating. Zir own wrists were sore, seemingly from the fall, but that was a minor inconvenience. Bruises healed, and the buzzing in zir head would dissipate with time. Savath didn't seem to be bothered, however, even with the sizable blood puddle pooling on the wood floor.

"Argh. Help!" Miketh was kicking the large, black bird away from her legs, one hand on her forehead. There was a faint trickle of blood near her right eye.

In one fluid movement, Savath stepped to Miketh, pushed the bird aside, and healed the wound. Savath's own wound continued to seep. "You're to see the lab tech now," Savath said. "She will guide you for the rest of your time on Ardulum." Without looking back, the gatoi eld stepped over the now unconscious bird and began to walk away, the glass shard still firmly embedded in layers of gold cloth and flesh. "I have great faith in you, Ekimet and Miketh. Listen to Ardulum. Follow its demands."

Savath disappeared around a corner, leaving Ekimet with a distinct emptiness that contrasted with the fullness in zir head. Savath had always been abstract, but to brush a wound like that aside, to have no time to even chat with Ekimet...what did that mean? Ekimet puzzled over this until Miketh took zir by the shoulder.

"Do you realize what the odds are of a bird that size fitting through a window frame that small?" she asked, looking down at the bird. "She had to do some amazing flying to make that fit happen."

Ekimet shook zir head, trying to clear it. The noise was making it hard to concentrate. "Miketh," Ekimet asked, hoping zir voice wasn't too loud. "Did the healing leave you with a really irritating sort of rustling in your head?"

"No. I'm completely back to normal." She looked quizzical. "Did you hit your head on the way down?"

"Must have." Zie looked at the broken sapling, thick sap running from the main break point, down the trunk, and onto the floor. "Looks like those epicormics are going to get their day in the sun after all."

"The tech is waiting for us, Ekimet," Miketh prodded. "Let the other lab sprouts worry about the broken andal." She led Ekimet out of the lab and to the left, where a dour-looking third *don* waited, tapping her foot impatiently.

"They still have andal on Neek, right?" Ekimet asked, more to zirself than Miketh.

Miketh shrugged. "Probably. Why?"

Ekimet sneezed and looked back the way they had come. A streak of broken glass trailed them as fragments continued to fall from their clothes, highlighting their path. "Because I might have a concussion from that fall. My head is...it isn't ringing so much as whispering. A hearty meal might help clear it."

Miketh raised a hand to her shoulder, pointing behind them. "I'm sure we have time for lunch if you really need to eat. We're already near the kitchen."

Ekimet shook zir head and continued walking, absentmindedly rubbing zir sore wrists beneath the thick fabric of the flight suit. "Not those," zie responded. "Genetically modified, low-lignin pot saplings are not going to cut it. Maybe I just need to lie down. I swear it sounds like andal is muttering in my head."

Chapter 16: *Scarlet Lucidity*

Somewhere beyond the heavens,
past our stars and the black of night,
lies Ardulum.
She sleeps unchained against her golden sun.
Free to wander, should she choose.
Free to stay, as she wishes.

She speaks to us only in ellipses and orbits,
gravitational pull, matter and radiation.
But look up, friend, between the stars.
See the lights that shine only in your mind.
For only with these lights, only with these thoughts,
will you lift the veil.
Only then will you find your home.
 —Excerpt from *The Book of the Departure,* second edition

SHE COULDN'T BRING herself to make the call. Frustrated, Emn melted into the thick cushioning of the central cockpit chair and stared at the viewscreen. Aided by the brightness of the stars, the screen shimmered as billions of cellulose strands shot across it, weaving in and out of their metal scaffolding and carrying information across computer systems. One touch would allow her to interface with the system. One small query would bring up the translated communication from the Eld. One command would send a hail across some unknown amount of space to the Ardulans, requesting an open communication line.

She shifted her feet underneath the chair, the carpet contouring her heels. If they answered, who would be at the other end? Would it be an eld? A generic operator? Maybe someone in the military? Did Ardulum have a military? What language would they speak, or would they speak at all? If they didn't speak, could a mental connection be made over such a distance?

Emn felt detached from what should have been a joyous, if not overwhelming, occasion. She'd sent everyone else back to the galley, thinking this moment would be one for just her and her mother—Emn's memory of her, that is. Yet, the more the *putput* of the ship's engine fell into rhythm with her heartbeat, the more trepid she became. This wasn't how she'd originally envisioned these events. The scenario in her mind had the *Lucidity*—well, the *Pledge*, really—being welcomed with open arms for returning a lost child to her home and family, the crew honored for their service. The Ardulans would be good people, sentients who cared about the Neek and the Keft and everyone else they'd ever encountered. They'd explain the Mmnnuggl situation, help Neek understand her history. They'd give Emn a home.

Now, however...now she was making a call to a probable bureaucratic operator under potential wartime conditions. She would have to ask for help. They wouldn't know her, so would the Eld even care about her? Or could her history with the Risalians pique their interest? Instead of returning as a long-lost daughter, she was a tourist trailing Mmnnuggls and Charted Systems baggage. Traveling to Ardulum could put everyone she cared about in danger, including the Ardulans.

She lifted her left hand and ran her fingertips over the console, sliding them into the small depressions still damp from Neek's fingers. Instantly, cellulose strands stalled their movements and hovered, waiting for direction from Emn. She watched them, marveling at the ordered and chaotic regions, at how delicate they were, at how easy it was to bind cellulose and release energy directly into herself. How easy it was to snap the bonds in the disordered regions and disintegrate the entire structure into glucose monomers. Could the other Ardulans—the actual Ardulans—manipulate cellulose in this same manner, or was this ability the product of Risalian tinkering and not actually Ardulan at all?

Emn's musings were interrupted by a tap on the cockpit door. She squirmed out of the recesses of the chair and swiveled around to face the entrance. "Who is it?" she asked, unnecessarily.

The door opened, and Neek stepped in. She'd changed, finally, out of the baggy, gray flight suit into a sharp, black one that hugged her hips and chest. Part of the overage supplies she'd negotiated during the ship trade, no doubt. No *stuk* trails were visible on the dark cotton fabric, but

Neek's hands were shoved into the hip pockets, which was more telling than the *stuk* would have been.

Neek let out a puff of air when Emn's stare lingered. "This was in the other bag I got from the shipyard. The other one was too big, I guess. I don't know. It looked silly when I saw it through your eyes." She sat down in the chair to the right of Emn and kicked back into a full recline. "How is it going in here? Made the call yet?"

"No." Emn stood and leaned back against the console. Neek was there at the corner of her mind, questioning, but Emn narrowed the connection. "I will. I just need a few more minutes."

Neek put her hands behind her head and closed her eyes. "Want some company?"

Emn nodded. She settled back into her chair, shifting against the foam padding, and kept her eyes to the viewscreen. This veneer Neek wore was new—nonchalant and relaxed, poorly concealing the reason she had come by. If it cracked, if Emn pushed too fast, she'd be picking up pieces for weeks. So, Emn reclined and waited. She counted heartbeats, paint drips on the wall, the rise and fall of Neek's chest...

Finally, Neek let out a long exhale and sat up, bringing the chair with her. She didn't turn to Emn, but instead kept her eyes straight ahead, staring at the stars.

"Ardulum means a lot to my people. Whatever the motives, your ancestral planet brought civilization to mine. Maybe the Keft were more advanced when the Ardulans came to them, so their feelings are different. But for us, the Neek, Ardulum made us who we are." She wiped her hands across the sides of her flight suit, finally marking the black fabric. "Maybe that does make Ardulum worthy of worship. Maybe it doesn't. A philosopher could answer that question better than me. The problem still remains... I don't know what to do about you. With you. Near you. Whatever."

Emn smiled. The meandering conversation was the most Neek had spoken to her since her metamorphosis. She decided to take it as an invitation.

"It's a strange time for both of us, I think. This body—" Again, Emn pulled at the front of her dress. "—takes some adjusting to, as does the mentality that comes along with it. My mother showed me images about what my metamorphosis would look like, and shared the emotions of her own, but she didn't really... She didn't have a chance to interact with other people or—" Emn paused and tried to gauge Neek's mood. When the pilot offered no additional cues, she continued, warily. "She didn't have a chance to really...bond with anyone."

Neek exhaled as some of the tension slipped from her shoulders. Emn's changes, apparently, were safer ground than her own troubles. "Yeah. Growth, puberty...it's hard no matter what species you are. You got to skip a lot of the awkwardness I had." Neek looked at the carpet and pursed her lips. "It's, uh...it's strange to think of your mind making the leap along with your body. That's...it's unusual, I think, at least by Charted Systems standards."

Frustrated with where that line of thinking would lead, Emn took back the reins of the conversation. "Should gods really be constrained by norms? I thought the whole point was that we were supposed to be magical."

Neek was taken aback. She blinked rapidly several times and then put her hands over her face and rubbed her forehead with her fingertips. "Yeah, but...you..."

"Aren't a god," Emn finished for her. "But I am an adult, so why are you still so skittish around me?" Hoping to mitigate her words so Neek wouldn't bolt, Emn knelt in front of the pilot and put her hands on top of Neek's. The *stuk* was thin and slippery, but Emn wove her fingers around it, determined to get a strong grip. "If you're going to avoid me, at least be honest about why you're doing it."

"I am being honest!" Neek sputtered. Emn felt her anger, but again, Neek didn't leave. "You're my history and my culture! Being in the same space with you it—it takes some getting used to." Neek shook her head emphatically. "And you're not exactly the same, you know, as the Ardulans who came to my world. You can do all these things that very well could be considered magic under the right circumstances."

"And that's all?"

Neek pulled her hands away, ran them through her hair, and then smacked the arm of the chair. "And... and the way you look at me, and when we're close... Argh! I'm not ready to have this conversation, Emn. We can deal with this after Ardulum. It's too much all at once." She leaned forward and closed her eyes. "Admiration, attraction, whatever this is—" Her voice fell. "—it deserves its own time, and I deserve whiskey." She looked up at Emn then, her eyes hesitant. "Don't you want time, too? To learn about yourself and your body and everything else that is out there in the world?"

Emn sat back against the console and considered that. Her body *was* continuously surprising her, in the new ways it moved and responded. Some things, though, hadn't changed and had just...intensified. Metamorphosed, it seemed, along with the rest of her. "I want a lot of things," she admitted. "I want a home. I want a family. I want to have friends, especially friends that are like me, but Neek...I don't want any of that without you."

Neek threw up her hands. Her mental defenses dropped, and a barrage of emotions hit Emn head-on.

"What do you want from me?!" The rawness of the words bit through Emn's mind. "You think I could just walk away from you? You think I haven't been bound to you since you walked into that hangar bay and toasted the Nugels, since you took command of your life and got this...presence?" She rubbed her temples and stared back down at the floor. Emn felt her trying to gather her emotions, but memories kept spilling out. "This whole thing is stupid. It's stupid, because you've been an adult for only a few months and you deserve time to figure out what that means. And yeah, I promised to help you, but the thing is, no matter what is best for the Neek people, I don't give a fuck about Ardulum itself. I don't care about the planet Neek either, for that matter." Neek looked up at Emn, her eyes challenging. "Is that enough?"

It felt...warm. Enveloping. The harsh tone cloaked feelings they'd been batting around for far too long. A smile crept across Emn's face, but she was careful to keep the little jumps in her stomach to herself. Neek put her hands on the armrests in preparation to stand. Emn stood but did not back away, hoping Neek wouldn't get up. Wouldn't run.

Neek set her mouth, her lips pursed. She made no attempt to move, locked in some internal battle that Emn couldn't see and would not intrude upon.

"I need you to hear me," Emn said after the silence hung for too long. "I want us to be something more than captain and pilot. Friends, definitely, but preferably something more. Please, Atalant."

"That isn't my name anymore!" Neek yelled and shot to her feet. "You know that. Why do you insist on using it?"

"You didn't seem to mind the last time, right after the war ended, when we were in your quarters."

Neek flushed and balled her hands into fists.

"You left your world. You rejected their way of life and their religion. Why should you bear the common name of your people?"

Neek moved behind the chair, placing a physical barrier between herself and Emn. "I didn't come here to argue, and I certainly didn't come here to have *this* conversation. I don't want to debate cultural assimilation practices. I just wanted to see if you were all right. You clearly are. I'll let you be." She turned sharply and stepped from the cockpit.

Before Neek could close the door, Emn called after her in one final effort to clarify what she was trying to say. "That's a shame. Stupid or not, I care about Atalant, not Neek. Even through all her religious indoctrination, she's seen me as an individual being. She protected me when I needed it most. I'd like to think that even in the face of mounting evidence for Ardulan deities, she would never stop seeing me as a person—that she would see me as her equal, not a child that needs protecting, not something to be worshipped. That I would be someone worthy of her, not she of me."

The door didn't close. Standing just outside, Neek turned and leaned against a bulkhead. She smashed a fist into the smooth, papered wall next to her thigh. "Fuck," she muttered.

"That's the hope." Emn felt warmth creep into her cheeks as she walked to the door and turned sideways, leaving enough room for Neek to pass if she wanted. She probably shouldn't have said that, but then again, maybe Neek needed a little nudge. "In the meantime, maybe we could talk? I know that's why you came to the cockpit. Your body language broadcasted it as much as your mind." Emn took a step back inside the room. "I would very much love to talk to you, Atalant. I'll close the door to give you space, but you're welcome in here, anytime."

Neek sagged against the bulkhead, folding until her head was on her knees, her arms wrapped around her legs. Emn's chest felt tight as she turned from Neek to the door controls. Her fingers hovered over the panel. It hurt to watch Neek battling against her past, but Emn couldn't fight those demons for her. All this stupid power, and she had to leave Neek curled in the hall.

She closed the door. Emn walked with heavy footsteps to the rightmost chair and sat, letting the cushion billow around her head. She had to resist the urge to touch Neek's mind and was surprised when, a moment later, a familiar voice muttered into her head.

A Neek can't date an Ardulan. It just sounds profane.

Emn hesitated before speaking, choosing her words carefully. If Neek still wanted to talk, there was a chance they might be able to clear the air before the *Lucidity* landed on Ardulum and everyone's lives became entrenched in dogma.

A Neek and Ardulan can be friends though, can't they? Emn asked.

Frustration filtered across the link. *Yeah, I suppose. Probably not. I don't know. But friendship...I was friends with Yorden. I am friends with Nicholas, sort of. I'd...want more than that, with you. Maybe just not now. Or maybe now. I don't know.*

Emn heard the sound of something hitting metal and a loud curse.

Neek? Emn laced the question with concern. Neek had a bad habit of punching walls and ending up bleeding.

I'm fine, came the terse reply. *Would...would it be all right if I came back in?*

Emn's heart skipped, and she swiveled her chair to face the door. She tamped down the emotion, terrified of scaring Neek away. *Of course.*

The door opened, and Neek stepped in. Her eyes were intent on Emn, searching the younger woman's face as if she expected to find answers there. Emn tried to smile, but her mouth wouldn't follow directions.

"The problem is being a Neek." Neek walked stiffly to the captain's chair and sat on the seat's edge, her body taut. "Sort of a perpetual problem for me."

Emn nodded, unsure if Neek was seeking comfort or just working through her past. Playing it safe, Emn refrained from commenting.

Neek looked down at her hands. *Stuk* strung from fingertip to fingertip, the consistency changing with Neek's varying emotional upheavals. She wiped her hands on the pants of her flight suit and then looked up at the ceiling. "If I let it go, who would I be? Just Atalant?"

"You'd still be an amazing pilot," Emn offered in a near whisper. "A great mentor and friend as well."

Neek's eyes met Emn's, finally, and stayed there. "You'd want more than that?"

Emn nodded.

"With Atalant?"

Emn nodded again.

Neek took a deep breath and exhaled loudly through her nose. She pushed herself from her chair and, without breaking eye contact, slowly extended a hand, palm out, to Emn.

Emn caught no trail of emotion from Neek. She was keeping her thoughts to herself, which surprised Emn. Unsure what Neek wanted, Emn took her hand and stood.

Neek took a step towards Emn and then stepped back. Her face flushed as her lips pressed into a tight line. She steadied her breathing and tried again, first stepping into Emn and then reaching a tentative hand up and onto the younger woman's shoulder.

Silence and starlight hung between the women for...minutes? Hours? Emn didn't know how long they stood a handspan apart, staring at each other. Neek's hand shook slightly on Emn's shoulder, but Emn made no move to still it. An image flashed across Emn's mind, of the two of them pressed against one another, lips together. Emn tried to control the smile that threatened.

Emn canted her head and raised an eyebrow.

A small nod accompanied a quiet *yes* in the back of Emn's head. Unable to contain the smile any longer, Emn placed her hands on either side of Neek's waist, tilted her head down slightly to match Neek's height, and leaned forward.

Before she could get much farther, a loud cough came from behind them. Startled, Neek backed away, and both turned towards the noise.

Nicholas stood in the doorway, looking sheepish and apologetic. "I, well, wasn't sure how much longer you were going, to, uh, be at it and wanted an update." He held his hands up in a defensive posture. "I swear I just got here."

"It's all right, Nicholas," Neek said, although Emn caught a tinge of frustration across their mental link. She smiled at Emn, who grinned back and tried to ignore the desire to push Neek up against a wall and continue what they were doing, regardless of whether Nicholas was there or not. If they let the moment go now, would they ever find time to get it back?

"Still going to call Ardulum?" Nicholas asked. He hesitantly moved one foot into the cockpit. "Can I watch? The call, obviously. Not anything else. I'm not gross."

That boy is adorable, Neek sent.

He's the same age as me, Atalant.

Point taken. Neek gestured for Nicholas to enter. "Ready then, Emn?"

Emn nodded and walked back to the console. When she placed her hand on the panel, it seemed less daunting now. Less still when she felt

Neek's hand land on her shoulder, the familiar presence in her mind now tinged with a hue of anticipation that had nothing to do with Ardulum.

"Time to call home," Neek said softly. "We're right here, if you need us."

Emn sank into the computer. She followed a small cluster of cellulose into the communications system and checked the origin stamp of the Ardulan message. She fed the coordinates back into the computer and initiated the call.

"We just have to wait now," she said. "I don't know if anyone will respond. If the planet moved..."

The connection established quickly. Too quickly. Emn had a brief desire to run from the cockpit, bury her face in Neek's neck, and avoid everything that was about to happen. Instead, she capped her emotions, pushed them down with the ones from earlier, and routed the response to the main viewer.

Emn gaped. The Ardulan gaped. It seemed impossible that the being on the other end would be as surprised as they were, but Emn supposed they made for an interesting sight if one were expecting a Keft crew. No one said anything for nearly a minute.

"Hello," Emn finally managed. The other being didn't look anything like her, not in facial structure, skin pigment, or markings. Had she expected someone identical? Maybe? She certainly hadn't expected this. "We're, well, tourists from the Charted Systems." Emn paused and was grateful for the reassurance Neek was sending. "Next to me is a Neek and Nicholas, a Terran Journey youth."

The being on the other end continued to stare. Emn wasn't sure how to address them, or even what gendered pronoun to use. Their appearance was ambiguous, with medium-length red hair, translucent gold skin, and deep-set green eyes. Lacking any better option, she nervously continued to fill the silence.

"We'd like to come visit Ardulum, request refuge from the Nugels, and get some help. We have some personal business, too. I came from the Risalians. They had me imprisoned and did experiments on my kind. There was a big war and all the Ardulans from the Charted Systems died except for us. I...I thought it would be nice to come home."

"Common. Right. From the Charted Systems." The being consulted something offscreen. "I'm Yarek, and this is way, way beyond my pay grade." Yarek leaned closer to the screen and squinted their eyes. "What is *wrong* with you?"

"Huh?" Emn looked down at her wrinkled dress and bare arms and realized what they were getting at. The two might both be bipeds with reddish hair, but she was the one covered in markings. "I don't know. I was like this when I left metamorphosis. The Risalians did strange things to us, I told you."

"Andal help us, it's hideous. You want to see a healer or something?"

Emn hadn't considered that. "Yes, actually. That would be perfect. Could you let someone know we're coming, so they don't shoot us out of the sky? Our vessel is Keft, so perhaps not as well-known."

"Yeah, okay," Yarek said. They got out a long stick of wood with a silvery tip and began to write on something out of view. "So you've got a human, a Neek, and...whatever you are. Risalian construct or something. Right? Anyone else?"

"That's all," Emn replied. "I beg your pardon, but I don't know how to address you. Is it sir? Madam?"

"Oh, sorry." Yarek put down the writing tool and straightened the front of their shirt. "I'm Yarek, male, third-*don* Hearth, chief operator of inter-planet communications. Pleasure to meet you."

"Nice to meet you. I am second *don*. I don't think I have a Talent specialization."

"Uh-huh. Right, got it." Yarek turned and disappeared offscreen for several seconds before popping back into view. "I just filed your ship registration with Patrol and your asylum request with the Charted Systems ambassador. They'll watch for you. Be sure to leave your beacon on before you initiate your tesseract so that you're broadcasting when you exit. It'll help them find you faster." Emn heard tapping, and a large packet of data appeared on one of the console screens. "The third month of Arath is a busy time for trade, and we're preparing to relocate so commerce is heavier than usual. I just sent three routes to you, along with the names and codes of all the traders in the system at this time. Patrol will advise on which route to take to land once you arrive, based upon traffic." He looked up. "Any questions?"

"No, thank you. We look forward to meeting you soon." Emn smiled, hoping for one in return.

"Not likely," Yarek replied. "I'm on one of our satellites. You'll end up at our immigration compound. All foreigners head there first for decontamination. Don't worry; it's usually pretty quick. Delicate ecosystem. Standard procedures, you know?"

Emn was unsure how to respond.

Yarek continued, ignoring the silence. "Great. Have a fun trip, and hey, welcome to Ardulum!" He terminated the connection, and the screen was once again filled with stars. Emn closed her eyes and reached for Neek, pleased when she found the comforting presence so near and her body even closer.

"I think I expected them to be...I don't know. Floatier. Maybe bearded and wearing robes." Nicholas stretched his arms behind his back. "For gods, they are kind of a letdown."

Emn nodded, Yarek's appearance still fresh in her mind. "He just looked...normal. Just a biped. We could have seen hundreds of Ardulans at Xinar and never have known."

"We'll go chat in the galley, Nicholas and I," Neek said. "Give you a few minutes." Her fingers ran across Emn's shoulder as she headed for the door, the hesitant tendril of images that accompanied the touch making Emn blush.

"Let us know when you're ready to go, okay?"

Emn nodded, grateful for the time alone, and turned to watch them leave.

Nicholas and Neek stepped in tandem down the three short steps that connected the cockpit to the main galley, but stopped when Nicholas rounded on Neek. "Does this mean you're going to stop being so awkward around her now?" he asked Neek. Emn smiled to herself. "No more flitting apologies when you've overstepped your imaginary boundaries? I mean, my timing wasn't entirely unintentional, Neek."

Neek laughed a little too loudly. "Of course it wasn't. And you *love* my apologies. Admit it."

Nicholas rolled his eyes and elbowed Neek in the ribs.

"Okay, okay. I can't promise anything, but speaking of awkward, we should have a quick conversation about my name."

"What's wrong with it?" Nicholas asked. "Tired of modifiers?"

Nicholas and Neek moved out of Emn's sight, but she heard the tail end of their conversation as they headed towards the galley. "No, it's just...well. I appear to have outgrown it."

Chapter 17: Research Station K47, Ardulum

We will wait no longer! The President is dead—the government overthrown. Rise up, children of Neek, and join us. The Ardulans returned, but we were not worthy. They chose from us our most reviled to bring us back to the right path, and we ignored her. Our government, our elected officials, brought this upon us. No more. The Priesthood will lead us into a new age—an age where we are worthy of Ardulum!
—Speech at a Neek religious rally, third lunar cycle, 230 AA

ARIK WAS BUZZING. No, he was glowing. No, he was buzzing *and* glowing as energy from the panel whipped into him. That he could somehow hold it, contain it around himself was even more surprising than the visualized cellulose. The shriek of the alarms didn't seem so urgent now, the guards shooting at them just a minor inconvenience. No wonder they hadn't been allowed cellulose. It was in *everything,* and he could manipulate it, break it apart, bring it together to release energy... He reverberated with limitless potential in a galaxy built and defined by one polymer. Was this what it felt like to be an eld? Was this what it felt like to be a god?

The flares were still in the same hall, having made little progress forward, but the number of people around them was steadily growing. How many guards were at the station? There had to be twenty or thirty already facing them, and more were pouring in from both ends of the hall.

Arik had formed a small circle with the other flares, with Ukie and Kallik facing the front, and Tik and Arik facing the rear. Kisak, finally, had joined them all, and now pulled back from the interface and moved next to Ukie. Arik counted another fifteen guards amassed at both ends of the hall. They weren't going to get out of the facility without someone getting hurt. As if on cue, a rifle discharge flew at his head but splattered widely as Arik disassembled the cellulose before it could hit him. The momentum pushed him sideways into Tik as a shower of crystallites burst across his vision, but he remained unharmed.

Another shot, this one of pure energy, streaked from behind him and caught the guard directly in the chest. The guard dropped to the floor, her body spasming for several moments before lying still. Tendrils of smoke curled out from her ears and nose and then dissipated.

That was very satisfying, Kisak said smugly. *You kids should try it, too.*

Arik hesitated. He hadn't planned on killing anyone. There had to be a way to simply knock the guards unconscious—

Shots, cellulose-laced and otherwise, arced throughout the hall. The air grew choked with acrid fumes. Arik stumbled forward, trying to find the wall, but ran instead into a male guard. The guard brandished a knife—a long, thin piece of metal slightly curved at the tip. Arik reacted. He pushed at the energy around him, focused on the man's face. The blast hit. The guard fell to the floor, jerking and smoking. Still clasped in his hand was the Dulan knife. Arik shuddered and kicked the weapon away. He'd not seen a ceremonial knife outside a museum, but he knew exactly what they were used for. That the guards here were carrying them...

There was no hesitation this time when three more guards rushed at him, grabbing Arik and forcing him to the ground. There was another glint of metal in the hand of the shorter female as they rolled Arik onto his stomach and pulled up the back of his shirt to expose the base of his spine. Arik waited until he felt coolness of the metal on his skin before releasing his remaining energy. It dispersed into his body and then radiated outwards and into the guards. Hands jerked away. The knife fell onto his back. Arik kicked himself over and sprang to his feet. On the ground around him lay three blackened corpses, curled and blistered and unrecognizable. Arik tried to think about their families, the first *dons* he had just robbed of a parent, but he couldn't take his eyes from the knife. Sacrificial Dulan knives hadn't been used in almost six thousand years. They had no place in modern society, not among civilized sentients. The guards had no right to use them against fellow Ardulans.

Stillness descended as Arik looked around. Crumpled, smoking bodies lay in clumps across the floor, some charred black, others simply frozen in wide-eyed shock.

That's all from this group, Ukie said. There was a smugness in her voice that Arik found disquieting. He'd culled sickly *titha* on his family's farm before, burned lesser trees to heat their home, but this smell, what he saw before him, was garish. Ardulans killing Ardulans was…it wasn't right. His parents would be horrified. He should have been horrified.

We should keep going, Arik suggested, stepping around bodies he didn't want to look at. *If we're lucky, we can find a way out before they call in more guards.*

Do you think we should go back for the others? Ukie asked as the group started walking. *If everyone can do this, we'd have no problems escaping.*

Kisak shot a scientist as she exited a room. Her body fell to floor in a heap, white lab coat billowing out from her waist. *The time it would take us to convince them to come along could mean the difference between a hasty, successful escape and a bloody, unsuccessful one,* Kisak said wryly. Three more scientists turned the corner and stood, wide-eyed, in front of the group before Kisak shot them as well. *We need to keep moving. We either need to find a ship or the central communications hub.*

What they needed was to stop killing people. Getting out of the hall was probably the fastest way to achieve that. *The hub sounds like a good idea,* Arik said as he stopped at a forked hallway. *Any of you want to make a guess? Left or right?*

Both, Tik suggested. *I'll go with Ukie and Kallik to the left, you and Kisak go to the right. If either group finds something worth mentioning, we'll call.*

Perhaps Arik could talk Kisak down from increasing the body count if they were together. He nodded, and the two resumed their quick pace down another identical hall. White and gray plastic buffered them as they wound through arced corridors devoid of any other beings. A final right turn brought them face-first to a closed door made of solid andal.

This looks promising, Kisak said. Zie grabbed the handle, turned it to the right, and then slammed into the door, throwing it open. Inside, a woman with short, black hair and a glass beaker in one hand stumbled from her chair and backed up against the wall. Kisak raised zir hand, but Arik stilled zir.

Wait! That one is a healer. He pointed to her exposed wrist—at the arcs of three circles peeking out just above the sleeve cuff—and then at the single circle embroidered on her lab coat lapel. *Let's get some information.*

Kisak rolled zir eyes but dropped zir hand, gesturing for Arik to move ahead.

Arik put both his hands out, palms up, and tried to smile reassuringly. *We just want to talk,* he sent to her, hoping she wouldn't mind communicating telepathically.

The woman continued to press up against the wall. The beaker fell from her hand and shattered against the floor, glass spilling over her feet. Her hands began to flutter, reaching for objects well outside her grasp as if holding something would bring solace.

"About...about what?" she replied. "I don't have anything of value. I can't cure you. Please, just leave me alone."

Arik reached to the left of the woman, righted her stool, and then patted the seat. *Sit down. We just want information. You're a healer, right?*

She nodded, but did not sit. Instead, she leaned over and grabbed a long glass pipette and began to turn it over and over in her hands. Arik pulled another stool from underneath her lab bench and sat down, facing her. *Do you work on us? Do research?*

"Yes." The bulb fell off the pipette, and the woman trembled.

Good. Can you tell me why we can't talk?

The woman placed the pipette gingerly back onto the bench and then brought her hands together over her nose and mouth. She kept her eyes on Arik, wariness replacing fear, as she rubbed the bridge of her nose. "The mechanism isn't entirely understood yet. Please understand that. We think that it is a side effect of flaring".

Arik looked at Kisak, who shrugged zir shoulders. *Sorry, the what now?*

"Flaring. It's the term used to describe manifesting another Talent at one's third *don*. It isn't common knowledge because it generally only happens once in a while, when we need a new eld."

Arik nodded in understanding. *Right. The Eld have two Talents each.*

The woman brought her hands down. Her head tilted slightly to the left as her eyes narrowed. She was getting irritated, which was a particularly reckless move considering Arik and Kisak were the ones with all the power.

"Yes. They get one when they emerge from first *don*, and a second when they become third *don*. But in some people, in flares...something goes wrong. A chain reaction starts, caused by your second *don* manifest. You get one Talent. Then you flare into a second Talent. Then the reactions keep happening all over your body, until every vein is emblazoned. The barrage of Talents...flares like you cannot process it at the rate they appear. We believe that it causes damage. Things rip— things break. You lose your ability to speak."

Arik put his hands on the woman's face, squaring it and forcing her to look at him. She flinched, but didn't pull away. If she was lying, he could see no trace of it, even under the growing disdain.

Can it be repaired? Kisak interjected. *It's just torn tissue and ligaments, right?*

The woman pulled herself from Arik's grasp. "Yes, I am sure it could be. Perhaps in five minutes, by a skilled healer."

Arik slapped the side of his stool. Five minutes? That's all it would take? Were their lives worth so little? Was his life on par with a subspecies, a Keft, a Yishin, a Neek? He spat. Surely not a Neek.

Why do you people keep us mute? Kisak asked her, zir tone too calm. Zie pulled the woman forward and slapped her across the face. She reeled back, cupping her cheek, eyes blazing. She balled her fists but held her arms at her sides, tense.

"We don't waste resources on superfluous tasks."

My speech isn't superfluous! Arik stood and kicked his stool. It fell to the floor and landed on a large piece of the beaker, crushing the glass further. The woman jumped back. He'd thought to reprimand Kisak for slapping the healer, but damn it, Arik was ready to do it himself. *Did you ever consider that treating us like people might have had this whole situation,* Arik said, gesturing widely, *end differently?*

The woman glared, silent and defiant.

Arik refused to rein in his anger. *Are Ardulan scientists just incompetent? How long has this been going on? Why don't you have a cure for flaring yet? Why are we sequestered like this? Are we contagious? If we are, does it matter? Wouldn't society be better with everyone having all the Talents?*

The woman took a step forward, fists balled, as if she were going to physically attack Arik. He laughed and shook his head. *He* was the one who had been locked up. *He* was the one who couldn't see his family, care for his plantations. It was *his* saplings that were dying now, because of all this. The problem wasn't them. It wasn't the flares. It was all the other Ardulans—all the petulant little single Talents too afraid to leave their comfort zone, to change the status quo. There was inferiority here, but it wasn't his. There was reason to be angry, but it wasn't hers.

Kisak reached out and put a hand on Arik's shoulder. *I really don't think you're going to get much else out of this one,* zie said. *If you want information, just query the computer. I'm sure the scientists keep data on all the experiments. We can take a look when we find the central communication hub.*

The warmth from Kisak's hand was soothing. Arik's anger refined, took on a more stable form. He punched the woman in the nose, chasing the hit with energy stolen from a nearby panel. The healer's head hit the wall and rebounded back before her entire body fell onto the floor amidst tiny pieces of glass.

Come on, Kisak chuckled, steering Arik out the door. *We'll retrace our steps and follow the others. We're done here.*

FOLLOWING THE OTHER group proved much easier than Arik had anticipated. Their route had obviously been closer to the central hub, as the body count increased the farther they went. After five minutes of winding around smoking corpses of guards and scientists, Kisak and Arik finally saw Tik's backside jutting out through the opening of a double door.

Tik! Arik called. *Our turn was a dead end. What did you find?*

Tik was still visibly charged, but his body slumped when he turned, his long, thin arms hanging dead at his sides. Arik thought he remembered Tik having more color to his face, but the skin now was ashen. *Want to know why there are so few staff here, Arik? Want to know why we were all shoved in that room together? Come see.*

He moved to the side to allow Arik and Kisak entrance. Arik stepped down into the circular room, stepping over bodies. It was definitely the central communication hub. Seven desks sat in a circle around a large projector. Each of the chairs held a body except for the one Ukie sat on, its former occupant slumped on the floor, disemboweled. Kallik stood next to Ukie, looking vaguely sick. Above the desk, a screen hung suspended from the ceiling. Arik marveled at the finely woven cellulose that made the screen shimmer before realizing that a feed was playing.

Look familiar? Tik asked.

The common area. Arik returned. *Where are the rest of us? Did they shove them all into the bedrooms? I can't imagine everyone would fit.*

No one answered. Instead, Ukie flicked the console, and the viewing angle changed. Now the screen showed the floor of the common room—a floor that wasn't visible because covering every centimeter were the bodies of the other flares. Dried blood was visible near their mouths and noses. Not a single person was moving.

Kisak pushed Arik out of the way and stood as close to the screen as zie could. Arik could make out Waiketh's form slumped in a corner, huddled next to two young second *dons* like himself. The edges of her mouth were stained maroon, as were patches of her clothes.

What happened in there? Arik demanded. *We disabled all the guards between here and our rooms. Did they kill them remotely?!* To himself, careful not to broadcast to the others, Arik offered up a small prayer. *I'm sorry, Waiketh. May you be with the andal. May we see you again.*

Kallik, trembling, tossed a rolled-up tablet to Kisak. *Read for yourself. The Eld are trying to save energy before the move. Bringing only some of us here was their first cull. Those of us that made it here were randomly selected from our peers to be housed at this facility. We were all supposed to live here until after the move, when they'd redistribute us, but it seems something changed their minds. Instead, the Eld ordered complete termination. Didn't even shoot them, although I can't figure out how they died. It wasn't chemically induced, of that I am sure. It's more like someone reached into their bodies and pulled bits apart.*

It felt colder in the hub, suddenly. Like someone had sucked the life from the station and left only dry air. Even *titha* were killed with more grace than the flares had been. The Eld *regulated* the slaughter of *titha* to ensure respectful treatment. This was...this was nothing. An absence of morality. A dismissal not only of sentience, but of inherent value. But it wasn't something the Eld would just jump to, Arik surmised. Actions like this had to be built over time, or something had to press the issue. Something had forced the Eld's hand in this, because no one was this callous. No one could be this callous. Right?

Arik tried to read the tablet over Kisak's shoulder, but the text was too small to make out. *Do we know what the catalyst was?* he asked Kallik finally, giving up on the tablet.

Kallik's bitter words echoed in his head. *Yes, we do. Did you hear about the war the Charted Systems had? It wasn't that long ago. The Mmnnuggls were part of it.* She pointed to the tablet in Kisak's hands. *The Risalians were apparently sold some 'sterilized' versions of us, whatever that means. It looks like they figured out a way to reverse whatever the Eld did, because a flare, their word for us—a talking flare, I should add—is heading to Ardulum. The Eld are terrified. She's trained, looks like, and powerful. Took out most of the Mmnnuggl fleet and a bunch of Systems ships.*

A free flare. A *trained flare.* Ideas flew around Arik's head faster than he could process them. The other flares were dead, simply discarded by the rulers they had all worshipped. There was majesty to the ancient andal—he'd never doubt that—but the Eld had clearly lost their course. As the only flares remaining, there was little the five of them could accomplish, little they could do to right this injustice. Not without training. But this new flare, this talking flare...that was promising.

Ukie, Arik asked. *Do you know where the foreign flare is now?*

Ukie tapped the interface again. Her shoulders sagged before she turned back to face him. *She's on her way to Ardulum.*

Great. She's walking right into their waiting syringes. Kallik snorted.

There was no time to debate. No time to discuss. If they were going to change anything on Ardulum, it had to be now. *We have to get to her,* Arik said. *Fast. If she knows how to use her Talents—really use them— we need her. This has to stop. The Eld have to go.* He pulled up his shirt sleeve, exposing hundreds of black veins streaking across translucent, yellow skin. *We have multiple Talents. If anyone is qualified to lead Ardulum, it's us. It should be us, because we have seen what happens when others try. We can never let flare containment happen again. We will lead Ardulum. That foreign flare is our key.*

Well, unless we have the capability for matter transport, there is no way we can get to her anytime soon. Ukie pointed to the hanging screen, which now showed a topographic map of their current location and the kilometers of water that rested on top of them. Over the water was a contiguous landmass, with an opening large enough to fit a small dive ship and nothing else.

Arik studied the image, considering. *The Eld really don't take chances, do they?*

The next submarine doesn't arrive for three days. There aren't any spares docked at the station. We're stranded here, and if the warnings that went off when Kallik connected with the console were sent to the Eld...that submarine may never come.

On the upside, Tik said, his voice devoid of humor, *by our count, we five are now the only living things left in this station.*

Arik's anger turned desperate. *Can't we just...* He searched for ideas. *Can we dig the station out? Float to the surface? Blast out with rockets or something? There has to be a way.*

Kisak grunted. *Maybe, if any of us had some level of training.*

Tik straightened, a smile creeping across his face. He moved between Kisak and Arik, placing an arm around each of them. *My family works in spaceship tech I've been building rockets and fuel cells since I could walk. How about we raid a few laboratories and see what kinds of chemicals the good scientists have here?*

Chapter 18: Neek

The planet Neek has officially withdrawn from the Charted Systems. Remove all Risalian sheriffs from the area and post a sentry at the entrance to the Neek Wormhole. Monitor all traffic in the Alusian System. Additional forces will be arriving shortly.
—Communication from the Markin Council to the Risalian fleet, December 18th, 2060 CE

"WE'RE HERE," MIKETH announced.

Ekimet watched the star field slow as the yellow and red swirls of the planet Neek came into view. Zie rubbed zir temples with zir palms, wishing the headache zie had had since the bird incident would go away. It had to have done something to Ekimet's hearing as well, because Ekimet couldn't seem to shake a persistent snapping sound, like branches cracking off in a storm. Maybe zie was just tired. They'd been put on their skiff so fast zie hadn't even had time for a shower or change of clothes—they'd had to don their golden robes directly over their flight suits, which made for uncomfortable sitting with so much bunched fabric in their way.

"Are you ready for first contact?" Miketh prodded. "It's been forever since an Ardulan was last here, and the Neek are still at least a century behind our technology. This is going to take some finesse."

"I'm prepared," Ekimet responded, more confidently than zie felt. "Just remember to leave the talking to me. This species is religiously delicate. Get their ships and defenses up to speed. Everything else is my purview."

Miketh nodded and fiddled with the interface. "You know that if the Eld were serious about building a defense force here, they'd have sent us with Aggression and Science Talents. Asking a Mind and Hearth to do this job alone...these people will be slaughtered. I realize that will placate the Mmnnuggls and keep the conflict from Ardulum, but it's a pretty harsh deal for the Neek. They could have at least chosen a species we weren't related to."

A thin, green line shot across the front console, distracting Ekimet before zie could reply.

"We were just hailed by what appears to be some type of customs official. There is a small fleet of skiffs on the other side of the planet, but the hail came from the surface." Ekimet watched Miketh's hand hover over the console, a slight shiver giving away her apprehension.

"Go ahead and answer it. I'm ready." Zie ran a hand down the front of zir robe, smoothing the wrinkles. Fashion had been very different the last time Ardulum had come this way, and Ekimet wanted to be as historically accurate as possible. Still, it put zir on edge to wear Eld robe colors, even if everyone had worn them in centuries past.

There was a brief flash of static, and then an image of a bored Neek filled the screen. The man's eyes—at least, Ekimet assumed they were male—were puffy and bloodshot. Combined with the thin sheen of *stuk* that glistened on the man's forehead, Ekimet concluded visitors, especially high-ranking ones, did not often visit the planet.

"State your business on Neek," the man said in the popping sounds of the Neek language, not bothering to look up. A small pendant bobbed on the male's neck—a tiny wood sphere suspended on a silver chain.

Ekimet chose zir words carefully, not wanting to make a mistake in a language zie was not entirely comfortable with.

"Your planet sleeps, Neek. Your andal wilts. The Charted Systems move against us, and so, too, they move against you." Ekimet looked sternly at Miketh, concerned that her stifled chortling could be heard over the audio. "We do not forget our children. We have heard the cries of your religious leaders, and we have come to answer them."

Slowly, the Neek's head rose. He studied Ekimet without speaking, mouth slightly agape. "I'm sorry," the man said, his voice thick. "You're here to...to what now?"

Ekimet was prepared. Zie stood and let the robe fall from zir left shoulder, where zie had already peeled away the flight suit, revealing the black outlines of four perfectly aligned hexagons. "I am Ekimet, second-*don* Hearth. Traveling with me is Miketh, a third-*don* Mind Talent. The Eld have sent us to Neek. We have been sent to aid you."

"Andal help us," the man breathed. His fingers flew across the screen, thin trails of *stuk* left in their wake. "Forgiveness, please, Ekimet and Miketh. The day is long. I should have recognized you. Why didn't I recognize you?" The man started babbling as he futzed with controls just below view. "I've contacted the High Priest of Neek. I'm sure you know, but we've had some reorganization as of late." A chime and several short beeps sounded from the Neek's console. "He'll meet you when you land. Your clearance is all set." The man took a number of shallow breaths and finally managed to close his mouth.

"We still require landing coordinates," Ekimet prodded.

The man's eyes flew wide open, and he smacked the screen. "Of course! I'm so sorry. Forgive me. There, sending now."

Ekimet looked to zir left and saw the confirmation nod from Miketh. "Thank you so much for your help, dear Neek. I am certain we will see you again."

The man puffed with pleasure but wisely refrained from talking. The connection terminated.

"How do you keep a straight face when you talk like that?" Miketh asked as she sent the navigation instructions to the computer. "I'd rather sheer a *titha* than keep up that façade."

"At least the Neek respect all of us." Ekimet sat back down and watched the thick clouds move past the viewscreen as the ship descended to the planet's surface. "They have a third gender here, too, with similar breeding mores. I'd rather be a god than have fruit pelted at me."

"Let's see if you change your mind after some time on-planet," Miketh said dourly. The ship gave the slightest jostle, and then the boarding hatch opened, sending sunlight streaming into the cockpit. "At least it smells better than Ggllot."

Ekimet stood, rearranged the collar of zir robe, and then stepped from the ship onto a wooden landing pad. Just beyond, an older male in similarly styled gold robes waited, flanked by a group of Neek bedecked in gold and green. Crimson settees sat in an arc behind the group, the nose of each tilted ever so slightly upwards, towards the heavens.

The old man took two steps forward, but then hesitated. Miketh gave Ekimet a nudge with her elbow. *They're waiting for you.*

Embarrassed, Ekimet took a deep breath, clasped zir hands behind zir back, and stepped forward into the sunlight. "Children of Neek." Zir voice boomed across the landing pad. "We have returned."

Chapter 19: Research Station K47, Ardulum

Tolerate no imperfection. Strive past your limits. Find within yourself the capacity for greatness. You are not tied to this world. You are not tied to your old ways. You are Neek, but this does not always have to be so.
 —Excerpt from *The Book of the Uplifting*, original edition

WE ARE EITHER going to kill ourselves instantaneously, or die a long, painful death from pressure changes, Kisak muttered. *This plan is terrible.*

We are going to die one way or the other, Arik countered. *We'll not leave you here to starve to death. You deserve more than that. We all deserve more than that.* He pointed to the large pile of glass drums filled with dichloromethane, all propped against the copper wall of the central core. *This does have a reasonable chance of working. Also—* He tugged on the sleeve of Kisak's wet suit, the cellulose fiber reinforcements coarse against his fingers. *This should help deal with the water. The inside tag says they are rated for this depth as long as you make sure there are no open seams between pieces.*

Arik heard wisps of grumbling in his mind as the gatoi latched the helmet onto zir suit and powered the flow of oxygen. Arik sent reassurance. This escape was daunting for all of them, but Kisak's age—combined with zir early life as a protected gender—would make the journey much more difficult for zir. Gatois seldom engaged in manual labor or strenuous activities unless they specifically requested them. The escape might be beyond Kisak's developed abilities.

Turn the heat on, too, or you'll freeze to death, he reminded the gatoi. *The switch is in the left armpit.*

Kisak's mental tone became a growl. *So let's say that stupid organic solvent does corrode at an acceptable rate and we get our exit hole. Then what? We are* underground, *not just underwater. How do we break the surface?*

I can answer that one. Ukie shuffled forward, her face obscured by the dense vein work of cellulose on her helmet. *I just finished sifting through the records in the computer about our location. There's a small fishing village not far from here, where the supplies for the station are purchased. There's a one-kilometer break in the bi-layer two meters west of our current location, which is the only route the ships can take to access the village. It was extensively detailed on that map we pulled earlier.*

We just need to aim ourselves up and a bit west, Arik sent. *If you miss the opening, in theory you can use the compass in the suit to navigate in the right direction.* To himself, Arik added that, if they died in the attempt, at least it would probably be quick, unlike the slow, lingering death that awaited them in the station. *Let's get to the surface, and we can plan from there.*

Everyone ready, then? Tik glanced around and received a nod from each of the flares before snapping his own helmet on. Using his right hand, he picked up a flask of water with a rubber stopper. *Okay, everyone back to the far wall. If something sparks, we're all in trouble. I'll let you know when it is safe to venture through the hole.*

Tik gave the stopper another firm push and then threw the flask at the farthest drum. The glass on both vessels broke. The dichloromethane mixed with the water and both seeped onto the wall, corroding the surface and allowing the ocean to pour in. Well, trickle in. The corrosion was slower than Arik had hoped, which meant more time to wallow in nervousness. He would have preferred using the extra air tanks as propulsion and just exiting out a door, but Tik was right. They needed a much more powerful boost to reach the surface. In theory, the suits could handle a quick change in pressure, but that, too, remained to be seen.

Get ready, Tik said as the hole widened from the size of a fingernail to the size of a fist. *We have to get out the moment the hole is big enough. Don't dawdle. Once the corrosion reaches the nitric acid in the main console, this whole place is going to explode. We need to be far enough away that we can ride the force without being torn apart. The cellulose in the suits makes them sturdy, but not enough to deal with a direct blast.*

The hole was growing faster now, the degradation of the copper increasing exponentially as more water entered in from the ocean. The trickle became a stream, knocking a drum into another and shattering both. After that, the reaction went much more quickly. The wall disappeared handspans at a time. Arik looked back at the wood barrier they'd built around the console. It was holding back the mix of water and chemicals for now, but he didn't think it would last much longer. Even he was having a hard time standing upright as the water beat against him.

Now! Tik shouted. He dove down and forced himself against the rush of the water. Ukie swam behind him and pushed him out, bracing herself against a quickly corroding wall.

He's out! she yelled. *Someone give me some help!*

Kallik grabbed Arik's hand, and the two waddled their way to Ukie. Arik managed to get one leg out and propped against the outer wall, bracing himself against the torrent of water. With Kallik's help, they got Ukie out and then Kisak.

You next! Kallik said, and Arik caught the worry in her tone. He wrapped his other leg around the wall edge and let Kallik push him the rest of the way into the ocean.

Arik heard a hiss against his ear as his suit compensated for external pressure and the internal heater moved into a higher gear. He pushed against the current, unable to see any of the other flares. The suits had limited oxygen—another safety precaution, no doubt, to keep escapes like this from happening. The extra tanks in the med unit didn't even connect to the suits. If any of them were going to make it to the surface alive, the water would have to breach their wood barrier soon. Hopefully not, however, before Kallik made it out.

Arik checked the elevation meter on his suit. He was moving closer to the surface at least, and in the direction of the land opening, although his frantic clawing didn't seem to be getting him anywhere. Getting distance from the station was the most important thing now, no matter whether he went up or down. Arik really didn't want to end up with a blasted helmet or brain hemorrhage if he was too close when the shock wave hit.

Anyone around? Arik sent, hoping for an answer. He was getting tired and was deeply regretting passing on swimming lessons as a first *don.* He'd never liked the idea. His mother had tried to get him in the water multiple times in his youth. Maybe she'd seen something in his future that he hadn't, because there was no clear reason for a plantation family's son to know how to swim.

The first wave hit him unexpectedly. The momentum came from below and shot Arik straight up. A loud screeching sound started in his suit, and Arik fervently hoped it would hold together. He felt lightheaded and nauseous as fish flashed past his field of vision. Colors from the internal indicators blurred together as the suit tried to compensate for the changing conditions. He was hot and then cold. His chest felt compressed, and he gasped for breath. Something pinged in his suit, and the internal monitors died. Then, as suddenly as it began, the force began to taper off. Arik slowed and then stopped altogether. He had one short moment to realize he had no idea where he was before the next wave hit. This time he was prepared and braced himself, closing his eyes so he wouldn't get quite so motion sick. By the time the third wave slackened, Arik could see light above and the edges of a landmass.

Arik covered the remaining distance at a feeble speed. He was exhausted, but the increasing sunlight kept him persistent. If there was light, then he'd managed to stay in the vicinity of the underground lab. He was near the village and, hopefully, food and rest. Whether the others had been as lucky, he didn't want to consider.

After three more minutes of swimming, Arik's head finally broke the surface of the water. He removed his helmet and took a long breath, drops of seawater creeping past his lips. It was very early morning, the sun just coming up over the horizon. Arik could see the village of Thannon in the distance, as well as scattered fishing boats, but all were well close to shore. The air smelled of algae and fish. Treading water as best he could in the bobbing current, Arik spun in a circle, trying to see if he could spot any of the other flares.

Hello? he called out when no other dark patches were readily apparent. Andal waved in the breeze from the shore and several tethered ships rocked on the waves. Energized from the sight, he gathered the remains of the energy he'd taken from the station and used it to amplify his reach, sending his thoughts as widely as he could and hoping that only the flares would be actively listening.

Anyone there? he yelled into the blankness. *Hello?*

He waited ten heartbeats and then began to count backwards from one hundred. When he reached fifty-seven, he finally caught the faintest response. Eagerly, Arik focused his energy on that connection, thickening it until the other's consciousness butted right up against his own.

Hello? a tentative voice responded, speaking in a language he recognized from his early schooling. *Who is this?* The voice was confused, and Arik could feel the apprehension coming from the other end.

He backed off quickly and tried to switch into...what was it? Common? The language of the backwater Charted Systems? He'd been decent at it long ago, but he'd not had a lesson in years. *Apologies. I...hope find...my friends.* The words sounded strained, even to him. He was about to terminate the connection and try again for the other flares when the other side reinforced it, bringing them back together.

Are you Ardulan?

Now that was a strange question. Curious, Arik followed the connection to the outermost thoughts of his new acquaintance. A jumble of emotions and images greeted him. She—and he was certain they were a she—was on a Keft ship, looking out the main screen at the inside of a docking bay. She was nervous, more than anything, but there was something else, too. Something was familiar about her.

Arik sank a little deeper, ignoring propriety, and tried to dig for more clues and a bit more of the language as well. He accessed her language center easily enough and then spun through internal images of the ship and another female in a black flight suit before he lost the ability to breathe.

Gasping and confused, Arik kicked at the water, hoping to scare off whatever had knocked his wind away.

You weren't invited in, the voice chastised him. *Do it again and you won't recover as easily.*

Arik shivered even though the sun was blaring down on him. The connection was powerful—like interfacing with a computer for the first time. He considered that for a moment as he returned to a respectful distance from the woman's mind.

Are you Ardulan? he asked finally.

The woman hesitated, her mind suddenly whirling in confused images. He caught one—of a bare arm covered in Talent markings—and suddenly realized exactly to whom he was speaking. He sent back an image of himself, highlighting the markings on his own skin, and then those of the other flares. He detailed the differences they'd noticed in the hall and laced the image with the feel of snapping cellulose, which he hoped she would relate to. Finally, he attempted words again. *Hello, cousin. My name is Arik, and I'm glad to meet you.*

Instead of a response, a string of profanities ripped through Arik's head, shattering the link to the off-worlder. *Kisak?* Arik called out, delighted to hear the older flare's voice. A strong hand gripped Arik's shoulder, and the hiss of a helmet release filled Arik's ears.

That was the absolute worst experience of my life, Kisak grumbled as zie gulped for air. *I must have rotated after the first wave hit, because the second one slammed me right in the hip and I rode it up laterally. I am certain I was hit in the face with a fish.*

I told you it would work! Tik's triumphant voice seemed strained to Arik, and it wasn't until he spotted the pair of hands waving above the water's surface a far distance away that he understood why. *I'll swim to you,* Tik sent. *Ukie is just beneath me. Stay put.*

What's wrong with you? Kisak asked Arik as Ukie's helmet finally broke through the surface.

Arik shook his head. *Sorry, I didn't see you swim up. I just connected with the off-world flare. She's still alive, mercifully. I'll try to get her again, once we are on land.*

Tik and Ukie reached them a moment later, their strokes sluggish. Even before they took off their helmets, Arik caught Ukie's leaking emotion. He scanned the area, and when Kallik was nowhere to be seen, drew an uncomfortable conclusion.

Kallik is dead, Ukie returned. Tendrils of emotion seeped from her mind, lapping at his consciousness. Images of a shattered helmet, a bare head buffeted by the explosive forces, sailed across his vision. *Her suit was faulty. It was the second blast that did it. She was with me for the first. I...* Ukie's thoughts jumbled, images overlapping. *I don't know where her body ended up. I couldn't find it. She's just under there. Trapped under the land. Alone.*

In between the lapping of the water, Arik thought he heard sobbing but kept his eyes on the horizon. No one said anything, but Arik surmised their minds were all on the same images. Kallik's body. The bodies of the other flares in the common room. The limp, hopelessness of the situation. The worth of their lives.

You okay to swim, Kisak? Ukie asked finally. Her eyes moved from where she'd come through the landmass to the gatoi's labored treading.

Yeah, I can make it. We're not far out.

We need a plan for what to do when we get there, Tik said. The group began to swim in long, languid strokes, Kallik heavy on their minds. Arik was tired and his muscles ached, but the land couldn't have been more than five kilometers away.

Does anyone know what this town is called? Arik asked.

What we just blew up was Research Station K47, Ukie responded. She was breathing heavily—more so even than Kisak. Arik splashed some water towards Tik, who paused to allow Ukie to catch up. *We're just off Cape Xallus—and ahead is the fishing village of Thannon, which is approximately fifty kilometers from the capital city.*

Arik spat seawater from his mouth. *I think we have to give up the illusion that we could get to shore unnoticed. Fishing boats are already out for the day, and the sun reflects pretty strongly off our helmets and suits. Chances are someone has already spotted us.*

Tik nodded and resumed swimming, this time at a slower pace. *I agree. I think the question is whether or not the residents of Xallus know about the station. If they do, we're going to be apprehended the moment we hit land.*

Ukie paused again to catch her breath. *Even if they don't try to imprison us again, what are we going to do? If we want the Eld to listen to us, if we seriously want to enact change, we need that flare—the one who is not of Ardulum. They'll listen for certain if she is with us.*

I know where she is, Arik responded. *She and I had a chat just now. She's just getting off her ship and into decontamination. Likely, she'll be in the capital by night.*

Ukie was falling behind again, but this time Tik swam back and wrapped his arm around her torso, propelling them both forward with his strong kicking. *We need to meet her,* Tik said as they rejoined the group. *If there is any chance of bringing her to our cause, we have to know.*

What is our cause? Kisak demanded. *We're fugitives right now. If you idiots want freedom, then we need to get on the nearest ship and leave the Alliance. With these Eld in power, andal help us, even with our current regulatory rules, flares have no chance at equality.* Zie spat into the water. *We are spots. Blemishes. If we stay, we have two options—blend in or be eliminated.*

Chances are the Eld have already sent a recovery team, Ukie added as she gulped air.

Kisak continued. *If we're lucky, which by very definition we are not, the Eld will be so caught up with the off-world flare that they won't be paying attention to little problems like research stations. We probably have a few hours, maybe even a day.* Kisak stopped swimming and tapped Arik's shoulder. *Here comes our chariot now.* He pointed to a small double canoe heading directly for the four flares. *What will it be, Arik? Escape? Or do you have some ridiculously noble aspiration of changing the cultural mores of Ardulum itself?*

The canoe slowed and a large, well-muscled gatoi wrapped an arm around Ukie and pulled her from the water. Tik accepted a man's hand up, while a woman dove into the water to aid Kisak.

Arik swam to the back of the far canoe and hoisted himself inside. A woman sitting at an oar spoke to him, but her voice was carried away in the wind. He smiled and then put his hands over his ears and pointed to the sky. The woman nodded in understanding, and Arik sat down. Once everyone was settled, the crew began to row, and the canoe glided back towards shore.

We're going to stay, Arik told the flares resolutely. *Right now, somewhere on this ridiculous planet, another flare is being born. Maybe that little one could grow up on an Ardulum where flares lead, where our Talents are put to use. Maybe that little one doesn't ever have to know what we went through.*

Arik felt Kisak's irritation, but Tik and Ukie were listening carefully. *I think we need to meet with the off-world woman—hear her story, tell her ours. Then, as a united force, we should have a long conversation with the Eld. Let them see who we are, what we are capable of.*

I suppose there is enough andal in that palace to fry each one of them to a crisp if we really need to drive a point home, Kisak returned.

A solid reminder of why you shouldn't anger people stronger than yourself, Tik added smugly. *There might even need to be a permanent change in leadership. If you think about it, who is best situated to lead— those who possess two Talents, or those who possess them all?*

Arik moved his arm out in an effort to highlight his markings, but then realized that his wet suit covered his body completely. With the bright sun overhead and the wet hair clinging to their faces, he suddenly realized why the canoers had not reacted to their appearance.

I am in complete agreement, Arik said. *Let me send an invitation to our cousin and see how soon she can join us.*

Chapter 20: Port 17, Ardulum

The Neek wormhole has collapsed! We are currently investigating the circumstances, but our sentry ships have been unable to enter since early this morning. We will update with more information when available.
—Encrypted communication from a Risalian sentry skiff to the Markin Council, December 19th, 2060 CE

ARDULUM SMELLED...WET. Tropical. There was a buzzing—and rustling, too—that seemed to tickle the back of Atalant's mind as she took the final step off the *Lucidity*'s boarding ramp and stood, feet together, on a planet that shouldn't have existed.

Emn came down the ramp next and stopped at Atalant's right, followed by Nicholas. Atalant couldn't begin to imagine what this meant for the younger woman. Curious, she brushed Emn's mind and was mechanically rebuffed, as if Emn was concentrating too hard on something else to notice. That was fair, Atalant supposed. She didn't press the connection. It was hard not to be overwhelmed.

"This is really strange," Atalant said into the empty hangar. There was a door in the far wall, open, but no one had yet come to meet them. It was possible they had flubbed entry protocol. "Any thoughts, Nicholas?"

"Because I find mythical planets all the time? This is beyond surreal."

"What do you think the rustling noise is?"

Nicholas turned to her, confused. "What rustling? I just hear the sounds of land skiffs in the distance."

Atalant rubbed her ears with her palms and frowned. It wasn't getting louder, but there was definitely a sort of hushed whispering in the background. Some type of insect, perhaps? It was soft enough that she might be able to ignore it, but then again, it also might drive away what little remained of her patience.

"Emn, do you hear it?"

Emn looked around, confused. "Sorry, what?" she asked. "I wasn't listening."

Nicholas raised an eyebrow and a grin spread across his face. "If you'd prefer, you two could go back into the ship and I could wait for the welcome party. Finish whatever it was you were discussing before in very close quarters."

"Funny," Atalant responded as she felt heat rising in her cheeks. "Just because *you* don't—" The rest of her retort faded when a tall Ardulan walked into the room. His thick, red hair fell in waves down his back, and he carried a rolled-up panel in his hand. Emn tensed beside Atalant as he approached, unrolled the panel, and tapped it a few times before addressing the group.

"Welcome to Ardulum," he said, his voice flat. His eyes flicked up, passed over Atalant and Nicholas, and then fell on Emn. His jaw dropped, and he took a step back.

"Uh, what exactly…"

"I'm Ardulan," Emn said. Atalant smiled at the firmness in Emn's voice. At least one of them was sure.

The Ardulan broke his gaze away and scanned his panel. "I've seen a lot of strange shit," he muttered as text flew over the surface. "This— Ah!" He tapped the screen twice. "Apparently, there is a precedent. You've already been granted visas, and I'll not argue with the signers." The Ardulan snorted but did not look up again. "Before proceeding to the scanners, there are some routine questions we need to ask. First—" The illuminated text scrolled down as the Ardulan flicked a finger, the text shining through the transparent panel. "Are you carrying any live cargo including but not limited to: bacteria, archaea, fungi, arthropods, mammals, or birds?"

"We have some perishable food we picked up before entering Alliance space," Nicholas responded. "Nothing still alive."

The Ardulan nodded. "Said food will need to remain on your ship. Please ensure you do not bring it with you through decontamination. Second, I need the ages of the human and the Neek. That information was not provided in the initial communication."

"I'm nineteen and Atalant is…" Nicholas trailed off, hesitant.

Atalant rolled her eyes. "I'm twenty-nine," she muttered.

"Thank you," the Ardulan responded, tapping furiously on the panel. "Now, if you follow me, we'll move through this door, which will scan you for any live artifacts you may still be carrying. After that, we will move to a small room where you will be asked to stand for a full minute until the xenon lamp can finish its arc. Then, you'll receive your official papers and be free to move about Ardulum as you will for the next two days. Be sure to be on your ship and out of Ardulum's atmosphere well before the move."

Atalant fell in step behind the Ardulan, but let her thoughts trail back to Emn as they moved through the wood and metal hangar. *We're out of our element here, Emn. We'll need you to warn us if something is going wrong.*

Emn's response was slow and meandering, and Atalant made a mental note to ask her what was wrong once they were clear of customs. Their surroundings—from the wood floors and walls to the markings of their guide—made Atalant feel like she was a little girl in a storybook. Emn's reaction was likely a lot more complex.

I don't know if I could tell you if something is going wrong, because I don't know what is supposed to be right, Emn finally responded. *There is too much going on. Everything is alive and talking in some form or another. I don't know how much protection I can offer here. My head is...my head is full of chatter.*

Emn, if I die before we finish our last chat, I am going to be very upset.

That did make Emn laugh. Warmth filled Atalant's mind, followed by a brush of Emn's hand against her own that made her body feel warmer still.

The crew passed through the doorway, and the Ardulan ushered them a few more meters before indicating a small room. "Everyone in, please. This won't take long. While you're here, I'll review your scans."

"I hate xenon arc lamps," Neek muttered as she stepped into the room. The door shut and then sealed with a thin, shimmering membrane. The lights dimmed to pale purple, and a bright, white beam shot from the floor and began to move slowly across the room. When it got to Atalant, she tensed even though the beam was painless. She and Yorden had had to go through decontamination procedures every time they stopped at Missotona, too. It was never a good way to start a vacation. At least they weren't going to be x-rayed. Atalant wasn't certain how to explain the vegetable peeler in her boot. Even so, she wished they'd had time to pick up a few more weapons before entering this fairy tale.

The beam hit the far wall and shut off. Immediately, the door reopened and the Ardulan male entered. He placed a thin, square film on the shoulder of each of the crew, except for Emn. Instead, he placed one near the hem of her dress. Atalant watched the film dissolve upon contact, leaving a wet patch and a faint smell of cinnamon.

"Your passport circuitry is now tied to your current apparel, so be sure to wear it when walking around Ardulum." He motioned for the crew to follow as he led them from the complex and outside into the orange glare of the rising sun. "If you walk to the corner of this road—" Atalant looked down and kicked the heel of her boot into the wooden pavement, briefly wondering how they managed to maintain it. "—and wait, there should be a ground transport arriving within the next ten minutes. The driver can take you wherever you desire, whether it be an eatery or lodging. Your ship will remain parked, without charge, at this berth for the duration of your stay. If you are interested in shopping, note that many of the stores—especially at the capital, which is a thirty-minute flight if you don't go into orbit—are having massive sales to prepare for the next move. You could find some bargains."

"Go back a minute," Atalant said when the customs official stopped talking. "Is Ardulum planning on leaving this system soon?"

He nodded. "Yes. The move is scheduled for two days from now. I hope you weren't planning on an extended stay. Visitors are not allowed on-world during a move."

"No, just a brief visit," Atalant replied quickly. "Before we head off on our exciting vacation—what currency is accepted here and in the capital?"

"Locals mostly use a barter economy. Foreigners can use any of the major currencies, including andal chits, sapphires, and diamonds."

"Lovely. Thank you very much." Atalant put her arm around Nicholas's shoulder and steered him away from a wooden posting board.

"Aren't we here to take in the culture?" Nicholas asked as his foot caught a bump in the road. "Are we in some sort of hurry?"

"That remains to be seen," Atalant responded tersely, "Take a look around."

Nicholas shrugged Atalant off and spun slowly in a circle, surveying. The buildings were short, most no more than two stories, and lined either side of the road they were currently walking on. The path itself was andal, but the buildings looked more yellowish, perhaps made from a different tree. Most of the shops looked closed, but several Ardulans were outside. A family was directly across the street from them, and just behind them an older man was sweeping the entrance near his shop. Nicholas stared at the old man, and then at the family, before realization dawned on his face.

"That guy made it seem like they get tourists," he said slowly. "So why the gawking? We're just normal bipeds."

Atalant felt the side of Emn's dress brush her hand as the young woman moved up next to her. "They're not staring at you all. They're staring at me. Only me."

"We need to get either somewhere less rural, so people aren't so wary of differences, or somewhere inside. Then, we need to discuss a plan. We have two days here and don't know what we hope to achieve, other than getting the hell away from the Nugels."

A small hovercraft pulled up near the curb where the crew stood, and the side door slid open. Atalant peered in. It certainly *smelled* like a taxi. Regardless of species, they all seemed to have a similar bouquet of unwashed feet and stale alcohol. She decided to chance it.

"Capital city?" Atalant asked the driver. She peered in to see a young woman, probably a second *don*, at the console. "We'd like lodging, if possible. Cheap lodging."

"Common..." the woman said under her breath. She tapped the console in front of herself a few times and then nodded. "Ride...long and much cost. Accept?"

"Accept," Atalant said and climbed into the craft. "Everyone in. It will be tight, but we'll make it work." It was clear the craft was meant to seat only two passengers, but with some rearranging and complete disregard for personal space, the door was finally shut and the craft took off.

"Emn," Atalant began as she shifted against the door. "The capital is probably going to be a safer place to start out. Could you give me an idea of what you are after? I know you're thinking of staying, but since off-worlders can't stay during a move, I... I don't want to leave you here after only two days on a planet we know nothing about." She thought about chasing the words with an *I don't want to leave you here at all*, but decided against it.

Emn leaned her head against the door, her eyes focused on the passing scenery. They sped past a plantation of andal trees planted in firm rows delighting in the bright sunlight. A group of first-*don* children waved at them, halting their chasing game between the rows to gawk.

"I want to see things, of course. Oceans, beaches, mountains, important cultural sites... But first—" She paused as the craft slowed through a small town. Paper banners hung across buildings, written in a script Atalant did not recognize. They passed a square where families in long dresses danced around the thick trunk of an andal. Green and gold sparkled and highlighted everything. Atalant turned from the window, uncomfortable.

"At some point, I want to see a doctor. I want...I want to know more about myself, about what the Risalians did and did not change. After I get some kind of confirmation that I am an Ardulan, that I really belong here, I'll consider what to do." The ship leaned starboard for a moment as the driver swerved around a herd of migrating *titha* before righting itself. Atalant pitched forward into Nicholas, steadying herself on the back of the seat in front of her.

"Let's not make any rash decisions, okay?" Atalant said. She righted herself and gave Nicholas a pat on the shoulder. "Sorry about that, Nick."

Nicholas snorted and nudged Emn's foot with his own. "Want to change seats?"

Emn looked over at her and tilted her head.

Atalant chose to ignore the images that popped, of their own accord, into her mind, coughed, and turned back to Nicholas. "We have another pressing problem." They were passing another town. Another festival. Another mass of colors that held too many memories.

"Money?" Nicholas nodded. "I figured. I have five diamond rounds left from what Chen gave us."

"I'm sorry, I didn't even think about currency," Emn said apologetically.

"I've got a small bag of sapphires I found on the Nugel ship, in addition to two diamond rounds left over from our trip to the Xinar System." Atalant lifted up her hip and fished into her deep side pocket, pulling out a heavy, woven bag. "I haven't counted them though. Glad I snagged it before docking the ship. Let's hope that altogether it's enough to uncover the mysteries of Ardulum."

ATALANT STOOD IN a mossy clearing, shaded by the canopy of one large andal tree. She could hear chirping and rustling, but didn't bother to look for the source. The wind was still, the temperature pleasant.

Slowly, she walked towards the andal's trunk. She ran her fingers across the curly bark, which flaked in her hand and fell to the forest floor. Curious, Atalant dug her fingernails underneath a large piece and pulled it back. She peeled away a long strip, exposing the pale sapwood. Thin droplets began to form on the edges of the rip, growing larger until they ran down the sapwood to the other end of the tear. Atalant watched as the drips came faster, the thin sap building to a milky white gel. The sapwood became difficult to see. She touched the white sap with her fingertip and was surprised to find it viscous, hardening in the open air. After several minutes, the sap crystalized, forming a protective barrier over the wound.

"I'm sorry about that," Atalant said to the tree. "I didn't mean to hurt you."

"Didn't mean to hurt whom?" a voice responded distantly. "Atalant, I think you're dreaming."

Confused, Atalant closed her eyes and counted to ten. When she opened them again, she was staring out a window overlooking a busy marketplace. Bipeds and a small spattering of quadrupeds were milling around brightly painted wood stands that gleamed in the rising sunlight. She could see wares of every sort, from furniture and textiles to paints and fresh fruit, although the majority of the crafts appeared to be made from wood. The species diversity was huge, and Atalant racked her brain to place the features she saw.

"Where..." She turned from her side to her back to see Emn peering down at her. The younger woman had one knee on the bed and a hand on Atalant's shoulder, which she was almost certain had shaken her awake. Her bearings came back quickly. They were in lodging above a bar, in the capital. They'd had enough rounds to get their own rooms. She'd collapsed immediately upon entering and hadn't even made it under the rayon blanket, which, with the damp chill in the morning air, she regretted. It was morning...still? No, again. She'd slept a day away, and the buzzing-rustling in her head was still there, and still just as irritating.

"I'm sorry. I heard you thrashing around from the hallway when I walked past your room. I wanted to make sure you were all right. We all slept through yesterday. There's been so much going on recently—I think we were all exhausted." Emn slid her hand from Atalant's shoulder and placed it on her own knee. The hem of her dress lay just above, clean of maroon stains. "Good morning, too. I can leave, if you like. I just wanted to be sure you were okay."

Atalant tried to shake the dream from her mind, focusing instead on the opportunity before her. The woman before her. There was so much to do, so much she didn't understand, and yet, maybe, there was time to...to what? Maybe to get to know adult Emn and stop hiding from a million silly, little fears?

"Good morning." Atalant propped herself up on an elbow and reached over with her free hand, pushing some strands of hair from Emn's face. Atalant's hand trembled, but only a little. She doubted that Emn noticed. "It was just a stupid dream. I think I've had it before." She tucked the strands behind Emn's ear. "You slept okay?"

Emn caught Atalant's hand and held it, a smile forming at the edges of her mouth. "Yes, but I could hear Nicholas snoring through the wall." She shifted to sit on the edge of the bed, frowned, and then stood back up again. "May I stay for a bit? Nicholas will be around in a few minutes to join us for breakfast, but before we're all together again, and before this day starts...it'd be nice to spend some time with you."

Atalant felt Emn's hesitant, unspoken question. There was an unfortunate time constraint this morning—she definitely remembered telling everyone to gather for breakfast upon waking. Now though, looking at the dark-haired woman in the thin, airy dress near the edge of her bed, Atalant wasn't the least bit interested in breakfast. She sat up, swung her legs around, and patted the mattress to her left.

"You're welcome to stay," Atalant said. She smiled, although it probably appeared more tentative than she planned, and pulled Emn towards her. The younger woman released Atalant's hand and sat, close enough that their hips touched.

There was silence then, both verbal and mental, as Emn watched Atalant and Atalant tried to force her eyes to Emn's instead of to the hemline of her dress, which was halfway up her thighs. The markings on each leg mirrored one another, and it was increasingly difficult not to imagine tracing those lines with her fingers as they spun higher, underneath the dress. Would the markings be raised from the skin there, too, or simply a part of it?

Atalant's breath felt heavy, but she was certain it was not from the humid air. Dark green eyes watched her—patient but with clear desire.

"Atalant?" Emn prodded. The look in her eyes turned to concern.

"You're sure about...me?" Atalant asked, cutting her off. Words seemed safer than letting her mind wander, and certainly safer than letting her hands wander. "We found Ardulum. We're *on* Ardulum. For all we know you're a god here, too, what with all the markings you have." She focused on the triangles under Emn's eyes and, with a visibly shaking hand, traced one with a fingertip. The marking was raised, ever so slightly, and felt warmer than the surrounding skin. Atalant wanted to cup Emn's cheek, to pull her forward and to let her hand slide down, but she drew back instead, putting her at arm's length. She had to be sure. *Emn* had to be sure. It wasn't even just about age. It was about status, and Talent, and, well, an *Ardulan* and a *Neek*. "There are other women here. Men and gatois too, if you are interested in them. People who would be closer to you. You know. In ability."

Emn sighed and smoothed out a wrinkle near the hem of her dress. "It's my markings that frighten you? If I had only the one, would it be any different?"

"Gods of any form just generally aren't my type," Atalant responded, trying to diffuse some of the hurt she heard in Emn's tone with humor. "Or at least, they generally don't go for me."

Emn didn't come closer, but she did take one of Atalant's hands in hers again and squeezed it. Her skin felt warm and inviting, and Atalant desperately wished her brain would shut up so she could collapse into Emn's arms and forget about Ardulum entirely.

"I'm not a god, Atalant—at least, not for you. I'm just Emn. Nothing else."

Atalant snorted good-naturedly. "I think that is a significant understatement." She flipped Emn's hand over and studied the pentagons that circled her palm. The lines here were more delicate than the ones on her face, and looked almost fragile. Atalant let her thumb glide over the markings once, twice, and then a third time. She looked up just before the fourth pass, caught Emn's delighted smile, and immediately released Emn's hand before looking back at the bedsheets.

"I was always an Aggression Talent, you know, when we played as kids. It never would have occurred to me to make up markings other than the ones we already knew about."

"Do you think they're not of Ardulum?" Emn asked in a tight voice.

Atalant looked up at her, eyes wide. "No, of course they're of Ardulum. They're just...unexpected. Like you. I don't do well with unexpected, but I'm...I'm working on it." Gah, she was babbling and probably just making Emn feel worse. She needed to change the subject.

"Do you think Ardulans only came to Neek to harvest our andal?" Atalant asked. She scooted back to Emn until their hips once again touched. She'd stay here, damn it, no matter how flustered she got. "Or do you think they genuinely wanted to help us be better?"

"Better than what, Atalant?" Emn seemed to relax with the change in topic, and to help make amends, Atalant wrapped her arm around the younger woman's waist. She felt Emn's relief instantly and puzzled over it. Did Emn really think Atalant wasn't interested? There was just so much else to contend with!

"Was there something wrong with Neek before the Ardulans came that needed fixing?" Emn continued. "Did you need to have spaceships and food printers? Did you need cellulosic technology?"

"We Neek do not look back fondly on our pastoral heritage. I think you could argue that we wanted more from life...we just didn't know how to get it." Atalant let her gaze fall back to Emn's exposed thighs and again felt the heat rise in her cheeks. This time she let the emotions leak through their bond as she let her head rest on Emn's shoulder. "I wonder, though, if the price was worth it."

"It wasn't for the Keft. Maybe it was for the Neek. Maybe the Ardulans were upfront about what they wanted to do, and the president at the time said it was all right. Maybe—" Emn wordlessly held out a hand, and when the Atalant offered hers, Emn placed the latter, cautiously, on her own knee. "Maybe they weren't gods at first. Maybe that happened later." *You are welcome here, Atalant, if you want.*

Atalant considered. While she did so, she traced the icosahedron that covered Emn's kneecap. "I don't know. My people need prodding. They need direction."

"I don't think that is unique to the Neek," Emn interjected. Atalant heard the catch in her breathing and couldn't help smiling. "A lot of species have a hard time with change. That's not so unusual a concept."

"I suppose not," Atalant agreed. She shifted so that she was facing Emn, their knees touching now instead of their hips. Now there was nowhere to look but into green eyes, at the swell of Emn's chest, or at the markings that spun across her thighs. Atalant stilled her hand but stayed locked in Emn's gaze, letting her mind work through its own hurdles while their conversation continued.

"I think Yorden would have agreed with me that the Neek are particularly hardheaded. Just being given technology wouldn't have been enough. Teaching them how to use it wouldn't have been enough. The old texts... I've been through almost all of the main ones now, and it's funny: the Ardulans never refer to themselves as gods."

"The Keft never even mentioned them as deities," Emn returned. A smile was playing at the corners of her mouth, which Atalant found both enticing and exasperating. Emn had endless fucking patience, it seemed. Had their roles been reversed, Atalant wasn't certain she'd have been able to be so calm. "They just called them explorers. Traders."

Atalant nodded and, without meaning to, slid her hand to the inside of Emn's knee. A grin threatened to break across Emn's face, but instead of calling attention to it, Atalant left her hand there and continued speaking. "So Ardulum came. Traded our land and andal for technology that advanced our civilization. Two years go by, the andal starts to crash, and they leave. The Neek...maybe they don't know what to do without someone prodding them. Someone in power gets an idea about how to keep things moving forward. History gets changed. The Ardulans become gods. Gods we could meet again, if we get our act together."

"Atalant," Emn said slowly, enunciating each syllable. "Is this really what you want to talk about?"

"No, of course not, but...well..." The once chilled room had become humid and overly warm, the sunlight now streaking through the window and hitting her black flight suit at least partly to blame. Atalant wanted to touch Emn, and be touched—her skin was on fire, but touching, kissing, or even something as simple as hugging seemed...abrupt. Not quite right somehow, like Atalant hadn't earned that privilege just yet, however stupid that sounded.

"I'm...I'm still working on this, the idea of us," Atalant said. She moved her hand to the top of Emn's thigh and pursed her lips. *It's not because of the markings, and it's not because I don't...have feelings for you. It's more that, well, we're on a planet that shouldn't exist, and you're sitting on my bed in a dress that—*

A loud, single knock came from the door.

"Go away!" Atalant yelled.

Another rap hit the door. "You said early morning, Neek. Atalant. Sorry. I went through the bother of getting up, only to find you not at breakfast. This is payback."

Emn sighed and put her hand on top of Atalant's. "We did promise we wouldn't be late. Maybe breakfast will give you some time to collect your thoughts?" She stood, smoothed her dress down, and offered Atalant a tight smile. "Maybe we could talk again, even if it's about something mundane? I really enjoyed this time with you, Atalant. It doesn't *have* to lead to something else."

"Yeah, but I *want* it to," Atalant grumbled unintelligibly to herself as she got up from the bed and straightened her flight suit. She was upset with herself over the intimacy issue—she'd never had a problem with women before, or men, or any other gender, for that matter. This was just so, so—she didn't know what. Dogmatic? That wasn't the right word, but she couldn't think of a better one. She clearly still had some mental hang-ups to get over if she really wanted a relationship with Emn.

She stretched, the flight suit far too snug for her liking, which brought her mind to how much she missed the comfort of weaponry against her skin. She briefly mused on what knives she might be able to pick up from an Ardulan retailer, and what she could probably flip them for back on Neek if she didn't grow too attached. The only weapon she'd managed to keep with her through the past several months was the funny knife she'd purchased from Chen—the one with the andal hilt and the curved tip. The one sitting, secure, just inside her boot and that she kept forgetting about but stubbornly refused to throw away. It wasn't a very effective weapon, but it was better than none at all.

"We're dressed," Atalant announced as she opened the door. Emn, looking much brighter in her gray dress, came up behind her. The image of Emn from moments before—her skirt riding up her legs, the intensity of her eyes—flashed across Atalant's mind. She pushed the image away and tried to rein in her own thoughts.

"All set," Emn said. She looked from Nicholas to Atalant and smiled. She was getting as good at hiding emotions as Atalant was. "I suppose here of all places I shouldn't have to worry about getting any andal to eat."

Nicholas nodded, looking anywhere but at the two women. "I saw steamed branches downstairs. Also—" He chanced a peek at Emn, but then turned away. "Kidding aside, do you two have this business figured out?"

Emn's smile faltered, but Atalant wasn't about to let their small amount of progress go unnoticed. She slipped her hand into Emn's, and the younger woman responded by smiling sweetly and leading Atalant out the door.

Atalant shot an apologetic smile at Nicholas as she was pulled down the hall.

"This is not what I signed up for," Nicholas muttered as he trailed them down the stairs.

ATALANT HAD TO shade her eyes from the morning sun that streaked through an open window as she sat down at a long wood slab table with the rest of the crew. It was still early, she reasoned, since there were only a few other patrons, and it seemed as if the bar could seat several dozen. A seasoned vegetable smell hung heavily in the air, which wasn't entirely unpleasant, but did not kickstart her appetite.

Disinterested in Nicholas's oration about some Terran sports team, Atalant traced the summerwood lines on the table. A surprising number were discontinuous, which, judging from what she assumed of the traveling planet, seemed both logical and concerning. If the planet moving interrupted the growth of the andal, why would the Ardulans do it? Andal was fragile enough—it certainly didn't need changing atmospheric conditions added to its list of triggers.

"Welcome, travelers!" A short, rotund Ardulan arrived at their table. Atalant searched for any visible markings or gaps in their clothing to indicate where markings might be, but failed to find any. The server noticed her bobbing head, laughed, and then continued in Common.

"Apologies, friend. I can see why you would be confused. My name is Kallum, and I'm first *don*. No Talent yet, but my parents, who own the bar, are both Hearths. I'll probably go that direction too. I'm also gatoi. We have a tri-gender system here on Ardulum. Different from the quad systems found on most Alliance worlds." Kallum opened zir arms wide and smiled. "Would you all like to try our standard Ardulan breakfast? It is very popular with tourists."

"Is it...wood?" Nicholas asked hesitantly.

Kallum laughed again. "Yes, but young shoots. Digestible even by off-worlders. Trust me and try it. You'll love it."

Emn, who was wedged at the far end of the bench behind Atalant, leaned forward so she would be heard. "Ardulans eat the young shoots often? Not the cooked branches?"

Kallum put zir hands behind zir back. "Well now, that is an unusual question. It's actually more of a regional preference..." zie trailed off, and Atalant watched zir eyes scan Emn, lingering on her uncovered arms littered with dark markings. "Sorry, but did you get discharged? Are you better?"

It took Atalant far too long to realize what the server was talking about. Trying to act as smoothly as she could, she smiled. "Yes, she's much better now. Thank you for asking, Kallum." Atalant wrapped an arm around Emn and pulled her back behind herself, out of view of the server. "Times have been hard, of course, but that's all behind us now. We are on vacation, but thought we should maybe hop to the local clinic, just for a checkup. Could you recommend one nearby?"

Kallum perked up. "Actually, yes! There is a great one about two blocks away. My older sisters went flare, too, when they manifested. It was really hard on my parents, especially since we're not allowed to talk about it. They're at the local treatment center." Zie leaned onto the table and tried to crane zir head around to see Emn. "You haven't heard anything about them, have you? Their names are Ukie and Kallik."

Emn scooted forward again. "No, I'm sorry, but I haven't."

Crestfallen, Kallum stood back up. "Well, it doesn't hurt to ask. I don't know how many flares there are. Guess too many for you to all know each other."

Atalant raised both hands. "Sorry, it's been a long time since we were last here. Refresh my memory on what causes someone to flare?"

"Don't know. I don't know if anyone does. Just happens sometimes. You go to see the Eld a few days after your metamorphosis. You get some synthetic mucus smeared on your forehead. You're *supposed* to get just one Talent, but sometimes...sometimes things go wrong." Zie lowered zir voice. "I'm scared about my metamorphosis. If it's genetic...maybe I'll end up with a bunch of Talents, too. It'd be really hard on my parents."

Nicholas reached over and patted Kallum on the shoulder. "I'm sure you'll be fine. Besides, she's okay, right?" He gestured at Emn, who waved.

Kallum nodded. "You're right, of course." Enthusiasm came back into zir voice. "So, three Ardulan specials then?"

"Uh, sure," Atalant said. She had no desire to eat wood, but doubted ordering bacon would be well received. "Add something to drink, too. Whatever you recommend is fine."

Kallum nodded. "Will you be taking the afternoon tour as well? It's the last one before the move. It's your best bet to see the palace. We have another one that runs to our main historic site, too. It's an old fishing village not far from here, a town called Thannon. They partially overlap, unfortunately, so you'll have to pick one or the other."

"How would one go about booking it?" Nicholas asked. "We're short on funds, so price matters."

Kallum brightened. "Well, the palace tour is free, per the dictate of the Eld. The historic site isn't too pricey—fourteen andal chits a head, two sapphires, or one diamond round. All galactic currencies are accepted. You can book with the tourist headquarters—their kiosk is just up the road from here. Should be open now."

Atalant held up a hand. "Wait, can we backtrack a minute. How exactly *does* Ardulum move?"

Kallum looked up at the ceiling and furrowed zir brow. "Don't know, really. That's Eld stuff. The planet travels on its own, but it's the Eld who steer the ship, if you follow. But that business is theirs, not mine." Zie looked back at Atalant, and zir eyebrows shot up. "Oh! You could ask during the palace tour! That'd be a good question!"

"Thank you very much. We'll discuss it." Nicholas started to salute, paused, and then waved instead. The server left, chuckling to zirself as zie went. "Any interest?" Nicholas asked, turning to Emn. "Your choice."

Atalant felt Emn's emotions flicker. She tried to chase the feeling, but Emn tucked it away as quickly as it arose. "Emn?" she asked. "You all right?"

Emn stood from the bench, straightened her dress, and then sat back down, tucking one leg underneath herself as she did so. "I'm going to the village," she said. Her voice was low, shadowy, and sent an odd shiver down Atalant's spine. "I also—" She paused and looked pointedly at Atalant, her expression softening. "I want to go alone."

Atalant smacked her palm into the table. "That is not safe!" she exclaimed, alarmed. *Also, completely unreasonable. You expect me to just play tourist while you wander?!*

"*Atalant.*" Nicholas's voice was grating.

Her first reaction was to yell at the Journey youth, but she held back. Instead, she grumbled and tried to settle her emotions. "It isn't a good idea," she muttered.

"Not our decision," Nicholas cautioned. "We can take the palace tour and all compare notes this evening. Wouldn't that work?"

"No," Atalant retorted. "Think about the reactions we've been getting. Separation is a terrible idea." She nudged the periphery of Emn's mind, trying to make her concerns clear. "At least let me come with you."

"Atalant, I don't need a chaperone." The response was warm but curt.

When no mental clarification followed, Atalant scowled and turned to Nicholas. "A little backup here?"

Nicholas sniffed and reached out to grab the long, narrow dish of steaming andal shoots offered to him by Kallum, who had walked up with a tray. The other dishes were passed around, including wooden mugs of something cool and sweet-smelling and a round, segmented dish of colored powders Atalant assumed were seasonings. When a stack of wooden discs was placed in front of her, she took one, grabbed a handful of hot twigs and the spice dish, stood, and brought the ensemble over to the corner of the table.

Atalant knelt down next to Emn and set the dishes down in front of her. "Could we please discuss this?" she asked, her voice low. Emn popped three shoot ends into her mouth, chewed quickly, and swallowed.

You could have asked to come, instead of demanding it, Emn returned.

Says the woman who cornered me in a cockpit, Atalant shot back. *What's this about?*

Atalant felt Emn's hesitation as the young woman munched on a shoot. Trying to be patient, Atalant took an exploratory sip from a cup and grimaced at the syrupy sweetness of the beverage. She placed the cup back down and scooted it as far away as her reach would allow.

I spoke to a flare from there, Emn responded finally. *I want to meet him, but...* She grew quiet, her eyes scanning Atalant's face. She pursed her lips and sighed.

"Yeah, I get it," she mumbled. Atalant got to one knee and clasped Emn's hand before standing and moving back to her own seat. "Guess I'm taking the palace tour too," she said loudly as she reached for the main dish of andal. "Someone pass the seasoning."

Chapter 21: Thannon, Ardulum

The Neek asked the Ardulan child, "What is Ardulum?"

The child responded by pointing at a small tree. "Ardulum is of the andal. Without it, we cannot live. Without it, we would not want to live. Without it, we would not know how to live."
—Excerpt from *The Book of the Uplifting*, original version

"...ROOT SYSTEM. NOTE the wide canopy and ample liana colonization, even over the buttress formation. Here, the sentinels have been trimmed back, but you can tell the age even without them." The tour guide, a tall woman early into her third *don*, gestured to the towering andal tree growing directly from the center of the village square in Thannon.

Emn nudged her way to the front of the crowd, keeping the sleeves of the flight suit she'd swapped with Atalant down over her hands. Her hair was loose and cascaded over her face, hiding, she hoped, most of her markings. Emn had suggested they swap the passport films, too, but Atalant had been firmly against it under some misguided heroic notion that if someone were to come for Emn, Atalant would be better prepared to defend herself. Emn hadn't bothered to argue.

A throaty sound wisped across her mind.

Hello? she asked. Guessing at its source, she added, *I speak Common.*

There was a momentary pause, and then a distinctly male voice addressed her. *Touch it. That old tree is sacred. It's said the roots of that one run to all four spires of the Eld Palace.*

No one will get mad? she asked.

Nope. We cherish our andal. Funny, because we clearly don't cherish all Ardulans.

Unable to resist, Emn ran her fingertips over the curly bark of the ancient andal, reveling in the texture. The bark unfurled with the pressure and then sprang back into place when she pulled her fingers away, resulting in a soft, wispy sound.

Hello.

Who...had that been the *tree*? Emn blinked several times, but then shook her head at the crazy notion of talking trees.

Not so crazy, the voice said. *The andal speaks to the Eld. Perhaps one day, it will speak to us, too.*

Emn tried to imagine what a tree might say, and if it would converse in words or in images, like the Risalian Ardulans. *Do you really think the andal would speak to those the Eld shun?* she asked, curious. *Especially if the Eld are the mouthpieces of the andal?*

A sort of mental shrug went through Emn's mind. *Even if it doesn't, we can speak to each other. Our telepathy is a lot stronger than a standard Ardulan's. The flares will always have that.*

Emn was surprised at the sudden warmth that brought to her chest. Telepathy was something even the Risalians had not managed to take away.

Are you going to meet us? This time, the voice was feminine.

I'd like to very much, Emn responded. It was hard to keep the excitement from her own voice. *Where are you?*

The female responded. *There is a small gazebo in a forested ravine north of town. We left a path that only you should be able to see.* An image filled Emn's mind of a stream of glittering cellulose that led into an old-growth andal forest. *It is a fifteen-minute walk from where you are now. The tours are highly regimented. It won't leave for three and one quarter hours more. Slip away, and we promise to have you back in time to return.*

Emn realized she was still touching the tree. She hastily shoved her hands back in her pockets. If she was radiating nervousness, none of the other tourists seemed to be aware of it. The two quadrupeds next to her barely glanced in her direction as they edged past, following the guide towards the pier. She was more excited to meet the flares than she had been to land on Ardulum, and although it would've been nice to have company, forcing Nicholas, or even Atalant, to sit through several hours of...whatever she was about to do seemed unnecessary.

I'll be there soon.

Weaving back through the crowd, Emn looked to the sky to get her bearings and then began to head north through narrow footpaths. Short, cylindrical houses with andal bark thatched roofs sat in haphazard rows, a beaten dirt path winding between them. It was still midmorning, but the tour guide had told them that the fishers had left much earlier and wouldn't be back until dusk. That left the streets empty and quiet save for a few older Ardulans tending to small gardens.

Another few minutes of walking brought her to the north side of town. The buildings cut off quickly, the houses built directly up to the edge of the ravine precipice. Emn jogged to the edge and peered down, hoping to find a cut staircase or some other means of descending. When none was readily apparent, she began to pick her way along the ledge, scanning for anything that would get her to her destination.

We left a ladder for you, a different male voice said. *It is hidden behind a buttress of an andal on the lane paved with bark.*

Emn slowly turned around. Behind her, and several rows of homes back, she could see a lane ending at a T-junction, the curls of the andal bark road dark against the pale sky. Emn send an affirmation and moved as quickly as she dared. She found the rope ladder under a pile of last year's leaves, one end already firmly embedded in the ground, tied to some andal roots. Giving a tug to ensure it was still sturdy, Emn tossed the end over the ledge and began her descent, hoping the ladder would still be at her disposal in a few hours.

It took about five minutes or so for Emn to follow the game trail to a gazebo tucked into an andal grove. As Emn came towards the structure, the flares stepped out, forming a loose semicircle around her. Arik—whom she quickly identified as the one she first spoke to—was smiling, as was the one female; the other two seemed wary. Scattered around the gazebo were little round tins. Some were open, and in them Emn saw powders of different shades. On the bench nearest the female, a stack of rolled biofilms was balanced precariously close to the edge. There were clothes too, stacked in a thick pile. Some had powdery fingerprints on them, and as Emn observed them, she realized all the flares had some level of the powder on themselves as well.

Emn offered her hand, palm up, and smiled back. "Hello," she said, unsure how low she needed to keep her voice, whether they were hiding or in the middle of some strange ritual. "I'm Emn. It's nice to meet you."

Arik offered his own hand, palm up. When Emn eyed the powder on his palm, he laughed and wiped it on his pants. *The fishers that picked us up told us we should come here. We found these baskets of makeup,* clothes, and instructions on how to blend in until we make it to the capital, where we are apparently supposed to go to meet up with some sort of flare underground.

Emn brought her hand back down and confusedly eyed the tin nearest to her.

Sorry, first things first. Let me introduce you. Arik nodded to each flare in turn, and they gave Emn a nod when their name was called. As they introduced themselves, Emn studied their markings. They all had the same facial markings, the same upside-down triangles under their eyes that, Emn assumed, indicated the microkinesis Talent. Everything else was different, save for the standard Talent markings. Tik and Kisak had hair so black it reflected an almost bluish tint in the steaming sunlight. Arik's and Ukie's hair was closer to hers, with more reddish highlights. All had their hair pulled back in some way. Suddenly self-conscious, Emn pulled her hair back into a tail and tied it.

She's young like you, Arik, Kisak sent, zir tone tinged with humor.

I'm very early into my second don, Emn returned, sending more confidence than she felt.

When did it happen? Ukie asked suddenly, cutting in. Emn relaxed as she recognized the voice. There was so much friendliness embedded in it that a smile tugged at the corners of Emn's mouth.

You have no Eld, so you would have had no ceremony. How did you get the markings? Ukie prodded.

Emn briefly tried to imagine what a metamorphosis ceremony on Ardulum would look like. They'd have wood, certainly. Maybe it would be over a fire? Burning wood seemed pretty ceremonial. Maybe there were costumes, too, and dancing, like she'd seen in the villages.

She felt a gentle nudge from one of the other flares and quickly cleared her mind, setting up a vision from her own memories. *I had some before my second* don, she said and pointed to the triangles under her eyes. *These came first. Then I took too much energy from a Risalian cutter and it launched me into metamorphosis. When I came out, I looked like this. I don't know what happened.*

Tik took a step forward, but then hesitated. *I don't mean to be rude, but would you mind if I looked a little closer?*

Emn shook her head as the flutters in her stomach turned to leaps. Would they connect, like she and Atalant had, at first touch? What did a solid connection to another Ardulan feel like?

Tik came close, taking her chin between his thumb and finger and gently turning her head left and right. His fingers were cool and slightly damp, but other than the sensations on her skin, there was no additional connection save his subtle presence in her mind. That was disappointing, although since she wasn't sure what was normal for an Ardulan telepathic connection, she held out hope that one of the others might form a stronger bond.

Emn was the taller of the two by several centimeters and had to suppress a smile when Tik turned her head upward, inspecting her neck. She wasn't quite sure why it was funny, and Tik didn't seem amused at all, which only made it worse.

Different methodology, same result, Tik said as he released Emn and rejoined the others. *Interesting, isn't it, that one can achieve Talents without the Eld?*

The flares began to discuss, but the words flowed out of Emn's mind as soon as they formed. She chased them, trying to make sense of the jumble, but finally conceded that she was likely not meant to be part of the conversation.

After several minutes, the words became clear again and came from Tik, whose tone was still hesitant. *We're very curious about your metamorphosis. Would you please provide some details?*

Emn gathered memories together—memories of Captain Ran, the Markin, and the cage in which she and her mother had lived. Finally, she showed the string of events leading to her emergence, including her harvesting masses of cellulose aboard the Risalian cutter and the backlash. *The Risalians,* she said after the images finished, pausing. *The Ardulans the Risalians had were their laboratory toys. We were slaves, kept in isolation until we were fully weaponized. We had been altered. Tinkered with.* She swallowed the lump in her throat and looked at Arik. *I was their prize. My genetic code was the product of decades of selective breeding and laboratory manipulation. That could be why we're different.*

There was an abrupt shift in the flares. The remaining cautiousness in their minds melted and their bodies lost their rigidness. Images spun—Arik on a medical table, Ukie being beaten by a guard, and Tik receiving undesired attention from his assigned lab tech. They were experiments, just like her—but she had had some worth, if only as a weapon.

Arik's smile turned from courteous to genuine. He extended a hand out to Emn and gestured towards the gazebo. *We have a lot in common, cousin. Come sit with us? I think there is plenty to discuss.*

THE SUN WAS directly overhead when Emn thought to check it again. She caught her breath from a fit of laughter. She and Ukie were enjoying a fourth round of Tik's impersonations of the female eld when she saw the light drip through the round opening in the gazebo top.

No, really! Tik insisted. *Asth moves just like that!* He wiggled his fingers in front of their faces and opened his eyes widely. *Come here, little second don. Let me smear viscous, synthetic goo all over you with my icy hands of death.*

Ukie laughed louder as she nudged Emn. *Seriously, you would not believe the stuff they use to initiate the metamorphosis! Our species stopped producing empathic convection mucus centuries ago when our telepathy became sufficiently powerful without it, so we have this synthetic counterpart that allows the Eld's powers to transfer to us and begin the process. My uncle works at the plant that manufactures it. You do not want to know how it is made!*

Emn wrapped her arms around her midsection and broke into another fit of laughter, even as the weight of Ukie's words settled in. She needed to remember the bit about the mucus. Atalant would want to know.

You all right, Emn? Ukie asked. *You got really serious all of a sudden.*

Emn brought back a smile. *That does sound pretty gross. It seems strange that Ardulans would evolve away from something so pivotal to their life cycle.* She caught her breath and leaned back on the wooden bench, letting the light breeze tickle her face. It was so calm here, in the clearing. When was the last time she had been this relaxed? Had she ever been? Emn looked to Ukie, who smiled and put an arm around her shoulder.

You okay, Emn? It's a lot, I know.

Emn nodded and rested against Ukie. *It was a lot to take in yesterday and this morning. Now it seems... Well, it is still a lot, but it's nice to have friends to face it with.*

Tik nodded and squeezed Emn's shoulder affectionately. *Being with flares is like being with family.*

Family. A question tugged at Emn's mind. *Ukie, do you have a...* Emn stumbled over the word. *A sibling?*

The mood of the flares dropped. Ukie's face turned ashen, and she brought her arm back in. *My sister, Kallik, was also a flare. She didn't make the escape.*

Emn grabbed Ukie's hand and squeezed. *I'm so sorry, Ukie. I... I wasn't sure. I meant, well, we're staying at an inn. A gatoi first don said zir sisters went flare. They were named Ukie and Kallik.*

Kallum!? Ukie sat up straight. Her grip on Emn's hand tightened painfully. *You saw Kallum? Andal help me, zie has to be about ready for zir Talent Day! How is zie, Emn? And my parents? Could I—* Emn felt a mental prod. *Could I see your memories? I want to see Kallum for myself, but only if it is all right.*

Emn nodded and relaxed her mind. Ukie's presence was warm as it carefully slid into Emn's own. Emn played the breakfast conversation in her head and felt Ukie's delight at seeing Kallum. Ukie catalogued every facial expression and movement, filing them into her memory.

When the scene finished playing out, Ukie retracted. A lingering warmth remained in Emn's mind.

Thank you for this gift, Emn. I'm glad you're here. We all are.

Tik nodded and squeezed Emn's shoulder. *You remind me of my little sister. She's tall, like you, with those same round eyes. I wish I could have seen her one last time, before I was locked away. It would have been nice to say goodbye.*

Arik gave Tik a one-armed hug. *You'll see her soon, Tik. I promise. I can feel my andal saplings calling me home. We just have to fix some things first.* He turned to Emn, and his smile faded. *As much as I hate to do this, we should probably talk about some serious matters. Emn,* he asked slowly. *I wonder if we might ask a favor of you.*

Emn grinned and nudged Ukie with her shoulder. *Want to have our next conversation out loud?*

You know how to heal well enough to do it right? Kisak asked gruffly.

Emn nodded. *Yes. I did it myself, intuitively, as a first don. I can heal all of you at the same time, too, unless you have objections.*

Arik's eyebrows raised. *How did you learn...never mind. Healing first—then questions. When you're ready.*

Emn reached out to each mind, establishing a firm connection, before moving down into identical throats. She knew the damage too well now, but was pleased that there did not seem to be any difference between the placement of the ligaments within the flares and herself. Confident, she reached into her breakfast reserves, overlaid the image of her throat onto each, and pulled.

No audible sound came at first, until she sat back and nodded. Then, a barrage of noises surfaced, from Ukie's whooping excitement to Tik's high tenor.

"Outstanding!" Arik clapped his hands together.

"That was amazing!" Ukie agreed, giving Emn a hug. "Thank you."

Emn smiled happily and dusted her hands on the front of her flight suit. "You're welcome. It's not too difficult to automate a push, once you get used to it. I can teach you all, if you'd like."

There was a long pause as Arik looked from Tik to Ukie and then to Kisak. Not wanting to intrude on a private conversation, Emn busied herself with the architecture of the gazebo's top. The dark wood was intricately inlaid with weaving tendrils of bark. It seemed like a lot of work for a gazebo in the middle of a forest, and Emn wondered idly about its purpose. It wasn't here for the flares...was it?

"We'd like to talk to you about that," Arik said finally, breaking the silence. "We've received no training, formal or otherwise. Flares on Ardulum are separated from the populace, deprived of wood, and used for experiments. We have no rights, and without andal, no way to learn our strengths." He sighed and sat on the rough-hewn bench. "From your description of the Risalians, you have experienced the same."

Emn felt old emotions swirl dangerously close to the surface. She could still taste her anger for Ran right before she shot hir in the head— twenty years of isolation and the murder of her mother culminating in one moment.

Emn didn't realize she was broadcasting until Ukie took her hand and squeezed it. "Yes," Emn muttered under her breath. "I have had a similar experience. I expected more from Ardulum, though. It is the reason I came." She picked up a tin and emptied the black contents onto her lap. "Perhaps I misjudged? It does sound like someone is trying to help you. You've been rescued, of sorts, sheltered, and given a way to blend in."

Kisak huffed and shoved zir gnarled hands into zir pockets. "We've been given a way to *hide*," zie said. "The films speak of an underground flare community. Flares that acquiesce to training, to rigid protocols, to *limiting* themselves to just one Talent. All so they can live within the population and not frighten anyone."

Emn blanched. Hiding. Always being afraid. She swirled the dark powder in her lap and experimentally rubbed some onto her arm. It was too dark for her skin tone, but it absorbed quickly, covering the markings there.

"Emn?"

Emn brought her head back up and faced Arik.

"We have a plan to petition the Eld. We're not going to hide anymore. We're going to meet with the Eld face-to-face and force them to explain their actions. There have to be different approaches to dealing with flares other than this..." Arik pointed to the streak on Emn's arm. "Other than pretending to be less than what we are for the rest of our lives. Pretending to be 'normal,' when we are so much more than that."

"I can't do that." Emn pushed the powder from her lap. It fell onto the tops of her feet, and she kicked at the fine particulate. "I lived most of my life in a cage. I won't put myself back in one, even if it doesn't have bars. This isn't right. Do they really all think we are just...just defective?"

Tik spat. "They say flares are unstable and too powerful. They say the flaring overpowers our circulatory system and our brain. We're more powerful, you see, but apparently more emotional as well, or some stupid drivel like that." He smacked a hand onto his chest. "I'd love to see some published data on that! How emotionally stable do they expect people to be when they are locked up in pens and fed meat? Why would we be happy being ripped from our families and treated as animals?"

Arik tugged Tik down onto the bench next to him and soothed his back with a palm. Tik's breathing slowed to a normal pace, but his face remained red. Emn watched him clench and unclench his fists and remembered her own anger at the Risalians, how good it had felt to exact even a small amount of retribution. Except here, the flares had a chance for real change.

"You have to learn to control your thoughts," Ukie said softly, nudging Emn. "We can all hear you when you wander like that."

"You could help us make this your home, too." Arik brought his hands back to his lap. "That way none of us have to hide. Help us change the minds of the Eld. Help us reeducate the populace." He tapped his temple. "We need you. Without your guidance, we're no better than a bunch of first *don*s. You have training."

"It's not training, it's just...luck, really. I—"

"You have experience, then," Arik said, cutting her off. "We need it if we are going to be successful."

"You also have an easy way to the Eld," Kisak added. "They've been watching you. You're quite the novelty."

Emn paled, remembering the transparent films that had been placed on their clothes by the customs official, and that she was officially "Atalant" at the moment. Unless the Eld were using some other method to track her? "A novelty?"

"Zie means they are going to want to see you, either by invitation or some other method. When you do get that audience, you'll have their undivided attention." Arik grinned. "It gives us an excellent opportunity to enter the palace and join you. A chance to get a full audience with the Eld without interruptions."

"That sounds promising, but I haven't been contacted by the Eld. We just arrived yesterday, and the planet is supposed to move tomorrow. If they're going to schedule some type of meeting, they're running behind."

"The Eld work on their own schedule," Kisak countered. Zie sat down on the floor of the gazebo, sending up a small cloud of dirt. "They're also cautious. They like to know what they are doing before they do it." Zie pointed in the direction from which Emn had come. "You need to head back to the capital and do something to force the issue. You need to get their attention."

Ukie pulled her hand from Emn's and traced the line work on the top of one of Emn's knuckles. Then, she placed her own hand next to it, touching their knuckles together. "We're so similar, yet you say you've been 'tinkered' with. It'd be natural, wouldn't it, to want to know more? Maybe get some testing to see how close you are to native Ardulans?"

Emn nodded. "It's been on my mind."

"There is a research hospital not far from the Eld Palace. It's the only one in the capital, actually, so everyone living there will be familiar with it. The doctors report directly to the Eld on their findings. They don't take walk-ins, but I'm sure if a flare on a tourist visa showed up, they'd find a way to fit you into their schedule." Tik looked to Arik. "What do you think?"

"I think it's perfect, if you're up for it, Emn. We can get a transport to the capital that arrives just when your tour group does. Unless the Eld contact you on your way back, once you disembark, head to the hospital and check in. Tell them your story. I'm sure half the hospital will be sending word to the Eld before you are even seated in an exam room."

"Then I…" She paused and considered. "I wait for the Eld to come while the doctors examine me? Why not just go to the palace and ask for an audience?"

Kisak rolled zir eyes. "We're playing a delicate game here, woman."

"Which won't work unless she gets it," Ukie snapped back.

"Agreed." Arik moved next to Emn and took her hands in his. "We need them to bring you in, need them to actually seek you out. It forces action on their part, shakes them up, takes them out of their comfort zone."

"It puts them off-balance," Ukie added wryly. She smiled at Emn. "Think how out of sorts you feel here, in a world you should belong to. They can't have all the power in this. You are an unknown commodity, and they don't know yet what to do with you. You can't be seen as passive, or even willing to play by the rules."

Arik nodded and squeezed her hands. "All right? The less they know about your motivations and goals, the more mysterious you are, the better."

Emn felt Arik at the edges of her mind. She touched his consciousness with her own, sinking into the hope and warm belonging that Arik projected. They would talk to the Eld. The Eld would see that Emn could control her Talents. That all the flares could control their Talents. They'd be welcomed back into society. Emn would really, truly, be an Ardulan.

It was an idealized scenario. Emn pulled from the warmth and sighed.

"What happens if they decide to lock us all up?" she asked, looking at each of the flares in turn. "You don't have high opinions of them, so why should my presence change ancient mores? Why should they listen to me? What happens if they don't?"

A curling tendril of energy twined from Kisak's fingertips and ran along the floor of the gazebo. When it hit the wooden rail of the archway, it sparked and puffed into a small column of smoke, leaving a black char on the wood and the faint smell of burning.

"I'm not interested in killing anyone." Emn took her hands back and crossed them over her chest.

"What do you suggest we do then, Emn, if they try to put us back in the compound?" Arik sent several images of his previous accommodations.

"Do you want to be separated from your friends? What about your Neek that you spoke so fondly of earlier?" He smacked his upper arm with his hand. "We are experiments. Rejects. If diplomacy fails, you have to be ready to take the next step. Failure to make that choice means all your future choices will be taken from you."

"You'll doom us, too," Ukie added, her voice soft. "We have to work together on this, or we will all likely die."

Emn let her head fall to her knees. She was tired of the constant life-or-death dynamic. Why did everything have to be so binary? Why did she relentlessly have to fight just for the basic right to live as a sentient being, for the right to belong?

"Emn?" Ukie prodded. Emn raised her head and looked at the other woman. She was tall, like Emn, with a more muscular build in her shoulders and chest. Her skin was a little darker, too—more olive in its translucency. Her hair was clipped short to just above her ears, although whether that was how she preferred it cut or whether that was done to her, Emn didn't have the courage to ask. Noting the usual genetic variations across a species, they could have been cousins. Their noses were the same shape, their mouths had the same bow lip. Maybe they *were* cousins, genetically—and Emn wondered briefly if she could snag the genome analyzer from the ship and get the flares to consent to a test.

"You're powerful," Ukie continued carefully, pointing to the veins on Emn's palm. "You're experienced. I'm sure you can make the Eld see reason, and the Ardulan populace after that."

Emotions followed. There were thoughts of friendship. Of family. Of stability. Images of Emn's mother floated in her vision. Warm arms were around her shoulders—her mother's or Ukie's, she wasn't sure. Emn relaxed into the embrace, let Ukie's mind wash away her fears.

"Ardulum is my home," Emn whispered, lingering on the last word as the breeze picked up and carried the sound away from the gazebo. She repeated herself, putting authority into the words and feeling surer of her decision, "Ardulum is my home. I'm ready to help my family."

Chapter 22: Sekreth, Ardulum

I had a bark doll as a child, made from an old-growth andal from my uncle's land. She was my confidant in all things. When I gave up my child-name, I gave her up, too, to a little neighbor boy who had no doll of his own. His older brother stole her not long after and used her to start a cooking fire. The boy came to me in tears, and we rushed to the fire, hoping to salvage some remains of the doll. We were unsuccessful, but I remember how much the smoke stung my eyes, how dried my skin became. I had intense dreams from that moment onwards, about trees, forests, andal. I used to think the doll was the catalyst—some shattered remnant of my childhood self burning in the fire. I wonder often, these days, if that's all it was.

—Excerpt from *Atalant's Awakening*, published in the Charted Systems, 235 AA

EMN SAT ALONE on a narrow wooden platform in the examination room and tried not to look nervous. She'd been ushered inside with whispers and stares after her sudden appearance at the Central Sekreth Clinic, where she'd gone immediately after getting off the transport from Thannon. She knew she should have contacted the rest of the crew first—Atalant especially—but couldn't shake the discomfort from the makeup and the biofilms she'd read. She couldn't hide anymore. Wouldn't hide. The flares shouldn't have to, either. She could rendezvous with Atalant and Nicholas in the palace if the Eld took her there. Their tour was supposed to include a dinner, and it was getting on towards evening. The timing would work out well.

The room's interior lighting was completely synthetic, which contrasted with every other building Emn had so far visited on Ardulum. Everything smelled sterile, the wood surfaces so highly polished that a visible finish could be seen. There were no wall decorations and no windows, containing nothing but what was absolutely necessary. The room itself looked so small that it might only accommodate two people— the patient and the doctor.

Emn began to tap her bare feet on the floor, toes gliding over the smooth wood surface. She pulled irritably at the flight suit, the tightness on her chest and hips increasingly uncomfortable in the warmth of the building. Was it a good thing or a bad thing that the doctor was taking so long? She shifted her position on the bench and started wondering what the Ardulan medical staff had against comfortable seating.

Finally, a short Ardulan in a thick, brown smock walked in. She was struggling to hold the three rolled tablets in her hands, which led to her kicking the door shut with a loud bang.

"So sorry," she said in hurried Common. "Sorry about the wait. Your visit was a bit of a shock. Actually, I would have been in to see you an hour ago, but then the Eld called and there had to be a conference."

"Oh?" Emn replied cautiously, hoping that she sounded surprised. "Is everything all right?"

"I don't know, really," the woman responded. She gave Emn a light tap on the knee, recoiled, and turned away. She moved to a table pushed up against the opposite wall and carefully unrolled the tablets. Bright text began to scroll across the surface in a language Emn couldn't read.

"My condition can't be unique, right?" Emn caught a toe on a small raised section of the floor and winced. "Right?"

"In that you are correct." The doctor turned back around and gave a tight smile. "Your condition is known as flare disease, or flaring, which manifests at the onset of one's second *don,* and for which there is no cure. Currently it afflicts zero point one percent of the Ardulan population. How you have it—and your relationship to native Ardulans—is still under some discussion."

Emn had a decent idea what those discussions probably entailed and hoped she would get to have them in person with the Eld soon. When the doctor continued to just stare at her instead of providing more information, Emn decided to prod a bit more. "Am I dangerous? Am I contagious?"

The doctor shuddered and ran her hands down her sides, straightening her smock. "Yes and no. The medical literature indicates that you are incapable of focus, as you have no directed Talent structure. Training you, as would normally be done in second *don,* is impossible."

She shifted her eyes from Emn and stared at the wall instead. "Flares are housed with other flares, away from the general populace, to avoid potential accidents and to allow our scientists as much time as possible to study and advance a cure."

Emn lost her patience, which she hadn't even realized had worn thin. "You think flares can't use their Talents?" she demanded.

The doctor took a step back and smacked into the rear wall. "Well, I suppose they can, theoretically, but not in the same way an Ardulan could. There is less focus, less ability to hone. Conversely, the reach is greater. It is a great danger to the general populace."

"I don't think I believe that," Emn said staunchly. "Sounds like conjecture to me. Do you even know what causes it?" She slid from the platform and stood, arms crossed over her chest. The fabric of the flight suit pulled tightly across her shoulders, but she ignored it.

"Ah." Without moving her eyes off Emn, the doctor reached for a tablet. It rolled into a cylinder, which she began to tap against her thigh. "It could be different with you, of course. I'm going to take a genetic sample shortly to determine just what the Risalians managed to do."

Emn tried to stifle her desire to strangle the doctor and decided to try a new line of questioning. "How did Ardulans get into Risalian hands? Were we captured? If you knew about us, why weren't we rescued?"

"Capture is probably the wrong word," a new voice said as the door opened. An old Ardulan, older than Emn had yet seen, shuffled into the room. Zir build looked similar to their breakfast server, so Emn assumed zie was gatoi, but the shocking mop of white hair and intense eyes made the hairs on her arm stand at attention.

The doctor dropped to one knee and bowed her head, the relief evident in her voice when she spoke. "It is an honor, Eld."

"Of course." The maybe-gatoi eld waved a hand dismissively, not bothering to look away from Emn. Zir stare was intense, and Emn shivered.

"You are dismissed, doctor. Leave the tablets, please." The doctor nodded, bowed stiffly, and hurriedly exited the room. The eld shuffled inside, moving as close to Emn as possible while zir eyes raked Emn from her head to her feet.

Zir presence was even more disconcerting up close. The maybe-gatoi eld brought a sort of bright fog with zir that fuzzed the edges of Emn's mind. The fog felt tangy, as if it were laced with raw energy. Emn tried to seal her mind to the fog, but it permeated and persisted. It didn't seem to interfere with her thinking, for which Emn was glad, but its presence made her nervous nonetheless.

"Eld." Emn clasped her hands behind her back and straightened her posture. "I'm sorry, but I'm unsure of the protocol for greeting you. It is an honor."

The eld offered zir right hand, palm up, to Emn, who placed her left hand in it. Short, stubby fingers curled around Emn's in a firm grip. "It is a pleasure to meet you, Emn. I am Eld Adzeek, the male representative. Your communication from the *Lucidity* came as quite a shock. We've been awaiting your arrival."

Now she was even more nervous—helped, no doubt, by her gender assumption. Ukie had tried to show her how to clamp down on the broadcasting before Emn left Thannon, but she doubted the trick would work on an eld. It would be better as an emotional cover. Of course she would be nervous meeting an eld for the first time. Who wouldn't be? The trick was going to be to maintain nervous and reverent, instead of nervous and angry, which was where she was heading.

"You have a most interesting history," Adzeek continued. "We have copies of the Risalian reports, of course. You are welcome to read them if you desire. They were very detailed. You might find information about your mother."

Hope flared inside Emn for a moment, but then extinguished. Was that the bait? Was that supposed to be what lured her to the palace? According to the other flares, the Eld gave nothing without demanding something in return.

"We would like to run some tests. You can understand why. I'm especially curious as to your capacity for speech, as our flares are incapable and, according to your oral account, you have not had time for extended surgery." The male eld smiled, white teeth gleaming in the bright lighting. The fog around Emn's consciousness thickened for a moment before receding.

"I did it myself," Emn said defiantly. "None of the Risalian Ardulans could speak, not even the normal ones. I, well—I copied the pattern of a throat belonging to a human friend of mine. It wasn't too difficult."

Adzeek rubbed his chin and nodded. "Telekinesis, I assume? Do you often heal things with intent?"

"I suppose so." Emn pursed her lips, unsure how much of her Talent she should disclose to an eld. "Though, I healed Atalant—a Neek—but that was by accident, or at least I didn't consciously do it."

Adzeek continued to nod. "This all seems in line with what we understand of flares. I do have many more questions though, and it is almost dinnertime. Would you care to accompany me to the palace? The staff has prepared a lovely meal, and we could spend some more time getting to know one another."

Dinner. She supposed that was a logical step, and she *was* hungry. Emn forced a smile as the male eld placed a hand on her elbow and escorted her out of the room. She could do this. She just had to keep her patience through dinner, and then the flares would have their chance at reconciliation.

ATALANT DROPPED TO her knees in the middle of the evening market. Around her, shoppers muttered and juked, trying to avoid her suddenly stationary form.

Nicholas had caught the movement in his periphery. He sidestepped two quadrupeds and ducked underneath the basket of a tall Ardulan male to reach Atalant, who was teetering dangerously close to the sharp edge of a stall. Her eyelids fluttered as she covered them with her palms, rubbing away something Nicholas couldn't see.

He caught her as an Ardulan knocked her over. "What's going on?" he asked. She was heavier than he expected and, with her height, surprisingly hard to hold upright. More concerning, however, were her eyes, which were now red and secreting what he hoped was *stuk* from the tear ducts.

The crowd pushed at them, threatening Nicholas's tenuous hold on her. It was quickly approaching late evening, and the square in front of the Eld Palace bustled with last-minute sales. After declining the dinner at the end of the tour, they'd milled around the market for over an hour, waiting for some word from Emn.

"Hey," Nicholas said, pulling Atalant's hands from her eyes when she didn't respond to his question. "They're irritated enough. Doing that will only make it worse. What is going on?"

Atalant swayed again, so Nicholas braced her with an arm around her shoulder. "I..." Her voice was as unsteady as her legs. "I'm not entirely sure. My vision has gone foggy, and I've completely lost my equilibrium." She wiped the side of her right eye on her shoulder. "My eyes burn, too, like I'm too close to fire."

"Emn?" Nicholas asked. "She get lost on her way back from the tour? Is she in trouble?" Atalant had been right, of course. They never should have split up. But if he had discovered his ancestral homeworld, he might have wanted some alone time, too, despite being treated like a leper by the locals. Maybe just not with a war brewing.

Atalant shook her head. "This isn't Emn, although my connection to her is thinner now—but that might just be because I can't seem to think straight." She blinked a few times at Nicholas and then squinted. "Our connection is too frayed to work. I want to try someplace quiet. Can you get me out of this crowd and back to the inn?"

"On it." Nicholas moved his arm under Atalant's shoulder and half dragged, half carried her from the square. Twice, he almost lost her as shops began to close and the owners jostled through evening strollers with their perishable wares. The pilot sagged more and more as they moved on, her head bobbing down onto her chest and back again as they approached the inn.

Atalant was nearly on her knees despite Nicholas's best efforts to keep her upright when they crossed the threshold. Nicholas waved to Kallum, who was bringing a steaming bowl of andal to another set of guests. The bar had filled considerably since breakfast, and now patrons sat not only at the tables, but at the area close to the computer screens as well. Nicholas was pleased to see a septped family in the far corner. At least they weren't the only tourists cutting it close. The planet would move in, what, a few hours? Hopefully not until daybreak? The market had slowly emptied of other species during the day. They'd all have to leave tonight, whether they wanted to or not.

"What happened?" Kallum asked, rushing over. Zie propped up Atalant's other side, and the two moved Atalant to a long, wooden bench. She sat and managed a short "thanks" before groaning and curling into a fetal position on her side.

"She ran into some bad telepathy. I think. I don't really know." Nicholas had thought to launch into more of an explanation, but in the dimmer lighting of the inn, Kallum looked much younger. The bright silhouette of morning had given zir a more commanding presence, but now zie seemed more like Emn had in her first *don*—uncertain and wary.

Atalant muttered something into the bench as she struggled to keep her eyes open.

"Is there a healer nearby, maybe? Could we take her to the hospital?" Nicholas regretted asking the moment it came out of his mouth. Good things did not happen to them in hospitals. "Maybe a Science Talent who doesn't ask too many questions? This doesn't have to be an interplanetary incident. Maybe her telepathy and Ardulan telepathy just aren't compatible on a large scale."

Kallum looked confusedly from Atalant to Nicholas and backed away. "If you did something to get invasive telepathy, you are in some real trouble. Bad trouble." Zie bit zir lower lip. "We have a boarder on the third floor, second door on the right. Retired woman who used to sit on the Eld council. She's of Science, but I don't remember her specialty. Maybe you could ask her?"

How was he going to get Atalant up three flights of stairs? She'd started to shiver, *stuk* now beading across her brow. It was like some sort of strange Neek fever, but one that was progressing way too fast to be natural. The mysterious Science Talent on the third floor would have to do.

"Thanks, then," Nicholas said to Kallum. The youth's shoulders relaxed in relief, and zie dashed off to a table where a patron was holding up an empty, wooden mug.

"We have to try walking, Atalant." Nicholas moved Atalant's legs from the bench. She set them on the floor and jolted upright, shuddering. Nicholas wrapped her right arm around his shoulder and pulled. Somehow, they managed to get Atalant standing and limping to the stairway.

"Hold on there!" A thick Keft female with very short claws scooped Atalant from her slant before Nicholas had time to object. He barely managed to loosen his grip on Atalant's shoulders before she was in the Keft's arms. "Bit early for this level of drunk. Where's your room?"

The familiarity was disquieting until Nicholas remembered that there weren't many visual differences between the Keft and the Neek. The woman could be a Neek, for all he knew—though given their xenophobic culture that seemed unlikely, and he was pretty certain none of the Neek had claws. He also couldn't recall any of the Neek being quite as hairy as this woman, but then again, he'd not met many Neek, or Keft for that matter. Relieved, he pointed up. "Third floor."

The Keft gave a knowing wink and then took the stairs, two at a time, to the top. She gingerly lowered Atalant, whose eyes had remained shut the entire time, back into Nicholas's grip. "Guess if you're going to drink this much, might as well do it right before the move." She tapped Nicholas on the back, a gesture he hoped was friendly, and then waved with sticky fingers. "Glad to see another Yishin, if only for a few minutes. Enjoy your evening!"

That seemed less likely with each passing minute. A Yishin? Nicholas's gaze wandered back to Atalant's prone form. They'd have to talk about that later, when she was conscious.

Instead of pondering more on that, Nicholas looked at the door in front of him. In the tiny gap above the floor, Nicholas could see a difference in the lighting. Hopefully that meant the tenant was in. He leaned Atalant against the wall, rapped three times, and then stepped back.

After a tense moment, a woman answered. She had to be third *don*— Nicholas had not yet seen so many wrinkles on an Ardulan before. Her white hair was piled neatly on her head, and her skin was so pale that Nicholas thought he could see her bones. She was dressed simply in a loose shirt and pants, the cuffs of which went well past her wrists and ankles.

"Terran?" she croaked, eyeing Nicholas suspiciously. "My Common is old. What business?"

Nicholas rocked Atalant to a stand. She twitched against his arms, but her eyes remained closed. "Our Neek is having some telepathy trouble, among other things. We were told you could help. Discreetly." He coughed uncomfortably. "May we come in? She really needs help."

The woman scowled and jabbed Atalant with a bony finger covered in fabric. "Messy," she muttered, pushing up the hem of the gray dress Atalant wore. Then, she ran the same finger along Atalant's arm. The hairs on the pilot's skin rose and then sat back down all at once.

"The Eld." The woman sighed, moved into her room, and looked back over her shoulder. "Follow. Her on floor." She pointed to a bark mat that lay in the center of the small room. "Quickly."

Nicholas eased Atalant into the room. "Can you do anything for her?" he asked as he lowered her onto the ground. Her body curled back into a fetal position, a groan escaping her lips. "We have sapphires to pay with. Not many, but maybe we could barter? Owe you some later?"

The woman waved Nicholas away from Atalant and bent over her. She moved Atalant's head back and forth in her hand.

Nicholas took a step back. Money was going to be a big problem. How he was going to get more, he couldn't begin to imagine. Maybe they could sell some of the interior furnishings on the ship? That'd take a particular type of buyer. Looking around the woman's sitting room, he supposed the Ardulan might have a similar aesthetic. Lidded boxes made of various wood species lay strewn about the furniture. Some were ornately carved, others plain, but all were smudged with what looked like a fine, white powder. One of the little boxes was open, and something that looked strangely like his mother's antique powder puff lay against its side.

"Neek are telepaths little bit," the woman said, breaking up Nicholas's thoughts. "Have to break it. Too many in there at once makes an overload. No recovery without." She tugged Nicholas's sleeve, her eyebrows arched. "Consent? She cannot."

A wheezing sound escaped Atalant, but Nicholas couldn't make out any words. He was not prepared to make this type of decision. Shutting off her telepathy, while it certainly—well, probably—wouldn't kill her, would take away their only connection to Emn. That alone would likely get him in deep trouble with Atalant. With it active... He puffed his cheeks and looked down at Atalant. She couldn't do a thing to help Emn like this. He couldn't just leave her here, either. Partially functional was better than not at all, right?

"Do it," he said, although the words wavered in his mouth. "Let's hope it can be undone later. Right now...right now, we need her conscious."

Nicholas caught what looked like a muscle spasm in Atalant's right leg. Her head moved, rolling from left to right, and then was still again. The old woman ignored both convulsions as she put her hands on Atalant's temples and closed her eyes.

Nicholas counted breaths. One. Two. Three. Four. Just as he was about to hit five, Atalant's eyes flew open. She sat up, pushed the old woman away, and spun at Nicholas, fury and confusion on her face.

"You can't do that!" she yelled, sputtering. "How dare you!" She jumped to her feet, trembling with rage. Her hands clenched to fists, but both stayed tight at her sides. "You had no *right*," she hissed at him.

Nicholas stood his ground, his breath coming in short gasps. He had to remain calm. He'd done the right thing. She was walking. Talking. Raging. They needed that.

"Atalant," he began.

"Bastard," she said, her anger turning to sobs. "She's *gone*."

"She can fix it, I'm sure," he offered. He hoped. "Right now, isn't finding Emn more important? I would have thought that would be the most important thing to you."

Atalant snarled, and Nicholas took an involuntary step back. "And just how do you suggest we find her when you have *shut off my telepathy*?" The pilot turned to the old woman, seething. "What was so wrong with me that you had to do this? What happened? Can it be undone?"

The old woman remained kneeling on the floor. Nicholas held out a small cluster of sapphires to the woman, hoping it was enough. She looked them over, holding each to the light individually, before placing them all back in Nicholas's palm. "I am Corccinth, advisor of Eld for flare relations—flares like your Emn. Retired, sometimes. Here, no coin. Information exchange. Sit. Down."

"Emn?" Nicholas sat promptly. Atalant followed, still shaking, but Nicholas could see color returning to her face. Corccinth stared at Atalant, and the pilot stared back, as if they were locked in an impossible telepathic battle. Nicholas frowned. If they were talking about Emn, or the Eld, he'd leave them to it. There was something about the room that was bugging him. When Corccinth did start to speak. Nicholas half listened to the conversation as he continued to survey the strange objects on the tables, the light powder in the air tickling his nose.

"—know of Eld?"

"Some sort of ruling power?"

"Control. They have found you much interest. Ardulum must move, and Emn must not be problematic."

Nicholas stood, picked up a rose-colored pot the size of his hand, and studied its white halo of floating granules.

"What was the point of cutting off my telepathy!?"

"Control. Always control. Her power is unmatched."

"Okay, but why *my* mind?"

"They test. Push. Define. Hope. It is the way of Eld."

Nicholas ran a finger through the powder, leaving a thin path in his wake. The substance was fine, light, and vanished into his skin. The result was a smoother area, the tip of his fingerprint indistinct. It distracted him from the other nagging question in his mind, about why the old woman knew so much about Emn.

"Why are you involvement?"

"She's our friend. Things are complicated."

Nicholas turned back around and watched the woman consider the words. Her mouth was pursed into a thin line that made wrinkles appear in her cheeks. He squinted. They weren't actually wrinkles. In fact, they looked more like cracks or fissures, with something dark underneath.

Like tattoos. Or veins. Or...

Suddenly, everything made sense.

Nicholas interrupted the conversation. "We're looking for her because she's part of our crew. She's family. I think you would understand that."

The woman raised an eyebrow. "Why you assume?"

Nicholas wiped his fingers across the white dust on the tabletop, gathering a small amount. He walked to the center of the room and then tipped his hand over, letting the powder snow onto the floor. "Because she's a flare. Just like you."

Chapter 23: Eld Palace, Ardulum

Everything is prepared per your orders. The Neek populace follows our commands. Our emissary of sorts, the president and high priest, anticipates our needs and has proven as a solid liaison with the people. The settee pilots have been trained, instructed, and are ready to meet the Mmnnuggl fleets.

—Encrypted communication from Ekimet, second-*don* Hearth, to the Eld of Ardulum, Third Month of Arath, 26_15

THE PALACE WAS breathtaking. Emn followed Eld Adzeek through the tall archways that framed each new hallway, the dark andal heartwood in stark contrast to the pale sapwood of the walls. They walked through adjoined rooms dedicated to each Talent, each done in a different style. Some rooms contained tapestries of woven bark—others, delicate marquetry in bright hues. Color was omnipresent. It saturated Emn's vision, overwhelming her. Her time on the Neek homeworld had shown her the rich blues of water and the coarse yellow of sand, but the palette presented in the Eld Palace was unlike anything she had ever seen before.

Every few steps, they paused as Adzeek pointed to another wonder. They were currently walking through an oddly shaped assembly hall, with walls covered in marquetry depicting a century of seeding events. They'd just come from a round room with a low ceiling, where marquetry dyed in fungal pigments gave a visual description of each Talent structure. Emn had let her eyes linger on the elaborate panel for the Aggression Talent. Was that what she should have been—would have been, perhaps—without Risalian tinkering?

Not paying attention to where she was walking, Emn caught the side of her hip on an ornate andal bench as she tried to keep up. A crash followed, and Emn cringed as a shallow pot skittered across the floor, broken into two pieces.

"Vessels are a sacred form," Adzeek informed her, his face unreadable. "We keep many here in the palace. They serve as a reminder." He reached down to one of the wooden halves and picked it up, turning it over reverently in his hand. The artificially tinted wood was covered with tiny depressions. Emn didn't recognize the significance.

"This is a wooden replica of an andal seed pod. From the oldest trees, these pods are produced. In the right soil, new andal will grow strong." Adzeek flipped the piece over so that the jagged end was on top. "In the wrong soil, nothing can survive."

Adzeek held the piece out to Emn. She turned it over in her hands, running her fingertips across the depressions. The wood was silken, and the dye moved with the pressure of her fingertips, but did not lift. She puzzled at the dynamics but decided against asking or looking inside the wood. Instead, she handed the fragment back to Adzeek, who set it respectfully on the bench and continued to move to the other end of the room.

Paying more attention this time, Emn followed. When she reached a panel showing what looked like the Neek homeworld, she stopped. Atalant. She deserved to be here, to see this. There were answers here for her, too. At the very least, Emn could share the image of this panel, let Atalant have a window to her history.

Now is not the time, Adzeek sent. Emn felt heat rise in her cheeks. She'd been trying not to broadcast. Adzeek placed a hand on a door handle and turned back to look at Emn. *This world is yours, not hers. Not theirs. They have no place here.*

Emn took one final look at the panel, trying to burn the image into her memory, before following Adzeek into a wide hallway. Here, the walls were only plywood, covered in tapestries. Old plywood, perhaps, as the surface was littered with tiny fissures. They passed a thick, dark door on the right, walked another five meters, and then pushed open another door.

They stepped into another round room, this one large, with a domed ceiling that looked like fuzzy glass, and some strange statues. Inside was another ancient Ardulan, sitting on a wood throne, her cinnamon hair gathered on top of her head in two long twists.

Adzeek sat down next to her on another wood throne, splaying his legs so that the Talent markings carved into the base could be well seen.

A carving Emn couldn't make out arced over the thrones, as if it might topple and consume the Eld at any moment. Just in front of the thrones was a square mat of bark—black, curly, and not very comfortable-looking.

"Come sit and talk to us, Emn," the female eld called. She gestured to the mat. Emn took a step, but then hesitated. The floor was littered with wood pots, one of which was on its side. Emn leaned over and inspected the inside of one just by her left foot. Something viscous glinted in the overhead light.

"Please, Emn," Adzeek prodded.

Cautiously, Emn picked her way across the floor until she was standing in front of the thrones.

"This is Asth," Adzeek said, standing. "She is of Mind and Aggression. Our gatoi representative, Savath, recently passed, and we are not yet aware of the andal's chosen successor."

Emn wasn't certain what to make of that. She nodded in deference to Asth and then considered the bark mat. She wasn't fond of kneeling—especially when another forced her to. The last being who had tried had...she'd killed hir. The Eld weren't the Risalians, but snippets of the conversation she'd had with the other flares would not leave her mind. Hiding. Lying. Being *less*.

The walls shifted. Emn jumped back, knocking over an almost-full pot. Her eyes darted around the room. Convex striations wove across the wall. They transformed into complex geometric patterns and then loosened, the shapes they made existing for only seconds before disappearing.

She'd seen the designs before—on herself, on Arik, on Ukie... The walls were mimicking her markings and, somehow, those of the other flares.

"I see you noticed the andal roots," Asth said, smiling. She gestured towards the wall. "Each of these striations is a root from a different tree, and all the andal of Ardulum have at least one root here. They circle this room and imprint the walls, leaving the designs you see."

"Every tree..." Emn whispered. She fell to her knees, trying to comprehend roots spanning oceans, continents, just to...what? Amass here and play with her mind? Be at the beck and call of the Eld? *Did* the Eld command the andal, or was it the other way around?

There *were* gods here then, potentially, one way or the other. Her gods. Roots or Eld, it didn't matter. She needed Atalant here. She couldn't kneel here in front of rulers of Ardulum and talk about inane things when trees wound through the palace, possibly even reaching into her mind. She needed support, and the blatant disregard for divinity that only came from Atalant. Emn reached back for their link, searching for assurance or comfort or anything that could ground her in this moment.

Nothing was there. Emn searched, lingering in the back of her mind, in the small corner where Atalant's consciousness resided. When she could still find nothing, she reached out as far as she could, pushing past the minds of the Eld, the outer palace guards, and into the throngs of evening shoppers in the square. The exercise was draining, and without thinking, Emn pulled at the first bits of cellulose that caught her attention, bringing them together and absorbing the released energy to fuel her search. She heard pots shatter, but ignored it. She scanned the inn, the market, and then all of Sekreth, but the familiar brightness of Atalant's mind was nowhere to be found.

"That will be quite enough of that!" Adzeek leaned over and placed a hand on Emn's shoulder. She got the distinct impression of a wet towel being thrown over her head as her focus snapped back to the room. "We did not invite you to the Talent Chamber to ruin our antiques and spill anointment oil all over the floor." He frowned at Emn. "You were brought before your Eld to provide information. That is the only task we currently require of you. Your Neek is well beyond your reach."

Emn jumped to her feet and pulled from Adzeek's grip. When the male eld again reached for her, she slapped his hand away and backed towards the door. *What did you do?* she hissed into their minds.

"You're a smart girl," Adzeek said, his eyes condescending. "You can't feel her anymore. What do you think?"

Chapter 24: Sekreth, Ardulum

Request to outfit Charted Systems ships with tesseract generators is approved.
—Communication of unknown origin to the Mmnnuggl flagship *Ittyrr*, December 20th, 2060 CE

"YOU MIND DEAD."

Corccinth pointed through the last-minute shoppers in the marketplace to a nondescript door at the side of the Eld Palace. In both hands, she carried large woven baskets, each packed tightly with powdered makeup in ranges of melanin tints and covered with black, cotton sheets. "Way to Emn. The Eld tell their lies to protect, but always flawed methodology. Here is primary hallway to throne room and Talent Chamber. Kitchens close."

Atalant rubbed at her temples. If only she could reach inside her own mind, like Emn. Just turn on switches or synapses or whatever and fix her telepathy. Atalant's mind ached without Emn's presence, and her own thoughts reverberated throughout the emptiness in her head. And if the Eld had sinister motives, it'd be easy enough to convince Emn that Atalant had died if this was what she was feeling as well. "Are you bringing those baskets with us?" she asked tiredly. "Are they really necessary?"

Corccinth narrowed her eyes, and Atalant looked away. It wasn't worth arguing over.

"We're not actually going in through the kitchens then?" Nicholas asked. "That would have to be the busiest part of the castle, I'd think."

Corccinth shook her head. A tall Ardulan barreled towards the tiny woman, but then sidestepped at the last minute. Atalant caught the confusion on his face as his foot landed apparently not where he had planned and his packages smacked against his leg. Corccinth sniffed and looked up at Nicholas. "Hall is near but not. Turn left upon entry and follow past door to throne room. End door is Emn and Eld."

A heavy-set gatoi bumped into Atalant from behind. With her equilibrium still shaky, she fell against Nicholas, who managed to keep her from landing on the wood path.

"You sure you're up for this, Atalant?" he asked seriously. "I could probably manage a rescue with Corccinth here. The palace layout doesn't sound complicated."

"No!" Corccinth slapped at the back of Nicholas's leg. He jumped away and eyed her warily. "I don't go in. I have old business." She hefted the baskets and gestured towards the north edge of the market.

"Corccinth—" Atalant began, but Corccinth cut her off, pointing a powdered finger up at Atalant and then to a group of people a few meters away.

"*You* have to heal the wound, Neek, not me. But I have some who may help. Wait."

"Yeah, fine." Atalant retreated again. The crowd around them continued to thin, and the walls of the palace became readily visible.

"So when should we—" She looked down, but Corccinth had disappeared into the crowd. Atalant turned to where the small woman had pointed and saw four people bent over and speaking to Corccinth. Atalant bobbed her head around weaving bodies blocking her line of sight and caught glimpses of Corccinth's hair, her clothing, and her baskets. The contents were being emptied and placed into pockets. There was hugging. Rolled up biofilm exchanged hands. A large man stepped right in front of Atalant to ask Nicholas for directions, realized Nicholas wasn't an Ardulan, and walked off in a huff. When Atalant looked back to where Corccinth was, the woman was gone.

The group that had been with her, however, were coming towards them. They all wore the same cream-colored shirts and pants, and their feet were clad in brown leather. As they approached, pockets bulging with Corccinth's gifts, Atalant could see makeup on their faces, hands, and necks. Sweat beaded near their temples, clumping the fine powder and unmistakably identifying the four as flares.

Atalant motioned to the south side of the square, where a thick clump of andal grew around two long benches. The area was deserted and therefore semiprivate.

"Flares, then?" Nicholas asked as he followed Atalant to the benches.

"Hope so."

There wasn't any time left to speculate. When the two turned around, the flares were just behind them. The one in front, a male with green eyes, searched Atalant's face. She returned the fascination, unable to look away from the two upside-down triangle marks insufficiently covered by the makeup and visible from a short distance.

"Are you with Corccinth?" Atalant asked. Her arm came up unbidden from her side to touch the flare's cheek. She checked herself before her hand was past her hip and clasped both hands behind her back instead.

"Yes. She asked us to meet you. You and the Terran named Nicholas." The man offered a small smile. "I'm Arik, and this is Tik, Kisak, and Ukie."

"Why—" Nicholas began, but Atalant cut him off.

"You're the flares Emn went to see, aren't you?"

At the mention of Emn's name, the group collectively relaxed. The woman pushed forward. Makeup had crumbled into her loose hair, streaking it brown. "You've seen Emn since her return?"

"No." Again, the triangles on her face were visible this close, even under the powder, and again Atalant caught herself trying to reach out. She crossed her arms over her chest and told them to stay there. "She's in the palace in the east wing. The Eld have cut off our connection. We're going in to get her. I think... I think you're supposed to help."

Arik barked a laugh and then covered his mouth with the inside of his arm when Atalant scowled at him. "Corccinth was very light on details, as if expecting us to shut up and follow her lead. As if we owe her something. As if she controls us." He wiped sweat from his brow, and the sleeve came away white with powder. "Apologies, Neek, but the business with the Eld does not concern you. We will be taking the palace, with Emn's help, momentarily. She doesn't need rescue, and your presence could put Emn in danger. Stay away. Emn will find you when she has finished her tasks and the Eld are quieted."

"Are you *serious*?"

Atalant had had enough. She'd lost her settee, her homeworld, and her connection to Emn, and there was no way she was going to sit back while a bunch of idiots manipulated Emn into overthrowing a government. If she was telepathically mute, then she couldn't broadcast or be read by the flares fast enough. Smug in that knowledge, Atalant threw a punch right at Arik's nose.

The sound of cracking cartilage was instantaneous and was followed by maroon blood. Nicholas pulled Atalant back before she could manage another swing, but when the other flares went for her, Arik held them back. "Stay out of our way, Neek," he warned in a nasally tone. "I'll not be responsible for your safety if you enter the palace."

"What exactly do you think you will accomplish by storming in there?" Atalant demanded as she struggled against Nicholas's desperate grip.

"Atalant," Nicholas begged, "Corccinth asked them to help us for a reason. We should remain civil and find common ground." Atalant ignored him.

"Can you hear her?" Atalant yelled. "If she is with the Eld now and you storm in there, what happens to her?" She jerked out of Nicholas's grip and stood nose-to-nose with Arik, her hands clenched into fists. "You're a child playing revolutionary." She pointed to the palace. "They're *Eld*. They're not going to listen to some escapees from a prison, especially not ones that break into their home."

Tik moved next to Arik and put a hand on his shoulder. Arik tried to shove him off, but Tik held tightly. "She's right, Arik," he said in a low tone. "They probably won't give her a long leash. Now they have something we value, and we have nothing. They certainly know we are coming. We need to balance the scales before we head in."

Arik stepped back. His face and the front of his tunic were stained with blood, and his jaw was clenched tightly shut. He kept his eyes locked on Atalant's. "Did you have something in mind?"

"The crowd." The gravelly voice of Kisak came up from the back. The—Atalant assumed—gatoi limped to Arik and then pointed at the marketplace. "We have the shoppers."

Nicholas pushed past Atalant, his face angrier than she had ever seen before. "These are your *people*." He said each word deliberately, as if that would help Kisak better understand. "They're *innocent*."

Kisak reached up and slapped Nicholas. Stunned, the Journey youth teetered on his feet, eyes wide. Atalant rounded on Kisak, but the gatoi held zir hands up. "We're all innocent here, Terran. Hard lessons have to be taught today. Grow up."

"It's a good idea," Ukie said. "They don't have to be hurt, necessarily, but riling them up would work." She eased up next to Kisak and nodded her head at Atalant. "Emn wouldn't want you getting hurt, Atalant, but from what she has told us about you, you'll not step away from this. If you stay out of our way, we will stay out of yours. Will you agree to that?" Ukie eyed Nicholas. "If we promise only to agitate?"

Atalant clasped Nicholas's hand and dragged the youth back behind her. He dragged his heels, and she could feel the tenseness in his muscles. Nicholas had never flat-out hit anyone, she was sure, but given much more of this conversation, he was likely to. Hitting Arik had not been the best example. Their fight wasn't with the flares, and as much as she disagreed with instigating a mob, she'd done the same in the past. Besides, their chances of sneaking into the palace unnoticed increased significantly with that level of diversion.

"Agreed," Atalant said. "But when we find Emn, she's coming with us."

"Atalant!" Nicholas hissed.

"I think that is her decision to make, not yours, Atalant," Ukie returned. "We'll see what happens when the time comes."

EMN SCREAMED INTO the silence in her head. She wanted to run at the Eld, but her feet were too heavy. She wanted to yell, but her tongue was too thick in her mouth. Sounds died in her throat. Death had come between her and Atalant once before, and it'd not stopped them. Emn just had to get out of the palace, away from the Eld so she could find the pilot and fix whatever was wrong.

A loud voice cut through her thoughts. *You will sit down! You will obey.* Asth stared at her, but her lips did not move. Emn would have sent every pot in the room at the eld then if she'd been able. But she did not obey. That time was behind her—Emn would not let it return.

"Sit," Adzeek ordered coolly, all traces of friendliness gone. "There are rules on Ardulum. If you wish to join this planet, you must learn to obey them."

Emn tore into the Eld's minds. *I didn't come here to obey, I came here to find my home. This—* She sent an image of the palace. *—is not my home. Ardulans who control others, who lock away those different from themselves out of fear, are not my people.* She resisted the pressure in her mind now telling her to walk closer to the Eld. *You fear me. I may not be able to feel your emotions, but I can see it in your eyes.*

I've done nothing to you, but if you have hurt my friends, if you have hurt Atalant... Emn lowered her tone and sent detailed images directly at the Eld. *I will destroy you.*

Asth rolled her eyes, but the set of her mouth spoke of tension. She looked at Adzeek. "Who is Atalant?"

"The Neek she keeps whining about. Emn came with some Charted Systems inhabitants—a Neek and a human."

"She couldn't have bonded with one of the more competent subspecies? Even a Keft would be better than a Neek."

"Agreed," Adzeek replied. "Conveniently, they were part of the tour this morning, so we have their images, and they've still got their passports on, though the Neek seemed to think swapping clothing with the flare would go unnoticed. The films track genetic makeup for a reason. A few moments ago, I heard from the kitchen staff on the comm. They're back now—came in the east door and are lurking in the hall, heading south. They know where they're going."

"Corccinth?" Asth asked.

Adzeek nodded. "Likely."

Asth looked pointedly at Emn. She chewed her lower lip and stared, unblinking. "Just have the guards lock the doors that connect to the east hall. It's a long corridor, but easy enough to contain," she said finally. "It will slow them down long enough for us to find separate places to hold them. Corccinth had best know what she is doing. A Neek. Seriously." Asth stood and moved briskly to the door. "You will come with me, Emn. Since you do not want to cooperate, we will move you to different facilities that are better suited to your condition until we are confident in your control. Follow."

Emn's feet began to move, trailing after Asth. Atalant and Nicholas were in the palace. Her mind processed the information while she continued to pull against the Eld's control. That meant Atalant wasn't dead, just... Emn didn't know what. Altered in some way? Had the Eld interfered with their bond?

"Wait a moment," Adzeek called out as Asth pushed the door open. "We have an unforeseen problem."

Asth turned back around. The rigidity slipped from Emn's body as Asth's mind connected with Adzeek's. Asth moved back into the room, past Emn, and took Adzeek by the hand. They bowed their heads together. Asth's face turned ashen. This time, it was the Eld who leaked.

Flares...

Idiots, Emn spat to herself. While her limbs were still locked, the inattention had freed her Talents. She pulled at the floorboards without preamble, binding cellulose into thick cords. Not waiting to see if the Eld would react, Emn pushed at their minds, hoping to disable them enough to escape.

She was unprepared for the images they projected in return. Instead of fighting, the Eld invited her in, linked her to their collective consciousness. She saw the square just outside the palace's main doors. It was quieter than it had been in the morning, but some fifty people still milled around the stalls. In the center of the square stood the four flares. Emn watched with horrified fascination as they began to wipe at the makeup covering their skin. Ukie brought the bottom of her shirt up—exposing her bare, marked skin—and rubbed the cotton over her face. Tik grabbed a canister of water and a dish cloth from a shopkeeper, wet the cloth, and then washed his hands and face. He handed the smeared cloth to Arik and Kisak, who did the same.

Why... Emn wondered across the link. *To not hide, yes, but in the square...*

The shoppers stopped. Stared and whispered. Somewhere outside of Emn's view, a child began to cry. The gawkers surrounded the flares in a ring, but Arik corralled them back and worked his way to the palace steps. The others followed and stood behind him in a semicircle.

"We are *flares!*" Arik boomed across the marketplace. Murmuring met the declaration as the vendors abandoned their stalls and gathered with the crowd. "We were taken from our families! Held in captivity! Told to hide who we are. *No longer!*" He took the canister of water and poured the remains over his head. The remaining makeup ran off his face and dripped onto his shirt in scaly patches.

A hush fell across the crowd. From the back, a female voice called out. "Call the medics!"

Sorrow filled Emn, but it was so deep that she doubted it was entirely hers.

"The people don't understand," Asth said, her voice tired and too loud in Emn's ears. "And the flares don't know any better."

Emn watched two Ardulans in medical uniforms push to the front of the crowd. They had been shopping—Emn saw the bags in their hands, which they dropped upon getting a full view of the flares.

"You…" the shorter one said, his voice stuttering. "You shouldn't be here. Come with me, now. You can't—you shouldn't touch the palace. You…you could contaminate it."

"Contaminate it?" A man standing nearby looked aghast and then started to shout back into the crowd. "It's *contagious*! The mutations are contagious! They're desecrating the Eld Palace!"

"We are not sick!" Arik yelled. The people were moving now, pushing one another. Some were trying to leave the square, but others jostled forward, towards the steps of the palace. The medics were pulled back into the people, their bags left behind. Taunts streamed up from the mob.

"They'll infect the Eld! Kill them! Save the Eld!"

"Save our children!"

"We *are* your children!" Arik shouted in return, his voice increasingly shrill. "We deserve rights!"

"You threaten the Eld. You deserve death!" A woman in the very front of the crowd leapt at Arik and grabbed his arm. She pulled, and Arik tumbled from the stairs into the surging crowd. Tik jumped down, punched the woman and a man trying to pin Arik to the ground, and hauled Arik back up. Five more Ardulans were on them again, dragging the men back down.

"Inside!" Tik shouted. "Now!"

Ukie and Kisak turned and ran. Tik pulled cellulose from the nearest stall. The wooden structure collapsed, crushing the pastries inside. Tik gathered the released energy, brought it to himself, and then sent it into the arms of the Ardulans holding him and Arik.

The people screamed. The ones holding Arik and Tik burned. Their skin charred and small flames erupted from their eyes and ears. The crowd fell back.

Emn tried to scream, but she couldn't. She had Atalant's memories from the Risalian cutter—the charred, blue bodies filled her mind's eye.

Finally free, Arik and Tik ran up the remaining stairs where Ukie and Kisak waited, pushed open the tall, arched doors of the Eld Palace, and fled inside. The mob, still screaming, pushed after them, and everyone flooded into the main throne room.

Help them! Emn cried to the Eld. *They don't deserve—*

Enough. Cellulose surged. The Eld took what was left of Emn's collected energy and added it to their own. Except… Emn traced the bonds. The Eld were pulling from the andal. The live andal. And they weren't pulling so much as having it handed to them by trees that she was almost certain were sentient enough to speak.

The crowd in the throne room were now climbing onto the Eld's dais to reach the cornered flares. The Eld's presence washed across the crowd. The rage bled from the people. They stilled and fell back from the dais. Several of the older Ardulans fell to their knees and began to pray.

The vision abruptly ceased as Emn was kicked from the connection. As if the rejection had been physical, Emn landed on her backside, palms slamming against the floor.

Adzeek turned and faced her. "The potential of abusing your Talents is too great. You alone, Emn, slaughtered every crew member of a Risalian cutter. You disabled hundreds of Mmnnuggl ships, leaving many of the species to be killed by their enemies. You are responsible for the deaths of every single Risalian Ardulan in the Charted Systems, which is both horrific and useful. You are just one. Imagine the damage from hundreds of flares, all on the same planet. You can see the need, surely, for control."

"Another common problem in flares is impulse control." Asth looked sternly at Emn as the younger woman pulled herself to her feet. "These are not your friends. They are genetic mutations, and we do our best to care for them as much as we can. We understand their circumstances are not their fault, but that does not mean we will allow them to run amok on the planet we are charged with protecting."

An image invaded Emn's mind. She watched the flares again as they taunted the now cowed populace from atop the great gold dais that housed the Eld thrones. The hairs on her arms rose. Cellulose began to swim through the air, channeling towards the flares. They pulled at every piece of wood—from the ceiling, the floors, the thrones...anything they could reach.

Come out, Eld, Arik sneered. *We came to talk, to negotiate, but we will not be manipulated further! Do your dirty work yourselves.*

Bonds formed. Energy surged. Arik stepped forward, heat radiating from him. *Come out or we burn the palace down, and everyone in it.*

"Enough," Asth commanded. The Eld linked elbows—and then a number of things happened at once. The energy Arik was collecting dissipated, as if he was releasing a breath after being punched in the gut. Arik dropped to his knees, followed by the rest of the flares, all gasping.

Cracks began to run up the walls of the throne room, and even though Emn's vision was spotty, she was certain that tree roots were starting to weave in through the openings.

"We are done dealing with defects who cannot or will not be trained," Asth said. She stepped forward and swiftly kicked Emn's legs out from under her. Emn fell to the floor, the vision clouding her mind.

"I'll go deal with the Charted Systems beings," she heard Asth say. "There are only the five flares. Put them all away until after the move. We can decide their fate then."

Emn lost consciousness.

Chapter 25: Eld Palace, Ardulum

Behold, the power of Ardulum! With the andal you have so carefully tended will your ships fly faster than your enemies! Your weapons shall fire truer. Your victories shall be of Neek, of Ardulum. They shall be the victories your children sing about to their children—the victory of Ardulum and Neek over blasphemers and idolaters—the return of the one, true religion.
   —Excerpt from Ekimet's worldwide broadcast on Neek, fourth lunar cycle, 230 AA

ATALANT OVERSTEPPED AND teetered, her grip on Nicholas's flight suit the only thing keeping her upright. Fucking telepathy and fucking balance. The world around her was muted and oddly two-dimensional, and it made walking difficult. That she was walking through a palace on a planet she had sworn didn't exist was not helping, either.

Nicholas tried another door, first by turning the handle and then by pounding on the front. Again, it was locked.

Atalant sighed and tried to straighten. That was the third door they couldn't open. They'd made fine progress—up to this point, Corccinth's directions had been perfect. Enter east of the kitchen. Turn left and keep left to where the hall ends, to the Talent Chamber. To Emn. Except immediately upon entering the corridor, all the doors had locked, including the one they'd come through. They'd made it all the way down the hall without incident, but the door to the Talent Chamber was also locked. They were trapped.

"Maybe we should rest." Nicholas walked them to the wooden wall and leaned her up against it.

Atalant dug her fingers into the soft sapwood, comforted by the familiarity of the andal. "I can't take much more of this," she breathed. "Any of this."

"We'll find her." Nicholas kept a steadying hand on her shoulder. "Just keep telling yourself—it's just a palace. Just a planet. Just some bipeds. Best part?" He leaned in conspiratorially. "You were *right!*" Nicholas left her against the wall and threw himself at the door to the Talent Chamber. A *thunk* reverberated through the wood, but it did not give.

Atalant chuckled. "I don't think 'right' is the word we should use here." Atalant pushed herself from the wall and walked tentatively forward, running her hands over the fungal demarcation lines in the door's paneling. "At least Corccinth and the flares got us this far. We should be able to figure out the rest on our own, right? We're resourceful. Chances are everyone in the palace is busy with the mob the flares riled up. We just have to find a way to break down one door. *One.*"

"Yeah, but Corccinth could have mentioned triggering an auto locking system, or whatever this is. Also, I would have liked a little more information on this underground flare community," Nicholas said as he rammed his shoulder into the softer white rot in the wood. The area dented, but again, the door did not move. "Flares are kept in containment, but some aren't? That doesn't make any logical sense. Also, ugh." He rubbed his shoulder and glared at the door. "This isn't working. Maybe we should try the ceiling. Maybe it's made of something softer..." Nicholas trailed off and pointed up, his eyes wide.

A large, silent crack was forming in the paneling just above the door, the wood splintering in unnatural patterns. Smaller fissures burst from the larger crack, crossed the ceiling, and meandered down the wall. Another few breaths and the two burst into the door. It happened in eerie stillness, each separation spiraling into another without any auditory clues. Atalant's arm hair stood on end. Something whispered in her mind. She chased it, but it was gone a moment later.

"Emn, maybe?" Nicholas asked. "If it is her, you'd think she could at least get us a path—"

The door before them burst into two pieces with a loud crack. The smaller of the pieces fell to the floor. "We're through!" Nicholas yelled triumphantly. "Go, Emn!" He wrapped an arm back around Atalant and motioned to the doorway. "Come on."

They didn't get far. As if his words had sparked a chain reaction, sound returned. Cracking wood crescendoed throughout the hall. The fissures deepened. The walls crumbled. The ceiling, now so striated that it looked like vein work, lost its integrity, and wood dust rained down on them. It fell into the cracks now forming in the floor, creating a strange waterfall of andal.

"Out of the hall!" Atalant yelled. She tugged at Nicholas, stumbling across the gaps in the floor. Once they moved past the doorframe, however, the conditions did not improve. They were definitely in the Talent Chamber, of that Atalant was certain. The small circular room held numerous wood pots, three thrones, and the Eld statues. It matched Corccinth's description perfectly. The thrones, however, were coated in dust, the fine, beige powder stark against the dark wood. Atalant looked up to gauge how bad the ceiling was and instantly regretted it when a large clump of wood dust fell into her eyes.

"Damn it," she muttered, rubbing furiously against the secreting *stuk*. She forgot to maintain one hand on Nicholas, lost her balance, and kicked over a large wooden vessel. It slammed onto the floor without breaking, but a thick, viscous liquid seeped over the side and began to pool.

"Aaaand there is another species with mucus." Nicholas carefully stepped around the growing puddle and offered Atalant a hand. "Emn may be helping, but she's not in here. No one is. We'll have to keep looking. Any ideas?"

"Hold on." Ignoring the crumbling infrastructure, Atalant grabbed onto Nicholas's shirt, bent down, and sniffed. "Know what's funny? It does smell like *stuk*. It is the right consistency, too, from the looks of it. I wonder why they keep it in pots?"

The back wall fell in, crashing to the floor. Atalant could now see clearly into the receiving hall and throne room, which was filled with praying patrons who seemed completely oblivious to the destruction around them. Back in the Talent Chamber, wooden pots were being crushed by the debris, their contents spilling across the floor.

"We can play guess the mucus later." Nicholas hurriedly pulled at Atalant's arm. "We have to go! The throne room looks stable. Let's head there."

Irritated with his tone, Atalant pulled herself back up, threatening to choke Nicholas in the process, and nudged him to a jog. The ceiling continued to rain as they skittered around holes and soft flooring. They narrowly avoided a thick shower of wood dust before Atalant stopped them again. Nicholas was about to object, when she pointed to the doorframe, just next to the gaping hole in the wall. Bulged striations wove across the surface. These weren't cracks, and they weren't forming at random. The patterns were ordered. Geometric. Atalant recognized a cluster of diamond markings from Emn's hips, the circles from her wrists. "Roots," she muttered, backing well away from the doorframe with Nicholas's help. "Andal roots."

"Does that make it more or less dangerous?" Nicholas asked. He eased Atalant over a raised piece of flooring. "If Emn is doing this, I wish she would wait until we found her. A crumbling palace is not—"

He was cut off as a large piece of the ceiling fell into the center of the room. Atalant pushed Nicholas out of the way and dove to the floor. Nicholas stumbled backwards and fell, catching himself on his palms as the floor began to ripple and another piece of ceiling hit right where he had been standing, obstructing Atalant's view of him.

"Leave me and run!" Atalant yelled in the direction she'd last seen Nicholas. She pushed off the floor and tried to skirt the rubble, looking wildly for the Journey youth, only to have her view blocked as the floor rose and curved away, forming a high ridge. It curled into her and pushed her against the wall, knocking over more pots and coating her boots in mucus. Disgusted, Atalant tried to edge back around the mass, but then froze.

From the opening in the floor, a tree was growing. It wasn't a whole tree, more just its trunk and roots, as if the tree were growing upside down. The trunk widened into a buttress, and then a thick branch spun off and swept the floor, knocking Atalant's legs out from under her. Four pots splintered as they broke her fall.

"Atalant!" Nicholas called from the other side of the tree. "Are you all right? I'm stuck under part of the ceiling. I can't get to you."

"I'm fine!" she yelled back. She sat up and heard Nicholas grunting in pain. "Just stay where you are! I'm coming to—"

The rest of the ceiling fell. The fragments of cellulose-glass and wood battered her head. She heard Nicholas yell, a crash, and then silence.

Atalant choked on the dust, tried to clear her eyes to stand, and had almost managed to pull herself back up when the wall she was leaning against fell forward onto her, crushing her against the curled floor. Her head hit something hard. She blacked out.

Chapter 26: Eld Palace, Ardulum

Permission to outfit Charted Systems ships with lasers and reflective plating is granted. Begin militia training for all interested parties, including tactics.
   —Communication of unknown origin to the Mmnnuggl flagship *Ittyrr*, First Month of Squinth, 27_15

EMN AWOKE WITH a start. The back, right section of her skull ached as if she had been hit, but she distinctly remembered passing out without trauma. She let her consciousness sink down, assessing the damage only to find that she was in perfect health. Perfect health, with a headache that would not quit.

Her bearings came back quickly as she tossed her legs over the side of the narrow bed. She was alone, sitting on a thick mattress in a room she could cross in perhaps five steps. It was dark, but enough light came through the gap under the door that she could make out some type of animal-hair blanket at the end of her bed, a small, plastic table, and a glass pitcher of water. She stretched her feet to the floor, surprised to find cool concrete instead of wood.

Was she even still in the palace? Where had the Eld taken her? Emn reached out with her mind, searching for the other flares, but connected only to Arik.

Emn. His tone was tired as he spoke to her, words chased by images of his former detention center, the bodies of flares overlapping on the plastic floor. *We're powerless.*

They weren't, though. Powerless was being a scared, little first *don* on a Risalian cutter, having your mother killed in front of you, being unable to communicate with people who wanted to help you. Here wasn't Risal, and they were adults, if only just. There had to be options.

Is everyone here? she asked.

A brief flash of anger, followed by a sense of depressed hopelessness. *I can only sense you. I don't know where the others are.*

"They're in a separate chamber, as a precaution." Adzeek's voice was dispassionate as it filtered under the door. "Sectioning you into pairs in our concrete chambers is for your, and our, safety. We can have you further moved to complete isolation, if you become troublesome. Remember that. We have the space."

Footsteps approached her door, and a moment later, it slid open. Light blinded her eyes, and Emn looked away as Eld Adzeek grabbed the front of her flight suit and pulled her out of the room. Arik knelt on the ground to the right, bound in tight plastic constraints. Emn glided across the floor in Adzeek's grip as if she weighed nothing at all, her feet only skimming the ground.

"How..." she began, but stopped just after. Cellulose crackled off Adzeek's skin, the strands dancing in a halo around his body. He released her, and Emn tumbled onto packed dirt, sending up a cloud of particulate. Her head hit the floor and rebounded, jostling her connection to Arik. She choked on the dust as she searched for his mind again.

"In deference to Corccinth, now is the time to discuss your situation," Adzeek said. He crossed his hands over his chest, the sleeves of his gold robe hanging in wide triangles. "You and the other flares were conspiring to overthrow the government. You are also charged with the murder of twenty-seven Ardulan scientists and inciting riots." He knelt next to Emn, his eyes unblinking. "You are a stunning example of why flares are not allowed within the general populace."

She'd expected more anger in his voice, considering this contrived list of crimes, but heard only disappointment. As if she had broken some family heirloom and was being reprimanded. It made no sense.

"I am Ardulan," she whispered defiantly. The words grounded her, helped her focus. "I've not killed anyone."

"Perhaps not here, but you have. We do not have much time." Adzeek brought out a long-handled knife with a hooked blade and ran the flat of it on the hem of his robe. Emn recognized the design and shivered. A Dulan knife. The same as the Risalians used to terminate their own Ardulans. A knife specifically designed to sever the column of veins at the base of an Ardulan spine, bringing instant death.

Adzeek grabbed Emn's front again and hauled her to her knees, briefly lifting her off the floor as he did so. His movements were rough but not overly so. Emn puzzled over them, over Eld Adzeek himself. Did he want something from her? Was this an exercise in humiliation? Confession?

He spun her around. She felt the knife's tip again at the small of her back as Adzeek turned it in a tight circle, separating the fabric of her flight suit. The metal of the blade was hot against her skin. Her heart was pounding, and she could feel a vein in her spinal column pulsing with the increase in blood flow.

This was it, then. The Eld wanted her dead for crimes she'd not participated in.

Fight, Emn, Arik whispered into her mind.

"You think," the male eld breathed into her ear, "that you are special? Think about what you have done—the pain and destruction you have caused. If you had listened to the Risalians, we never would have had to send the Mmnnuggls. Millions would still be alive. The Charted Systems would still be at peace. Now, because of you, Ardulans have died as well. The flares escaped their compound and came here to find *you*. All those people yelling outside—that is because of you."

He's twisting events, Emn! Arik yelled. *We broke out before we knew of you. We would have come here anyway, eventually. All of this still would have happened. The Eld brought it upon themselves.*

The ceiling above them shifted, and a sudden surge of wood dust rained down. Emn grasped at the cellulose, pulling it to her.

"I'm not sorry," she stated, managing a quarter-turn, "for wanting to be in control of my own life. I will not have choices made for me, and I will not bear the guilt of others."

Adzeek brought the hilt of the blade down between Emn's shoulder blades. Pain reverberated down her spinal column. She fell to her hands and knees as she brought the cellulose together, collecting the released energy. She corralled it, formed it into a packed ball of heat, and let it hover just to her left. Ready for dispersal.

"We all have choices made for us, Emn. Even the andal of Ardulum must leave the fate of its planting to lesser beings."

Emn pushed herself into kneeling, but Adzeek pressed the heel of his foot firmly into Emn's midsection, kicking her onto her back. She pushed at the energy, trying to send it at the eld, but Adzeek was there, in her mind. He was past her barriers. Emn lost her grip on the energy, and it dissipated, heat radiating outwards but causing no harm. She searched for more cellulose only to find the dust now a fragmented lignin shell, and nothing more.

You see what they are like! Tossing us about like thrashed andal. We have no value to the corrupt Eld of Ardulum. Emn, please! Arik struggled against his invisible bonds. *You know more than us. Do something!*

She could do something. She could automate bonding of the loose cellulose. She could start a reaction that would burn Adzeek and the Eld, the flares, and the palace. She *could* do it, but the memory of the Crippling War, of the death of the Ardulans, tugged her back from the decision.

The knife stilled in his hand. Adzeek backed away. "Perhaps Arik, then?" Emn listened to Eld Adzeek's footsteps as he walked to Arik, saw through the other flare's eyes as Adzeek approached, turned Arik around, and lifted his shirt.

Emn couldn't breathe. *Is this what Atalant feels like sometimes?* she wondered. *Powerless around those so powerful. Outcast when she should belong. Forced to make decisions when those in power make poor choices.*

Adzeek traced the Dulan knife down Arik's spine, his eyes never leaving Emn's. Like he was challenging her. Baiting her. Almost like he *wanted* her to do something rash. Like a flare could choose nothing but destruction.

Except Emn could.

She sprang to her feet and ran at the eld, prepared to ram him if necessary. She'd take the knife. She'd protect Arik. They'd find a way out without burning the palace down and everyone in it.

She made it five steps before a loud *CRACK* came from the ceiling.

A thick andal root twirled lazily downward from an opening in the floor above. When it hit the dirt floor of the containment room, smaller roots broke off from the main one and embedded themselves in the ground. Moonlight filtered down through the opening in the ceiling. More importantly, the wood in the upper stories of the palace was now available to her.

Adzeek clasped his hands behind his back and closed his eyes. He nodded, his body taut. The Dulan knife dropped from his hands, landing an arm span away from Arik.

"The andal speaks," Adzeek murmured. "I listen. If you find Corccinth, tell her I did my best with you two. I know it doesn't make up for her tochter, but perhaps it is a start."

Long, thin spines were beginning to grow from the tops of the smaller roots. They were short at first, but after several heartbeats, the room was filled with sharp quills, each as long as Emn's arm and glistening black in the scattered sunlight.

"Andal has spines?" Emn whispered, so shocked that Adzeek's words melted from her mind.

"It doesn't," Arik said.

Adzeek's concentration wavered, and a spine from the andal pierced Arik's bonds, separating the plastic. Immediately, Arik reached out and ran a finger down the length of a nearby spine, carefully avoiding the tip. When he reached the base, he grasped the spine and broke it off. "Sometimes, sentinel trees grow around andal, when it grows wild. These are their spines." Arik turned the spine over in his hand and then looked towards Adzeek. His eyes unfocused, and Emn thought she heard faint whispers leaking from his mind into hers.

"The palace always comes down just before the move." Arik gripped the spine tightly in his fist. "Do you believe in dreams, Emn? Do you believe in gods? That we're all meant to do something? Or maybe the andal just controls us all, or makes suggestions, and all we can do is follow."

"Arik!" Emn broke into a run, tried to grab the spine, but Arik jerked away. Before she could try again, he had Adzeek's robes parted and the spine at his back. The whispering in her mind turned to incoherent shouting.

"Monstrosity," Arik spat as he plunged the spine into the male eld.

Emn couldn't breathe. The air was suddenly heavy and thick with humidity. The crowd's voices turned to anger. More black spines began to spring from the andal stem, some diving deep into the male eld's flesh. Adzeek remained motionless, the pool of maroon blood at his feet absorbing into the dirt. Unlike the spines from the smaller roots, however, these did not stop growing at a given length. Instead, they continued their progress, running through Adzeek's hand and into his throat and back out again. Several pierced his abdomen and a large cluster shot directly through his head.

Arik backed away, rejoining Emn. The spines grew longer, split Adzeek's body in half, and pinned each side to the wall. "It's over," Arik said. "The reign of terror from these Eld is over, and we won't let the new ones make the same mistakes." No emotion chased the words. There was just the simplicity of the statement, the blood pooled on the floor. The sounds of screaming came from the throne room.

"He didn't... I don't think..." Emn stuttered, trying to form coherent thoughts. There was something else going on down here. Eld Adzeek could have killed her, but didn't. He could have killed Arik, but didn't. All the flares could have simply been killed while they were unconscious. Why bring them here? Why torment them? And why would the andal kill an eld?

Arik wiped his hands on his shirt and looked up at the broken ceiling. "As long as they live, we can't. We have to stop the cycle, Emn, and if we can get through the move without the Eld, then maybe we have a chance at really changing things." He pointed to the stem. "We need to go up, find the other flares. We can use the spines as a ladder. The ones on the opposite side of the eld aren't growing anymore."

Emn looked up the trunk. Small roots continued to branch and sink into the dirt floor, and the spines were multiplying quickly. If they stayed put, they would likely be impaled. Climbing seemed their best option. She'd focus first on getting out and finding Atalant, Nicholas, and the other flares. Dealing with dead bodies, even those of the rulers of Ardulum, would have to wait.

She didn't want to step into more trouble, however. Emn reached out with her mind to the floor above, checking for cellulose. They appeared to be just one floor below the main palace level, as she found copious supplies of andal and other woods and—

"Nicholas!"

Emn heard the cry in Atalant's voice from somewhere above. Her chest tightened. With the palace coming down, Atalant and Nicholas were in desperate risk of being crushed. Emn searched for the pilot, tried desperately to make a connection, but she could not locate Atalant's mind.

"We have to find the other flares, Emn," Arik said. He was now well above her, his right heel teetering on a short, fat spine. "Then there are the other elds. Loose ends. Other things we need to deal with."

Emn grabbed a horizontal spine on the main root and began to climb, ignoring the cellulose that bled over her hands the moment she made contact with the andal. "There's only one eld left. Asth and Adzeek told me that Savath had passed. Regardless, I have to get to Atalant and Nicholas. After that, if we combine our skills, we should be able to rescue the other flares. Then...then..." Emn trailed off. Then what? They'd overthrow the government? She wanted a home, not anarchy.

"Not anarchy," Arik agreed. He reached the top and scrambled onto the floor, bits of wood flaking off as he kicked. "We take control. We make this planet a home for everyone. You could live here, unafraid, with your friends. Even the subspecies would be welcome, if you desire. There would be a place even for your Neek, Atalant."

"How...?" Emn didn't finish the question. She reached the battered remains of the floor above and cautiously leapt from the root to a patch of solid-looking floor. Arik's words continued to tumble in her mind. It was so tempting to think of what they could accomplish. A real home for her and Atalant. Freedom for the flares.

"It sounds like a dream," she returned.

"Not a dream. An eventuality." Arik placed his hand on her shoulder. "I know you don't like the methods, but there is no other option. The planet moves tonight. It can only do so with all three elds in place to direct the andal. Without a strong governance, the planet will break apart in the move. Everyone will die, Emn. Everyone. But we are flares. We have all the Talents. We can be that governance, remake Ardulum. We don't have to hide." He took his hand away and looked at her. "Now is our time. We will be the Eld Ardulum needs. Without us, everyone will die."

Emn imagined then, living with Atalant in an apartment in the capital, Nicholas stopping by to visit during trade runs with his own ship. She imagined shopping in the market square in a sundress, bare arms showing and no one staring—people chatting with her about mundane things without their eyes darting across her exposed skin. She thought about being judged on her interactions with people, not on her potential to destroy. She thought about having control of her body, her mind, her Talents. It was what she had always wanted, wasn't it?

Except maybe what she wanted wasn't the most important thing right now. She had to help move a planet, had to teach the flares to use their Talents so Ardulum itself wouldn't spiral into space. Finding Atalant was part of all of that, but she couldn't allow herself to become myopic. She was partially responsible for Adzeek's death. She had to deal with the consequences.

"I'll help, but we have to find Atalant and Nicholas in the process. Where do we begin?" Emn asked as the trunk they'd just climbed up expanded, sealing the hole in the floor. A root covered in curly, black bark spun off and twirled past an open door and into a hallway.

"Where the andal leads," Arik said. He took Emn's hand. "Let's go."

Chapter 27: Eld Palace, Ardulum

Cellulose isn't our greatest weapon—it is our only weapon. How has this planet not progressed past our last visit? What in the name of andal have these people been doing during these last centuries? Worshiping us makes no logical sense if it hinders social and technological progress.

—Overheard conversation by an attending Neek in the Eld's Chambers, fourth lunar cycle, 230 AA

A COOL BREEZE skimmed past Atalant's face, and she opened her eyes, completely disoriented. Hadn't she been in a room with Nicholas? Wasn't the Eld Palace falling down around them? How had she ended up lying on a thick pile of leaves under the immense canopy of an andal forest?

Atalant sat up and brushed her hair. Brown leaves crinkled against her fingertips and fell lazily to the moss-covered ground. She brought her fingertips to her pants to rub away the inevitable, congealed mass of leaves and *stuk*, but was surprised when her skin slid smoothly over the fabric. Confused, Atalant studied first one set of fingers and then the other. Both were dry.

"Not normal," she muttered to herself as she looked around. There was no understory to speak of, lacking even small ground plants. The andal dominated, and Atalant wondered briefly if she was in a plantation instead of a natural forest.

"Hello?" she called out, loudly. "Anyone around? Nick?" The breeze picked up and carried her words away, chapping her lips in the process. "This is why we have *stuk*," she muttered as she stood. "This is ridiculous. Where the fuck is everyone?"

Another breeze kicked up, this one sending a cyclone of dead leaves spiraling near her feet. Atalant kicked at it, but the leaf formation backed away, staying just out of reach. It suddenly occurred to Atalant that she was probably dreaming. As she looked around, pieces of her last andal dream returned. The trees looked the same, and the lack of understory was familiar. Mystery settled, Atalant leaned against a thick andal trunk, trying to will herself awake, and thunked her head on the bark.

Instead of a crumbly, rough surface, however, Atalant's head met something wet and sticky. No longer relaxed, she pulled away and turned to see what bug or small mammal she had inadvertently crushed. Where her head had been, however, there was only a long, horizontal gash that looked like someone had cut a strip of bark away. Sap oozed from the wound, the smell and viscosity reminding her strongly of *stuk*. That was stupid, of course, because andal trees produced a latex that was nothing at all like *stuk*. Her mind was obviously having a great time with this dream.

"No sense in wasting a natural lubricant," she said as she rubbed her fingers in the sap. She brought her smallest finger to her lips and coated them, easing the chap. "Much better," she said, smacking her lips together.

Atalant wiped the excess onto her pants and looked back down at the ground. The little leaf cyclone was still hovering near her right leg, unchanged despite the lack of wind.

"What the hell are you supposed to represent?" she asked sourly. "My life?"

As if in response, the cyclone began to intensify, bringing in more leaves as it did so. Its core was thick with brown now, and Atalant could no longer see through it. It continued to grow in height until the top was just above Atalant's head, whereupon it filled out sideways in a rough approximation of a biped.

"This is the part where the dream turns into a nightmare, isn't it?" Atalant breathed. "Great."

The leaves swirled tighter and tighter as they picked up the loose strands of Atalant's hair and blew them in every direction. An opening formed near what Atalant considered the head, releasing a loud whistling sound. From within, Atalant was sure she heard actual words.

"We waited a long time for you," the leaf cyclone breathed. "We know you through our brothers and sisters, through the seeds of our children spread long ago."

Atalant blinked several times and opted to keep silent. She was fine unless the leaf thing started coming after her with a knife. Until then, why not indulge in a little dream absurdity?

The arm of the cyclone reached out and pointed to the gash in the tree trunk. "You accepted our offering, and we are pleased."

"My lips were chapped," Atalant countered. "What offer?"

"To accept the flaring is to carry the torch of Ardulum. We honor you, Atalant, for being what many could not." A handful of leaves spun off the arm and stuck to the gash in the trunk, covering it.

Atalant squinted at the leaf thing. Was it her imagination, or was it not as compact as it was a moment ago? Moreover, why was she having dreams about being a flare? Courting a relationship with one was more than enough to bring her religion into a dangerous tailspin. Being one was just absurd.

"Protect us during the move, Atalant, and for future generations." She was certain now that the leaf thing was destabilizing. "In return, we shall continue to serve as the trophobiont for the Ardulan people, as we always have."

Atalant saluted. "Sure thing, leaves. I'll just go be an Ardulan and move a planet. Why not?" She raised her hand to salute again when the cyclone stopped. The leaves that were left drifted slowly back to the moss and lay still. There was no more breeze, and for the first time, Atalant noticed the eerie silence of the forest, as if there were no other living beings except the moss, the andal, and herself.

That thought was more disconcerting than having an entire conversation with a pile of leaves. Atalant rubbed her chest, finding it suddenly difficult to breathe. Why was there so much pressure? She took long, deep breaths that made her cough. There was even pain in her legs now, which didn't make any sense at all.

Can you drown in a forest? she wondered, trying to push something she couldn't see off her chest. Her vision was getting murky, the trees blurring together into brown fog. Atalant rubbed her eyes, and when she opened them, all she could see was brown with hints of light peeking through. The pain was much more intense now—too intense to be a dream.

Groaning, Atalant opened her eyes, but it was too dim to make out her surroundings. She tried to move and realized she was on her back, not standing, and there was something on her chest after all. Her legs were caught as well, and sharp fragments of something were poking her back. She was also completely drenched in a viscous material she sincerely hoped was her own *stuk*.

"Hey!" she called out, her voice croaking. "Is anyone there? Can someone hear me?"

"Atalant!" Nicholas's jubilant voice came from somewhere to her right. "You're alive! I'm here, but pinned under part of the roof. I think I blacked out, too. I haven't been able to break free. I am so glad you're okay!" Nicholas's words tumbled over each other, and Atalant smiled.

"Relax, Nicholas. I'll see if I can get out. I think I'm fine." Atalant tried to shift her hip, using the maybe-*stuk* as a lubricant to slide partway out from one of the beams that pinned her to the ground. She managed several centimeters before something shifted and the entire load slammed back down onto her, holding her more tightly than before.

"That didn't sound good!" Nicholas called out, his tone worried. "Atalant?"

"Still fine," she replied crossly. Her breath was wheezing now with the additional pressure on her lungs. She needed help fast. "Just had to have that telepathy shut down," Atalant muttered to herself. "Never seems to be a god-like friend around when you need one."

"Are you saying something, Atalant?" Nicholas asked. "I thought I heard you say something."

"Nothing, Nicholas. Ignore it," she replied. "Just trying to find a way out." Atalant could feel her fingertips drying, which was not a good sign. If her circulation was being cut off, she didn't have long.

Just in case that crazy woman screwed up the telepathy blocker, is there anyone who can hear me? I need help! she yelled into her mind, towards the place Emn used to occupy. The words spiraled in her head, but then slowly died away.

Atalant coughed again, wheezing as she tried to inhale. Suddenly, another crushing sensation overtook her, but this time, it was in her mind. A huge, multifaceted presence broke into her consciousness, tendrils of thought, each distinct but feeding into a whole, curled into her brain. Atalant screamed—a full, well breathed scream—and brought her hands to her head, pushing in with her palms. Outside of her head, she could hear scraping and banging before the pressure on her chest eased and then disappeared. Opening her eyes, Atalant clamped her hands over her mouth and scuttled to the wall. She rammed her back against it as several large andal roots cleared away the debris from where she had been lying.

Her panicked thoughts turned to Nicholas, an image of him floating to the front of her mind. Instantly, the roots changed direction and moved to the other large pile of debris, where Atalant could make out one of Nicholas's arms lying outstretched on the floor.

"Atalant?!" she heard Nicholas call over the din in her ears. "What is going on? Why did you scream? Did you get out? What..." As the last piece was cleared, Nicholas sat up and gawked, wide-eyed, at the roots that were standing somehow at attention, their tips pointed at Atalant.

The pressure in Atalant's head was waning. The presence pulled back, the whispering faded to what almost sounded like a gentle rustling of leaves. Atalant gulped air and stared at the roots, unblinking.

"Fuck." Nicholas said slowly. "Just...fuck. Where are they going? Where's the puppet master of these roots?"

Atalant stopped rocking—having not noticed when she'd started—and brought her hands back up to her face. *Stuk* production had resumed, though looking around, she wasn't sure where she would clean her hands if she needed to. She was sitting in a pool of the Ardulan pot-goop, her dress completely saturated and her hair hanging in wet strands that stuck to her face and neck.

"I am sitting in someone else's *stuk*!" she yelled out, not caring how crazy she sounded. She shook her hands and feet and tried to wring out the bottom of the dress. The goopy-whatever just smeared further onto her skin. "Fuck this whole situation!" The scattering sound in her head began to grow louder. Atalant clamped her hands back over her ears, forgetting the slime that covered them, and put her head between her legs, trying desperately not to scream again.

There was a squishing sound and then an arm curled around her bare shoulder. "Atalant?" Nicholas asked, worried. "Are you hurt? Is there something I can do to help?"

"I am covered in *mucus*!" Atalant screamed again. "Fuck Ardulum, it's *everywhere*." She shook her arms violently. "I can't. It's too much. My head will not shut up. The leaves won't leave me alone. Damn it, Nicholas, the wetness is *disgusting!*"

"Okay, okay," Nicholas placated. "Stand up, and we'll get you out of the dress. That should help." He helped Atalant stand, whereupon she frantically grasped the front of the dress and ripped it apart, shedding the whole garment in one throw. The pieces landed on her feet in a sticky pile.

"Get it *off!*" she yelled, hopping from the puddle onto a clear patch of floor, kicking the remains of the dress away as she did so. She crossed her arms and stepped farther away, breathing heavily as Nicholas joined her. The tips of the andal roots followed her as she moved, but without the dress, for some reason, she was feeling calmer.

"Better now?" Nicholas asked.

"Yeah," she responded noncommittally. The rustling had fallen back to a whisper, so Atalant tried to collect herself. The resulting breeze from the caved-in roof was cool against her skin, the sky above dotted with stars. "I need to find something else to wear, I think."

"You're sure you're not hurt?" Nicholas asked. He tilted his head and looked around Atalant's back. "You fell hard and didn't respond for a while. If you have a concussion..." Nicholas trailed off and took a step behind Atalant, staring down at her legs. "Neek," he said, slipping on the name. "You're twenty-nine? Today wouldn't be your thirtieth birthday, would it?"

Atalant rolled her eyes. "Nicholas, is that really a pertinent question right now? What are you even looking at?" She craned her neck around, trying to get a similar vantage point.

"I don't see..." Except, there they were. Three equilateral triangles all meeting at one apex on the very bottom of her left calf, near the ankle. The markings for a Mind Talent. Bruising surrounded the new pattern, tinted blue.

"There's another one," Nicholas said cautiously, "on your right side. I can see the start of hexagons from here."

Atalant lifted her right arm and looked down. Seven tiny, linked hexagons hovered just above her hipbone in an elongated oval shape. The markings for an Aggression Talent. Of course.

"First *don* lasts twenty years," Nicholas breathed. He moved to face Atalant and clasped his hands behind his back. "Second *don* lasts ten years." He nodded at the andal root tip that was pointing now at Atalant's calf markings. "Happy birthday, Atalant."

Atalant slowly worked through all the information her brain was trying to process. Today *was* her birthday—she had completely forgotten. Who kept track of those things when you were an adult, anyway?

The andal was here, in the palace. It was alive, as far as she could tell, and sentient, each tree with a distinct identity, and they were all in her head, chatting and waving. And somehow, inadvertently, she'd agreed to be an eld because she'd had chapped lips and hated her fingertips being dry. *Why* was she an eld? Why *her*? Was there no one else of suitable age around? Was it some sort of joke where the andal got fed up with the Eld and picked a Neek in retribution? How in the world was she going to explain this at home? How was she going to explain it to Emn? She poked at one of the markings and winced at how tender the area was. Was this how Emn had felt, coming out of the chrysalis? Had her whole body hurt with the stupid tattoos of Ardulum?

Emn. Her priorities crashed around her. *Please stop destroying the palace,* Atalant sent fervently to the rustling in the back of her head. *People are in here that I care about.*

The din Atalant hadn't realized she was hearing came to a halt. Weaving roots fell slack to the floor, and a calm overtook the shattered room. Every branch, every root, stilled and hovered, waiting for directions. At least part of her telepathy was back, although she'd have much preferred talking to Emn than a bunch of roots.

Nicholas stared, wide-eyed, at Atalant. "Not at all creepy. I guess that explains your piloting skills though. You had a Talent, just not the markings. Weird."

"I wasn't...I mean..." Atalant brushed her hand dismissively over her hipbone and then winced at the pain. "It isn't supposed to work like this! I'm a *Neek.*"

Nicholas snorted. "You're an eld, too, looks like. It's kind of funny, if you stop and think about it."

Atalant glared at him. "I could terminate your contract right now. You know that, right?"

"Yeah, but then you wouldn't have anyone to corroborate your story, your eldness." He pointed to the giant gap in the wall. It was now completely filled in with writhing andal roots. "If you're ready to move on from this weirdness to something worse, that should be the way to the throne room, if you can convince the andal to move. I can hear the people more now that the tree has died down, but it looked stable before our roof caved in. Might be a good place to start. Maybe it's still in one piece."

Atalant nodded and began to pick her way carefully to the gap, grateful that her boots were still intact. She simply motioned for Nicholas to follow. Three andal roots snaked after them, trailing a respectful distance behind. Atalant chose to ignore them.

As they reached the mass and Atalant reached out to prod a thin filament, the andal roots became active again. Six shot across the gap and a seventh smacked her hand away. "Apparently we are not going this way," she muttered. She threw up her hands in defeat. "Okay, I give in. Which way *are* we going?"

The andal responded by retracting from the gap and slithering across the broken floorboards to another, smaller, oval door on the opposite end of the room. It had been hidden by a throne before, Atalant thought, or maybe obscured by one of those ridiculous statues. Two thin roots wiggled beneath the lower frame, and the door swung open, revealing steps with a dim light coming from below.

"Ominous," Nicholas commented. "This is creepy as fuck, Atalant. What is going on?"

"I am working on a theory that this planet is actually a giant, sentient ball of andal."

"I don't do sentient trees." Nicholas walked to the open door and peered down. "I can't hear anything down there. Your call. You're the god."

The whispering in Atalant's mind increased slightly in pitch as she neared the doorway. She could barely hear anything outside the andal in her head. Root tendrils lapped at her ankles, urging her forward. "I don't think I'm being given much of a choice," she murmured.

Cautiously, she moved down the steps, Nicholas close behind. A damp dirt smell filled her nose, and she coughed as the relative humidity increased. Her last hop off the stairs made a squelching sound, but in the dim overhead lighting, Atalant could only make out a dark puddle below her.

Nicholas brushed past her shoulder—she flinched when she saw the dark liquid ooze up between his bare toes. "Atalant, the andal." Nicholas pointed to two thick roots that were skirting the edges of the puddle, which ran in a wandering stream to an unlit section of the chamber.

Forward. The word rustled in Atalant's head, sending shivers down her spine.

"Nicholas," she began softly as the andal's touch lightened. "I am being given hazy directions from a planet."

Nicholas considered for a moment and then gave a lopsided smile. "That falls under the same category as sentient trees. However, I think if a planet talks to you, you listen. Where sentient andal leads, you follow." He gestured towards the wet trail. "After you, your highness."

"I really don't like you sometimes," Atalant snapped.

When Nicholas remained silent, she took a deep breath and began to slowly follow the trail. Several times, she attempted to step out of the liquid and onto the dry packed dirt, but the andal kept her on the path. The squelching of their feet was sufficient to drown out the remaining noise of the crowd above, but nothing seemed to override the rustling in her mind.

"Oof." Nicholas stumbled, catching himself on Atalant's shoulders. "Sorry, Atalant. Why didn't they install lights over..." he trailed off. Atalant followed his gaze downwards. There was a vague form a few meters on their left, but it was too dark to make out much more.

Curious, she closed the distance and nudged the lump. It emitted a low groan, and Atalant could see labored movement in the shadows.

"Hey," Nicholas said as he edged his way past Atalant into the darkness. "Are you okay? Do you need help?"

Atalant crouched down to get a closer look, but stopped just short of the floor. The smell that filtered through her nostrils was unmistakable this close to the source. She could almost taste the metallic odor.

The groan came again, followed by more movement. At an achingly slow pace, a hunched, female form emerged from the shadows, supported by Nicholas. Her long cinnamon hair was matted in blood, her clothes dripping. Atalant recoiled from the stench.

"There's a big hole at the base of her spine," Nicholas wheezed as he tried to pull the woman straighter. "And there is a lot of blood. Looks like hers."

Choking back bile, Atalant ran to the other side of the woman and relieved some of the weight from Nicholas. Her arm wrapped around slick, wet fabric. It wasn't until they reached the light streaming from the door from which they'd entered that Atalant was able to get a good look at whom she was carrying.

"You're one of the Eld, aren't you?" Atalant glanced behind the woman and saw the large cut in the back of her gold robe, blood still flowing freely from the wound. "The andal led us here, but I don't know what we can do. Neither of us have medical training. We could try to stop the bleeding maybe. Do you have some bandages or towels somewhere?"

The female eld shook her head and coughed, the sound wet and harsh. "I am Eld Asth. The andal whispers of you, Atalant."

"Yeah, well, andal is pretty chatty," Atalant retorted. She released Asth, and without the extra support, the older woman fell to her knees, taking Nicholas partially with her. "Where is Emn?"

The eld doubled over, her forehead touching the dirt floor. Andal roots spooled around her ankles and traveled over her legs and torso, weaving into a tight net. Nicholas backed away, startled by the sudden increase in activity. Atalant smacked a third root that was heading for Asth's head.

Leave her be! she shouted at it. *She owes me answers.* The root stopped, hovering just over Asth's head, its tip pointing to the center of her forehead.

Asth began to chuckle. The sound was low and muffled, but Atalant could see her chest vibrating even through the layers of andal roots. "Flares must learn control, young Atalant. Unchecked, they will tear this planet apart and crush the minds of all its inhabitants."

Atalant grabbed a handful of bloody hair and yanked, pulling Asth's face up to hers. "Where is Emn!?" she yelled. "I don't give a fuck about your damn planet!"

The eld opened her mouth to respond, but before she could, the hovering root plunged into her forehead. Her skull cracked in two and fell apart, each half splashing into the small puddle of blood that surrounded the torso. Roots surged from the walls and floor, covering the body and pulling it back into the shadows across the wet, sticky trail Nicholas and she had just walked down.

"I am officially uncomfortable with this situation." Nicholas grimaced, and Atalant thought he looked a bit ill. "We need to find Emn and get off this planet. Come on, Atalant." Hopping over one of the skull fragments, Nicholas grabbed Atalant's wrist and began to climb the stairs to the main floor.

Atalant followed silently, her mind a cacophony of wisps and images utterly alien to her. When they reentered the Talent Chamber, Atalant stopped walking. The gap in the wall had been cleared, and she could see directly into the throne room. Looking up, she could see moons in the sky through the hole in the ceiling, their light burning away most of the stars. Tendrils of andal snaked across the remains of the roof, coming together to form complex geometric patterns that formed and reformed continuously. The yelling of the crowd, that she had only just been able to make out before, completely died away in Atalant's mind. The whispers of the andal turned into trumpeting, and Atalant found she couldn't tear her gaze away from the ceiling. Sounds rang in her ears: the sounds of the forest, the wind in the leaves, the pit-pat of andal sap oozing from a broken stem... Images followed, visions of new andal forests springing into life on virgin soil and heavy winds dispersing seed pods across a field.

Realization snapped Atalant out of her trance. Wide-eyed, she turned to Nicholas, grabbed his hand, and sprinted towards the gap in the wall.

"What the hell, Atalant!?" Nicholas sputtered as his toes caught on debris.

"You're right, Nicholas," Atalant gasped as the andal roots spiraled from the door and it opened into a crowd of people. "We can't waste any more time. The planet has decided to move itself. Now."

Chapter 28: Eld Palace, Ardulum

Testing is complete. Xylan weaponry is online, and all Alliance ships are equipped. Per your instructions, cellulosic materials have been minimized and replaced with petrochemical counterparts. There will be a sacrifice of speed and accuracy—however, we trust your advice in this matter.
—Tightband report from the *Ittyrr* to an unknown recipient, January 5th, 2061 CE

"THE PLANET IS going to tear itself apart." Emn braced herself against the wall as another tremor shook the ground. They'd left the guest quarters where they'd surfaced and were now angling through the hall to the decorative rooms, which Adzeek had shown her, in the center of the palace. She vaguely remembered the route they'd taken to the Talent Chamber as well, but she wasn't entirely confident they still wouldn't end up in the kitchens. "I don't know if killing an eld was a wise choice so close to the move."

Privately, Emn wondered too what the death of Adzeek had done to the crowd in the throne room. She could still feel them all, but their emotions were chaotic and dense enough that it was difficult to pick apart meaning. Without the Eld's influence, had they reverted back to a mob? Would they still be intent on the death of the flares?

Arik stumbled and caught himself. As the tremor eased, he gestured towards the middle of a common room, where they were currently walking. If they turned left or right they would enter the gatoi chambers. If they continued forward, they would eventually hit...what? The kitchens? Emn couldn't remember well enough, so she turned around and headed back the way they'd come.

"I think we have to turn around. I think."

Arik shrugged and followed. "Wise choice or not, it had to be done. Your story is different than ours. You don't understand. The Eld killed hundreds, possibly thousands, of flares, because they needed to lighten the load for the move. I was taken from my family, leaving them unable to care for our plantations. My saplings will have died by now. Thousands of andal trees, thousands of flares, dead. They're dead because of this."

He stopped, turned to Emn, and pulled up his sleeve, revealing his markings. "You know this pain. I'm not looking for your approval, but I do need your help. You don't know where your Neek is, and I don't know where the other flares are. We've only got the andal for help, so let's try and work together, all right?" They passed the guest quarters again, this time exiting into a hall.

Arik pointed to the snaking root that was coiled next to the door as if preparing for a nap.

"Those smaller doors lead to the basement, where we were. The circular chambers down there are the original flare containment cells, back when we were routinely culled. Corccinth had a map of the underground parts for us in her bags at the gazebo. I can't feel the other flares, so likely they're in containment. That is where I am going. That is where the andal points."

Emn hesitated. She'd heard Atalant yelling for Nicholas above, not below. If he was trapped—if Atalant was trapped...

We don't have time! Arik sent. *If your Neek is crushed, there is nothing we can do for her. The flares need us. Now! Ardulum needs us now!*

A crash came from behind the oval door. The andal shuddered. Another crash followed, and the door burst open, releasing a large cloud of dirt. Tik's and Kisak's presences bled into her mind, bringing with them a surge of adrenaline. A moment later, the flares themselves appeared at the top of the stairs. Both were covered in brown dirt, and Kisak's limp had gotten worse—but they were alive.

"Ukie?" Arik asked, embracing Kisak. The gatoi, much to Emn's surprise, hugged back, zir head resting momentarily on Arik's shoulder.

"Not with us," Tik said. "No one was with us. The andal went wild, broke the doors off the cells. We climbed up."

The andal root quivered, almost like it was pleased with itself. The hair on Emn's arms rose. More cracking sounds came from above, as if trees were falling over. There was a thunderous bang, and then a rumble began that grew steadily in pitch. As it got louder, the ceiling above Emn's head began to shake. She looked up and then back at the root, the end of which was bobbing right at head level. That was even more disturbing than it emoting. What was going *on*?

Suddenly, a yell rang out in the distance—a yell in Atalant's voice. Emn forgot everything else.

"Atalant!" she yelled down the hall. "Where are you? I'm coming! We're coming!" Almost in response, the andal shot off in the direction of Atalant's voice. Was it...leading Emn to her? Did it care? Did Emn care, as long as she found Atalant? She needed to *go,* but she couldn't just leave the flares, either. She needed them to come with her, before even more things unraveled.

"Atalant is being crushed!" Emn yelled. "We will be too, if we don't move. We're only missing Ukie, and there are no more basement doors in this hall. There might be on the other side of the gatoi chambers, which is also the way the andal is leading. We can go through there, find Atalant and Nicholas, and then check the basements."

She didn't wait for assent, didn't bother to listen to the words Arik sent to her mind. She'd lost her mother. She'd never had a home. She would not lose Atalant.

The thundering of the palace grew louder as Emn pushed past Tik and broke into a run, heading back down the hall, following the root. She turned back past the guest quarters and raced through the gatoi commons, ignoring the half-opened doors and confused looks of those roused from the noise. Emn pressed on, out through the door on the other end of the chambers and into another long hallway. Here, she heard the sounds of the crowd again—were they *still* upset?—and she turned towards the throne room. This area of the palace, at least, she was familiar with. She ran faster, Arik close behind. The people were still chanting, even shouting, for the Eld. Demanding to see the Eld. Demanding the flares. The andal dogging at her heels, Emn ran to the door connecting the hallway to the throne room.

"Emn, stop!" Arik yelled after her.

Emn did stop, but only when she was pressed just against the door, the andal weaving across her feet. She could hear the crowd's words distinctly through the wood.

"The Eld told us to wait!"

"The Eld aren't here, and the palace is crumbling! The flares have done something to them. We have to find them!"

"We will *all* be killed if we stay here! Why are we waiting here, to be slaughtered?"

"Let's just kill the lot of them!"

Arik and the other flares caught up to her. There were sounds of shuffling on the other end of the door and then the sounds of one of the thrones creaking.

"Death to the flares!" a voice screamed.

The crowd screamed back, "Protect the Eld!"

A solitary shriek stilled the crowd. A loud thump followed.

Emn shivered. *We have to find the other eld.*

They couldn't go into the crowd, not like this. Those people out there didn't *understand.*

Agreed. Arik gestured for her to follow, Tik and Kisak close behind. *We should go back near the kitchens. You passed the corner near the Records Room and Adzeek's chambers. There's another stairwell there to the basement. If Ukie is there, then likely an eld is, too.*

Actually, I'm out here. Ukie's voice broke across their connection, startling all the flares. Emn hadn't felt her reestablish the link, but her presence was clear, strong, and coming from...the dais in the middle of the throne room.

The floor began to move. The solitary root that had led the flares joined the other roots crisscrossing the floor and gathered into a thick mass, spinning into a rope. It flowed towards the closed door. Smaller roots slipped under the gap. A moment later, the door swung open, the andal separated and dispersed, and harsh whispering flooded the hall. Past the door was a mob of Ardulans spanning every *don.* They were whispering, but their voices were getting louder as they pushed against one another. Above their heads, Emn saw the raised dais and the three Eld thrones.

Ukie sat in the middle one, smiling. A dead gatoi lay at her feet, zir maroon blood dripping over the side of the dais and seeping into the people beyond.

The crowd exploded a moment after, screaming. Ardulans tried to climb the dais and pull Ukie down, but each time, they fell back via some invisible force. People wailed for the Eld. Hurled abuse and food, but Ukie only stood and smiled.

Come on, Emn! Arik yelled. He ran through the doorway, Tik and Kisak just behind, and began to fight through the people. Ardulans fell. Struggled to get back up. Tried to fight the flares. The flares pushed back, with hands, with cellulose.

We need you, Emn, Arik called as he reached the dais. *Can't you feel it? Can't you feel Ardulum? We can link here, in this central location. We need to guide the planet.*

Emn couldn't feel anything, in fact, but the state of the palace, the lack of ceiling, and the andal roots that coated the walls of the throne room was concerning. Saving Atalant and Nicholas was what mattered, but if they were in the crowd, or on the other side, she'd never find them before the palace collapsed. She pulled away from her hazy thoughts and tried to push forward, but she was too far behind Kisak. The opening zie had created was thick again with bodies. A woman fell into her.

Then, she saw it. Strawberry-blonde bound into a braid. A mass of dark curls. Just a flash near the far wall, possibly even inside the Talent Chamber. They were there! They were alive! She just had to get to them—she could worry about the planet later.

A man turned, noticed her, and punched her in the gut. Another Ardulan shoved her onto her stomach, and a booted foot came towards her face.

I don't have time for this! As gently as she could manage, Emn pulled cellulose from the flooring, bound it, collected the energy, and pushed it at the Ardulans near her. They flew back, knocking into others, but were otherwise unhurt. Emn stood and repeated the process again and again as more Ardulans came towards her. She began to walk towards the thrones, which sat in the middle of the room. She had to get around the dais before she could reach the Talent Chamber. Taunts followed.

"Mutation!"

"Unclean!"

"Killer!"

Emn pushed three women to the side. A gatoi stepped into her path, a wooden staff in zir right hand. Zie spoke before Emn had a chance to send zir away. "Where are the Eld?" zie asked. The gatoi gripped the staff with both hands and braced.

A crack opened in the floor, right underneath the gatoi. It widened too quickly, and before Emn could react, the gatoi's foot had fallen through and zie was on zir back, yelling for help. Emn reached down to the gatoi and tried to help zir up.

Emn! We don't have time! Ukie yelled from the dais as four more Ardulans fell back from her, smoking from the ears.

The gatoi smacked Emn's hand away, so she stood and tried to find a way around zir and past the others. *You can't just kill them, Ukie!* Emn fought through her own panic, desperate for options. She needed to get to the other side of the room! Could she push all the Ardulans back and maybe pin them to the walls? No, there were too many. Force them out the door? No, that would take time to corral them that she did not have. Make them unconscious, maybe?

Yes, and the flares could help. It would forward their goals as well.

Here. Emn pushed herself into the minds of the other flares. *Do what I do. Watch.* Emn reached for the first cellulose she could find. She followed it as the disordered areas hopped along the crystalline matrix, gathering each adjacent strand and then the strands touching those. Meticulously, she mapped the strands within the palace—from the floor and walls, to the woven tapestries and small pots—against the pull of the people in the hall. She skirted the people and moved into the detritus in the soil upon which the palace stood. When she had mapped every millimeter of the palace, she shifted into the mind of the gatoi on the floor, still struggling against the floor gap. She rifled through zir brain until she found the spot that controlled consciousness. Then, she addressed the four flares.

Push here. Gently. Just enough for them to collapse. Have in your mind the basics of the operation. When I pull, I'll send the energy to you. Each of you can then disperse it to as many minds as you can reach. If you hold the idea of what you want to do in your head and don't get distracted, the process should automate. Don't screw up. We can fix them after the planet moves. It'll just take me a bit to figure out how. Ready?

Eager assent came back from all of them.

Here we go.

Emn let her mind calm, probing the edges of her cellulose net. When she was sure of the boundaries, she collapsed the framework and brought every strand together.

A thick, crystalline structure materialized at her feet. The crowd around her fell to stillness for a brief second, and then everything happened simultaneously. The palace, devoid of its wood matrix, crumbled to the ground as bits of lignin and paint rained down on the crowd. The shell that remained was entirely composed of living andal roots, weaving together and continuously changing form. Microscopic fissures opened in the ground where Emn removed decaying plant matter, leaving unseen weak spots that sent many of the milling Ardulans to their knees. The crowd quelled, shocked, but they did not pass out. Instead, they began to wander, confused, bumping into each other as if they had no concept of their surroundings. Their minds sent confused images to Emn, which she worked desperately to sort through. It was as if...

As if...as if their minds had been fractured.

Like the Risalian Ardulans.

Like her mother.

Emn held the energy for a moment, the horror of what she had accidentally done slowly bleeding into her mind. The stillness of the moment swung delicately in front of her. The flares looked at her expectantly. She had too much energy. Again. It had to go somewhere, and the chain reaction was already in place. The flares were already pulling at the energy, desperate to try the trick themselves.

Don't, Emn sent, barely able to breathe. *Please don't.*

The stillness broke. The consciousness of the other flares bled back into her mind, and Emn couldn't fight the pressure. She sectioned the energy to the flares and felt them reach out and touch the minds of each Ardulan in the palace. Eyes glassed over. Dialogue ceased. The crowd stopped.

"You're brilliant, Emn!" Arik said when he expended the last of the energy. "It would have taken us hours, maybe a day to reach that many people." Arik hopped onto the dais, joining the other flares.

Emn couldn't move, staying rooted to the floor, witness to her destruction. A child to her left toddled on uneven steps. Zir eyes were unfocused, zir hands pulling at zir tunic and then gliding over the fabric as if zie had never touched it before. Why was there a child here? Why had someone brought a child with them from the market? A third-*don* woman allowed herself to be moved by the crowd. She offered no resistance, her eyes blank. A man and a gatoi huddled close together, backs to the wall, trembling.

Kisak lumbered from the dais and cleared a path to Emn, pushing Ardulans to either side as zie walked. "Adzeek is dead. Ukie confirms Asth is dead through her doing, and she found Savath's body laid out in a death shroud. We don't have time to dally. We can repair their broken minds later. We haven't gotten to them all yet, anyway. Right now, we need your help." When zie grabbed Emn by the arm, she pulled back, but Kisak's grip was strong. All the fractured minds pulled at her, threatening to drown her in their vacant swirling.

She was hauled onto the dais, her arms linked with Kisak's and Arik's. Flare minds pushed the other Ardulans away. "NO!" Emn screamed at them, adding weight to the words with her mind, but Arik pushed his consciousness deeper, bringing her to focus.

"Emn," he said, too calmly. "Would you just listen?"

An oppressive weight landed in her mind, pushing it down. It smothered her thoughts with a million sprigs of consciousness, unwilling, teeming, trying to break free.

Emn struggled to breathe. Her mind was in danger of ripping apart. "I feel...covered," Emn said to Arik, no longer struggling against the flares. She couldn't. The weight of the planet was too much, its need too great. "The andal feels foreign, like it doesn't belong. Like I am being crushed. The planet is going to come apart, isn't it?"

Arik's response was distant due to the weight of the andal. "Yes, but we can guide it. It will fight us, but we are its only choice."

"What do we do now?" Emn asked as the sense of urgency grew. Something, something unfathomable, shrieked into her head. Her skin felt like it was cracking apart. "I've never done anything like this before!" Emn yelled. "What do we do?"

Arik gestured to where one of the thrones had once stood. "We save the planet, Emn. Just like the Eld."

Chapter 29: Eld Palace, Ardulum

Current tally of outfitted Charted Systems ships:
Fourteen Risalian cutters
Three hundred and twenty-two Risalian stellar skiffs
Eight Minoran galactic liners
Eighty-seven Oorin dredgers
Five Alusian barges
Two hundred and fifty-one Alusian tramps
Twelve Terran shuttles
One hundred and eighty-six unidentified tramps

In addition, fifteen of our skiffs and four cutters are now completely cellulose-free.
    —Report to the Markin Council, January 8th, 2061 CE

EMN WAS ALIVE.

Atalant saw her, grouped with other flares, on a metal dais in a sea of people who were...confused? What had happened? They'd been upset just moments before and now the lot of them were acting like the Risalian Ardulan woman they'd met on Neek—before she had disobeyed the Risalians and saved all of their lives. And what had happened to the *ceiling*? The two things weren't related, right? They couldn't be related. There was no way Emn would do...whatever this was... *Right*?

Atalant would have to get to her to ask, regardless. At least Emn's—Atalant's, technically—flight suit was distinct from the cream-colored outfits of the others, her height unmistakable. Atalant wanted to reach out, to call to Emn, to ask what the hell was going on, but all she could access was the twisting consciousness of the andal and the flares, just beyond, holding hands with their eyes closed as they tried to interface with something far beyond their capabilities.

The tight patchwork of andal roots above shielded her from the falling remains of the palace. With the walls down and no more physical barriers in place, she could see the remains of the marketplace and the inn where they had stayed. People stood near their homes, their closed-down carts, staring blankly. Children sat on packed dirt, crying out for comfort only a parent could provide.

Nicholas was talking to her—she was aware of the sounds but not able to process the words. Instead, the andal whispered to her in whipping tendrils of vibrations and smells. Atalant felt the determination of the andal to relocate, felt its desire for a new start, to begin a new line. She felt it push back against the flares, recoiling at their touch. Through the hair-like roots that rested on her shoulders, she felt the very matrix of the planet begin to make a subtle shift. The movement was jerky, somehow uncertain. That did not give her a great deal of confidence.

"Hey, are you even listening?" Nicholas's voice finally registered. She turned. He seemed different, too, as he wobbled, trying to keep his balance on the uneven ground. Maybe he was a little taller, or maybe it was the way he stood now, fully upright instead of slouched, sounding confident and snarky where once he had only been whiny. His shoulders were broad. Strong. He looked...competent, she admitted to herself. Adult.

"I need your help, Nicholas." The words didn't taste as funny as she had worried they might. "I have to get to Emn, and I have to deal with the flares. This all has to get sorted so I can babysit a giant root ball across space." Atalant smiled a small but genuine smile and held out an open palm.

Nicholas grinned and clasped her hand. "What's the plan? Take out the flares? Save the damsel?"

Atalant opened her mouth to speak, but then closed it as two thick andal roots surged forward, the long and golden robe of an eld stretched between them. It was Asth's robe. Atalant recognized the stains. The andal roots paused in front of her feet and drew back, the robe falling into her hands.

"I don't like this," Atalant muttered. She rubbed the fabric between her fingertips. Silk? Silk and andal rayon? It was smooth, whatever it was. Atalant brushed dirt from the robe, the bloodstains crumbling off in tandem and powdering to the floor.

"Better than being mostly-naked?" Nicholas shrugged his shoulders. "Maybe?"

"I suppose," Atalant grumbled as she slipped the garment over her head and tied the waist sash. The urgency of the andal was increasing exponentially, threatening to tear her mind apart along with the planet. The whispering presences bucked against the flares, tried to throw them off and out, but their combined strength tethered the andal in place and caused it to pull against itself. The ground trembled. She didn't have time to care about clothing—or what it signified.

"Nicholas, I need help getting to that platform."

"On it." Without waiting for further instruction, Nicholas pushed his way into the crowd. The people stumbled from him as he gently herded them, opening a path. The andal trailed after, roots twirling together in thick, trunk-like clumps that held back the crowds from recovering the space.

With the andal wisps still on her shoulders, Atalant moved down the aisle, being careful to step around the divots in the dirt. Eyes stared at her from behind the andal fence. Occasionally, a hand reached out and then retracted. Whenever an Ardulan brushed the roots, Atalant received an impression of their mind. They were tortured and unsure, swirling and searching, with no refuge from the confusion in their heads.

Nicholas reached the center. The andal surged around the dais, creating a buffer. Another tremor hit, sending Ardulans to their knees. Atalant's path was now completely clear. Nicholas looked back to her, saluted once, pushed back into the sea of people, and disappeared from sight.

What did he think he was doing? Gah, Atalant didn't have time to chase after him and stop whatever silly-yet-heroic act he had in mind. Atalant reached into her boot and pulled the knife with the curved tip from the sunken sheath—the knife whose use she finally understood. A Dulan knife, once used by the Risalians to keep their Ardulans under control. It shouldn't have come as a surprise that Ardulum was responsible for its creation. Corccinth had discussed it with her in the marketplace before they'd reentered the palace. Guided her through Ardulan anatomy. Showed her how to sever the primary artery in the Ardulan spinal column, bringing death. Atalant didn't want to use it, but would, if necessary. There were too many lives at stake. With quiet footsteps, she approached the dais, knife at her side, her grip tight.

Again, the ground rocked. Atalant barely felt it. She hopped onto the platform and circled to Emn. The flares remained linked, eyes closed, unmoving.

"Emn," she called out. Atalant placed a hand on the woman's shoulder, hoping to find the presence she had come to rely upon.

Emn turned her head, eyes slitting open. She searched Atalant's face and then glanced at her robe. She blinked, rapidly, shaking her head as she did so. "Who…"

Atalant stared. Processing. Emn didn't know her. The fucking planet was moving, she was an eld, and *Emn didn't know her.* She didn't know what had happened—she didn't care what was happening. The remains of her patience frayed. Atalant stifled a scream.

The wisps on her back began to wave rhythmically. Words formed in her mind: *move move move move.* The planet was ready. The planet was impatient.

"Emn, just— Come on!" Atalant ducked under two entwined arms and stood in the center of the ring, facing the younger woman. She put both hands on Emn's shoulders and ran them down her arms. Emn's skin was hot, the Talent marks burning. Atalant caught the other woman's presence, then, in the andal. Emn was guiding the flares, driving them forward in their mad quest. Without her, they couldn't succeed. Atalant just had to figure out how to break their link.

Physically breaking it seemed a good place to start. Atalant pulled Emn's hands away from the flares, nearly bringing the younger woman into an embrace. Emn's consciousness appeared to remain entwined, as her eyes did not focus on Atalant's, but one presence did break away.

Arik moved forward, with what looked like a smile persistently twitching at the corners of his mouth. He picked up the hem of Atalant's sleeve and then tossed it aside in disgust, his hand still reaching towards her. "A subspecies wearing an eld robe. You do not stand with us. You were not to get in our way."

Atalant batted Arik's hand away, balancing against the swaying of the ground. Emn moved from her arms and rejoined the group.

"Right now, I stand with getting Ardulum through the move in one piece." She jabbed the knife tip towards him. "*You* are getting in the way. This—" She gestured to the crowd. "—isn't helping anything, and you all trying to connect with the andal is muddying my connection. *Stop it.*" Atalant's voice dropped as she let the anger at her present circumstances, the anger at her lost connection to Emn, and her general frustration with the entire situation come forth. "And you will let Emn out of whatever mind thing you've done to her."

Arik grasped the knife's blade. Blood streamed as his eyes unfocused. "*We* will move the planet," he said, dropping his hold on the knife before rejoining the circle. "We're not interested in an eld, imposter or otherwise, and we've done nothing to Emn. The complexity of the andal engages her. You have no place here, Neek. Go back to your planet. Leave ours."

Andal surged across the dais, lapping at Atalant's ankles. The ground fractured around her, fissures opening across the landscape. The metal and plastic structures that remained collapsed, falling amongst confused Ardulans who did not move out of the way.

"You have to stop!" The dais was rising, the ground around it falling away in fissured sinkholes. The andal teetered, awaiting a command. The knife in Atalant's hand was sticky with blood and *stuk*. She could use it on the other flares, but their deaths would not change anything. Emn was the one she had to reach, and Atalant would let the planet break apart before she'd use the knife on Emn.

She grabbed Emn's hand, trying to force out her *stuk,* desperate for a connection. "Emn, *please.*"

Emn turned her head, eyes still focused on something far away. She reached for the gathering of fabric at Atalant's hip with her free hand and ran her fingers over the silky weave. Her eyes met Atalant's, but the confusion lingered.

Flares, the andal whispered into Atalant's mind. *An open wound.*

Unhelpful, Atalant sent back. *What the hell do you want me to do about them?* When the andal offered no solution, she offered her own. *Can you connect me to Emn? Fix me?* She sent an image of grassland, andal saplings swaying gently in a breeze. *You want this? You need to help me make it happen.*

Flaresssss, the andal hissed. Then, there was streaking pain in her head, as if the roots were physically inside her brain. She felt squirming and teeming threads rearrange, focus, and break apart. Her vision broke to gray, color bleeding from the world around her.

Atalant fell to her knees, clutching her head in her hands. The pain ebbed, slowly, but the roots continued wiggling through brain crevices Atalant had been unaware even existed. When they finally slid away, she opened her eyes to patches of color. Blue spotted in first, and then yellow. Red followed, green dotting in and blending. Just beyond the spots of color was Emn. Their connection snapped back into focus almost painfully and with it, telepathy. Complete telepathy—a link with every goddamned Ardulan around her.

Atalant blocked them all as soon as they surfaced, keeping only her connection to Emn open. But there was still the andal, too, its seemingly limitless power at her control. Atalant grasped at it. She didn't know what she was doing. She didn't care. Somehow, cellulose came together and gave her the strength to reinforce her connection with Emn. She reached into the younger woman's mind and severed her link to the other flares.

Without Emn's lead, the flares could not maintain their control. They broke apart, their consciousnesses kicked from the andal and Atalant's mind. Vibrations built under Atalant's feet, this time without pauses. Emn fell into Atalant's arms as the others stumbled, gripping one another for stability.

"Atalant!"

Clear eyes looked up at her. Then, there were hands in her hair, Emn's cheek pressed against her own. The andal swirled in her mind, but Atalant ignored it. She grounded herself in Emn's touch, in the slender form pressed against hers. Atalant allowed herself one moment, arching her chest into Emn's, lingering in the contact. She wanted time to talk. To explain. To apologize for all the stupid avoidance and fear she'd been dragging between them.

The planet, Emn sent.

I know. Emn—

She didn't get a chance to finish. Hands dragged Atalant backwards, and Tik and Kisak threw her to the ground. Emn yelled, tried to reach her, but Atalant did not land. A thick mat of roots shot up underneath her, cushioning the fall. A veined fist came towards her face, but she rolled onto her side, kicking the flare's shins as she did so. Tik yelled in pain while Kisak brought zir heel to the base of Atalant's spine. Atalant fell onto her front, dirt in her mouth, whereupon Ukie straddled her back and began to land blows to her kidneys.

"We don't have time for this!" Atalant gasped as she leaned first to the right and then shifted her weight quickly to the left, flipping the woman off. She slashed the knife behind Ukie's knee, severing the connecting tissue, and leapt to her feet. This had to stop. She had to grab Emn and get someplace quiet so she could—

Kisak spun and lunged for her midsection. Atalant sidestepped and landed a fist to zir stomach, knocking out zir wind. Desperate to quickly resolve the situation, she slashed the knife along the gatoi's outer thigh, opening a shallow but long wound she hoped would be painful enough to keep zir from standing. Before she could see the results of her handiwork, Tik wrapped his arms around her from the back and tried to wrestle the knife from her hands. Atalant let her body go slack and slipped through his hold into a crouch. She brought her elbow upward and made contact with his groin, collapsing the flare in one blow. Without pause, she took the hilt of her knife and brought it down on top of his skull, knocking him unconscious.

She could see Emn just ahead, struggling against Arik. His hands were squeezing her arms to her sides. It looked like he was talking to her, perhaps trying to draw her back in. Emn struggled, but did not break away. Atalant puzzled over the situation. Emn was the strongest one here. Why she wouldn't pull cellulose...

Kisak rammed into her, ignoring zir wound. She fell onto her back, the impact again buoyed by several thick andal roots. Ukie clawed at her from her spot on the ground, fists and fingernails flying everywhere. Their desperation was palpable, even without the connection to the andal. They searched for cellulose—in the ground, the metal of the dais...the people.

Cellulose in the cotton. Atalant hadn't thought about that, hadn't thought the flares would be so callous. A sea of Ardulans lost their garments.

A moment later, she was burning. At least, that was what it felt like as the flares both shot a continuous stream of heat energy into her. Her eyes dried, and her skin felt like it was melting off as her *stuk* production went into overdrive. Atalant dropped to her knees as the flares continued their telekinetic assault. *Stuk* poured from every pore on her body, pushing off the remains of the synthetic compound she had inadvertently bathed in, coating her hair and skin. Instead of dripping to the floor, however, it built like lacquer, and with each layer, the burning feeling gradually lessened.

Open wound, the andal sent again, its tone pleading.

Busy here! Atalant yelled back. The pain was bearable. They'd run out of clothing quickly with this level of usage, and then the only cellulose left was in the people themselves. Atalant's free hand moved to her stomach, to her scar. The sound of her flesh separating was still crisp in her ears. She'd survived, but only because a medical facility had been close by. Here, there would be no hope—unless Emn could help...

Emn was sparring with Arik. Atalant felt her desperation, dodging energy, determined not to pull more to herself. Arik, however, was not so careful. The last of the mob's clothes disappeared.

"You have to stop!" Atalant yelled to the flares, hoping the command carried through the andal.

Whether the *stuk* lacquer inhibited her telepathy or whether the flares ignored her, she wasn't sure. The inevitable occurred. Ardulans began to collapse, row by row. As entire families crumpled to the ground—the cellulosic components yanked from their bodies, leaving spills of entrails and blood—Atalant understood, finally, the motivation of the previous Eld. The importance of Corccinth's work. That level of power...it would take a lifetime to wield properly. There was no way to train everyone. Those that proved they could remain in control, that escaped and lived peacefully among the rest, like Corccinth, could be trained. The rest had to be kept away from civilization. Stored. Goaded to find some internal motivation to control themselves so that *this* would never happen.

Atalant couldn't fix this. Couldn't reach all the flares to explain, not in the time she had remaining. She wasn't going to save the planet by saving the flares. Choices had to be made.

Atalant dropped the knife, her layer of *stuk* shedding as she did so. Startled at the sudden change, the flares paused long enough for Atalant to form a picture of each in her head and send a silent command.

The andal did not hesitate. Whipping strands surrounded Ukie and Kisak, pulling them down. They shrieked, struggled, released energy to burn the roots...but the andal did not react. In a sweeping movement, two thin tendrils rose and struck out at their eyes. The flares stopped moving.

The pressure in Atalant's mind raged. Wetness began to run from her ears down her neck, and when she checked it, her fingertips came back red. She could feel the impatience of the andal, its yearning to begin the move. *Just a few more minutes,* she pleaded. *We're almost sorted here.*

Heal the wound, Atalant. A chorus of trees chanted the words, each voice distinct. *Healthewoundhealthewoundhealthewound.*

Decided that arguing with trees was a waste of time, Atalant ran to the other side of the dais. There was no one blocking her field of view. Naked appendages of all melanin contents overlapped one another in a sea of death. There was no movement. No wind. There was only the vibrating planet and snap of energy from Emn and Arik, locked in one another's grip, legs braced back and arms interwoven.

She wouldn't chance the andal mistaking Emn for one of the other flares. *I want them to stay in one place,* she sent. *Leave their arms free, just root their feet and legs. I'll do the rest.*

The andal seemed pleased, she thought, as roots snaked across the clearing and began to wrap themselves around the legs of the flares. With a sudden tug, they were pulled apart, and they fell to the ground.

"Enough!" Atalant ordered in a low, cool tone. As if the trees agreed, the andal scaffolding of the palace began to unwind, branches and roots slowly receding into the ground. A breeze picked up, slowly at first, but then sent several large gusts, blowing the leaves from every tree. Just as suddenly, the breeze stopped, and the leaves swirled lazily to the ground, forming a still blanket over the Ardulan bodies.

Arik struggled against the andal, reaching for Atalant. Emn was quiet, breathing heavily, her eyes scanning the clearing.

"Do you—" Atalant paused and tried to control her breathing as she addressed the flares. "Do you have *any* concept of the magnitude of your argument here?"

A crunching sound came up behind her, and Atalant spun, reaching for a knife she no longer had. Nicholas walked towards the trio, Corccinth trailing behind him. Relief flooded through her. He was alive. The damn Journey youth. Somehow, however improbably, he had survived.

"How..." Atalant asked, choking on her relief as Nicholas reached them.

"She protected us," Nicholas answered flatly, indicating the older woman. His voice was emotionless. "I wish she wouldn't have. *Look* at this."

Arik did look, then. He dropped his arms to his sides and turned as much as he could, surveying the destruction. He paled, his breathing becoming shallow.

"It's just the capital," Corccinth croaked. She grabbed onto Nicholas's sleeve for support as a string of coughs wracked her body. "Enough of the underground flare community here to block the idiots' attack going any farther. Our network is strong, but not strong enough to protect against the move. That is your burden, Atalant. The rest of Ardulum is safe, if only for the next few minutes."

Atalant returned her attention to Arik. He looked younger, suddenly—like a lost Journey youth on his first day away from his family. Like Nicholas after that first battle on the *Pledge*.

"We..." He began to shake, small tremors stuttering through his body. The roots around both flares slowly unwound and slunk back into the ground.

"We need training," he said finally to the old woman. "I didn't... I'm *sorry*." Arik fell to his knees, gasping for breath.

Atalant stepped up to Arik, grabbed his wrist with her free hand, and jerked him to standing. She brought up her knife so it rested just below his sternum, the blade piecing the thin fabric. "An apology isn't enough. Not after this." She lowered her voice as the remains of the *stuk* patina began to move from her skin, rolling off her hair and face. Atalant pushed the knife tip in slightly, bringing a droplet of maroon to the surface of his skin.

"Emn, I can deal with. You—I'll gut you where you stand."

Still, she hesitated. In that moment, Arik turned to watch Emn, and Atalant did the same. Emn was staring at Atalant, her breath stilted. Slowly, as if she was afraid Atalant might object, Emn reached for Atalant's robe. Her fingers touched the fabric, lingered on the delicate weave, but then pulled away.

"Are you really an eld?" Emn asked in a whisper.

Heal the wound, Atalant. The Eld are threethreethree. Arik is threethreethree.

What the hell did that even mean? The command came again, a single, solitary voice that echoed through her mind, much louder than before.

Atalant scowled. *I'm not a healer. You are out of luck.*

The wound, Atalant. The wound of threethreethree. The command was back to communicating in shadowy wisps, as if the andal was trying to decide which tone she reacted better to.

"Argh!" she yelled out loud, startling Emn. *Stop speaking to me in fucking nonsense!*

Two images clouded her mind, so dense that she was briefly disoriented. The first showed Arik, on his stomach, the Dulan knife arching from his back. The second showed him dressed in the same golden robe she wore. The second Arik smiled and held out a hand, but melted with the first image back into reality.

"Okay, right." Atalant muttered. "Clearer, I guess. He's an eld—I'm an eld. We're all elds, even though he is only second *don* and this is technically impossible. Great." She offered Emn a smile. "The andal seems to think so, anyway. I'm still working on it."

Emn nodded and backed away, so Atalant returned to Arik. She twisted his wrist, her *stuk* production increasing. The pores on her right hand opened, and *stuk* poured onto Arik and hardened, the casing joining their arms. Arik moved his hand away from his face and straightened. In his eyes, she could see a mixture of defiance and hope.

"Sentient beings live by the rules their society sets, or they work within the system to change them." Atalant's voice was hard, unwavering. "The flares need help, maybe more intense training, or maybe genetic counseling, but whatever it is, I'm willing to work with you and the rest to figure it out." She moved the knife away and tossed it towards Corccinth. "I need your help. The planet is moving. The andal is prepped. The mental weight is below the threshold. Everything is prepared, but I can't guide it alone. There are supposed to be three of us, but there's only me. I need you, and the andal seems to think you are just the guy for the job. But if you do this—" Atalant paused and pointed to the leaf-covered ground, "—you do it right. You follow the rules. You agree to training. You atone for what you did here today."

As if in response, the andal tendrils riding on Atalant's back swarmed over her front and around her arm, further binding her to Arik.

Arik watched the roots, steadying his breathing. Atalant caught fragments of memory. Arik was planting seeds in a field he'd turned by hand. He was watering first-year saplings, picking insects from their leaves. He was a first *don*, sitting between rows, reading his favorite stories to trees no taller than he was. The andal swayed to his words. The leaves curled at his touch. They listened.

"The andal..." he whispered. "I had a dream like this once, you know."

"Yeah," Atalant returned, as the wisps of andal consciousness seemed to flow through her mind and into Arik. "I've had a couple of those, too."

Arik's eyes closed for a moment. "I know these whispers, Atalant. I heard them in my saplings. Heard them before I killed Adzeek." He looked at her with wide eyes. "I just wanted to get back home. How much of this did the andal plan, do you think?" His voice cracked with emotion as his hand began to shake. "Since my time on the plantation? When I was tending all those saplings, pretending to talk to them..."

"Damned if I know," Atalant responded, a small smile breaking across her face. "Sometimes you just have to roll with it, you know? Like a root ball."

Arik laughed—a short, barking sound. Following the andal, his mind fell into hers.

"Time to heal the wounds," she whispered. "All of them."

Chapter 30: Eld Palace, Ardulum

Proceed to Neek space.
—Broadband command to the Alliance and Charted Systems fleets, January 12th, 2061 CE

THE GROUND WAS shaking again. The whispering in Atalant's head turned into a whirlwind. Her vision blanked as Arik's consciousness rose back up, clear and focused, and slammed into hers as wave after wave of andal linked and corded around their minds. Atalant couldn't tell if her sudden motion sickness was from the actual movement of the planet or from the image of swirling andal connections she was somehow visualizing.

It's too chaotic, Arik yelled over the mental din. *We have to order it or the planet will unravel. Sort of like cellulose, I think, except now, we get to be the interfacial agent and the planet is the lignin.*

What the fuck are you talking about? Atalant yelled back. She batted at the bustling andal wisps, trying to clear a space for her own thoughts. More and more entered—twisting, seething, pushing Arik's mind from hers. She could feel him slipping to the periphery.

Where are you? she yelled through the mass in her mind. It was increasingly difficult to remain connected to Arik. The andal caught her thoughts, twisted and consumed them.

We are supposed to have a third anchor, filtered back through the noise. *It's.... cellulose...for the third....*

He was gone, then, tangled in the andal sentience and too buried to reach. Panic surged through Atalant—except it wasn't her own, and it definitely wasn't Arik's. She fought the foreign feeling, tried to calm it, but the emotions grew stronger. She needed to scream. She needed to run. She needed to *go.* It didn't matter where, she just couldn't be here anymore. Here wasn't where she belonged.

A connection sparked as the andal dove deeper into her mind.

Abruptly, Atalant was on the beach of her home province, her brother by her side. The tide was out, and there was a seemingly endless sandbar ahead, pristine and sparkling. They stood at the water's edge, letting the waves wash the sand underneath their feet.

"You should apply," her brother said. He had an application in his hand. It was on paper—the crisp, white pages batted in the wind. Atalant didn't have to look at it to know what it was for. Only the Heaven Guard used such old technology.

"I like it here. Besides, I want to be a pilot, but not *that* kind of pilot." Atalant scowled at the paper and then up at her brother. Her hair blew in front of her face, and she pulled at the strands with sticky fingers. "Why do we always talk about this, about me leaving Neek? This is my home. In a few years—"

"In a few years, Atalant, things will be very different." Her brother knelt down, took her hand in one of his, and pressed the crumbled paper into the other. "Sometimes, home isn't where we belong. Right now, this, here—" He tugged at the paper. "—is what you need to do. You don't have to believe in Ardulum to be a heaven guard. Just push all the religion crap from your mind. Piloting is a science, just like anything else. Nothing magical about it."

Atalant clasped her hands across her chest and kicked at the sand. "Yeah fine," she muttered. "It still sounds like a stupid idea."

The sounds of the ocean gave way to the cracking of ground—to its separation and its reforming. The memory drifted away but her brother's words lingered. He'd always been the one to encourage her disbelief, to argue for rational thought. Maybe she was making this whole moving thing too complicated. Atalant considered what she knew about Talents, about the flares' unique gifts and their microkinetic abilities. What had Nicholas said back on the *Pledge* the first time Emn had fried a Risalian ship—she tried to remember as the andal chased her thoughts—about cellulose, about wood structure, about microfibrils...?

Atalant needed to find Arik again. She could test her hypothesis without him, but needed his greater reach—his ability to automate processes that came from his being a flare—to make any significant change.

She needed a path in her mind. Atalant lashed out at the andal, pushing the wisps off her, out of her, *away*. The mass recoiled and compressed and then began to slide back—individual consciousnesses snaking at the periphery. Like filaments. Like cellulose. Just like cellulose, she hoped, it could be ordered, stacked, and bound.

This time when Atalant reached out, she pulled a handful towards herself, maneuvering one over the other, interweaving each triad into a chain. Just like she had seen Emn do all those months ago, back on the *Pledge,* when Ardulum had still been a fairy tale. She stacked the chain as it grew, forming a lattice that looked almost crystalline. Now there was breathing room. She formed another chain, stacked, and was able to push her mind forward again. Pull, push, overlap, and reorder. Arik's presence began to filter back in.

...out of the way...

She lost him as another influx of andal pressed forward. Unfazed, Atalant wove it into the matrix. Fibrils formed. Space cleared. She gained ground.

...Atalant! I...in the andal...you need to order the filaments.

I hear you! Push. Pull. Overlap. Reorder. Repeat. Then, he was there, a solid presence again in her mind. Arik was tired, his fatigue radiating across the andal.

Emn can automate her microkinesis, Atalant sent as she continued to order the andal around her, creating a sort of clear path forward. *Create chain reactions. You'll have to do the same. I can't keep up this level of interaction and neither can you. Without a third eld, it's our best chance at succeeding.*

As if emboldened by her thoughts, the andal presence increased. Strands whipped through Atalant's mind, pushing at her, threatening her connection with Arik. She tried to send words of encouragement, but the thoughts boomeranged back, encased in andal. She was hearing words, however, through the mass. Not words made of letters—they were more like dreams, fanciful modifiers. It reminded Atalant of Emn's speech, before she could speak. A child's mind and a child's game, the naming of objects with pictures.

Those pictures wove through the andal and through Atalant's mind: a stream green with algae, a purple meadow flower, an ant triumphant atop its mound... Hundreds more, each unique, and all seeming to search for someone. They queried her, searched her mind, and swooped away to the place where Arik's consciousness lay. His trees. His saplings. They had found him.

Her path filled, and once again it was oppressively hard to breath. Atalant felt physical roots on her arms and shoulders, pulling her down to the earth. They were on her legs, binding them together, across her throat—

Color surged. Roots and the consciousness fell back, snapped to order as Arik plowed into the andal. Push. Pull. Overlap. Reorder. Repeat. Except, Arik's abilities were exponentially greater than hers. He called some of the andal by name and they followed—curling into other strands, winding the wilder cousins together. With each reach, he bound thousands of consciousnesses, setting into motion the command for thousands more. The andal fell from Atalant, from both her body and her mind, as Arik stacked, ordered, and latticed. His cellulose reserves were gone. With the concentration and energy required for his task, Atalant felt Arik reach into his own circulatory system, desperate to fuel his Talents.

Then, it was done. The last wisp fell into structure—a perfectly ordered crystalline framework where fibrils alternated directions to form interlocked connections. Arik sagged behind the andal, exhausted.

All done? Atalant queried the andal. *Time to actually move the planet now that you're all packed?*

Alldonealldonealldone, the andal echoed smugly.

The andal slipped from Atalant's mind, dragging Arik behind it and leaving Atalant alone with her thoughts. Something like grass tickled Atalant's knees. Unsure of what to expect, she opened her eyes to bright daylight instead of moonlight. The andal was gone from her body. The *stuk* had melted off.

She released Arik's wrist and, as she pulled her hand away, paused. She tightened her fingers again, this time catching just Arik's two longest digits, as she pulled his arm up closer to her face.

The direct sunlight from above reflected harshly off of Arik's yellow skin—unmarked save for the three interlinked circles she saw on the inside of his wrist. A Science Talent. Before Arik had a chance to react, she grabbed his other hand and moved it palm up, confirming matching symbols on his right wrist as well.

Arik grimaced. "I think they're on my right side, as well," he said. "The skin feels tender there, anyway. The rest...I think they burned off. I had to use so much blood..."

Atalant released his hands and pointed to the hem of his shirt. "Do you mind?" she asked.

Arik shook his head and lifted the corner of his shirt, exposing the right side of his torso. His nearly translucent skin shone in the light. Atalant squinted and leaned in. Faint red hexagonal forms were just visible beneath his armpit—the marking for his new Aggression Talent. She wasn't sure how many, nor if the light was just playing tricks with her eyes.

"My head is a lot lighter," Arik said as he put his shirt down, "and we've moved, obviously." He sagged against Atalant, leaning heavily on her shoulder, but kept his eyes on the overhead sun. "I thought it would involve a lot more physics than that."

Atalant took a moment to look around as well. Just off to her right stood Nicholas and Corccinth, Emn in front of them. All three had wary expressions. They were lightly dusted in dirt, as if they had fallen several times. Except, the ground, Atalant noted, wasn't just dirt anymore. It had flattened and come back together. The Ardulan bodies had disappeared and the marketplace and building structures had vanished, replaced with thousands of first-year andal saplings, each busily unfurling new leaves and bobbing gently in the breeze. Looking up, Atalant saw buds forming on the older trees and smelled the rich scent of pollen in the air. A bright, red sun hung overhead.

Finally, Atalant's eyes settled on Emn. The younger woman took a step forward, paused, and stepped back. She looked away.

"Damn," Atalant muttered to herself. She glanced at Arik, making sure he could keep himself upright, and took three quick steps over to Emn and tilted her head up with a *stuk*-covered finger. Emn's eyes searched Atalant's, unsure.

That was... Emn trailed off. She ran fingertips down the length of Atalant's gold sleeve, lingering on the cuff.

"Hey," Atalant said softly, offering a reassuring smile. "It's just a robe, right?"

Emn nodded but remained silent. Her presence was back, however, in Atalant's mind. It was much subtler than the andal, which, despite its complacency, still murmured. Comforted that at least their connection had not changed, Atalant took Emn's hands. She wanted to kiss Emn— here, finally, in this field of andal saplings and bright sunlight—but understood what sat behind Emn's hesitancy.

"Eld, what happened?" Emn's voice was whispery. "Did you cure Arik?"

"Nothing's cure." Corccinth stepped past Atalant and grabbed Arik, bringing him closer to the group. "Flares are not broken. Eld of old had correct intentions, but makings were poor. Of this we often spoke." She looked pointedly at Atalant. "Here new Eld can make changes. Reconsidered policy." She brought up Arik's wrists one by one and studied them, making little chortling noises as she did so. When she was satisfied, she released his arms, hiked up his shirt, and moved her face so close to his side that her nose touched his flesh.

Arik raised his eyebrows at Atalant, who shrugged.

Corccinth raised her hand and slapped the red outlines on his side. Arik yelled, pulling his shirt down, and rubbed the bruised area. He glared at the woman. "What in Ardulum's name was that for!?"

"A Neek and a not-flare," she muttered to herself. "About time." Corccinth brought a long sleeve to her face and wiped off the makeup. Underneath the heavy foundation, Atalant saw the outline of two black triangles just under her eyes.

"About time for what?" Arik asked irritably. He looked over at Atalant. "Does she ever speak straight to you?"

The woman rounded on him and shoved a finger at his face, glowering. "You have ten years for train. You must learn to focus!"

"When you're ready, Atalant," Nicholas said, "and no rush, but when you're ready, we'd better start walking. The flares took out every building and being in a ten-kilometer radius, and it is another ten from the outskirts of the capital to the next town over. If we want shelter tonight, we'll need to get going, unless you want to create some magical andal tents for us to sleep in."

Atalant sighed and straightened her sash. She caught the quirking of Nicholas's mouth and glared at him. "You don't have any quips about the intolerable irony of my current situation? No words of solace or congratulations? I did just move a planet, after all."

Nicholas snickered as he wrapped an arm around Atalant's shoulders. Together, they began to pick their way across the andal field. The others fell in step behind them, and Emn's presence lingered in Atalant's mind, swaying with her own thoughts.

"Nope," the Journey youth said, failing to keep the mirth from his tone. "I know better than to poke a god. At least not on the first day of the job. We'll see about tomorrow."

Chapter 31: Sorin, Ardulum

I don't know how to describe the early days. I'm not sure I could even describe my current state. I certainly don't know what the future holds. Words like "confident" and "drowning" come at the same time to my mind. I suppose I can understand, now, why the Eld would cut themselves off from the populace, fear the flares. When you have this, this encasing presence in your mind—both awesome in its state as a trophobiont, providing food for the Ardulans in exchange for the Eld's guidance through space and reproduction assistance, and also terrifying in its abilities, especially those it confers to the Ardulans— how could you not be overwhelmed? Isolation provides comfort—I know that all too well. It gives you a sense of control over your life and circumstances. Unfortunately, that control is an illusion when you are interwoven into something like this. Ardulum...being an eld...being responsible for a collectively conscious biome—I know there's a word for this job. I just don't want to use it.

—Excerpt from *Atalant's Awakening*, published in the Charted Systems, 235 AA

ATALANT AWOKE TO the chirping of a small insect on the windowsill near her head. Her calf and side itched, and she gave each a furious scratch before turning onto her back. The shutters to the window were open, and despite the night sky, her room was bright with the reflection from three moons. She heard movement from the room next to her, the creaking of floorboards, and then a steady fall of water. A tube bath seemed like a sound idea—she just didn't think she could get out of bed to bother with it.

She knew she needed to sleep more. They'd arrived just after dusk at the outskirts of Sorin—a busy suburb which, from the number of inns lining the main road, was part of a bustling tourist trade. Atalant's and

Arik's markings had been enough to get them a host of rooms and dinner, no questions asked. She'd taken her share of dinner to her room, picked at the andal stalks that she supposed she'd have to develop a taste for, and then collapsed onto the soft bed.

How long had she been asleep? Only the first moon had started to show when she'd closed her eyes, but since she had no idea where they were, that meant nothing. How far could Ardulum travel in one move? Did planets use wormholes or did a giant, sentient root ball have some type of space flagella that it could retract when not in use? What the hell was she going to do if they were in an inhabited system and the neighbors decided to drop by?

Atalant covered her face with her hands and blew against them, willing her fatigue to exit along with her breath. When that didn't work, she swung her legs over the side of the bed and stood, deciding to give up on sleep. At their suggestion, the inn owners had provided her with a change of clothing while they attempted to remove the stains from Asth's robe. Her robe. Whatever. The point was that she didn't have to wear it currently, which was what mattered.

The cool linen pants and cotton shirt they'd provided were appropriately sized for her frame and were by far the most formfitting clothes she'd worn in a long time. Her boots had made it through the whole ordeal completely unscathed aside from some minor staining, but Atalant decided against wearing them. Instead, she lightly walked from her room, into the corridor, and to the main dining hall. She wasn't at all surprised to find Nicholas sitting outside just next to the door, his head leaning against the wall, staring at the moons.

"You'll probably go blind if you keep that up," she said as she sat next to him. "Hope you don't mind some company."

Nicholas grinned but kept his eyes upwards. "Knew you wouldn't be sleeping either." He pointed to the moon on the far right. "That one sort of looks like Earth's moon—even has craters in the same place. Looks kind of like a face, if you squint just right."

Atalant squinted and tried to see it. She tilted her head and then elbowed Nicholas playfully. "Sure this isn't a 'make the Neek look stupid' game?"

Laughing, Nicholas finally turned his head to look at her. "No, it isn't. I promise. You ever been to Earth, Atalant?"

She shook her head. "Never. Yorden kept saying we should go, but none of our runs ever took us past Mars. Earth is a little backwater. Not like Neek, but close."

Nicholas nodded and looked back up. "So, we only have one moon. One sun too, but that is pretty normal, and only one wormhole connection. Our people never really unified, like on a lot of other worlds, so we're still pretty culturally diverse, too. Probably have a couple of thousand gods, if not more. Some are more popular than others, but trends in that change over time, too."

"I really don't want to talk about this, Nick," Atalant said, tension creeping into her voice. "It has been a long day."

"Then why are you out here with me, sitting on a wood slab, instead of talking to Emn?" Nicholas turned onto his right hip and regarded Atalant. "I know things got out of control. But this is a big deal, Atalant."

"Seems like everything we do these days is a big deal," she muttered.

"No," he countered. "Rescuing and defending a lost child was the right thing to do. Trying to even the odds in the Crippling War was a reaction to circumstances. This—" He pointed to her calf. "—is different. This isn't us mucking about in events beyond our control, or even us trying to alter someone's fate. This is something cosmic, maybe mythical. I don't know the right word. You're the leader of a planet that is worshipped by other planets, including your own. That's *big*."

"Yeah," she muttered in response. "I know." Atalant kicked her heel at a pile of leaves and sent them skittering into the wind as she debated her next words. "My telepathy is back, but I still get all this feedback from the andal. All the time. It's sort of like the whole planet is breathing in my head, if that doesn't sound too nuts."

Nicholas bumped his shoulder into hers and grinned. "Nope. Sounds just nuts enough for this crew."

Atalant shifted and leaned against the youth. "Arik's in it too. The andal wants him—for a decent reason, I suppose—except he's too young to flare into his Aggression Talent or some nonsense like that, so he's got training marks instead. Old Corccinth was trying to explain it to me on the walk, but eventually, I stopped listening." She picked up one of the leaves and traced its veins with her thumb, soothed by the topography. "There has to be a third, logically, since the Eld are a triarchy, but who knows when zie will flare or, if zie has, where zie is hiding out. I've got a populace to soothe, a capital to rebuild, and a bunch of families to apologize to for the death of their loved ones. I don't have time to go looking for another eld."

Atalant took a deep breath and blew as she exhaled, making a loose whistling sound with her lips. "Oh, and the andal wants to reproduce. Did I mention that? I assume that means there are some suitable planets in this system, and tomorrow I have to go down to meet the inhabitants, convince them to plant andal monocultures, and, according to Ardulum, interbreed with their populace."

"Or you could, you know, fuck history," Nicholas offered. "You're in charge now, more or less."

"Technically, I think the andal is in charge," Atalant returned.

"But it listens to you, doesn't it? Can't you make suggestions? Have deep, philosophical conversations about invasive species and the long-term health effects of andal plantations?"

Atalant sighed. "Probably. I'm taking the night off though." She caught herself as Nicholas moved away, taking her support along with him. He stood, brushing the dust from his pants. "Hey!" she called out, indignant. "I was comfortable."

"Our time is up," he quipped, moving back inside. "I'll bill you for the whole hour. Besides, there is someone here to see you."

As Nicholas moved back through the doorway, a taller figure took his place. Her long hair was tied back, and she was wearing fresh clothes similar to the ones the inn owners had given Atalant.

"Hey," Atalant said gently as Emn took Nicholas's spot on the wood step.

"Hey," Emn returned, looking at anything but Atalant. They'd been keeping their distance, both mentally and physically, since the move. Atalant didn't want to pry, so instead, she studied Emn, visually tracing the black patterns on her skin in the moonlight. Flares. She'd have to do something about them, too, pretty soon—and that didn't even include "unfracturing" the Ardulans the flares hadn't managed to kill, if there were any. She wanted to curse, but realized that most of the Neek and Terran curses she knew involved a form of the word "god." She'd have to come up with some more colorful language.

"Lot of things to come to terms with," Atalant said, hoping she wouldn't scare Emn off. It wasn't fair that Atalant had managed to work through all her baggage just in time to have the tables turned. The andal probably thought it was funny—like her life was some big cosmic joke.

"Yeah," Emn returned, her voice muffled in her legs.

When Emn didn't continue, Atalant decided to let that conversation die. She'd have to have a discussion, a long one, with the underground flares soon. Now, however, wasn't the time. Instead, Atalant let the silence stretch, filling her mind with the sounds of night—the strange insect chirps and leaf rustling that reminded her so much of her own homeworld.

When Emn turned her face to Atalant, the pilot tried again to engage her. "Want to see them?"

"See what?"

"The markings."

"Oh." Emn sat up, curiosity evident on her face. Atalant grinned and hoisted the right side of her shirt, exposing the hexagons. She let Emn trace each with a soft fingertip before letting the shirt down and showing her calf. Atalant hadn't realized how intimate the touch could be. Maybe her markings were more sensitive because they were new. Maybe they were more sensitive because this was Emn. Either way, she wanted Emn's hand to stay there, on her skin, instead of pulling back. Maybe if they went inside...

Whoa. No. Now she was the one that was pushing. And blushing. She could feel the heat in her cheeks. She decided to diffuse the situation. That was what she did best, wasn't it? Avoidance? "You didn't tell me they hurt when they come in," she joked. "They itch, too."

Emn pulled her hand back, and her face fell. "I guess I didn't think about that. I'm sorry."

They were back here again. Damn it. Atalant sighed silently and again tried to change the subject. "How are you feeling?"

"I don't think there are Common words for it," Emn responded as she rested her head back on her legs.

That reminded Atalant—she had to start learning the native Ardulan language as well, and probably the dominant language of this new system. She could possibly squeeze that in between tomorrow and the end of her sanity, which was a quickly narrowing time frame.

"Yeah," Atalant agreed. She reached over and put a hand on Emn's shoulder. They were still at the shoulder stage, right? That wasn't intruding, surely. She'd need to do something more, though, to put them back on track. Not something big, just...something familiar. "I get that. We'll talk—you, me, Corccinth, and Arik. But not tonight." She moved her hand to Emn's head and tucked a stray lock of hair behind her ear. "Come sit with me?"

Without looking up, Emn scooted herself over to Atalant until their hips touched. With a sigh, she turned her head and looked up at Atalant. "You're my Eld," she said in a soft tone.

"I'm your friend, too," Atalant responded. "Unless things have changed." It didn't come out as a question, although she realized it probably should have been.

In a surprising move, Emn sat up and wrapped an arm around Atalant's shoulder, pulling her in. The gesture was relaxing, and Atalant gratefully rested her head. The multitude of tasks ahead slipped from her mind, drowning in Emn's heartbeat and the chirping of nighttime insects. The andal rested, for now, in the corners of Atalant's mind—stacked neatly in its crystal latticework and content with its present form. Here, now, in Emn's arms, Atalant almost felt the same. Friends. It wasn't what Atalant wanted—it wasn't what either of them wanted—but it was a good place to start.

They sat together in silence. Atalant watched the slow progression of the moons, every so often finding her eyelids too heavy to keep open. Her telepathy was back to rights, but her link with Emn was different now. Sharper. Her link with everything was sharper, which meant the needs of the flares, her friends, the populace, and the andal all rang in her head. Why did there have to be so much to do? Maybe if she asked Emn really nicely, she could convince her that they should all fly somewhere remote...

WISPS OF GOLD and orange were just starting to color the horizon when Atalant next opened her eyes. Her body had slouched in sleep, and her head now rested in Emn's lap. The morning was chilly, and despite the warmth coming from Emn's arm and the thickness of her shirt, Atalant shivered. Her hip was sore from digging into the wooden platform beneath her, but she felt rested, if only a little.

"Morning?" she asked as she sat up. She rubbed her eyes and yawned, keeping her body close to Emn for warmth.

"I think so," Emn responded. She pointed up at where Atalant could see faint gray streaks in the auburn sky. "Flybys are happening. I've seen at least four different shapes of craft, already."

Atalant groaned and put her head on Emn's shoulder. The fabric smelled of andal sap and the scented water the young woman used to wash her hair. It took her a moment to realize that other smells were starting to waft to her as well—andal cooking, along with the blissful aroma of frying meat. That likely meant Nicholas was up.

"Nicholas and I have been watching them for the last two hours." Emn ran her hand up and down Atalant's arm, and the pilot smiled, grateful for the warmth. "He's got a communicator hooked up to the Ardulan grid. You can broadcast to the planet whenever you're up to it."

"Anyone tried to contact the ships, by chance?" Atalant asked, refusing to move her head. "Maybe apologize for screwing up gravitational forces or whatever else Ardulum managed to do when it got here?" The waft of meat was growing stronger, overtaking the andal and making her stomach rumble.

Emn's hand stilled. "No, not yet. That's your call to make, not ours."

That made Atalant scowl. The rest of them were just as capable of making decisions today as they were yesterday, godhood or not. In fact, screw yesterday and everything that had led up to it. *She* was going to make some decisions, right now, that she probably should have made a long time ago. Atalant raised her head and caught Emn's eyes, bringing a cold hand to the young woman's cheek before she could turn away. "I'm not interested in a solo gig. I'm doing this with you, or not at all. And I want..." She paused, fumbling for the words as Emn's eyebrows rose. "Friendship is great, but I'd like something more. With you."

Emn's face broke into a smile, the tension smoothing from her forehead. Atalant couldn't help the smile that spread across her face in response. Emn took Atalant's hand from her cheek and stood, pulling Atalant with her. "Breakfast is ready—yours and mine. Best to address the planet on a full stomach."

"Is that a yes, then?"

Emn paused and turned back, meeting Atalant's eyes. There was humor playing at the corners of her mouth, but Atalant caught the hesitation as well. "What is it you're asking for, Eld?" she whispered.

Exasperated, Atalant dropped Emn's hand and pointed to the stars. "I'm asking for your help! Arik is too young for flaring and has to go through some weird training with the andal, and I have no clue who the third eld is. I refuse to do this alone!" Her tone softened. "I need your guidance. I need your power, in as much as you can handle safely. Help me guide these people and this ridiculous planet, Emn. Please."

Emn stared, unblinking. That question—the one Atalant had been avoiding, that hung unspoken between them, was back. Atalant looked at the ground. She dug her big toe into the soft springwood of the flooring and thought about the andal groves her brother had shown her as a child. She thought about her uncle, how proud he'd been when she'd applied to join the Heaven Guard. She thought about her family, the loss of her mother, and what it would be like to walk into her childhood home in the robes of an eld.

She thought about the woman in front of her, who had been so patient, and who was waiting, now, for words Atalant owed her a dozen times over.

Atalant raised her head, looking into green eyes, nervous and hopeful. "I'm ready to stop running."

Emn's arms were around her then, the younger woman's cheek against hers, a heartbeat—hers? Emn's?—loud in her ears. "From everything?" Emn asked cautiously, her voice barely above a whisper.

Atalant laughed then—happily, loudly—a sound she couldn't remember having made in a long time. She pulled the tie from Emn's hair, ran a hand through the thick strands, and then pushed up ever so lightly on her toes so she could meet Emn's lips. The kiss started as a light brush, but Emn was pulling Atalant in a moment later. Atalant hadn't known what to expect—her time on the *Pledge* hadn't often come with enough shore leave to explore something as intimate as kissing, but Emn had no problem taking the lead. She pressed their bodies tightly together, their breasts aligning almost perfectly thanks to their near identical heights. Atalant's tongue gained entrance and gave ground as Emn pushed back, exploring territory no longer restricted. Then, Emn's lips were on her cheek, and then her jawline, before they met her own once again. The silly remainder of Atalant's hesitation sparked into desire. Why had she waited so long for this? Why had she ever thought this would be anything less than perfect?

They stayed there, kissing and laughing and holding one another, until the sunlight on Atalant's neck became too hot and she had to step away, moving into the shade of the main room. Emn followed, their hands still gripped together. Inside, a long wood table was set up, covered with a dark tablecloth of woven andal bark. Nicholas was already seated with his elbows on the table and a smug grin on his face. Atalant knew her face had to be crimson, but fuck it all, she didn't care. She was an eld, wasn't she? She'd kiss whomever she damn well pleased.

Two pots of steaming andal sat in the middle of the table, surrounded by small platters of *bilaris* fruit and thin strips of crisp meat. The inn owners stood just behind the chair at the head of the table—two elderly men in pressed cotton suits. The taller man pulled a thick wood chair out for Atalant, bowing his head as he did so.

"Take it." Arik approached from her right. His skin wasn't as sickly today, although the dark circles under his eyes told Atalant plenty about his night. "Emn will be welcome next to you. I'll take the other end, if it is all right."

Nicholas held up a small disc communicator and waved it in the air. "When you're ready, it's all yours. Just hit the main button and you can talk to the whole planet." His grin got wider. "Some of us were working this morning."

Emn laughed and squeezed her hand. Their time had been much better spent, in Atalant's opinion, but her smile broadened anyway as she looked around the circular room. The Ardulan patrons lined the walls, staring at her with a mixture of awe and confusion. She felt their hesitation and reverence and wondered how she looked to them in her crumpled clothing, dried *stuk* still clinging to parts of her skin.

Nicholas threw a soft piece of andal at her arm. It slid from the slippery fabric and hit the floor with a wet plop. "You going to sit and eat so the rest of us can? You can contemplate godhood after breakfast."

She and Emn likely wouldn't have a chance to be alone again for a long time, so Atalant leaned to her right and kissed Emn, in front of everyone, shaking off the events of yesterday as easily as she had Asth's robe the night before. Keeping a tight grip on the younger woman's hand, Atalant moved to the head of the table and sat, releasing Emn at the chair nearest hers. Their eyes met for a long moment and the warmth Emn sent along their bond buoyed Atalant's confidence enough for her to turn away and address the room.

"Okay, everyone," she said, clapping her hands together, and reached for the bacon. "Food first. Then, we figure out how to fix this mess."

Glossary of Ardulan Talents

SCIENCE: Skills of creation, including biology, chemistry, agriculture, design, art, healing, and telepathy.

    Markings: Three linked, black circles on the inside of each wrist.

AGGRESSION: Skills of assertion, including innate knowledge of weapons, warfare, trade, land development, leadership, and exploration.

    Markings: A variable number (usually seven to ten) of hexagons linked across the right side of the torso. Can span from armpit to hip.

HEARTH: Skills of domesticity, including the arts of protection, shielding, child rearing, teaching, spiritual guidance, animal husbandry, public relations, and construction.

    Markings: Exactly four hexagons aligned side by side on the left shoulder.

MIND: Skills of critical thinking, including piloting, problem assessment, mathematics, music, and physics.

    Markings: A set of three equilateral triangles, intersecting at one point on the back of the left calf.

About the Author

J.S. Fields is a scientist who has perhaps spent too much time around organic solvents. She enjoys roller derby, woodturning, making chain mail by hand, and cultivating fungi in the backs of minivans. Nonbinary, but prefers female pronouns. Always up for a Twitter chat.

Email: chlorociboria@gmail.com

Website: http://www.jsfieldsbooks.com

Twitter: @galactoglucoman

Also by J.S. Fields

Ardulum: First Don

Coming Soon from J.S. Fields

Ardulum: Third Don

Prologue

JANUARY 12TH, 2061 CE

"I've just lost my last engine! We're making repairs, but if we can't dodge another hit—" The audio cut off. A small, blue light on Ekimet's console went dark.

Inside the Neek's main temple to Ardulum, Ekimet laid zir head in zir hands and, not for the first time, tried to will the light to come back on. It didn't work. It never worked. All the power of Ardulum, and Ekimet couldn't save even one Ardulan life.

The andal bench upon which zie sat lacked cushioning, and the wood was warm through Ekimet's gold robes. Zir tailbone hurt from sitting and waiting—and zir heart hurt from watching and trying to coordinate a battle zie had no skills for. No one in the room did. The Eld had ensured that.

Ekimet brought zir head back up. Next to zir, Miketh tapped on the andal table, a thin sheet of bioplastic just beyond her reach. Her black hair had lost its red highlights. Ekimet hadn't noticed until now, and zie didn't have time to consider what it meant aside from neither of them having gone outside in a month.

The High Priest of Neek was on the other side of the wooden table. He was supposed to be helping, inasmuch as he could as a subspecies Neek amongst Ardulans. Right now, however, he sat, eyes unfocused, wringing his robes as he whispered, "Seven. Seven Ardulan cutters and fourteen skiffs lost."

"Central, copy? Copy, please!" The Neek accent was clear over the transmission and startled Ekimet. It was a settee pilot, one of the Heaven Guard.

"We hear you, guard," Miketh answered. Her hand shook as she reached for the bioplastic sheet. It was just far enough on the other side of the table that the high priest had to push it towards her. "Report?"

"The Mmnnuggl pods in orbit, both big and small, are now guarded by at least four of the oval ships the Ardulans can't seem to hit. There are Risalian cutters out here too, and a bunch of ships I don't recognize. No matter how much interference we run for the Ardulans, it isn't making any difference. Nothing is making a difference. The Mmnnuggls are picking off the cutters one by one."

"Is your squadron still intact?" Miketh asked. "No Neek casualties?"

The voice came back confused. "No, no casualties to report on our side. The Mmnnuggls only seem interested in..." On the computer console in front of Ekimet, another pale blue light went dark.

"We lost another skiff," Ekimet reported in a monotone. Zie and Miketh knew how the battle would end. The Ardulans in the ships...they didn't, and the Neek certainly didn't. Leadership was needed, not tears. "Only four remain, along with two cutters."

"One cutter," the guard reported hesitantly. A red light went out on Ekimet's console. "A group of four pods just disintegrated the largest one."

Ekimet squeezed zir eyes shut. There were over forty Ardulans on each cutter and two per skiff. It had been less than an hour since the Mmnnuggls had engaged the Ardulan fleet. What was happening? That the Ardulans and Neek would lose had never been in question, but they weren't meant to lose like *this*.

Ekimet leaned towards Miketh and the speaker. "Tell the remaining cutter to—"

One of the skiff pilots cut into the feed. "We just lost our last cutter!" The last red light on Ekimet's dash went out. "Ekimet, we have to land. We haven't got a chance with the—" The line went dead. The final three blue lights died in quick succession.

There was silence for a long moment, followed by the uncomfortable shuffling of feet. The Ardulans were dead. Every ship the Eld had sent, every Ardulan onboard, was now scattered in fragments across Neek space. Ekimet and Miketh were...they were stranded. Again. They, and the Neek planet, had no protection.

"My lords?" The settee pilot was back. "The Mmnnuggl forces are leaving the engagement zone. Their allies are following. The Heaven Guard are still in orbit. Would you like us to follow instead of simply watching and reporting?"

"No!" Miketh said quickly before Ekimet could answer. "You have no weapons or shields. Don't make a threat you can't carry through. Just...just come back." She looked at Ekimet, moisture beading in her eyes. She hastily wiped at it with the back of her hand. "Just come home, okay?"

Relief flooded the pilot's voice. "As you say, my Eld. I'll tell the rest of the Heaven Guard."

The transmission ended. Miketh sniffed, and Ekimet did the same, although zie was far too well trained to let tears form.

"Is it over?" The high priest pushed his chair back from the dark andal table, his eyes on Ekimet's chin, never higher. "Will they leave? What do they want?"

We are about to find out. Miketh pointed at the yellow line streaking across the dash. *Call for you, Eki. We both know how this ends.*

Indeed. They'd been sent here to die, the same as the fleet. Sent to appease the Mmnnuggls. Sent to keep Ardulum safe. Ekimet slid zir finger across the yellow line, and an audio feed beeped. Zie could have turned on the Neek's archaic hologram projector, but...zie couldn't look at a Mmnnuggl. Not right now. Not with so many dead bodies floating above zir.

"You have lost," a monotone voice said over the comm.

"We understand that. Only two Ardulans remain, and we are prepared to surrender. We...we thank you for not harming the Neek forces."

A low trill resounded before it changed to words. "Only Ardulans harm unarmed civilians. Only *Ardulans* would use a seeded planet of primitive sentients as a sacrifice." The Mmnnuggl screeched. "Do you think we do not see a ruse when we see one? We have no hands and no feet, so therefore we have no *minds*?"

Ekimet tried to cut in. "We never meant—"

"*You* are of no concern to us. Two Ardulans mean nothing." There was a whirring in the background, and then a new voice came on.

It didn't have the usual clicking undertones of a Mmnnuggl accent. This voice, although deep and throaty, carried Common with ease. "Call your planet," it said. It sounded male, by Ardulan standards. "Call your planet and tell them to send the Eld of Ardulum and the flare named Emn. You have one week to comply."

"One week!" Miketh said, her voice unusually high. "The Neek operate on *stable wormhole* technology. The time frame is unmanageable. Beyond that, if you aren't bargaining with Neek lives, what is your collateral? The Neek planet is self-sustaining. They don't care to travel. If you think Ekimet and I will get frustrated enough to call the Eld here so you can slaughter them, you're as dumb as we thought!"

Laughter, biped laughter, came from the other end. "Underestimating the Nugels is a really, really stupid thing to do. One week, Ardulans. I suggest you start moving the Neek people to the cities. In one week, if we don't have the Eld and the flare in-system, then we are coming down to the planet. Well, the smaller pods are, anyway. They'll come down in the middle of the night when all the little Neek children are tucked snugly in bed, and they will set your forests on fire."

"You will destroy the Systems if you destroy the andal of Neek!" Miketh exclaimed. "Their entire cellulose infrastructure is rooted in this planet. What happened to not harming the defenseless?"

Chittering rose up from the feed before the male voice drowned it out. "The whole of the Charted Systems is behind this decision. They understand the threat Ardulum poses. Physically, the Risalians are here, along with Minorans, the Oori, and more than a dozen other species from the Systems and the Alliance. A week is plenty of time to move the forest-dwelling Neek out of harm's way. The Nugels are going to have their vengeance, Ardulans, and we will find the altered Ardulan woman. You just have to decide how much of your planet you want burned."

Also Available from NineStar Press

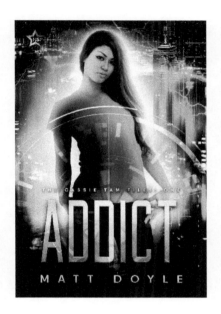

Connect with NineStar Press

Fic   Fields, J. S.,
Fields   author
v.2   Second don

CPSIA information can be obtained
at www.ICGtesting.com
Printed in the USA
LVHW111032080519
617046LV00005BA/88/P

9 781947 139961